P9-DTK-728

RED

teddekker.com

DEKKER FANTASY

BOOKS OF HISTORY CHRONICLES

THE LOST BOOKS
Chosen
Infidel
Renegade
Chaos
Lunatic
Elyon

THE CIRCLE SERIES
Green
Black
Red
White

THE PARADISE BOOKS
Showdown
Saint
Sinner

Skin
House
(WITH FRANK PERETTI)

DEKKER MYSTERY

Blink of an Eye
Kiss
(WITH ERIN HEALY)
Burn
(WITH ERIN HEALY—JANUARY 2010)

MARTYR'S SONG SERIES
Heaven's Wager
When Heaven Weeps
Thunder of Heaven
The Martyr's Song

THE CALEB BOOKS
Blessed Child
A Man Called Blessed

DEKKER THRILLER

THR3E
Obsessed
Adam

THE CIRCLE SERIES

RED

THE HEROIC RESCUE

TED DEKkER

THOMAS NELSON
Since 1798

NASHVILLE   DALLAS   MEXICO CITY   RIO DE JANEIRO   BEIJING

Red © 2004 by Ted Dekker
Red Graphic Novel © 2007 by Thomas Nelson

All rights reserved. No portion of this book may be reproduced, stored in a retrieval system, or transmitted in any form or by any means—electronic, mechanical, photocopy, recording, scanning, or other—except for brief quotations in critical reviews or articles, without the prior written permission of the publisher.

Published in Nashville, Tennessee, by Thomas Nelson. Thomas Nelson is a registered trademark of Thomas Nelson, Inc.

Published in association with Thomas Nelson and Creative Trust, Inc., 5141 Virginia Way, Suite 320, Brentwood, TN 37027.

Thomas Nelson, Inc. titles may be purchased in bulk for educational, business, fund-raising, or sales promotional use. For information, please e-mail SpecialMarkets@ThomasNelson.com.

This is a work of fiction. Names, characters, places, and incidents either are the product of the author's imagination or are used fictitiously. Any resemblance to actual persons, living or dead, events, organizations, or locales is entirely coincidental.

Library of Congress Cataloging-in-Publication Data

Dekker, Ted, 1962–
    Red : the heroic rescue / by Ted R. Dekker.
      p. cm.
    ISBN 978-0-8499-1791-2 (hardcover)
    ISBN 978-1-5955-4000-3 (international)
    ISBN 978-1-5955-4034-8 (trade paper)
    ISBN 978-1-59554-434-6 (repackage)
    ISBN 978-1-59554-731-6 (2nd repackage)
    I. Title.
    PS3554.E3R43 2004
    813'.6—dc22   2004004529

Printed in the United States of America

10 11 12 13 RRD 6 5 4 3

For my children.
May they always remember
what lies behind the veil.

WHERE DOES THE CIRCLE START?

Unlike most series, the Circle Series is truly circular, meaning *Green*, Book Zero, both begins the series for those who have not yet read *Black*, *Red*, or *White*, and it ends the series for those who have read *Black*, *Red*, and *White*. Have no fear, the story works seamlessly either way, like a circle or a zero. The choice is yours. Start with *Black*, then read *Red*, *White* and end with *Green*. Or start with *Green* and move on to *Black*, *Red* and *White*.

Dive Deep.

Bangkok

KARA GOT halfway to her door and stopped. She and Thomas were in a large hotel suite with two bedrooms. Beyond her bedroom door was a short hall that ran to the living room and, in the other direction, to the adjoining suite. Across that hall—her brother's room, where he lay dead to this world, dreaming, oblivious to the news she'd just heard from Deputy Secretary Merton Gains.

The virus had been released exactly as Thomas had predicted just last evening.

Half an hour, Secretary Gains had said. *Bring him down in half an hour.* If she woke Thomas now, he'd demand to go down immediately. Every minute of sleep—for that matter every second—could be the equivalent of hours or days or even weeks in his dream world. A lot could happen. Answers could come. She should let him sleep.

Then again, Svensson had released the virus. She should wake her brother now.

Right after she used the bathroom.

Kara hurried to the side room, flipped the light switch, turned on the water. Closed the door.

"We've stepped off the cliff and are falling into madness," she said. Then again, perhaps the fall to madness had started when Thomas had tried to jump off the balcony in Denver. He'd dragged her to Bangkok, kidnapped Monique de Raison, and survived two separate encounters with a killer named Carlos, who was undoubtedly still after them. All this because of his dreams of another reality.

Would Thomas wake with any new information? *The power was gone from the colored forest,* he'd said. The colored forest itself was gone, which meant that his power might be gone as well. If that was the case, Tom's dreams might be useless except as fantasies in which he was falling in love and learning to do backflips off a pinhead.

The water felt cool and refreshing on her face.

She flung the water from her hands and stepped to the toilet.

1

THOMAS URGED the sweating black steed into a full gallop through the sandy valley and up the gentle slope. He shoved his bloody sword into his scabbard, gripped the reins with both hands, and leaned over the horse's neck. Twenty fighters rode in a long line to his right and left, slightly behind. They were unquestionably the greatest warriors in all the earth, and they pounded for the crest directly ahead, one question drumming through each one's mind.

How many?

The Horde's attack had come from the canyon lands, through the Natalga Gap. This was not so unusual. The Desert Dwellers' armies had attacked from the east a dozen times over the last fifteen years. What was unusual, however, was the size of the party his men had just cut to ribbons less than a mile to the south. No more than a hundred.

Too few. Far too few.

The Horde never attacked in small numbers. Where Thomas and his army depended on superior speed and skill, the Horde had always depended on sheer numbers. They'd developed a kind of natural balance. One of his men could take out five of the Horde on any bad day, an advantage mitigated only by the fact that the Horde's army approached five hundred thousand strong. His own army numbered fewer than thirty thousand including the apprentices. None of this was lost on the enemy. And yet they'd sent only this small band of hooded warriors up the Gap to their deaths.

Why?

They rode without a word. Hoofs thundered like war drums, an oddly comforting sound. Their horses were all stallions. Each fighter was dressed in the same hardened-leather breastplate with forearm and thigh guards. These left their joints free for the movement required in hand-to-hand combat. They strapped their knives to calves and whips to hips, and carried their swords on their horses. These three weapons, a good horse, and a leather bottle full of water were all any of the Forest Guard required to survive a week and to kill a hundred. And the regular fighting force wasn't far behind.

Thomas flew over the hill's crest, leaned back, and pulled the stallion to a stamping halt. The others fell in along the ridge. Still not a word.

What they saw could not easily be put into words.

The sky was turning red, blood red, as it always did over the desert in the afternoons. To their right stretched the canyon lands, ten square miles of cliffs and boulders that acted as a natural barrier between the red deserts and the first of seven forests. Thomas's forest. Beyond the canyon's cliffs, red-tinged sand flowed into an endless sea of desert. This landscape was as familiar to Thomas as his own forest.

What he saw now was not.

At first glance, even to a trained eye, the subtle movement on the desert floor might have been mistaken for shimmering heat waves. It was hardly more than a beige discoloration rippling across the vast section of flat sand that fed into the canyons. But this was nothing so innocuous as desert heat.

This was the Horde army.

They wore beige hooded tunics to cover their gray scabbed flesh and rode light tan horses bred to disappear against the sand. Thomas had once ridden past fifty without distinguishing them from the sandstone.

"How many, Mikil?"

His second in command searched the horizon to the south. He followed her eyes. A dozen smaller contingents were heading up the Gap, armies of a few hundred each, not so much larger than the one they'd torn apart thirty minutes ago.

"Hundred thousand," she said. A strip of leather held her dark hair back from a tanned forehead. A small white scar on her right cheek marred an otherwise smooth, milky complexion. The cut had been inflicted not by the Horde, but by her own brother, who'd fought her to assert his strength just a year ago. She'd left him unscathed, underfoot, soundly defeated.

He'd died in a skirmish six months after.

Mikil's green eyes skirted the desert. "This will be a challenge."

Thomas grunted at the understatement. They'd all been hardened by dozens of battles, but never had they faced an army so large.

"The main body is moving south, along the southern cliffs."

She was right. This was a new tactic for the Horde.

"They're trying to engage us in the Natalga Gap while the main force flanks us," Thomas said.

"And they look to succeed," his lieutenant William said.

No one disagreed. No one spoke. No one moved.

Thomas scanned the horizon again and reviewed their bearings. To the west the desert ended in the same forested valley he'd protected from the Horde threat for the past fifteen years, ever since the boy had led them to the small paradise in the middle of the desert.

To the north and the south lay six other similar forests, inhabited by roughly a hundred thousand Forest People.

Thomas and Rachelle had not met their first forest dweller until nearly a full year after finding the lake. His name was Ciphus of Southern, for he came from the great Southern Forest. That was the year they gave birth to their first child, a daughter they named Marie. Marie of Thomas. Those who'd originally come from the colored forest took designation according to which forests they lived in, thus Ciphus of Southern. The children who were born after the Great Deception took the names of their fathers. Marie of Thomas.

Three years later, Rachelle and Thomas had a son, Samuel, a strong lad, nearly twelve now. He was wielding a sword already, and Thomas had to speak loudly to keep him from joining the battles.

Each forest had its own lake, and Elyon's faithful bathed each day to keep the painful skin disease from overtaking their bodies. This ritual cleansing was what separated them from the Scabs.

Each night, after bathing, the Forest People danced and sang in celebration of the Great Romance, as they called it. And each year the people of all seven forests, roughly a hundred thousand now, made the pilgrimage to the largest forest, called the Middle Forest—Thomas's forest. The

annual Gathering was to be held seven days from today. How many Forest
People were now making the exposed trek across the desert, Thomas hated
to imagine.

Scabs could become Forest People, of course—a simple bathing in
the lake would cleanse their skin and wash away their disgusting stench.
A small number of Scabs had become Forest People over the years, but
it was the unspoken practice of the Forest Guard to discourage Horde
defections.

There simply weren't enough lakes to accommodate all of them.

In fact, Ciphus of Southern, the Council elder, had calculated that the
lakes could function adequately for only three hundred thousand. There
simply wasn't enough water for the Horde, who already numbered well
over a million. The lakes were clearly a gift from Elyon to the Forest People
alone.

Discouraging the Horde from bathing was not difficult. The intense
pain of moisture on their diseased flesh was enough to fill the Scabs with
a deep revulsion for the lakes, and Qurong, their leader, had sworn to
destroy the waters when he conquered the much-coveted resources of the
forest lands.

The Desert Dwellers had first attacked thirteen years ago, descending
on a small forest two hundred miles to the southwest. Although the clumsy
attackers had been beaten back with rocks and clubs, over a hundred of
Elyon's followers, mostly women and children, had been slaughtered.

Despite his preference for peace, Thomas had determined then that
the only way to secure peace for the Forest People was to establish an
army. With the help of Johan, Rachelle's brother, Thomas went in hunt
of metal, drawing upon his recollection of the histories. He needed copper and tin, which when mixed would form bronze, a metal strong
enough for swords. They'd built a furnace and then heated rocks of all
varieties until they found the kind that leaked the telltale ore. As it
turned out, the canyon lands were full of ore. He still wasn't sure if the
material from which he'd fashioned the first sword was actually bronze,
but it was soft enough to sharpen and hard enough to cut off a man's
head with a single blow.

The Horde came again, this time with a larger force. Armed with swords and knives, Thomas and a hundred fighters, his first Forest Guard, cut the attacking Desert Dwellers to shreds.

Word of a mighty warrior named Thomas of Hunter spread throughout the desert and forests alike. For three years after, the Horde braved only the occasional skirmish, always to their own terrible demise.

But the need to conquer the fertile forest land proved too strong for the swelling Horde. They brought their first major campaign up the Natalga Gap armed with new weapons, bronze weapons: long swords and sharp sickles and large balls swinging from chains. Though defeated then, their strength had continued to grow since.

It was during the Winter Campaign three years ago that Johan went missing. The Forest People had mourned his loss at the Gathering that year. Some had begged Elyon to remember his promise to deliver them from the heart of evil, from the Horde's curse, in one stunning blow. That day would surely come, Thomas believed, because the boy had spoken it before disappearing into the lake.

It would be best for Thomas and his Guard if today was that day.

"They'll be at our catapults along the southern cliffs in three marks on the dial," Mikil said, referring to the sundials Thomas had introduced to keep time. Then she added, "Three hours."

Thomas faced the desert. The diseased Horde army was pouring into the canyons like whipped honey. By nightfall the sands would be black with blood. And this time it would be as much their blood as the Horde's.

An image of Rachelle and young Marie and his son, Samuel, filled his mind. A knot swelled in his throat. The rest had children too, many children, in part to even odds with the Horde. How many children in the forests now? Nearly half the population. Fifty thousand.

They had to find a way to beat back this army, if only for the children.

Thomas glanced down the line of his lieutenants, masters in combat, each one. He secretly believed any of them could capably lead this war, but he never doubted their loyalty to him, the Guard, and the forests. Even William, who was more than willing to point out Thomas's faults and challenge his judgment, would give his life. In matters of ultimate loyalty,

Thomas had set the standard. He would rather lose a leg than a single one of them, and they all knew it.

They also knew that, of them all, Thomas was the least likely to lose a leg or any other body part in any fight. This even though he was forty and many of them in their twenties. What they knew, they'd learned mostly from him.

Although he'd not once dreamed of the histories for the past fifteen years, he did remember some things—his last recollection of Bangkok, for example. He remembered falling asleep in a hotel room after failing to convince key government officials that the Raison Strain was on their doorstep.

He could also recall bits and pieces of the histories, and he drew on his lingering if fading knowledge of its wars and technology, an ability that gave him considerable advantage over the others. For in large part, memory of the histories had been all but wiped out when the black-winged Shataiki had overtaken the colored forest. Thomas suspected that now only the Roush, who had disappeared after the Great Deception, truly remembered any of the histories.

Thomas transferred the reins to his left hand and stretched his fingers. "William, you have the fastest horse. Take the canyon back to the forest and bring the reinforcements at the perimeter forward."

It would leave the forest exposed, but they had little choice.

"Forgive me for pointing out the obvious," William objected, "but taking them here will end badly."

"The high ground at the Gap favors us," Thomas said. "We hit them there."

"Then you'll engage them before the reinforcements arrive."

"We can hold them. We have no choice."

"We always have a choice," William said. This was how it was with him, always challenging. Thomas had anticipated his argument and, in this case, agreed.

"Tell Ciphus to prepare the tribe for evacuation to one of the northern villages. He will object because he isn't used to the prospect of losing a battle. And with the Gathering only a week away, he will scream sacrilege, so I want you to tell him with Rachelle present. She'll make sure that he listens."

William faced him. "Me, to the village? Send another runner. I can't miss this battle!"

"You'll be back in time for plenty of battle. I depend on you, William. Both missions are critical. You have the fastest horse and you're best suited to travel alone."

Although William needed no praise, it shut him up in front of the others.

Thomas faced Suzan, his most trusted scout, a young woman of twenty who could hold her own against ten untrained men. Her skin was dark, as was the skin of nearly half of the Forest People. Their varying shades of skin tone also distinguished them from the Horde, who were all white from the disease.

"Take two of our best scouts and run the southern cliffs. We will join you with the main force in two hours. I want positions and pace when I arrive. I want to know who leads that army if you have to go down and rip his hood off yourself. In particular I want to know if it's the druid Martyn. I want to know when they last fed and when they expect to feed again. Everything, Suzan. I depend on you."

"Yes sir." She whipped her horse around. "Hiyaaa!" The stallion bolted down the hill with William in fast pursuit.

Thomas stared out at the Horde. "Well, my friends, we've always known this was coming. You signed on to fight. It looks like Elyon has brought us our fight."

Someone humphed. All here would die for the forests. Not all would die for Elyon.

"How many men in this theater?" Thomas asked Mikil.

"With the escorts out to bring the other tribes in for the Gathering, only ten thousand, but five thousand of those are at the forest perimeter," Mikil said. "We have fewer than five thousand to join a battle at the southern cliffs."

"And how many to intercept these smaller bands of Horde that intend to distract us?"

Mikil shrugged. "Three thousand. A thousand at each pass."

"We'll send a thousand, three hundred for each pass. The rest go with us to the cliffs."

For a moment all sat quietly. What strategy could possibly overturn such impossible odds? What words of wisdom could even Elyon himself offer in a moment of such gravity?

"We have six hours before the sun sets," Thomas said, pulling his horse around. "Let's ride."

"I'm not sure we *will* see the sun set," one of them said.

No voice argued.

2

CARLOS MISSIRIAN stared at Thomas Hunter.

The man lay on his back, sleeping in a tangle of sheets, naked except for boxer shorts. Sweat soaked the sheets. Sweat and blood. Blood? So much blood, smeared over the sheets, some dried and some still wet.

The man had bled in his sleep? *Was* bleeding in his sleep. Dead?

Carlos stepped closer. No. Hunter's chest rose and fell steadily. There were scars on his chest and abdomen that Carlos couldn't remember, but no evidence of the slugs Carlos was sure he'd put into this same man in the last week.

He brought his gun to Hunter's temple and tightened his finger on the trigger.

3

A FLASH from the cliff. Two flashes.

Thomas, crouched behind a wide rock, raised the crude scope to his eye and scanned the hooded Scabs along the floor of the canyon. He'd fashioned the spyglass from his memory of the histories, using a resin from the pine trees, and although it hardly functioned as he suspected it should, it did give him a slight advantage over the naked eye. Mikil kneeled beside him.

The signal had come from the top of the cliffs, where he'd positioned two hundred archers each with five hundred arrows. They'd learned long ago that their odds were determined by the supply of munitions almost as much as by the number of men.

Their strategy was a simple, proven one. Thomas would lead a thousand warriors in a frontal assault that would choke the enemy along its front line. When the battlefield was sufficiently cluttered with dead Scabs, he would beat a hasty retreat while the archers rained thousands of arrows down on the crowded field. If all went well, they could at least slow the enemy down by clogging the wide canyon with the dead.

Two hundred cavalry waited with Thomas behind a long row of boulders. They kept their horses seated on the ground with gentle persuasion.

They'd done this once before. It was a wonder that the Horde was subjecting itself to—

"Sir!" A runner slid in from behind him, panting. "We have a report from the Southern Forest." Mikil shifted next to him.

"Go on. Quietly please."

"The Horde is attacking."

Thomas pulled the scope from his eye, then peered through it again.

He lifted his left hand, ready to signal his men's charge. The runner's report meant what?

That the Horde now had a new strategy.

That the situation had just gone from terrible to impossible.

That the end was near.

"Give me the rest. Quickly."

"It's said to be the work of Martyn."

Again he pulled the glass from his eye. Returned it. Then this army wasn't being led by their new general, as he'd suspected. They'd been tracking the one called Martyn for a year now. He was a younger man; they'd forced that much out of a prisoner once. He was also a good tactician; they knew that much from the shifting engagements. And they suspected that he was a druid as well as a general. The Desert Dwellers had no declared religion, but they paid homage to the Shataiki in ways that were slowly but surely formalizing their worship of the serpentine bat on their crest. Teeleh. Some said that Martyn practiced the black arts; others said he was guided by Teeleh himself. Either way, his army seemed to be advancing in skill quickly.

If the Scab called Martyn led his army against the Southern Forest, could this army be a diversion? Or was the attack on the Southern Forest the diversion?

"On my signal, Mikil."

"Ready," she replied. She slipped into the saddle of her seated horse.

"How many?" Thomas asked the runner.

"I don't know. We have fewer than a thousand, but they are in retreat."

"Who's in charge?"

"Jamous."

He jerked the lens from his face and looked at the man. "Jamous? Jamous is in retreat?"

"According to the report, yes."

If such a headstrong fighter as Jamous had fallen back, then the engaging force was stronger than any he'd fought before.

"There is also the warrior named Justin there."

"Sir?" It was Mikil.

He turned back, saw movement cresting the swell a hundred yards ahead, and took a deep breath. He lifted his hand and held it steady, waiting. Closer. The stench from their flaking skin reached his nostrils. Then their crest, the bronzed serpentine bat.

The Horde army rose into view, five hundred abreast at least, mounted on horses as pale as the desert sands. The warriors rode hooded and cloaked, grasping tall sickles that rose nearly as high as their serpent.

Thomas slowed his breathing. His only task was to turn this army back. Diversion or not, if he failed here, it made no difference what happened at the Southern Forest.

Thomas could hear Mikil breathing steadily through her nose. *I will beg Elyon for your safety today, Mikil. I will beg Elyon for the safety of us all. If any should die, let it be that traitor, Justin.*

"Now!" He dropped his hand.

His warriors were moving already. From the left, a long row of foot soldiers, silent and low, crept like spiders over the sand.

Two hundred horses bearing riders rolled to their feet. Thomas whirled to the runner. "Word to William and Ciphus! Send a thousand warriors to the Southern Forest. If we are overtaken here, we will meet in the third forest to the north. Go!"

His main force was already ten yards ahead of him, flying for the Horde, and Thomas wouldn't allow them to reach the battle first. Never. He swung into his saddle and kicked the stallion into a gallop. The black leaped over the boulders and raced for the long line of surprised Desert Dwellers, who'd stopped cold.

For a long moment the pounding of hooves was the only sound in the air. The sea of Scab warriors flowed down into the canyon and disappeared behind the cliffs. A hundred thousand sets of eyes peered out from the shadows of their hoods. These were the very ones who despised Elyon and hated his water. Theirs was a nomadic world of shallow, muddy wells and filthy, stinking flesh. They were hardly fit for life, much less the forests. And yet they would likely defile the lakes, ravage the forests, and plant their desert wheat.

These were the people of the colored forest gone amuck. The walking dead. Better buried at the base of a cliff than allowed to roam like an unchecked plague.

These were also warriors. Men only, strong, and not as ignorant as they had once been. But they were slower than the Forest Guard. Their debilitating skin condition reached down into their joints and made dexterity a difficult prospect.

Thomas pounded past his warriors. Now he was in the lead, where he belonged. He rested his hand on the hilt of his sword.

Forty yards.

His sword came free of its scabbard with the loud scraping of metal against metal.

Immediately a roar ascended from the Horde, as if the drawn sword confirmed Thomas's otherwise dubious intentions. A thousand horses snorted and reared in objection to the heavy hands that jerked them back in fear. Those in the front line would surely know that although victory was ultimately ensured today, they would be among the first to die.

The Forest Guard rode hard, jaws clenched, swords still lowered by their legs, easy in their hands.

Thomas veered to the right, transferred his sword to his left hand, and raked it along the breasts of three Scabs before blocking the first sickle that compensated for his sudden change in direction.

The lines of horses collided. His fighters screamed, thrusting and parrying and beheading with a practiced frenzy. A pale horse fell directly in front of Thomas, and he glanced over to see that Mikil had lost her sword in its rider's side.

"Mikil!" With her forearm, she blocked a nasty swipe from a monstrous Scab sword and twisted in her saddle. Thomas ripped at the cords that held his second scabbard and hurled it to her, sword and all. She caught it, whipped the blade out, twirled it once through the air and swung downward at a charging foot soldier.

Thomas deflected a swinging sickle as it sliced for his head, jumped his stallion over the dying horse, and whirled to meet the attacker.

The battle found its rhythm. On every side blades broad and narrow, short and long, swung, parried, blocked, swiped, sliced. Blood and sweat soaked man and beast. The terrible din of battle filled the canyon. Wails and cries and snorts and moans of death rose to the sky.

So did the battle cries of one thousand highly trained warriors facing an endless reservoir of skillful Scabs.

Not three years ago, under the guidance of Qurong, the Horde's cavalry never failed to suffer huge losses. Now, under the direct command of their young general, Martyn, they weren't dying without a fight.

A tall Scab whose hood had slipped off his head snarled and lunged his mount directly into Thomas's path. The horses collided and reared, kicking at the air. With a flip of his wrist, Thomas unleashed his whip and cracked it against the Scab's head. The man screamed and threw an arm up. Thomas thrust his sword at the man's exposed side, felt it sink deep, then wrenched it free just as a foot soldier swung a club at him from behind. He leaned far to his right and slashed backward with his sword. The warrior crumpled, headless.

The battle raged for ten minutes in the Forest Guard's unquestioned favor. But with so many blades swinging through the air, some were bound to find the exposed flesh of Thomas's men or the flanks of their horses.

The Forest Guard began to fall.

Thomas sensed it as much as saw it. Two. Four. Then ten, twenty, forty. More.

Thomas broke form and galloped down the line. The obstruction from fallen horses and men was enough. To his alarm he saw that more of his men had fallen than he'd first thought. He had to get them back!

He snatched up the horn at his belt and blasted the signal for retreat. Immediately his men fled, on horse, on foot, sprinting past him as if they'd been firmly defeated.

Thomas held his horse steady for a moment. The Scabs, hardly used to such wholesale retreat, paused, apparently confused by the sudden turn of events.

As planned.

The number of his men among the dead, however, was not planned. Maybe two hundred!

For the first time that day, Thomas felt the razored finger of panic slice across his chest. He whirled his horse and tore after his fighters.

He cleared the line of boulders in one long bound, slipped from his horse, and dropped to one knee in time to see the first barrage of arrows from the cliff arc silently into the Horde.

Now a new kind of chaos ensued. Horses reared and Scabs screamed and the dead piled high where they fell. The Horde army was temporarily trapped by a dam made of its own warriors.

"Our losses are high," Mikil said beside him, breathing hard. "Three hundred."

"Three hundred!" He looked at his second. Her face was red with blood and her eyes shone with an unusual glare of defiance. Fatalism. "We'll need more than bodies and boulders to hold them back," she said. She spit to the side.

Thomas scanned the cliffs. The archers were still sending arrows down onto the trapped army. As soon as the enemy cleared the bodies and marched fresh horses up, twenty catapults along each cliff would begin to shower the Horde with boulders.

Then it would begin again. Another head-on attack by Thomas, followed by more arrows, followed by more boulders. He quickly did the math. At this rate they might be able to hold off the army for five rounds.

Mikil voiced his thoughts. "Even if we hold them off until nightfall, they'll march over us tomorrow."

The sky cleared of arrows. Boulders began to fall. Thomas had been working on the counterweight catapults for years without perfecting them. They were still useless on flat ground, but they did heave big rocks far enough over a cliff to make good use of gravity. Two-foot boulders made terrible projectiles.

A dull thump preceded the ground's tremor.

"It won't be enough," Mikil said. "We'd have to bring the whole cliff down on them."

"We need to slow the pace!" Thomas said. "Next time on foot only, and draw the battle out by withdrawing quickly. Pass the word. Fight defensively!"

The boulders stopped falling and the Horde cleared more bodies. Thomas led his fighters in another frontal assault twenty minutes later.

This time they played with the enemy, using the Marduk fighting method that Rachelle and Thomas had developed and perfected over the years. It was a refinement of the aerial combat that Tanis had practiced in the colored forest. The Forest Guard knew it well and could play with a dozen Scabs under the right circumstances.

But here in crowded quarters with so many bodies and blades, their mobility was limited. They fought hard for thirty minutes and killed nearly a thousand.

This time they lost half of their force.

At this rate the Horde would be through their lines in an hour. The Desert Dwellers would stop for the night as was their custom, but Mikil was right. Even if the Guard could hold them off that long, Thomas's warriors would be finished in the morning. The Horde would reach his undefended Middle Forest in under one day. Rachelle. The children. Thirty thousand defenseless civilians would be slaughtered.

Thomas searched the cliffs. *Elyon, give me strength.* The chill he'd felt earlier was spreading to his shoulders.

"Bring up the reinforcements!" he snapped. "Gerard, your command. Keep them on that line, by whatever means. Watch the cliff for signals. Coordinate the attacks." He tossed the lieutenant the ram's horn. "Elyon's strength," he said, holding up his fist.

Gerard caught the horn. "Elyon's strength. Count on me, sir."

"I am. You have no idea how much I am." Thomas turned to Mikil. "With me." They swung into their horses and pounded down the canyon.

His second followed him without question. He led her up a small hill and then doubled back along the path toward an overlook near the top.

The battlefield stretched out to their right. His archers were raining arrows down on the Scabs again. The dead were piled high. To see the Horde's front lines, an observer might think that the Forest Guard was routing the enemy. But a quick look down the canyon told a different story.

Thousands upon thousands upon thousands of hooded warriors waited in an eerie silence. This was a battle of attrition.

This was a battle that could not be won.

"Any word from the three parties to the north?" Thomas asked.

"No. Let's pray they haven't broken through."

"They won't."

Thomas dismounted and studied the cliffs.

Mikil nudged her horse forward, then brought it snorting around.

"Yes, I know you're impatient, Mikil." There was something about the cliffs that bothered Thomas. "You're wondering if I've gone mad; is that it? My men are dying in a final battle and I've dismounted to watch it all."

"I'm worried about Jamous. What's your plan?"

"Jamous can take care of himself."

"Jamous is in retreat! He would never retreat. What's your plan?"

"I don't have a plan."

"If you don't come up with one soon, you may never plan again," she said.

"I know, Mikil." He paced.

Mikil spit again. "We can't just sit here—"

"I'm *not* just sitting here!" Thomas faced her, suddenly furious and knowing he had no right to be. Not at her.

"I am thinking! You should start thinking!" He thrust an arm out toward the Horde now being pounded by boulders again. "Look out there and tell me what could possibly stop such a monstrous army! Who do you think I am? Elyon? Can I clap my hands and make these cliffs crush—"

Thomas stopped.

"What?" Mikil demanded. She glanced around for an enemy, sword in hand.

Thomas spun toward the valley. "What was it you said earlier?"

"What? That you should be with your men?"

"No! The cliffs. You said we'd have to bring the whole cliff down on them."

"Yes, but we might as well try to bring the sun down on them."

It was an insane thought.

"What is it?" she demanded again.

"What if there *was* a way to bring the cliff—"

"There isn't."

He ran to the edge. "But *if*! If we could bring down the canyon walls near their rear, we could box them in, bring them down here, and we would trap them for an easy slaughter from above."

"What do you want to do, heat the whole cliff with a giant fire and empty the contents of the lake on it so that it cracks?"

He ignored her. It was reckless, but then so was doing nothing.

"There's a fault along the cliff there. Do you see it?"

He pointed and she looked.

"So there's a fault. I still don't see how—"

"Of course you don't! But if we *could*, would it work?"

"If you could clap your hands and bring down the cliff on them, then I'd say we have a chance of sending every last one of the Scabs to the black forest where they belong."

A battle cry filled the canyon. Gerard was leading his newly reinforced ranks into the battle again.

"How long do you think we can hold them?" Thomas demanded.

"Another hour. Maybe two."

Thomas paced and muttered under his breath. "That may not be enough!"

"Sir, please. You have to tell me what's going on. There's a reason I'm your second in command. If you can't, I am needed back on the battlefield."

"There was once a way to bring a cliff like this down. It was a long time ago, written about in the Books of Histories. Very few remember, but I do."

"And?"

Exactly. And what?

"I think it was called an explosion. A large ball of fire with tremendous strength. What if we could figure out how to cause an explosion?"

She looked at him with a wrinkled brow.

"There was a time when I could get specific information about the histories. What if I could retrieve specific information on how to cause an explosion?"

"That's the most ridiculous thing I've ever heard! We're in the middle of a battle here. You expect to go on some kind of expedition to find information on the histories? You have battle fatigue!"

"No, not an expedition. I'm not sure it would even work. I've taken the fruit so long." The idea swelled in his mind and with it an excitement. "It would be the first time in fifteen years I haven't eaten the fruit. What if I can still dream?"

She stared at him as if he'd gone mad. Below them the battle still raged.

"I would need to sleep; that's the only problem." He paced, eager for this idea now. "What if I can't sleep?"

"Sleep? You want to sleep? Now?"

"Dream!" he said, fist clenched. "I need to dream. I could dream as I used to and learn how to blow this cliff down!"

Mikil had been struck dumb.

"Do you have a better idea?" he asked forcefully.

"Not yet," she managed.

What if he couldn't dream? What if the rhambutan required several days to wear off?

Thomas faced the canyon. He glanced at the far cliff, its fault line clear where the milky white rock turned red. In two hours all of his men would be dead.

But if he did have an explosive . . .

Thomas bounded for his horse and swung into the saddle.

"Thomas!"

"Follow me!"

She followed at a gallop up the path to the cliff's lip. He swept past the first post and yelled at a full run.

"Delay them! Do whatever you must, but hold them until dark. I have a way."

"Thomas! What way?" came the cry.

"Just hold them!" And then he was past.

Do you have a way, Thomas?

He ran all the way down the line of archers and catapult teams, passing encouragement to each battery. "Hold them! Hold them till dark! Slow the pace. We have a way. If you hold them until dark, we have a way!"

Mikil said nothing.

When they passed the last catapult, Thomas pulled up.

"I'm with you only because you've saved my life a dozen times and I've sworn my own to you," Mikil said. "I hope you know that."

"Follow me."

He led her behind an outcropping of boulders and looked around. Good enough. He dismounted.

"What are we doing here?" she asked.

"We're dismounting." He found a rock the size of his fist and weighed it in one hand. As much as he disliked the thought of being hit in the head, he saw no alternative. There was no way he could fall asleep on his own. Not with so much adrenaline coursing through his veins.

"Here you go. I want you to knock me on the head. I need to sleep, but that's not going to happen, so you have to knock me unconscious."

She looked around uncomfortably. "Sir—"

"Knock me out! That's an order. And hit me hard enough to do the job on the first try. Once I'm out, wake me up in ten minutes. Do you understand?"

"Ten minutes is enough to retrieve what you need?"

He stared at her, struck by the sound of the questions.

"Listen to me," she said. "You've turned me into a lunatic. The Horde's druids might practice their magic, but when have we ever? Never! This is like their magic."

True enough. The Horde druids were rumored to practice a magic that healed and deceived at once. Thomas had never seen either. Some said that Justin practiced the way of the druids.

"Ten minutes. Say it."

"Yes, of course. Ten minutes."

"Then hit me."

She stepped forward. "You really—"

"Hit me!"

Mikil swung the rock.

Thomas blocked the blow.

"What are you doing?" she demanded.

"Sorry. It was reflex. I'll close my eyes this time."

He closed his eyes.

His head exploded with light.

His world faded to black.

4

THOMAS HUNTER awoke in perfect stillness, and he knew three things before his heart had completed its first heavy beat.

One, he knew that he wasn't the same man who'd fallen asleep just nine hours ago. He'd lived fifteen years in another reality and had been transformed by new knowledge and skills.

Two, none of those skills, unfortunately, included surviving a bullet to the head, as was once the case.

Three, there was a bullet in the barrel of the gun that at this very moment pressed lightly against his head.

He kept his eyes shut and his body limp. His head throbbed from Mikil's blow. His mind raced. Panic.

No, not panic. How many times had he faced death over the last fifteen years? Even here, in this dream world, he'd been shot twice in the last week, and each time he'd been healed by Elyon's water.

But this time there was no healing water. It had disappeared with the colored forest fifteen years ago.

A soft, low whisper filled his ear. "Good-bye, Mr. Hunter."

Carlos Missirian let the last satisfying moment linger. A line from a movie he'd once seen drummed through his mind.

Dodge this.

Yes, Mr. Hunter, just try to dodge this. He tightened his finger on the trigger.

Hunter's body jerked.

For a split second, Carlos thought he'd shot the gun and sent a bullet through the man's brain, which explained Hunter's sudden jerk.

But there had been no detonation.

And his gun was flying across the room.

And his wrist stung.

In one horrifying moment of enlightenment, Carlos saw that Thomas Hunter had slapped the gun from his hand and was now rolling away from him, far too quickly for any ordinary man.

Nothing of this kind had ever happened to Carlos. It confused him. There was something very wrong about this man who seemed to retrieve information and skills from his dreams at will. If Carlos were a mystic, as his mother was, he might be tempted to think Hunter was a demon.

The man came to his feet and faced Carlos on the opposite side of the bed. He had no weapon and wore only boxer shorts. He was bleeding from a fresh cut on his forearm that Carlos hadn't put there. Curious. Perhaps that explained the blood on the sheets.

Carlos withdrew his knife. Ordinarily his next course of action would be straightforward. He would either bear down on the unarmed man and slash his abdomen or neck, whichever presented itself, or he'd send the knife flying from where he stood. Despite the ease with which actors knocked aside hurling blades in the movies, deflecting a well-thrown stiletto in real combat wasn't an easy task.

But Hunter wasn't an ordinary man.

They faced off, both cautious.

It occurred to Carlos that Thomas had changed. Physically he was the same man with the same loose brown hair and green eyes, the same strong jaw and steady hands, the same muscled chest and abdomen. But he carried himself differently now, with a simple, unshakable confidence. He stood tall, hands loose at his sides. Hunter watched Carlos with unwavering eyes, the way a man might look at a challenging mathematics equation rather than a threatening foe.

Carlos knew that he should be diving for the gun on the floor to his left or throwing the knife he'd drawn. But his fascination with this man delayed his reactions. If Svensson knew the full extent of Hunter's capabilities, he might insist he be taken alive. Perhaps Carlos would take the matter up with Armand Fortier.

"What's your name?" Thomas asked. His eyes glanced sideways, to the gun and back.

Carlos eased to his left. "Carlos."

"Well, Carlos, it seems that we meet again."

They both went for the gun at the same time. Hunter reached it first. Kicked it under the bed. Sprang back.

"I never did like guns," Thomas said. "You wouldn't by any chance be interested in a fair fight, would you? Swords?"

"Swords would be fine," Carlos said. There was no way to get the gun now. "Unfortunately, we don't have time for games today."

The woman would be coming. At any moment she'd knock on the door and wake her brother as promised. If either of them raised an alarm . . .

Carlos lunged for Thomas.

The man sidestepped his thrusting blade, but not quickly enough to avoid it. The edge sliced into his shoulder.

Thomas ignored the cut and leaped toward the door.

You're fast, but not that fast. With two long steps to his right Carlos cut the man off.

"You've slipped through my fingers twice," he said. "Not today." He backed Thomas into the corner. Blood ran down his arm. How he'd once managed to survive a high-velocity slug to the head, Carlos had no clue, but the cut on his arm wasn't healing now. One well-directed slash, and Thomas Hunter's blood would turn the beige carpet red.

Hunter suddenly spread his mouth and yelled at the top of his lungs. "Karaaa!"

~~~

Kara had just flushed the toilet when her brother's voice sounded through the walls. "Karaaa!"

He was in trouble?

"Karaaa!"

She flew through the bathroom door. The bedroom door. Across the suite's hall. Slammed into Thomas's door and wrenched the knob. Threw the door open.

Thomas stood in the corner, all boxers and muscles and blood. A man of Mediterranean origin by all appearances had put him there with his knife. Carlos?

They both turned to her at the same time. She saw the long scar on his cheek then. Yes, Carlos. The man about to shove his blade through Thomas was the same who'd shot him a few days earlier.

She looked at Thomas again. He wasn't the same man she'd kissed on the forehead last night before retiring.

She'd told him to dream for a long time and become the kind of man who could save the world. She didn't know who he'd become in his dreams, but his eyes had changed. The sheets on the bed were stained with blood, some of it fresh, some dried black. He was bleeding from his shoulder and his forearm.

"Meet Carlos," Thomas said. "He hasn't heard about the antivirus that we have, so he thinks it's safe to kill me. I thought it would sound more convincing coming from you."

Had Thomas learned something about the antivirus from his dreams? Carlos's eyes jerked between them.

"What neither of you know," Thomas continued, "is that I have to take explosives of some kind back with me. The Horde is slicing my army to ribbons as we speak. I have fewer than five thousand men against a hundred thousand Scabs. I absolutely have to succeed. You understand? Both of you? I have to get this information and get back!"

He was babbling.

"The water doesn't work anymore, Kara. There's a gun under the bed. You don't have much time."

Carlos lunged at Thomas. Her brother slapped away the first blow with his right hand. The man followed with his left fist, which Thomas also deflected. But blocking the successive blows had left him exposed, and Kara had seen enough street fights in Manila to know that this was precisely what his attacker intended.

Carlos drove on, straight into Thomas, using his head as a battering ram. It connected solidly with Thomas's chin. Her brother dropped like a rock.

Kara dove for the bed and hit the carpet with a grunt. She rolled under the bed, saw the gun, and clawed for it.

5

A HORRENDOUS din filled the air.

The din of battle. Of death.

Thomas's eyes snapped open. He sat up and winced at the pounding pain in his head.

"Did you get it?" Mikil asked, dropping to one knee beside him.

"Get what?"

"I knew it!" She stood and walked away.

Of course, he'd gone for the explosives! His mind scrambled. "How long have I been unconscious?"

She shrugged. "Five minutes."

"Five minutes! I told you ten!"

"I didn't wake you. You woke on your own. Maybe it was Elyon waking you to go and lead your men."

"No, I have to go back!"

She looked at him. "Go back where?"

"I didn't have enough time. I have to get back to learn how to make explosives."

"This is nonsense. What would you have me do? Hit you on the head with another rock?"

"Yes!" He clamored to his feet. "It works. I'm dreaming again. I was there, Mikil!"

"And what did you do there?"

"I fought a man who was trying to shoot me with a gun. It's another kind of explosive device. He fights—he's very good. I think he knocked me out."

27

Thomas turned from her, remembering. "And Kara—" An ache in his shoulder stopped him.

There was a gash about three inches long just above his right bicep. He ran a finger along it, trying to recall if it had come from the battle below or from his dreams.

"Did I have this cut?" he asked her.

"You must have. I don't remember when—"

"No! It wasn't here when I came up. No one cut me while I was sleeping?"

"Of course not."

"Then it's from my dreams!" He grabbed Mikil's arm. "Knock me out! Now! Hurry! I have to get back to save my sister!"

"You don't have a sister."

"Hit me!" he cried. "Just hit me."

"It's not within me to strike my commander twice in the space of ten minutes, even if—"

"I order it." A tremor ran through his hands. "Pretend I'm not your commander. I'm a Scab and smell of rotten meat and I will knock your head off your shoulders if you don't defend—"

She was airborne and he made no attempt to deflect her blow. The leather sole of her boot struck him above his right ear, and he collapsed.

6

KARA'S HAND found the cold steel. She'd never felt such an intense sense of relief. She wrapped her fingers around the gun.

But her relief was premature. She was on her stomach, face planted in the carpet, useless. She twisted and rolled to her back. The gun clanged against the metal bedframe. A thunderous roar ripped through the cramped space.

She'd discharged the gun! Had she hit anyone? Put a hole in the wall or window? Maybe she'd hit Carlos. Or Thomas.

She twisted and saw that Thomas still lay on his back by the far wall. No bullet holes that she could see.

Something bounced on the bed. Carlos.

She fired into the mattress, wincing with the explosion. Again. *Boom, boom.*

She watched Carlos's feet land on the floor. Two long strides and he was into the hall.

Kara jerked the trigger and sent another shot in his general direction.

Carlos vanished toward the adjoining suite at the end of the hall. The door banged.

What if he hadn't really left? What if he was hiding around the wall, waiting for her to stand up and put the gun down before he rushed in and cut her throat?

She scooted into daylight, keeping the gun trained on the doorway as best she could considering all her nervous energy. She carefully stood, edged to the door, and circled to her left in a wide arc until she could see through the door into the hall.

No Carlos.

The door at the end of the hall was open. This man hadn't acted alone. Someone in the hotel had helped him access their suite through the one next to it.

"Thomas?"

Kara ran around the bed and knelt beside him. "Thomas!" She slapped his cheek lightly.

Someone was banging on the front door. They'd heard the shots. Carlos had fled because he knew they would hear the shots. Her accidental discharge may very well have saved both of their lives.

"Thomas, wake up, honey."

He groaned and slowly opened his eyes.

⎯⎯⎯

Thomas and Kara sat on the sofa in Merton Gains's suite, waiting for the deputy secretary of state to end a string of calls. He'd greeted them briefly, noted the details of the attack on Thomas, ordered more security for his own suite, and then excused himself for a few minutes. The world was unraveling behind closed doors, he said.

They could hear the secretary's muffled voice down the hall behind them. Kara spoke quietly, nearly a whisper.

"Fifteen? Fifteen years? You're sure?"

"Yes. I'm quite sure."

"How's that possible? You're not fifteen years older, are you?"

"My body isn't, nay—"

"Nay?"

"Sorry."

"Nay," she said. "Sounds . . . old."

"As I was saying, I'm about forty there. Honestly I feel forty here as well."

Amazing.

"So these wounds of yours are a definite change in the rules between these two realities," she said, indicating Thomas's arm. "Knowledge and skills have always been transferable both ways, but before the colored forest turned black, your injuries in that world didn't cross over here;

only injuries from this world crossed over there. Now it goes both ways?"

"Evidently. But it's blood that transfers, not merely injuries. Blood has to do with life. Actually, blood defiles the lakes, the boy said. It's one of our cardinal rules. In any case, it's going both ways now."

"But when you first hit your head—when this whole thing first started—it bled in both worlds."

"Maybe I really did wound it in both worlds at the same time. Maybe that's what opened this gateway." He sighed. "I don't know, sounds crazy. We'll assume that knowledge, skills, and blood are transferable. Nothing else."

"And that you're the only gateway. We're talking about *your* knowledge, your skills, your blood."

"Correct."

"It would explain why you haven't aged here," Kara said. "You get cut there and you get cut here, but you don't age the same, or gain weight the same, or sweat the same. Only specific events tied to the spilling of blood show up in both realities." She paused. "And you're a general over there?"

"Commander of the Forest Guard, General Thomas of Hunter," he said without batting an eye.

"How did that happen?" she asked. "Not that I don't think you couldn't be Alexander the Great himself, you understand. It's just a lot to digest. A little detail would help."

"Must sound pretty crazy, huh?" A grin played on his lips. This was the Thomas she knew.

He squeezed the leather cushion by his side. "This is all so . . . so strange. So real."

"That's because it *is* real. Please tell me you're not going to attempt another leap off the balcony."

He released the pillow. "Okay. Obviously both places are real. At least we're still assuming so, right? But you have to understand that after fifteen years in another world, this one here feels more like the dream. Forgive me if I behave rather oddly now and then."

She smiled and shook her head. He was half "rather oddly" and half the old Thomas.

"It's funny?" he asked.

"No. But just listen to you. 'Forgive me if I behave rather oddly now and then.' No offense, brother, but you sound a bit conflicted. Tell me more."

"After the Shataiki spread their poison through the colored forest, a terrible disease overtook the population. It makes the skin flake on the surface and crack underneath. It's very painful. The eyes turn gray and the body smells, like sulfur or rotten eggs. But Elyon made a way for us to live without the effects of this disease. Seven forests—regular forests, not colored ones—still stand, and in each forest is a lake. If we bathe in the lake each day, the disease remains in remission. The only condition we have for living in the forest is that we bathe regularly and keep the lakes from being defiled with blood."

She just looked at him.

"Unfortunately, I'm in a battle with the Horde at this very moment that may end it all."

"What about the prophecy?"

"That Elyon will bring down the Horde with one blow? Maybe dynamite is Elyon's answer." He stood, eager to move forward with this plan. "I have to figure out how to make dynamite before I go back."

"So I take it you're still dreaming," Gains said behind them.

Kara stood with her brother. Hearing the conviction in his voice and seeing the light in his eyes when he talked, she was tempted to think that the real drama was unfolding in a different reality, that the Raison Strain was only a story and the war in Thomas's desert was the real deal.

Gains brought her back to earth.

"Good," he said, rounding the sofa. "I have a feeling we're going to need these dreams of yours. Never imagined I would ever say something like that, but then again, I never imagined we would ever face such a monster either. Can I get either of you a drink?"

Neither responded.

"Again, the lack of security for your suite was my oversight. I hate to admit it, but we've underestimated you from the beginning, Thomas. I can guarantee you that has just changed."

Thomas said nothing.

Gains eyed him. "You sure you're okay?"

"I'm fine."

"Okay." He glanced at Kara, then back. "We need you on this, son."

"I'm not sure I can help anymore. Things have changed."

Gains stepped forward, took Thomas's arm, and guided him toward the window. "I'm not sure you realize the full extent of what's going on, but it's not looking good, Thomas. Raison Pharmaceutical has just concluded the examination of a jacket that was left on a coatrack in the Bangkok International Airport. A man reportedly harassed several flight attendants before walking to the first-aid station, hanging his coat on the rack, and leaving. Any guesses as to what's on the coat?"

"The virus," Kara said.

"Correct. The Raison Strain. As promised by Valborg Svensson. As predicted by none other than Thomas Hunter, which makes you a very, very important man, Thomas. And yes, the virus is airborne. Which means that if the three of us aren't already infected, we will be before we leave for D.C. Half of Thailand will be infected by week's end."

"Leaving for D.C.?" Thomas asked. "Why?"

"The president has suggested that you tell a committee he's pulling together what you know."

"I'm not sure I have anything to add to what you know."

Gains smiled nervously. "I know this hasn't been the easiest week for you, Thomas, but I'm not sure you're seeing the picture clearly here. We have a serious situation on our hands, and we don't have the first idea how to effectively deal with it. But you predicted the situation, and you seem to know more about it than anyone else at the moment. That makes you a guest of the president of the United States. Now. By force if necessary."

Thomas blinked. He glanced at Kara.

"Makes sense to me," she said.

"Any word on Monique?" Thomas asked.

"No."

"But you do understand what's happening now," Thomas said. "Svensson may not have the antivirus yet, but with her help, he will. When that happens, we're finished."

This was more like her old brother.

"I don't know what we are. At this point it's been taken out of my hands—"

"You see? I tell you something and you start in with the doubt. Why should I think that Washington will be any different?"

"I'm not doubting you! I'm just saying that the president has taken this over. I'm not the one who needs persuading; he is."

"Okay. I'll go. But I need your help too. I have to figure out how to create an explosion large enough to knock down a cliff before I fall sleep again."

Gains sighed.

Thomas stepped up, took Gains by the arm in almost the same fashion that Gains had taken his, and walked him slowly toward the same window.

"I'm not sure you realize the full extent of what's going on, but it's not looking good, Merton," he mimicked. "Let me help you. As we speak I am leading what remains of my army, the Forest Guard, in a terrible battle against the Horde. We number fewer than five thousand now. They number a hundred thousand. If I don't find a way to bring the cliff down on top of them, they'll overrun us and slaughter our women and children. That may be so much hogwash to you, fine. But there's another problem. If I die there, I die here. And if I'm dead here, I won't be of much help to you."

"Isn't that a bit of a stretch?"

Thomas thrust out his arm and pulled up his sleeve. "This bandage on my forearm covers a wound I received in battle today. My sheets upstairs are covered with blood. Carlos didn't cut me while I was sleeping. Who did? My temples are throbbing from a rock I took in the head. Believe me, the other reality is as real as this one. If I die there, I can guarantee you I die here."

And the opposite was true as well, Kara thought. *If he died here, then he would die in the forest.*

He pulled down his sleeve. "Now I'll do everything in my power to help you, if you'll help me stay alive. I would say that's an even exchange. Wouldn't you?"

An unsure grin crawled across the secretary's face. "Agreed. I'll see what I can do, on the condition that you won't talk about these kinds of details in front of the media or the establishment in Washington. I'm not sure they will understand."

Thomas nodded. "I see your point. Maybe, Kara, you could do some research for me while the secretary fills me in."

"You want me to figure out how to make explosives?" Her brow arched.

"I'm sure Gains can put a call in to the right people. We're in canyon lands. Lots of rock, rich in copper and tin ores. We make bronze weapons now. Even if we withdraw, we'll only have a few hours to find whatever ingredients you come up with and make explosives. It has to be strong enough to knock down canyon walls along a natural fault."

"Black powder," Gains said.

Thomas faced him. "Not dynamite?"

"I doubt it. Black powder was first made by combining several common elements. That's your best bet." He shook his head. "God help us. We're casually discussing which explosive will best blow up this 'Horde' while breathing in the world's deadliest virus."

"Who can help me?" Kara asked Gains.

He flipped open his cell phone, walked into the kitchen, punched up a number, spoke briefly in soft tones, and ended the call.

"You met Phil Grant last night. Director of the CIA. He's next door, and he'll put as many people as you need on it."

"Now?"

"Yes, now. If black powder can be found and made in a matter of hours, the CIA will find the people who can tell you how."

"Perfect." Thomas said.

Kara liked the new Thomas. She winked at him and left.

※

Thomas turned to Gains. "Okay now, where were you?"

It was all coming back to Thomas. Not that he'd forgotten any of the details, but he'd felt a bit disoriented thus far. He could only be spread so thin. With each passing minute in this world, his sense of its immediate crisis swelled, matching the crisis that depended on him in the other world.

"Washington."

Thomas ran a hand through his hair. "I can't imagine a group of politicians listening to anyone as forthright as me. They'll think I'm insane."

"The world's about to go ballistic, Thomas. The French, the British, the Chinese, Russia . . . every country in which Svensson has released this monster is reeling already. They want answers, and you may be the only person other than those complicit in this plot to give them answers. We don't have time to debate your sanity."

"Well said."

"You made a believer out of me. I've gone out on a limb for you. Don't back out on me, not now."

"Where has Svensson released the virus?"

"Come with me."

※

There was a sense of déjà vu to the meeting. Same conference room, same faces. But there were also some significant differences. Three new attendees had joined through video conference links. Health Secretary Barbara Kingsley, a high-ranking officer of the World Health Organization, and the secretary of defense, although he excused himself after only ten minutes. *Something was odd about his early departure,* Thomas thought.

Eyes flittered about the room on high-strung nerves. The confident glares of last night were gone. Most of them had trouble meeting his stare.

They spent thirty minutes rehashing the reports they'd received. Gains had been right. Russia, England, China, India, South Africa, Australia,

France—all of the countries that had been directly threatened this far were demanding answers from the State Department. But there were none, at least none that offered the slightest sliver of hope. And by end of day, the number of infected cities was promised to double.

Raison Pharmaceutical's report on the jacket left in the Bangkok airport took up fifteen minutes of speculation and conjecture, most of it led by Theresa Sumner from CDC. If, and it was a big *if*, she insisted, every city Svensson claimed to have infected actually had been infected, and if—again it was a big *if*—the virus did indeed act as the computer models showed it would, then the virus was already too widespread to stop.

None of them could quite grasp such a cataclysmic scenario.

"How in the name of heaven could anything like this have possibly happened?" Kingsley demanded. She was a heavy-boned woman with dark hair, and her question was greeted with silence.

This same simple question would be asked a hundred thousand times in as many clever ways as possible in the next week alone, Thomas thought.

"Mr. Raison, maybe you can give me an explanation that I would feel comfortable passing on to the president."

"It's a virus, madam. What explanation would you like?"

"I know it's a virus. The question is how is this possible? Millions of years of evolution or however we got here, and just like that a bug comes out of nowhere to kill us all off? These aren't the Dark Ages, for crying out loud!"

"No, in the Dark Ages the human race didn't have the technology to create anything this nasty."

"I can't believe you didn't see this coming."

It was as close to an accusation as one could make, and it silenced the room.

"Anyone who understands the true potential of superbugs could have seen something like this coming," Jacques de Raison said. "The balance of nature is a delicate matter. There is no way to predict mutations of this kind. Please explain that to your president."

They looked at each other as if at any moment one of them would surely say something that would set this terrible mistake straight.

April fools!

But it wasn't April and no one was fooling.

They rallied around Sumner's repeated announcement that the virus had only been verified in Bangkok. No one else knew quite what to look for, although the CDC was working feverishly to get the right information into the right hands.

"Don't we have a plane to catch?" Thomas finally asked.

They looked at him as if his statement should require some examination. Everything Thomas Hunter said was now worthy of examination.

"The car will take us in thirty minutes," Gains's assistant offered.

"Good. I'm not sure we're doing any good here."

Silence.

"How so?" someone finally asked.

"For starters, I've already told you all of this. And all the talk in the world won't change the fact that we're facing an airborne virus that will infect the world's entire population within two weeks. There's only one way to deal with the virus, and that is to find an antivirus. For that I believe we'll need Monique de Raison. The fate of the world rests on finding her."

He pushed back his chair and stood.

"But we can't speak of finding Monique de Raison here, because in doing so we'll probably tip our hand to Svensson. I believe he has someone on the inside."

Gains cleared his throat. "You're suggesting there's a mole? Here?"

"How else did Carlos know exactly where to find me? How else did he gain access to my suite through the adjoining room? How else did he know I was sleeping when he entered?"

"I have to agree," Phil Grant said. Thomas wondered if the man's trust of his colleagues had kept his own suspicions at bay until now. "There are other ways he could have gained access, but Thomas makes a good point."

"Then I must say that the French government would like custody of Thomas Hunter," Louis Dutêtre said.

All eyes turned to the French intelligence officer.

"Paris has come under attack. Mr. Hunter knew of that attack before it occurred. This places him under suspicion."

"Don't be ridiculous," Gains said. "They tried to kill him this morning."

"Who did? Who saw this mysterious intruder? As far as we know, Thomas is the mole. Isn't that a possibility? My country insists on the opportunity to interrogate—"

"Enough!" Gains stood. "This meeting is adjourned. Mr. Dutêtre, you may inform your people that Thomas Hunter is in the protective custody of the United States of America. If your president has a problem with that, please advise him to call the White House. Let's go."

"I object!" Dutêtre jumped to his feet. "We are all affected; we should all participate."

"Then find Svensson," Gains said.

"For all you know, this man *is* Svensson!"

Now there was an interesting idea.

Gains walked from the room without a backward glance. Thomas followed.

———— ✸ ————

The small jet winged westward over Thailand, bound for Washington, D.C., six hours after the first fax to the White House informed the world that everything had just changed for Homo sapiens. The CDC had now verified the virus in two new cities: New York and Atlanta. They started with the airports, following indications in Bangkok, and they hadn't needed to go any farther.

Svensson was using the airports.

Had used the airports.

The first critical decision was now upon the world leaders. Should they shut down the airports and by so doing slow the spread of the virus? Or should they avert public panic by withholding information until they had something more concrete?

According to Raison Pharmaceutical, closing the airports wouldn't slow the virus enough to make a difference—it was too widespread already. And panic wasn't a prospect any of the affected governments were willing to deal with yet. For now, the airports would remain open.

Thomas had been awake for only four hours, but now he was eager to fall asleep. He held the thin manila folder in his hands and read the contents for the fifth time.

Kara frowned. "It might not have the kind of power you need—it's pretty slow burning—but Gains was right. Black powder is the only explosive you have any chance of pulling together in the middle of nowhere."

"How am I going to find this stuff?"

"They tell me the kind of firepower you need isn't impossible. The Chinese figured it out nearly two thousand years ago by accident. You can be nearly 50 percent off on the combination of ingredients and still get a decent bang. And the three ingredients you'll need are very common. You just have to know what you're looking for, which you now do. Do you have sugar there?"

"Some, yes. From sugarcane, just like here."

"If you can't get to the charcoal quickly enough, sugar will work as a fuel as well. Here's a list of more substitutes. The ratios are all there. Stall the Horde, and stall them hard. Deploy a thousand soldiers to find what you need."

"A little research and you're ready to start commanding armies?" He grinned. "You'd be good there, Kara. You really would be."

"You like it better there than here?"

He hadn't considered the comparison. "I'm not sure there is a 'there' that's not also 'here.' Hard to explain and it's just a hunch, but both realities are actually very similar."

"Hmm. Well if you ever figure out how to take others with you, promise to take me first."

"I will."

She sighed. "I know this isn't exactly the best time to bring this up, but do you remember the last thing I told you before you disappeared for fifteen years last night?"

"Remind me."

"It was only twelve hours ago. I suggested that you become someone who could deal with the situation here. Now you've come back a general. It just makes me wonder."

"Interesting thought."

"You really have changed, Thomas. And I hate to break it to you, but I really think you've changed for the sake of this world, not that one."

"Maybe."

"We're running out of time. You've got to start figuring things out. Get past all this noncommittal 'maybe' and 'interesting thought' stuff. If you don't, we just may be toast."

"Maybe." He grinned and closed the folder. "But unless I can figure out how to survive as General Hunter there, I won't be around here to figure anything out. Like I said, if I die there, I think I die here."

"And if you die here?" she asked. "What happens if the virus kills us all?"

He hadn't connected the dots in that way, and her suggestion alarmed him. But it only made sense that if he died here along with the rest, he would die in the forest.

"Let's just hope this black powder of yours works, sis."

"Sis?"

"I've always called you that."

She shrugged. "Sounds odd now."

"I *am* odd, sis. I am very, very odd." He sighed, leaned his head back, and closed his eyes. "Time to get back into the ring. I'm almost tempted to ask you to rub my shoulders down. Fourteenth round and I'm dead on my feet."

"Not funny. You have everything you need?"

He tapped his head. "I've read the material a dozen times. Let's hope I can remember it. Let's hope I can find what I need."

"Elyon's strength," she said.

He cracked one eye and looked at her. "Elyon's strength."

7

"WAKE UP."

His cheek stung. A hand slapped it again several times.

Thomas pushed himself up. "I am awake! Give me a moment!"

Mikil stepped back.

Thomas's mind spun. After so long, transitions of his dreams felt surreal.

He looked at his second in command. Mikil. She could probably walk into any bar in New York and clear the place. She wore battle moccasins, a kind of boot with hardened-leather soles but cured squirrel hide around the ankles and halfway up the calf. A bone-handled knife was strapped to her lean, well-muscled leg. She wore thigh guards for battle and a short hardened-leather skirt that would stop most blows. Her torso was covered in the traditional leather armor, but her arms were free to swing and block. Her hair ordinarily fell to her shoulders, but she'd tied it back today for battle. She'd strapped a red feather to her left elbow, a gift from Jamous, who was courting her. A long scar ran from the dangling feather up to her shoulder, the work of a Scab moments before she'd sent him screaming into hell during the Winter Campaign.

Mikil's eyes had begun to turn gray. The report of skirmishes at the Natalga Gap had come during the night—she'd left the village without her customary swim in the lake. The Forest Guard Oath required all soldiers to bathe at least once every three days. Any longer and they would risk becoming like the Desert Dwellers themselves. The sickness affected not only the eyes and the skin, but the mind as well. The Guard had to either carry large amounts of water with them on campaigns or draw the battle lines close to home. It was the single greatest limiting factor a tactician could be handed.

Thomas had once been stranded for four days in the desert without a horse. He had two canteens, and he'd used one for a spit bath on the second day. But by the end of the third day, the onset of the disease was so painful that he could hardly walk. His skin had turned gray and flaked, and a foul odor seeped from his pores. He was still a day's walk from the nearest forest.

In a fit of panic he'd stripped naked, flung himself on the sand, and begged the blistering sun to burn the flesh from his bones. For the first time he knew what it meant to be a Desert Dweller. It was indeed hell on earth.

On the morning of the fourth day, he began to see the world differently. His craving for fresh water diminished. The sand felt better underfoot. He began to think that living life in this new gray skin might not be impossible after all. He wrote the thoughts off to hallucination and expected to die of thirst by day's end.

A group of straying Horde found him and mistook him for one of their own. He drank their stale water and donned a hooded cloak and demanded a horse. He could still remember the woman who'd given him hers as if he'd met her yesterday.

"Are you married?" she asked him.

Thomas stood there, scalp burning under the hood, and stared at the Desert Dweller, taken aback by her question. If he said yes, she might ask who was his wife, which might cause problems.

"No."

She stepped up to him and searched his face. Her eyes were a dull gray, nearly white. Her cheeks were ashen.

She drew back her hood and exposed her bleached hair. In that moment Thomas knew that this woman was propositioning him. But more, he knew that she was beautiful. He wasn't sure if the sun had gotten to him or if the disease was eating his mind, but he found her attractive. Fascinating, at the very least. No, more than that. Attractive. And no odor. In fact, he was sure that if he were somehow miraculously changed back into the Thomas with clear skin and green eyes, she would think that *his* skin stank.

The sudden attraction caught him wholly off guard. The Forest People followed the way of the Great Romance, vowing not to forget the love Elyon had lavished upon them in the colored forest. The Scabs did not.

Until this moment he'd never considered what a man's attraction to a female Scab felt like.

The woman reached a hand to his cheek and touched it. "I am Chelise."

He was immobilized with indecision.

"Would you like to come with me, Roland?" He'd given her the fictitious name knowing that his own was well known.

"I would, yes. But I first must complete my mission, and for that I need a horse."

"Is that so? What is your mission?" She smiled seductively. "Are you a fierce warrior off to assassinate the murderer of men?"

"As a matter of fact, I am an assassin." He thought it might earn him respect, but she acted as if meeting assassins in the desert was a common thing. "Who is this murderer of men?"

Her eyes darkened and he knew that he'd asked the wrong question.

"If you're an assassin, you would know, wouldn't you? There's only one man any assassin has taken an oath to kill."

"Yes, of course, but do *you* really know the business of an assassin?" he said, mentally scrambling for a way out. "If you are so eager to bear my children, perhaps you should know with whom you would make your home. So tell me, whom have we assassins sworn to kill?"

He could tell immediately that she liked his answer.

"Thomas of Hunter," she said. "He is the murderer of men and women and children, and he is the one that my father, the great Qurong, has commanded his assassins to kill."

The daughter of Qurong! He was speaking to Desert royalty. He dipped his head in a show of submission.

She laughed. "Don't be silly. As you can see, I don't wear my position on my sleeve."

The way her eyes had darkened when she spoke his name alarmed Thomas. He knew he was as despicable in the eyes of the Desert Dwellers as they were to him. But to discuss such a thing around the campfire after routing the enemy was one thing; to hear it coming from the lips of such a stunning enemy was quite another.

"Come with me, Roland," Chelise said. "I'll give you more to do than run around making hopeless assassination attempts. Everyone knows that Hunter is far too swift with his sword to yield to this senseless strategy of my father's. Martyn, our bright new general, will have a place for you."

It was the first time he'd heard the new general's name.

"I beg to differ, but I am the one assassin who can find the murderer of men and kill him at will."

"Is that so? You're that intelligent, are you? And are you bright enough to read what no man can read?"

She was mocking him by suggesting that he couldn't read?

"Of course I can read."

She arched an eyebrow. "The Books of Histories?"

Thomas blinked at the reference. She was speaking about the ancient books? How was that possible?

"You have them?" he asked.

Chelise turned away. "No. But I've seen a few in my time. It would take a wise man to read that gibberish."

"Give me a horse. Let me finish my mission, then I will return," he said.

"I'll give you a horse," she said, replacing her hood. "But don't bother returning to me. If killing another man is more important to you than serving a princess, I've misjudged you." She ordered a man nearby to give him a horse and then walked away.

His own Guard had nearly killed him at the edge of the forest. He bathed in the lake on the eve of the fourth day. Normally the cleansing of the disease felt soothing, but at this advanced stage of the disease, the pain was nearly unbearable. Entering the water had been not unlike pulling his skin off. It was no wonder the Scabs feared the lakes.

But the pain was only momentary, and when he emerged from the water, his skin was restored. Rachelle had finally and passionately kissed him on the mouth, now rid of its awful odor. The village had celebrated the return of its hero with more than its usual nightly celebration.

But the memory of that terrible condition with which the Horde lived every day never left him. And neither did the image of the woman from the desert. The only thing that separated her from Mikil was a bucket of Elyon's water.

Regardless of what he might want to think about the Desert Dwellers, one thing was indisputable: They had rejected the ways of Elyon. They were the enemy, and it wasn't their rotting flesh that Thomas hated as much as their treacherous, deceitful hearts. For the sake of Elyon, he and the Forest Guard had taken an oath to wipe the Horde from the earth or die in their attempt to do so.

"Did it work?" Mikil asked.

"Did what work?" His head throbbed. "The dreaming? Yes, yes it worked."

"But no way to bring down the cliff, I take it."

Hoofs pounded around the corner. William and Suzan rode on sweating mounts. The cliff?

The cliff! Black powder.

William pulled up and dropped to the ground. "Thomas! Our lines are breaking! I've brought two thousand from the rear and another two thousand will arrive in the night, but they're too many! It's a slaughter out there!"

"I have it!" Thomas cried.

"You have what?"

"Black powder. I know how to make black powder. In fact, I know a dozen ways to make it."

Suzan dismounted. All three looked at him, at a loss.

"Thomas ordered me to hit him on the head so that he could dream," Mikil said. "Evidently he has the ability to learn things from his dreams."

William blinked. "You do? What could you possibly learn that—"

"I've learned how to make black powder," Thomas said, marching past them. He turned back. "If we can make black powder, we have a chance, but we have to hurry."

"You plan to defeat the whores by sprinkling powder on them?" William demanded. "Have you gone mad?" His designation of the Hordes as whores had become commonplace among the Forest Guard.

"He plans to use the powder to break the cliff off," Mikil said. "Isn't that right, Thomas?"

"Essentially, yes. Black powder is an explosive, a fire that burns very fast and expands." He demonstrated with his hands. "If we could pack black powder into the crack at the top of the cliff and ignite it, the entire cliff might break off."

William was stupefied.

"You actually know how to make this black powder now?" Mikil asked.

"Yes."

"How?"

He recited the information from his memory. "Black powder is composed of three basic ingredients in roughly the following proportions: 15 percent charcoal, 10 percent sulfur, and 75 percent saltpeter. That's it. All we have to do is find these three ingredients, prepare them in tightly packed pouches, lower them—"

"What is sulfur?" Suzan asked.

"What is saltpeter?" Mikil asked.

"This is the most absurd thing I've ever heard anyone without scales for flesh utter!" William said.

Thomas began to lose his patience. "Did I say it would be easy? We're being slaughtered down there! You can't build such a devastating device without a bit of work. Charcoal we have, right? We burn it. A few fast riders can retrieve an ample supply and have it here by midnight. Sulfur is the sixteenth most common element occurring in the Earth's crust. And I do believe this is the same Earth's crust. Never mind that; just know that sulfur is found in caves with pyrite. Never mind that as well. The caves at the north end of the Gap. We'll need to break off the cones, heat them in a large fire, and pray that sulfur flows from the pores. Much like the metal ore."

An excitement was starting to show in Mikil's eyes, but William was frowning. "Even with the reinforcements we're badly outnumbered."

"What about the salt?" Mikil asked.

Thomas ignored William. "Saltpeter." He ran his fingers through his hair. "It's a white, translucent mineral composed of potassium nitrate."

They looked at each other.

"You see?" William asked. "He wants to make our fighters look for postass . . . a name he can hardly say, and in the dark? Because he dreamed—"

"Silence!" Thomas's voice rang over the sounds of battle. "If I fail this time, William, I will give you command of the Guard!"

"Where do we find this saltpeter?" Mikil pushed.

"I don't know."

"Then . . . what do you mean, you don't know?"

"We're looking for a translucent, milky rock that's salty."

William crossed his arms in disapproval.

"And if we do find these ingredients, what then?" Mikil asked.

"Then we have to grind them, mix them, compress the powder, and hope they ignite with enough force to do some damage."

Three sets of eyes locked on his. In the end they would agree because they all knew they had no viable alternative. But never had the stakes been so high.

"You do realize that if we must hold them off while we try this trick of yours, we lose the opportunity to evacuate the forest," William said. "If we leave now, we will have a half day start on the Horde because they won't march during the night. We could gather up the village and head north as planned."

"I realize that. But to what end? The Horde is overtaking the Southern Forest as we speak. Jamous is retreating. The Horde—"

"The Southern Forest?" William said. He hadn't heard.

"Yes. The Horde will take this forest and then move to the next."

Mikil looked to the west where the sounds of battle continued. "Maybe it would be wiser to retreat now, make this black powder of yours, and then, when we know it works, we blast the Horde to hell."

"If they take the Middle Forest—" He stopped. They all knew the loss of this forest was unacceptable. "When will we ever have them in a canyon like this? If this works, we could take out a third of their army in one blow. We can still order the evacuation, even if we aren't there to help." He followed Mikil's gaze westward. His men were dying and he was toying with wild dreams. "What if this is what the prophecy spoke of?"

"'In one incredible blow you will defeat the heart of evil,'" Suzan said, quoting from the boy's promise. "Qurong is leading this army while Martyn is attacking Jamous." A glimmer of eagerness lit her eye. "You think it will work?"

"We will know soon enough."

⸻

The moon shone high in the desert sky, surrounded by a million stars. Thomas sat on his stallion and studied the canyon floor. The Horde had settled in for the night, thousands upon thousands of Scab warriors, half sleeping in their cloaks, half milling in small groups. No fires. They'd won the battle and they'd celebrated their victory with a cry that had roared through the canyon like a mighty torrent.

Thomas had ordered his army back in a show of retreat. They'd hauled their catapults from the cliff and shown every sign of fleeing to the forest. Seven thousand of his men had joined the battle here in the canyon. Three thousand had given their lives.

It was the worst defeat they'd ever suffered.

Now their hope rested in a black powder that did not exist.

The Guard waited a mile to the west, ready to make for the forest at a moment's notice. If they could not find the saltpeter within the hour, Thomas would give the order.

They had enough charcoal already. William had led a contingent of soldiers to the caves for sulfur. They hauled nearly a ton of pyrite rock to a pit two canyons removed, where they'd built a fire and coaxed liquid sulfur from the stone. The stench had risen to the sky and Thomas couldn't remember ever being so ecstatic about such a horrible smell.

It was the odor of Scab flesh.

But the saltpeter eluded them. A thousand warriors searched in the moonlight for the white rock, licking when necessary.

"We could bring the archers back and at least give the Horde a parting surprise," Mikil said beside him.

"If we had any arrows left, I would shoot a few myself," Thomas said. He looked up at the moon again. "If we can't find the saltpeter in an hour, we leave."

"That's cutting it close. Even if we do find it, we have to mine it. Then grind it into powder, mix it, and test it. Then—"

"I know what we need to do, Mikil. It's my knowledge, remember?"

"Yes. Your dream."

He let the comment go. She'd always been a strong one, the kind of person whom he could trust to take his place at the head of this army if he were ever killed.

"If we are forced to flee, what will become of the Gathering?" she asked.

"Ciphus will insist on the Gathering. He'll hold it at one of the other lakes if he has to, but he won't neglect it."

She sighed. "And with all this nonsense of Justin coming to a head, I'm sure it will be a Gathering to remember. There's been talk of a challenge." Thomas had heard the rumors that Ciphus might press Justin into a debate and, if necessary, a physical contest for his defiance of the Council's prevailing doctrine. Thomas had witnessed three challenges since Ciphus had initiated them; they reminded him of the gladiator-style matches of the histories. All three usurpers had lost and been exiled to the desert.

"If there isn't, I may challenge him myself," Mikil continued.

"Justin's treachery is the least of our concerns at the moment. He will fall in battle like all of Elyon's enemies."

She dropped the subject and looked westward, toward the Middle Forest. "What will happen if the Horde overtakes our lakes?"

"We may lose our army, we may even lose our trees, but we'll never lose our lakes. Not before the prophecy delivers us. If we lose the lakes, then we will become Desert Dwellers against our will. Elyon would never allow it."

"Then he'd better come through soon," she said.

"You may not remember, but I do. He could clap his hands and end this tonight."

"Then why doesn't he?"

"He just might."

"Sir!"

A runner.

"William calls you. He says to tell you he may have found it."

———∞∞∞———

"Here! We'll do it all right here." Thomas gripped the large mallet in both hands and slammed it into the glowing rock. A slab of the cliff crashed down.

It was translucent and it was salty, and of all people to find it, William had. If it wasn't saltpeter, they would know soon enough.

Thomas grabbed a handful of the fragments. "Bring it down. All of it." He turned to William. Bring the charcoal and the sulfur. We will set up a line here for crushing the rock into powder and we'll mix it under that ledge. Put a thousand men on this if you have to. I want powder within the hour!"

He ran to his horse and swung into the saddle.

"Where are you going, sir?"

"To test this concoction of ours. Bring it down!"

They descended on the cliffs with a vengeance, swinging with bronze mallets and swords and granite boulders. Others began to crush the suspected saltpeter into a fine powder. They hauled the charcoal in and ground it further down the line. The sulfur caked the bronze bowls into which they had poured it. The cakes ground easily.

Very few knew what they were doing. Who'd ever heard of such a way to conduct a battle? But it hardly mattered—he'd ordered them to crush the rock, and the powder that was this rock would crush the enemy. He was the same man who'd shown them how to coax metals out of rocks by heating them, wasn't he? He was the man who had survived several days as a Scab and returned to wash in the lake. He was the man who had led them into battle a hundred times and emerged the victor.

If Thomas of Hunter told them to crush rocks, they would crush rocks. The fact that three thousand of their comrades had been killed by the Horde today only made their task more urgent.

Thomas knelt on the large stone slab and looked at a small pile of ground powder he had collected above the quarry.

"How do we measure it?" Mikil asked.

Despite his active participation, William's frown persisted.

"Like this." Thomas spilled the white powder in a line the length of his arm and tidied it so that it was roughly the same width for the entire length. "Seventy-five percent," he said. "And the charcoal . . ." He made another line of charcoal next to the white powder.

"Fifteen percent charcoal. One-fifth the length of saltpeter." He marked the line in five equal segments and swept four of them to one side.

"Now 10 percent sulfur." He poured the yellowed powder in a line two-thirds the length of the black powder.

"Look right to you?"

"Roughly. How exact does it have to be?"

"We're going to find out."

He mixed all three piles until he had a gray mess of powder.

"Not exactly black, is it? Let's light it up."

Mikil stood and backed away. "You're going to light it? Isn't it dangerous?"

"Watch." He made a trail of it and stood. "Maybe it's too much." He thinned the line so that it doubled in length to the height of a man.

William backed up a few steps, but he was clearly less concerned than Mikil.

"Ready?"

Thomas withdrew his flint wheel, a device that made sparks by striking flint against a rough bronze wheel. He started to roll the wheel on his palm but then opted for his thigh guard because his palm was moist with sweat. He lit a small roll of shredded bark.

Fire.

Mikil had backed up another few paces.

Thomas knelt at one end of the gray snake, lowered the fire, and touched it to the powder.

Nothing happened.

William grunted. "Huh."

And then the powder caught and hissed with sparks. A thick smoke boiled into the night air as the thin trail of black powder raced with fire.

"Ha!"

Mikil ran over. "It works?"

William had lowered his arms. He stared at the black mark on the rocks, then knelt and touched it. "It's hot." He stood. "I really don't see how this is going to bring down a cliff."

"It will when it's packed into bound leather bags. It burns too fast for the bags to contain the fire, and *boom*!"

"Boom," Mikil said.

"You've frowned enough for one evening, William. This is no small feat. Let your face relax."

"Fire from dirt. I will admit, it's pretty impressive. You got this from your dreams?"

"From my dreams."

Three hours later they had filled forty leather canteen bags, each the size of a man's head, with black powder, then wound these tightly in rolls of canvas. The rolls were hard, like rocks, and each had a small opening at its mouth, from which a strip of cloth that had been rolled in powder protruded.

Thomas called them bombs.

"Twenty along each cliff," Thomas instructed. "Five at each end and ten along the stretch through the middle. We have to at least box them in. Hurry. The sun will be up in two hours."

They crammed the bombs deep into the fault lines of each cliff for a mile on either side of the sleeping Horde. The strips of canvas rolled in powder ran up and then back, ten feet. The idea was to light them and run.

The rest was in Elyon's hands.

Placing the bombs took a full hour. Light already grayed the eastern sky above. The Horde began to stir. A hundred of the Forest Guard had been sent for more arrows. In the event that only half of the army below was crushed by rock, Thomas determined to fill the remainder with arrows. It would be like shooting fish in a barrel, he explained.

Thomas stood on the lookout, balancing the last bomb in his right hand.

"Are we ready?"

"You're keeping one out?" William asked.

Thomas studied the tightly rolled powder ball. "This, my friend, is our backup plan."

The canyon was gray. The Horde lay in their filth. Forty of Thomas's men knelt over fuses with their flint wheels ready.

Thomas took a deep breath. He closed his eyes. Opened them.

"Fire the north cliff."

A soft whoosh sounded behind him. The archer released the signal arrow. Fire shot into the sky, trailing smoke.

Twenty stood with Thomas on the ledge. They all stared at the cliff and waited.

And waited.

Nausea swept through Thomas's stomach.

"How long does it take?" someone asked.

As if in answer, a spectacular display of fire shot into the sky far down the cliff.

But it wasn't an explosion. The trapped bomb hadn't been strong enough to break its wrappings or the stone that squeezed it tight.

Another display went off closer. Then another and another. One by one the bombs ignited and spewed fire into the sky.

But they did not break the cliff.

Scabs began to scream in the canyon. None had seen such a show of power before. But it wasn't the kind of power Thomas needed.

He dropped the last bomb into his saddlebag and swung onto his horse. "Mikil, do not fire the southern cliff! Hold for my signal. One horn blast."

"Where are you going?"

"Down."

"Down to the Horde? Alone?"

"Alone."

He spun the stallion and kicked it into a full gallop.

Below, the Horde's cries swelled. But by the time Thomas reached the sandy wash, their fear had abated. Fire had erupted from the rocks above them, but not one Scab had been hurt.

Thomas entered the canyon and rode straight for their front lines at a full run. The sky was now a pale gray. Before him stretched a hundred thousand Scabs. Eighty thousand—his men had killed twenty thousand yesterday. None of this mattered. Only the ten thousand directly ahead, packed from side to side and watching him ride, mattered right now.

He leaped over the boulders the Forest Guard had used as a fighting base yesterday. If Desert Dwellers had trees and could make bows and arrows, they could have brought him down then, while he was still fifty yards out.

Thomas slid to a stop just out of spear range. *Elyon, give me strength.*

"Desert Dwellers! My name is Thomas of Hunter! If you wish to live even another hour, you will bring me your leader. I will speak to him and he will not be harmed. If your leader is a coward, then you will all die when we rain fire down from the skies and burn you to cinders!"

He calmed his stamping stallion and reached for the bomb in his saddlebag. He was playing this by ear, and it was a dangerous tune.

A loud rumble suddenly cracked the morning air and rolled over the canyon. A small section of cliff crashed down so far to the back of the army that Thomas could hardly see it. Dust rose to the sky.

A bomb had actually exploded! One bomb in twenty. Maybe a spark that had smoldered and fumed before detonating in a weak spot.

How many had been crushed? Too few. Still, the Horde shifted away from the cliff in a ripple of terror.

Bolstered by this good fortune, Thomas thundered another challenge. "Bring me your leader or we will crush you all like flies!"

The front line parted, and a Scab warrior wearing the black sash of a general rode out ten paces and stopped. But he wasn't Qurong.

"We aren't fooled by your tricks!" the general roared. "You heat rocks with fire and split them with water. We can do this as well. You think we fear fire?"

"Then you don't know the kind of fire that Elyon has given us! If you lay down your weapons and retreat, we will spare your army. If you stay, we will show you the fires of hell itself."

"You lie!"

"Then send out a hundred of your men, and I'll show you Elyon's power!"

The general considered this. He snapped his fingers.

None moved.

He turned and barked an order.

A large group marched out ten paces and stopped. It was a very dangerous tune indeed. If the bomb in his lap didn't detonate, there would be no bluffing.

"I suggest you move to the side," Thomas said.

The general hesitated, then walked his horse slowly away from his men.

Thomas withdrew his flint wheel, lit a two-foot fuse, and let it burn halfway before urging his horse forward. He ran the steed directly at the warriors, hurled his smoking bomb among them, and veered sharply to his right.

The smoldering bag landed in the middle of the Scabs, who instinctively ran for cover.

But there was no cover.

With a mighty *whump,* the bomb exploded, flinging bodies into the air. The concussion hit Thomas full in the face, a hot wind that momentarily took his breath away.

The general had been knocked off his horse. He stood calmly and stared at the carnage. At least fifty of his men lay dead. Many others were wounded. Only a few escaped unscathed.

"Now you will listen," Thomas cried. "You doubt that we can bring these cliffs down on you with such a weapon?"

The general held his ground. Fear wasn't common among the Horde, but this man's steel was impressive. He refused to answer.

Thomas pulled out the ram's horn and blasted once.

"Then you will see another demonstration. But this is your last. If you do not withdraw, every last one of you will die today."

The fireworks started at the far end, only this time on the southern cliff. Thomas desperately hoped for at least one more explosion. One weak spot along the cliff, and one bag stuffed with black powder to send tons of rock—

Whump!

A section of cliff began to fall.

Whump! Whump!

Two more! Suddenly a full third of the cliff slipped off the face and thundered down onto the screaming Horde. A huge slab of rock, enough to cover a thousand men, crashed to the ground, and then slowly toppled over and slammed into the army. The earth quaked, and more rock fell. Dust roiled skyward. Horses panicked and reared.

The Horde weren't given to fear, but they weren't suicidal either. The general gave the order to retreat only moments after the stampede had begun.

Thomas watched in stunned silence as the army fled, like a receding tide. Thousands had been killed by the rock. Perhaps ten thousand. But the greater victory here was the fear he'd planted in their hearts.

His own army cautiously edged to the lip of the northern cliff. What remained of it. Like him, they watched in a kind of stupefied wonder. They could have killed even more Scabs with the arrows that had just arrived, but the Forest Guard seemed to have forgotten those.

It took only minutes for the last of the Horde to disappear into the desert. As was their custom, they killed their wounded as they retreated. There was enough meat in this canyon to feed the jackals and vultures for a year.

Thomas sat alone on his horse staring down the deserted canyon, still unnerved by the devastation they had wrought upon the enemy. This enemy of Elyon.

His whole army had gathered above, seven thousand including those who'd arrived in the night. They began to chase the fleeing enemy with a chant of victory.

"Elyon! Elyon! Elyon!"

After a few minutes the chant changed. From the west toward the east, a single name swept along the long line of warriors. The chant grew until it filled the canyon with a thunderous roar.

"Hunter! Hunter! Hunter!"

Thomas slowly turned his horse and walked up the valley. It was time to go home.

8

CRISIS WAS a strange beast. At times it united. At times it divided.

For the moment, this particular crisis had at least forced a few of Washington's elite to lay aside political differences and submit to the president's demands for an immediate meeting.

Clearly, a virus was neither Democrat nor Republican.

Even so, Thomas sat at the back of the auditorium feeling out of place in this company of leaders—not because he was unaccustomed to leadership, but because his own experience in leadership was vastly different from theirs. His leadership had more to do with strength and physical power than with the manipulative politics that he knew would assert itself here.

He gazed out over the twenty-three men and women whom the president had gathered in the conference hall off the West Wing. Thomas had flown westward, over the Atlantic, and with the time change arrived midday in Washington. Merton Gains had left him with the assurance that he would be called upon to address their questions soon. Bob Stanton, an assistant, would answer any questions in the meantime. Bob sat on one side, Kara on the other.

Funny thing about Kara. Was he older than her now, or still younger? His body was still twenty-five, no denying that. But what about his mind? She seemed to look to him more as an older brother now. He'd given her the details of his victory using the black powder, and she'd mostly listened with a hint of awe in her eyes.

"They're late," Bob said. "Should've started by now."

Thomas's mind drifted back to the victory in the Natalga Gap. There, he was a world-renowned leader, a battle-hardened general, feared by the Horde, loved by his people. He was a husband, and a father to two children.

His fifteen years as commander had been gracious to him, despite the mis-judgments that William was kind enough to remind him of.

The chant still echoed through his mind. *Hunter, Hunter, Hunter.*

And here he was what? The twenty-five-year-old kid in the back who was going to talk about some psychic dreams he was having. *Grew up in the Philippines. Parents divorced. Mother suffers from manic depression. Never finished college. Mixed up with the mob. No wonder he's having these crazy dreams. But if President Robert Blair says he goes on, he goes on. Privileges of the office.*

A tall gray-haired man with a beak fit for a year bird walked on the stage and sat at a long table set up with microphones. He was followed by three others who took seats. Then the president, Robert Blair, entered and walked to the center seat. The meeting had the aura of a press conference.

"That's Ron Kreet, chief of staff, on the left," Bob said. "Then Graham Meyers, secretary of defense. I think you know Phil Grant, CIA. And that would be Barbara Kingsley, health secretary."

Thomas nodded. The big guns. The front row was crowded with vaguely familiar faces. Other cabinet members. Senators. Congressmen. Director of the FBI.

"Not often you get such a broad spectrum of power in one room," Bob said.

Ron Kreet cleared his throat. "Thank you for coming. As all of you know, the State Department received a letter by fax roughly fourteen hours ago that threatened our nation with a virus now known as the Raison Strain. You'll find a copy of this fax and all other pertinent documents in the folder you were given."

It was clear that not all of them had read the fax. A number flipped open their folders and shuffled through papers.

"The president has asked to speak to you personally on this matter." Kreet faced Robert Blair. "Sir."

Robert Blair had always reminded Thomas of Robert Redford. He didn't have as many freckles, but otherwise he was a spitting image of the actor. The president leaned forward and adjusted his mike, face relaxed, stern but not tense.

"Thank you for coming on such short notice." His voice sounded shallow. Blair shifted his head to one side and cleared his throat.

"I've thought of a dozen different ways to proceed, and I've decided to be completely candid. I've invited a panel to answer your questions in a moment, but let me summarize a situation that we're now opening up to you."

He took a deep breath. "A group of unconventional terrorists, whom we believe to be associated with a Swiss, Valborg Svensson, has released a virus in numerous cities throughout the world. These cities now include six of our own, and we believe that number will increase with each passing hour. We have verified the Raison Strain in Chicago, New York, Atlanta, Los Angeles, Miami, and Washington."

The room was still enough to pick out heavy breathers.

"The Raison Strain is an airborne virus that spreads at an unprecedented rate. It is lethal and we have no cure. According to our best estimates, three hundred million Americans will be infected by the virus within two weeks."

The room itself seemed to gasp, so universal was the reaction.

"That's . . . what are you saying?"

"I'm saying, Peggy, that if all the people in this room weren't infected ten minutes ago, you probably are now. I'm also saying that unless we find a way to deal with this virus, everyone living between New York and Los Angeles will be dead in four weeks."

Silence.

"You *knowingly* exposed us to this virus?" someone demanded.

"No, you were probably exposed before you set foot in this building, Bob."

Then noise. Lots of it. A cacophony of bewilderment and outrage. An older gentleman stood to Thomas's left.

"Surely you can't be sure of this. The claim will cause a panic."

A dozen others offered slightly less restrained agreement.

The president lifted his hand. "Please. Shut up and sit down, Charles! All of you!"

The man hesitated and sat. The room quieted.

"The only way we're going to make it through this is to focus on the problem. My blood has been drawn. I've tested positive for the Raison Strain. I have three weeks to live."

Smart man, Thomas thought. He'd effectively if only temporarily shut down the room.

The president reached to one side, lifted a ream of paper, and stood it on end using both hands. "The news doesn't get any better. The State Department received a second fax less than two hours ago. In it we have a very detailed and extensive demand. The New Allegiance, as they call themselves, will deliver an antivirus that would neutralize the threat of the Raison Strain. In exchange they have demanded, among other things, our key weapons systems. Their list is very specific, so specific that I'm surprised. It demands that the items be delivered to a destination of their choosing in fourteen days."

He lowered the paper with a gentle thump. "All of the nuclear powers have been given the same ultimatum. This, ladies and gentlemen, is not a group of schoolboys or some half-witted terrorists we're dealing with. This is a highly organized group that has every intention of radically shifting the balance of world power in the next twenty-one days."

He stopped and scanned the room. They were in a freeze frame.

A man in the front voiced the thought screaming through each of their minds. "That's . . . that's impossible."

The president didn't respond.

"Is that possible?" the man asked.

Bob leaned over to Thomas. "Jack Spake, ranking Democrat," he whispered.

"Is what possible?"

"Shipping our weapons in two weeks."

"We're analyzing that now. But they've been . . . selective. They seem to have considered everything."

"And you're telling us that with the brightest scientists and the best health-care professionals in the world, we have *no* way to deal with this virus?"

The president deferred to his secretary of health. "Barbara?"

"Naturally, we're working on that." Feedback squealed and she backed off before regaining the mike. "There are roughly three thousand virologists in our country qualified to work on a challenge of this magnitude, and we're securing their, um, assistance as we speak. But you have to understand that we're dealing with a mutation of a genetically engineered vaccine here—literally billions of DNA and RNA pairs. Unraveling an antivirus may take more time than we have. Raison Pharmaceutical, the creator of the vaccine from which the virus was adapted, is providing us with everything they have. Their information alone will take a week to sort through, even with the help of their own geneticists. Unfortunately, their top geneticist in charge of the project has gone missing. We believe she has been kidnapped by these same terrorists."

The magnitude of the problem was beginning to settle in.

A dozen questions erupted at once, and the president insisted on a semblance of order. Questions on the virus were fired in salvos and answered in fashion.

What about other forms of treatment? How does the virus work? How fast does it spread? How long before people start dying?

Barbara handled them all with a professionalism that Thomas found admirable. She showed them the same computer simulation that he'd seen in Bangkok, and when the screen went blue at the end, the questions came to a halt.

"So basically, this . . . this thing isn't going away, and we have no way to deal with it. In three weeks we'll all be dead. There's nothing . . . nothing at all that we can do. Is that what I'm hearing?"

"No, Pete, we're not saying that," the president said. "We're saying that we don't know of any way to deal with it. Not yet."

To their right a man with black hair and a perfectly round face stood. "And what happens if we give in to their demands?"

Bob leaned over. "Dwight Olsen. Senate majority leader. Hates the president."

The president deferred to the secretary of defense, Graham Meyers.

"As we see it, giving in to their demands is out of the question," Meyers said. "We don't deal with terrorists. If we were to hand over the weapons systems they've demanded, the United States would be left defenseless. We assume that these people are working with at least one sovereign nation. In the space of three weeks, that nation would hold enough power to manipulate whomever it wishes through threat of force. They would essentially enslave the world."

"Having a military doesn't give a nation control of the world," Olsen said. "The USSR had a military and didn't use it."

"The USSR had an opponent with as many nuclear weapons as they did. These people intend to disarm anyone with the will to deter them. You have to understand, they're demanding the delivery systems, the nukes, even our aircraft carriers, for crying out loud! They may not immediately have the personnel to man a battle group, but if they have our delivery systems, they won't need to. They're also demanding evidence, very detailed I might add, that we have disabled all of our early warning systems and long-range radar. Like the president said, we're not dealing with Boy Scouts here. They seem to know what they're talking about."

"What if one of the other countries hands over their weapons?" someone asked.

"We're doing our best to make sure that doesn't happen."

"But the alternative to handing over our weapons is death, right?" Dwight Olsen again.

The president reasserted himself. "Both are death. The only alternative that has any merit in my mind is to beat them up-front before the virus does its damage."

"The virus is already doing its damage."

"Not if we can find them and the antivirus in the next three weeks. It's the only course of action that makes any sense."

"Which I can assure you we're working on as we speak," CIA Director Phil Grant said. "We've temporarily suspended all other cases, over nine thousand, and directed all of our assets at locating these people."

"And what are your chances of doing that?" Olsen asked.

"We'll find them. The trick will be to find the antivirus with them."

The president leaned forward into his mike. "In the meantime, I think it's important that we confront this in the strictest of confidence. We need some ideas. Anything you can think of—I'm all ears. I don't care how crazy it sounds."

A kind of mad chaos overtook the room for the next hour. *They all seemed to function in it, but to say they controlled it would be wrong,* Thomas thought. *The chaos controlled them.*

He watched the verbal sparring, taken by it. It was not so different from his own Council. Here was an advanced civilization doing precisely what his own people did, exploring and vigorously defending ideas, not with swords, but with tongues as sharp as swords.

He stopped keeping track of who asked questions and who answered, but he mulled each one carefully. Americans really did have a kind of uncommon resourcefulness when pressed.

"It would seem that slowing the spread of the virus could at least buy us time," a handsome woman in a navy business suit observed. "Time is both our greatest enemy and our greatest ally. We should shut down travel."

"And cause widespread panic? A threat of this magnitude would bring out the worst in people."

"Then offer them another reason," the woman responded. "Issue a heightened terror alert based on information we can't disclose. They'll assume we're dealing with a bomb or something. Ground air travel and shut the airports. Stop all interstate travel. Anything we can to slow the spread of the virus. Even a day or two could make the difference, right?"

Barbara, the secretary of health, responded. "Technically, yes."

No one objected.

"Frankly, we might be better off concentrating on the antivirus and the means to distribute it on short notice. Getting a vaccine out to six billion people isn't an easy chore."

"But you're saying that everyone here is supposedly infected?" someone asked. "Shouldn't we isolate whatever command and control hasn't been infected? Keep them in isolation as long as is necessary."

"Can you insulate people from this thing?" someone else asked.

"There has to be a way. Clean rooms. Put them on the space shuttle and send them to the space station for all I care."

"To what end? What good are a couple hundred generals in the space station if the rest of the world is dying?"

"Then isolate the scientists who are working on the antivirus. Or give the space station the codes to launch a few well-aimed nukes down the throats of whoever's caused this thing if it ever gets to that."

To what end? Thomas wondered. Retaliation felt hollow in the face of death. The debate stalled.

"We lead this country, we die with this country if it comes down to that," the president finally said. "But I don't see the harm of insulating a thread of command and control and as many scientists as possible."

The chaos gradually gave way to a sober tension. Crisis sometimes divided and sometimes united. Now it united.

At least for the moment.

———— ✖ ————

The meeting was two hours old when the question that brought Thomas forward was finally asked.

The blue-suited woman. The smart one. "How do we know that they actually have an antivirus?"

No answer.

"Isn't it possible that they're bluffing? If it takes us months to create a vaccine or an antivirus, how is it they have one? You said the Raison Strain is a brand-new virus, less than a week old, a mutation of the Raison Vaccine. How did they get an antivirus in under a week?"

The president glanced toward Thomas near the back, then nodded at Deputy Secretary Gains, who stood and walked to an open mike. He'd spoken only a few times during the entire discussion, deferring to his superior, Secretary of State Paul Stanley, as a political courtesy, Thomas assumed.

"There's more to this. Nothing that changes what you've heard, but something that may assist us in a more . . . unconventional way. I hesitate because I'm about to open Pandora's box, but considering the situation, I think it best to go ahead."

Any trace of desire Thomas had to speak to this group suddenly vacated him. He was no more a politician than he was a rat.

"Roughly two weeks ago a man called one of our offices and claimed that he was having some strange dreams."

Thomas closed his eyes. Here they went.

"He came to the conclusion that the dreams were real, because in his dreams there were history books that recorded the histories of Earth. He could go to these history books and learn who won the Kentucky Derby this year, for example. Which he did, *before* the Derby was run, mind you. And he was right. Actually made over three hundred thousand on the long shot. The information in the history books from his dream world was real. Exact."

Thomas was a little surprised there weren't at least a few snickers.

"The reason he called our offices was because he learned something rather disturbing, namely, that a malicious virus named the Raison Strain would be released around the world this week. Again, this was nearly two weeks ago, before the Raison Strain even existed."

They were at least listening.

"No one listened to him, of course. Who would? He went to Bangkok and took matters into his own hands. For the past week he has been feeding us a steady diet of facts, all in advance of their happening."

He paused. No one was moving.

"I flew to Bangkok yesterday on the request of the president," Gains said. "What I have seen with my own eyes would leave you in shock. Like me, you've probably come to the conclusion that our nation is in a very, very bad place. The situation seems hopeless. If there's any one person who can save this country, ladies and gentlemen, it might very well be Thomas Hunter. Thomas?"

Thomas stood and stepped into the aisle. He walked toward the front, feeling self-conscious in the black slacks and white shirt he'd purchased at the mall on their way here from the airport. He must look very, very strange. *Here is the man who has seen the end of the world.* He was as disconnected from their reality as the Hulk or Spiderman.

He covered the mike. "I'm not sure this is going to do any good," he said quietly. The president held him with a steady gaze.

"Make them believe, Thomas," Gains said. "Let them ask their questions." He offered an anemic smile and stepped aside.

Thomas faced the audience. Twenty-three sets of eyes, as unsure and awkward as he was, stared at him.

He felt sweat bead on his forehead. If they knew how uncertain he felt, his information would fall on deaf ears. He had to play his part with as much conviction as he could muster. It didn't matter if they accepted him or liked him. Only that they heard him.

"I know this all sounds pretty crazy to some of you, maybe all of you. And that's okay." His voice sounded loud in the still room. "My name is Thomas Hunter, and the fact is, no matter how I know what I know—no matter how incredible it sounds to you—I do know a few things. If you follow what I'm about to tell you, you may have a chance. If you don't, you'll probably be dead in less than twenty-one days."

He sounded far too confident. Even cocky. But it was the only way he knew in this reality.

"Should I continue?"

"Continue, Thomas," the president said behind him.

His reservations fell like loosed chains. The plain truth was that he probably had more to offer the country than any other person in this room. And not because he wanted to carry such a responsibility. He had nothing to lose. None of them did.

"Thank you."

Thomas strolled to his right, then remembered the mike and walked back, studying them. He may get only one shot at this, so he would give it to them in a language that would at least cause a stir.

"I've lived a lifetime in the past two weeks. I've also learned some things in that lifetime. In particular, that most men and women will yield to the strong currents sucking them into the seas of ruin. Only the strongest in mind and spirit will swim against that current. A bit philosophical maybe, but it's what some people say where I come from, and I agree."

He paused and made eye contact with the navy-suited woman whose question had led to Gains's introduction.

"You'll all be sucked out to sea if you're not very, very careful. I know I must sound like a spiritual adviser to you. Not so. I'm only speaking what I know, and here's what I know."

The woman was smiling gently. Support or incredulity, he didn't know. Didn't care.

"I know that the Swiss will have the antivirus if he doesn't already. I know this because that's what the history books say. Some people survive. Without an antivirus any survival would be impossible."

Thomas took a breath and tried to read them, but the difference between being shocked by a speaker's knowledge and being shocked by his audacity was a difficult thing to gauge.

"Furthermore, I know that the U.S. will eventually yield to his demands and hand over its weapons. I know that the whole world will give in to this man, and even then, half of the world's population will die, though I can only guess which half. This will lead into a time of terrible tribulation."

He sounded like a prophet, or like a schoolteacher lecturing children. It was the last thing he wanted, although he supposed in some unconventional way he was a prophet. Was it possible that he was meant to be here today?

"If you give in to the Swiss, you'll follow the course of history as it's written. You'll be sucked out to sea. Your only hope is to resist those who demand you yield. You'll either find a way to change history, or you'll follow its course and die, as it is written."

"Excuse me."

It was Olsen, the black-haired man who Bob claimed was an enemy of the president. He was grinning wickedly.

"Yes, Mr. Olsen?"

The man's eyes twitched. He hadn't expected to be called by name.

"You're saying that you're a psychic? The president is now counseling psychics?"

"I don't even believe in psychics," Thomas said. "I am simply someone who knows more than you do about a few things. The fact, for example, that you will die in less than twenty-one days due to massive hemorrhaging in your heart and lungs and liver. You will have less than twenty-four hours from the onset of symptoms to your death. I know it all sounds a bit harsh, but then I'm assuming none of you has the time for games."

Olsen's smug grin vanished.

"I also suspect that within one week you will lead a motion to give in to Svensson's demands. That's not from the Books of Histories, you understand. It's my judgment based on what I've observed of you today. If I'm right, you are the kind of man the rest in this room must resist."

Gains chuckled nervously. "I'm sure Thomas isn't entirely sincere. He has unique . . . wit, as I'm sure you can see. Are there other questions?"

"Are you serious?" Olsen demanded, looking at Gains. "You actually have the audacity to parade a circus act in front of us at a time like this?"

"Dead serious!" Gains said. "We're here today because we didn't listen to this man two weeks ago. He told us what, he told us where, he told us when, and he told us why, and we ignored him. I suggest you take every word he speaks as though it were from God himself."

Thomas cringed. He hardly faulted the group for their doubt. They had no reference against which to judge him.

"So you learned about all of this because it's all recorded in some history books in another reality?" the navy-suited woman asked.

"Your name?" Thomas asked.

"Clarice Morton," she said, glancing at the president. "Congresswoman Morton."

"The answer is yes, Ms. Morton. I really did. Any number of events can confirm that. I knew about the Raison Strain over a week ago. I reported it to the State Department and then to the Centers for Disease Control. When neither was helpful, I flew to Bangkok myself. In an admittedly desperate act, I kidnapped Monique de Raison—perhaps you heard about that. I was attempting to help her understand how dangerous her vaccine really was. Needless to say, she now understands."

"So you convinced her before this all happened?"

"She demanded specific information from me. I went into the histories and retrieved the information. She knew then. That was before Carlos shot me and took her. They're undoubtedly using her now to create the antivirus."

"You were shot?"

"A very long story, Ms. Morton. Moot at this point."

Gains was having difficulty suppressing a small grin.

"So if this really is all true, if you can get information about the future as a matter of history—and for the moment I'm going to believe you can—then can you find out what happens next?"

"If I could find the Books of Histories, technically, yes. I could."

She glanced at the president. "And if you can find out what is going to happen, then we might be able to find out how to stop it, right?"

"We might be able to, yes. Assuming history can be changed."

"But we have to assume it can be, or all of this is all moot, as you say."

"Agreed."

"So then can you find out what happens next?"

Thomas had understood where she was going, but not until now did her simple suggestion strike a chord in his mind. The problem, of course, was that the Books of Histories were no longer available. He'd lived with that realization for fifteen years. But rumor was they still existed. He'd never had reason to search them out. Defending the forests from the Horde and celebrating the Great Romance had been his primary passion in the forest. Now he had a very good reason to search them out. They might provide a way out of this mess, precisely as Clarice was suggesting.

"Actually, the Books of Histories . . . are not presently available."

A murmur rippled through the room. It was as if this little bit of information actually interested them. They were incensed. *How convenient. The Books of Histories have gone missing! Yes, of course, what did you expect? It always works that way.*

Or maybe they were disappointed. Some of them at least wanted to believe everything he had said.

And so they should. Decent men and women could see sincerity when it stared them in the face.

"This is absurd!" Olsen said.

"Then I'm afraid that I'm leaning toward the absurd, Dwight," the president said. "Thomas has earned himself a voice. And I think Clarice is on to something. Can you find anything more for us, Thomas?"

Could he? His answer was as calculating as it was truthful. "Maybe."

Olsen muttered something, but Thomas couldn't make it out.

The president closed his folder. "Good. Ladies and gentlemen, please send any additional thoughts and comments through my staff. Good evening. And may God preserve our nation." He stood and left the room.

Now the crisis would divide.

"Six more cities," Phil Grant said, slapping the folder down on the coffee table. His maroon silk tie hung loose around his neck. He ran a finger under his collar and loosened it even more. "Including St. Petersburg. They're climbing the walls. If the Russians keep this under their hats, it'll be a miracle."

"This . . . this is a nightmare," his assistant said. Thomas watched Dempsey walk to the window and stare out with a lost gaze. "The Russians have decades of experience keeping things under the lid. I'd worry about the United States. If I were a betting man, I'd say Olsen's already leaking this. How many did you say?"

"Twenty. All airports. Like clockwork."

"We *aren't* closing the airports?"

"CDC ran another simulation using the latest data. They say closing the airports won't help at this point. There've been over ten thousand flights in the continental U.S. since the virus first hit New York. Conservative estimates have a quarter of the country exposed already."

Grant put his elbows on his knees and formed a tent with his fingers. A slight tremor shook his hands. Dempsey paced back from the window, frowning. Sweat darkened his pale blue shirt at the armpits. The full reality of what had been delivered to the United States of America was finally and terribly settling into the CIA.

Grant had brought Thomas to the CIA headquarters in Langley forty-five minutes ago.

"You're convinced this psychologist is worth our time?" Thomas asked. "It just seems like a lot of downtime."

"On the contrary, trying to unlock that mind of yours is the only thing that makes sense where you're concerned," Grant said.

"Memories, maybe. But I wouldn't assume that whatever is happening is happening in my head," Thomas replied.

"I'll settle for memories. If you gave the antivirus characteristics to Carlos like you think you may have, that information would be a memory. With any luck Dr. Myles Bancroft can stimulate that memory. You have no information, none whatsoever, on where Svensson might be holing up?"

"None."

"Or where he could have Monique?"

"I assume she's wherever he is. The only communication has been through the faxes, sent from an apartment in Bangkok. We took it down six hours ago. It was empty except for a laptop. He's using relays. Smart to stay off the Web by using facsimile. The last fax came from an address in Istanbul. As far as we know, he has a hundred relays. Took us how long to track down Bin Laden? This guy could be worse. But in a few days I doubt it will matter. As you pointed out earlier, he's undoubtedly working with others. Likely a country. You'll know where to look then."

"But only because he wants us to know. We can't very well bomb Argentina or whatever country he's using. Not as long as he has the antivirus." The director stood and grunted. "The world's coming apart at the seams and we're sitting here, blind as bats," Grant replied.

"Whatever happens, don't let anyone talk the president into compromising," Thomas said.

"I think you'll have the opportunity to do that yourself," Grant said. "He wants to meet with you personally tomorrow."

The phone rang. Grant snatched it up and listened for a moment. "On our way." He dropped the phone in its cradle. "He's ready. Let's go."

Dr. Myles Bancroft was a frumpy, short man with wrinkled slacks and facial hair poking out of his orifices, overall not the kind of man most people would associate with the Pulitzer Prize. He wore a small knowing grin that was immediately disarming—a good thing, considering what he played with.

People's minds.

His lab occupied a small basement on the south side of Johns Hopkins's campus. They'd flown Thomas in by helicopter and hurried him down the steps as if he were a man committed to the witness protection program and they'd received warnings of snipers on the adjoining roofs.

Thomas faced the cognitive psychologist in the white concrete room. Two of Grant's men waited with crossed legs in the lobby. Grant had remained in Langley with a thousand concerns clogging his mind.

"So basically you're going to try to hypnotize me, and then you're going to hook me up to these machines of yours and make me fall asleep while you toy with my mind using electrical stimuli."

Bancroft grinned. "Basically, yes. I describe it using more glamorous, fun words, but in essence you have the picture, lad. Hypnosis can be rather unreliable. I won't josh you. It requires a particularly cooperative subject, and I would like you to be that subject. But even if you're not, I may be able to accomplish some interesting results by Frankensteining you." Another grin.

Thomas liked this man immensely. "And can you explain this Frankensteining of yours? In terms I can understand?"

"Let me give it a whirl. The brain does record everything; I'm sure you know that. We don't know precisely how to access the information externally or to record memories, et cetera, et cetera. But we are getting close. We hook you up to these wires here and we can record the wave signatures emitted by the brain. Unfortunately, we're a bit fuzzy on the brain's language, so when we see a zip and a zap, we know it means something, but we don't yet know what zip or zap means. Follow?"

"So basically you're clueless."

"That about summarizes it. Shall we get started?"

"Seriously."

"Well, it's rather . . . speculative, I must admit, but here you go: I have been developing a way to stimulate memories. Different brain activities have different wave signatures. For example, in the simplest of terms, conceptual activity, or waking thought, looks different from perceptual, dream thought. I've been mapping and identifying those signatures for some time. Among countless other discoveries, we've learned that there's a connection between dreams and memories—similar signatures, you see. Similar brain language, as it were. Essentially what I'm going to do is record the signatures from your dreams and then force-feed them into the section of your brain that typically holds memory. This seems to excite the memory. The effect isn't permanent, but it does stimulate the memories of most subjects."

"Hmm. But you can't isolate any particular memories. You just have a general hope that I wake up remembering more than when I fell asleep."

"In some cases, yes. In others, subjects have dreams that turn out to be actual memories. It's like pouring liquid into a cup already brimming with water or, in this case, memories. When you pour the liquid in, the water is displaced over the lip. Quite fun actually. The memory stimulation even seems to help some subjects remember the dreams themselves. As you know, the average person experiences five dreams per night and remembers one at the most. Not so when I hook you up. Shall we begin?"

"Why not?"

"First, some basics. Vitals and whatnot. I need to draw some blood and have it analyzed by the lab for several common diseases that affect the mind. Just covering our bases."

Half an hour later, after a brief battery of simple tests followed by five failed attempts to lure Thomas into a hypnotic state, Bancroft changed tracks and hooked him up to the EEG machine. He connected twelve small electrodes to various parts of his head before feeding him a pill that would calm him without interfering with brain activity.

Then he turned down the lights and left the room. Moments later, soft music began to play through ceiling speakers. The chair Thomas lay in was similar to a dentist's chair. He wondered if there was a pill that could block his dreams. It was the last thought he had before slipping into deep sleep.

———

Mike Orear left his office at CNN at six and struggled through traffic for the typical hour it took to reach Theresa Sumner's new home on the south side. He hadn't planned on seeing her tonight, though he wasn't complaining.

She had been called off to some assignment in Bangkok for the CDC and returned earlier today to another private meeting in Washington. A bit unusual, but only a bit. They both lived lives full of curve balls and sudden changes in plan.

Theresa had called him from the tarmac at Reagan International, telling him to get his sorry self to her house tonight by eight. She was in one of her irresistibly bossy moods, and after giving her a piece of his mind, mostly nonsense that made for good drama, he agreed as they both knew he would before she'd even asked. He'd only been to her new house three or four times in the ten months they'd dated, and he never left disappointed.

A white box-looking car—a Volvo—rode to his right and a black Lincoln to his left. Neither of the drivers looked at him when he drilled them with a good stare. This was the rush hour in Atlanta, and everyone was lost in his own world, oblivious to anyone else's. These zombies floated through life as if nothing would ever matter in the end.

Three years ago, his reassignment to the Atlanta office from North Dakota to anchor the late-afternoon hours was a good thing. Now he wasn't so sure. The city had its distractions, but he was growing tired of pursuing them. One of these days he would have to quit playing the tough guy and settle down with someone more like Betty than Theresa.

On the other hand, he liked playing most of this game he was playing.

He could turn the tough act on or off with the flip of a hidden switch, a real advantage in this business. To the audience and some of his peers, he was the genuine North Dakota face with a GQ shadow and dark wavy hair that they could always trust. To others, like Theresa, he was the enigmatic college quarterback who could have made pro if not for the drugs.

Now he threw words instead of balls and could deliver them at any pace required by the game.

He finally pulled his BMW in front of the white house on the corner of Langshershim and Bentley.

He sighed, opened the door, and unfolded himself from the front seat. Her car was in the garage. He could just see the SUV's roof rack through the window.

He sauntered up to the door and rang the bell.

Theresa opened the door and walked back into the kitchen without a word. See, now Betty, the girl he'd dated for two years during college, never would have done that—not knowing he'd driven for an hour to see her. Well, maybe she would as a come-on now and then, but never while wearing this distant, nearly angry look.

Her short blond hair was disheveled and her face was drawn—not exactly the tempting, sexy look he had expected. She pulled a wineglass from her rack and poured Sauvignon Blanc.

"Am I wrong, or did you actually invite me out here?" he asked.

"I did. And thank you. I'm sorry, I just . . . it's been a long day." She forced a smile.

This wasn't a game. She was obviously bothered by something that had happened on her trip. Theresa put both hands on the counter and closed her eyes. He registered alarm for the first time.

"Okay, what's wrong?"

"Nothing. Nothing I can tell you. Just a bad day." She took a long drink and set the glass down. "A very bad day."

"What do you mean you can't tell me? Your job's okay?"

"For the time being." She took another drink. He saw that her hand was trembling.

Mike stepped forward. Took the glass from her hand. "Tell me."

"I can't tell—"

"For crying out loud, Theresa, just tell me!"

She stepped away from the counter and ran her hands through her hair, blowing out a long sigh. He couldn't remember ever seeing her in this condition. Someone had died, or was dying, or something terrible had happened to her mother or the brother who lived in San Diego.

"If you're trying to scare me, you've already done it. So if you don't mind, let's cut the games. Just tell me."

"They'd kill me if I told you. *You* of all people."

"'You' meaning me in the news?" She'd said too much already, and her quick side glance confirmed it. Something had gone down that would make her sweat bullets and send a newsman like him into orbit. And she was sworn to secrecy.

"Don't you kid yourself," he said, grabbing a glass from the rack. "You called me down here to tell me something, and I can guarantee you I won't leave until you do. Now we can sit down and get sloshed before you tell me, or you can tell me straight up while we still have our full wits about us. Your choice."

"What kind of assurance that you don't go public with this?"

"Depends."

"Then forget it." Her eyes flashed. "This isn't the kind of thing that 'depends' on anything you think or don't think." She wasn't in complete control of herself. Whatever had happened was bigger than a death or an accident.

"This has something to do with the CDC, right? What, the West Nile virus is loose in the White House?"

"I swear, if you even breathe—"

"Okay." He lifted both hands, balancing the glass in his right. "Not a word about anything."

"That's not—"

"I swear, Theresa! You have my complete assurance that I won't breathe a word to anyone outside this house. Just tell me!"

She took a deep breath. "It's a virus."

"A virus. I was right?"

"This virus makes the West Nile virus look like a case of hiccups."

"What then? Ebola?" He was half-kidding, but she glared at him, and for a horrible moment he thought he might have hit it.

"You're kidding, right?"

Of course she wasn't kidding. If she was kidding, her upper lip wouldn't be misty with sweat.

"The Ebola?"

"Worse."

He felt the blood drain from his face.

"Where?"

"Everywhere. We're calling it the Raison Strain." The tremor had spread from her hands to her voice. "It was released by terrorists in twenty-four cities today. By the end of the week every person in the United States will be infected, and there is no treatment. Unless we find a vaccine or something, we are in a load of hurt. Atlanta was one of the cities."

He couldn't quite sort all of this into the boxes he used to understand his world. What kind of virus was worse than Ebola?

"Terrorists?"

She nodded. "They're demanding our nuclear weapons. The *world's* nuclear weapons."

Mike stared at her for a long time.

"Who's infected? I mean, when you say Atlanta, you aren't necessarily saying—"

"You're not listening, Mike. There's no way to stop this thing. For all we know, everyone at CNN is already infected."

He was infected? Mike blinked. "That's . . . how can that be? I don't feel like I have anything."

"That's because the virus has a three-week latency period. Trust me, if we don't figure this out, you'll feel something in a couple weeks."

"And you don't think the people deserve to know this?"

"Why? So they can panic and run for the hills? I swear, Mike, if you even look funny at anyone down at the network, I'll personally kill you! You hear me?" She was red.

He set his glass on the counter and then leaned on the cabinet for balance. "Okay, okay, just calm down." There was still something wrong with what she'd told him. He couldn't put his finger on it, but something didn't compute.

"There has to be a mistake. This . . . this kind of thing just doesn't happen. No one knows about this?"

"The president, his cabinet, a few members of Congress. Half the governments in the world. And there is no mistake. I ran some of the tests myself. I've studied the model for the past twelve hours. This is it, Mike. This is the one we all hoped would never come."

Theresa dropped into an armchair, rested her head, closed her eyes, and swallowed.

Mike straddled a table chair, and for a long time neither spoke. The air conditioner came on and blew cold air through his hair from a ceiling vent. The refrigerator hummed behind him. Theresa had opened her eyes and was staring at the ceiling, lost.

"Start at the beginning," he said. "Tell me everything."

There was a problem with the EEG.

Bancroft knew this wasn't true. He knew that something strange was happening in that mind that slept in his chair, but the scientist in him demanded he eliminate every possible alternative.

He switched out the EEG, plugged the twelve electrodes back in, and reset it. Wave patterns consistent with conceptual brain activity ran across the screen. Same thing. He knew it. Same thing as the other unit. There were no perceptual waves.

He checked the other monitors. Facial color, eye movement, skin temperature. Nothing. Not a single cottonpickin' thing. Thomas Hunter had been asleep for two hours. His breathing was deep and his body sagged in the chair. No doubt about it, this man was lost to the world. Asleep.

But that's where the typical indications ended. His skin temperature had not changed. His eyes had not entered REM. The signatures on the EEG did not show a hint of a perceptual signature.

Bancroft walked around the patient twice, running down a mental checklist of alternative explanations.

None.

He walked into his office and called the direct line Phil Grant had given him.

"Grant."

"Hello, Mr. Grant. Myles Bancroft with your boy here."

"And?"

"And I think we have a problem."

"Meaning what?"

"Meaning your boy's not dreaming."

"How's that possible? Does that happen?"

"Not very often. Not this long. He's sleeping, no doubt. Plenty of brain activity. But whatever's going on in that head of his isn't characterized by anything I've seen. Judging by the monitors, I'd say he's awake."

"I thought you said he was sleeping."

"He is. Ergo, the problem."

"I'll be over. Keep him dreaming."

The man hung up before Bancroft could correct him.

Thomas Hunter wasn't dreaming.

9

RACHELLE HEARD the ululating cries on the edge of her consciousness, beyond the sounds of Samuel's singing and Marie's hopeless efforts to correct his tone deafness. But her subconscious had been trained to hear this distant cry, day or night.

She gasped and jumped to her feet, straining for the sound. "Samuel, hush!"

"What is it?" Marie asked. Then she heard the warbling cries too. "Father!"

"Father, father!" Samuel cried.

They lived in a wooden hut, large and circular with two floors, both of which had doors leading to the outside. The doors were one of Thomas's pride and joys. Nearly ten thousand houses circled the lake now, most of them among the trees set back from the wide swath cleared around the waters, but none had a door quite like Thomas's. It was the first and best hinged double door in all the land, as far as Thomas was concerned, because it could swing both ways for fast entry or exit.

The top floor where they slept had a normal locking door that opened onto a walkway, which was part of a labyrinth of suspended walkways linking many homes. The bottom floor, where Rachelle was ladling hot stew into tin bowls, boasted the hinged double door. The hinges were made of leather, which also acted as a kind of spring to keep the doors closed.

Marie, being the oldest and fastest at fourteen, reached the door first and slammed through it.

Samuel was right behind. Too far behind. Too close behind. He met the doors as they released Marie. They smacked him in the forehead and dropped him like a sack of potatoes.

"Samuel!" Rachelle dropped to her knees. "Those cursed doors! Are you okay, my child?"

Samuel struggled to a sitting position, then shook his head to clear it.

"Come on!" Marie cried. "Hurry!"

"Get back here and help your brother," Rachelle yelled. "You've knocked him silly with the doors!"

By the time Marie returned, Samuel was on his feet and running through the doors. This time the doors struck Rachelle on the right arm, nearly knocking her down. She grunted and ran down the stone path after the children.

The doors had hurt her arm, she saw. They had opened a very small cut that could hardly concern her now. She ignored the thin trail of blood and ran on.

Streams of women and children ran the paths that led toward the gate where the high-pitched cries continued with growing intensity. They were definitely home. The only question was how many.

On every side grew winding puroon vines with lavender flowers similar to what Thomas described as bougainvillea and large tawii bushes with white silken petals, each spreading their sweet scent through the air. Like gardenia, Thomas said. Every home was draped in similar flowering vines according to a grand master plan that rendered the entire village a garden of beauty. It was the Forest People's best imitation of the colored forest.

Rachelle ran with a knot in her throat. Thomas may be the best fighter among them, but he was also their leader and the first to rush into the worst battles. Too many times he'd returned carrying the body of the soldier who'd fallen beside him. His good fortune couldn't last forever.

And William's order to prepare for evacuation had set the entire village on edge.

They converged on a seventy-foot-wide stone road that cut a straight line from the main gate to the lake. Night was falling, and the people were ready for celebration in anticipation of the Forest Guard's return. They mobbed the front gate, bouncing and dancing. Torches and branches were raised up high. The army was mounted, but with children on their mother's shoulders, the view was blocked.

A loud voice screamed above the din. This was the assistant to Ciphus—Rachelle could pick out his voice from a hundred yards. He was trying to move the people to the side as was customary.

The crowd suddenly settled and parted like a sea. Rachelle pulled up with Marie on one side and Samuel on the other. Then she saw Thomas where she always saw him, seated on his black stallion, leading his men, who stretched behind him into the forest. A bucket of relief washed over her.

"Father!"

"Wait, Samuel! First we honor the fallen."

The people parted farther, leaving a wide path for the warriors. The *clip-clop* of the horses' hoofs was now clearly audible.

Ciphus approached the front line and Thomas stopped his horse. They talked quietly for a moment. To Rachelle's right, thousands continued to line the road that led to the distant lake, now shimmering in rising moonlight. About thirty thousand lived here, and in the days to follow, their number would swell to a hundred thousand as the rest arrived for the annual Gathering.

Ciphus seemed to be taking longer than usual. Something was wrong. William had been emphatic about the seriousness of the situation when he'd ridden in yesterday to demand they prepare to evacuate, but they had won, hadn't they? Surely they hadn't come to announce that the Horde was only a day's march behind.

Ciphus turned slowly to face the throng. He waited a long time, and for every second he stood, the silence deepened until Rachelle thought that she could hear his breathing. He lifted both hands, tilted his face to the sky, and began to moan. This was the traditional mourning.

Yes, yes, Ciphus, but how many? Tell us how many!

Soft wails joined him. Then in a loud voice he cried, "They have taken three thousand of our sons and daughters!"

Three thousand! So many! They had never even lost a thousand.

The wails rose to fever-pitch cries of agony that reached out to the surrounding desert. First Thomas and then the rest of his men dismounted and sank to their knees, lowered their heads to the ground, and wept.

Rachelle fell to her knees with the rest, until the whole village knelt on the side of the road, weeping for the wives and mothers and fathers and daughters and sons who'd suffered such a terrible loss to the Horde. Only Ciphus stood, and he stood with arms raised in a cry to Elyon.

"Comfort your children, Maker of men! Take your daughters into your bosom and wipe away their tears. Deliver your sons from the evil that ravages what is sacred. Come and save us, O Elyon. Come and save us, lover of our souls!"

The custom of immediately marrying the widows to eligible men would be stretched very thin. There weren't enough men to go around. They were all dying. Rachelle's heart ached for those who would soon learn that their husbands were among the three thousand.

The mourning continued for about fifteen minutes, until Ciphus finished his long prayer. Then he lowered his arms and a hush fell over the crowd now standing.

"Our loss is great. But their loss is greater. Fifty thousand of the Horde have been sent to an appropriate fate on this day!"

A roar erupted down the line. The ground trembled with their throaty yells, motivated as much by the fresh horror of their own loss and their hatred of the Horde as by their thirst for victory.

Thomas swung back into his saddle and walked his horse up the road. At times like this he would sometimes acknowledge the crowd with nods and an uplifted hand, but tonight he rode with sobriety.

His eyes found Rachelle. She ran to him with Samuel and Marie. He leaned over and kissed her on the lips.

"You are my sunshine," he said.

"And you are my rainbow," she replied, tempted to haul him off the horse right now. He felt her teasing tug and grinned. Their sappy exchange was refreshing because it was so genuine. She loved him for it.

"Walk with me."

He kissed Marie and smiled. "As beautiful as your mother." He ruffled Samuel's hair.

They walked down the cheering line like that, Thomas in the saddle, Rachelle, Samuel, and Marie walking proudly on his right side. But there was a tension in Thomas's face. It wasn't only the price they had paid in battle that occupied his mind.

The moment they reached the wide sandy shores to the lake, Thomas dismounted, handed the horse off to his stable boy, and turned to his lieutenants.

"Mikil, William, we meet as soon as we've bathed. Suzan, bring Ciphus and whatever members of the Council you can find. Quickly." He kissed Rachelle on her forehead. "We need your wisdom, my love. Join us."

He hugged Samuel and Marie, whispered something in their ears. They ran off, undoubtedly up to some mischief.

Thomas took Rachelle's hand and led her to one of the twenty gazebos that overlooked a large amphitheater cut from the forest floor. The lake lay two hundred yards distant, just past a swath of clean white sand. They'd cleared the forest over the years, and as the village grew, they expanded the beach by relocating houses that had once been near the lake, such as their own. In their place they planted thick, rich grass and more than two thousand flowering trees, carefully positioned in concentric arcs leading to the sand. Hundreds of rosebushes and honeysuckles spotted the grass in tidy enclaves with benches for sitting. This end of the lake had been landscaped as a garden park fit for a king.

The lake's waters were not for drinking or washing—such water came from the springs—but only for bathing and only then without soap. The lake's shores were reserved for the nightly celebrations, which were getting underway around a large firepit.

Thomas and Rachelle would normally be among the first at the celebration, dancing and singing and retelling stories of Elyon's love that would stretch into the night. It had always been the highlight of their day. But at the moment Thomas's mind was a hundred miles away.

"Thomas. What is it?"

"It's the Southern Forest," he said. "We may lose the Southern Forest."

⸺◈⸺

Thomas paced along the gazebo's half wall deep in thought. Torches blazed from each post. Down the shore, delighted laughter rose from the celebration. A long line of dancers, dressed in fabrics made from dark green leaves and white flowers, had linked arms and were moving in graceful circles around the bonfire. They were undoubtedly light with wine and stuffed with meat. Out on the lake, moonlight shone in a long white shaft.

For so long Thomas's people had waited for Elyon's deliverance. They'd spun a thousand stories about the way he might ultimately deliver them from the Horde. Would he rise from the lake and flood the desert with water to drown them? Or would he ride in on a mighty white horse and lead them in one final battle that rid the earth of the scourge once and for all?

Thomas turned to the gathered elders and lieutenants. "If there are two armies, there may be three. Otherwise, yes, Ciphus, I wouldn't hesitate to lead five thousand men to Jamous's aid tonight. But it's a full day's journey—nearly three days there and back. The Horde has never attacked us on two fronts until now. If our Guard vacate this forest while so many are coming for the annual Gathering—"

"Well, we won't change the Gathering. I promise you that."

"Half of our forces are out escorting the tribes. We're already stretched way too thin. To send more men to the Southern Forest puts us at great risk."

Mikil stood. "Then let me go with just a few of the Forest Guard. Jamous is still fighting, Thomas. You heard the runner!"

The runner had met them at the gates with fresh word from the south. Jamous was holding strong against the Horde. His first retreat had been a strategy to draw the Horde near the forest where his archers had the distinct advantage of cover. They had been fighting for three days now.

"How many men?"

"Give me five hundred," Mikil said.

"That would leave us weak here," William objected. "Here where the whole world will be gathered in less than a week. What if the Horde is weakening us for an assault on the forest, here, next week, when they can take us all in one blow?"

"He's right, Mikil," Thomas said. "I can't let you take five hundred."

"You're forgetting the bombs," Mikil said.

The news of their stunning victory was spreading like fire. He looked at Rachelle. They hadn't been alone yet, when he knew he'd get her true reaction to the fact that he'd started dreaming again. Still, with such a victory, what could she say?

What none of them knew was that he'd dreamed not once, but twice, the second time when they'd stopped for sleep returning from the battle. He'd dreamed that he'd gone before a special meeting called by the president of the United States and then been put to sleep by a psychologist. In his dream world, he was at this very moment lying in a chair in Dr. Bancroft's laboratory.

And he intended to dream again, tonight. He had to. If he could only make Rachelle understand that.

"Using the black powder, we could destroy the Horde!" Mikil said.

"Not on the open desert we won't," William said. "You'll kill a handful with each blast; that's it. And you're forgetting that we don't have any bombs at the moment."

"Then three hundred warriors."

"Three hundred," Thomas said. "But not you. Send another division and tell them to ride along the runners' route." They continually sent messengers on fast horses between the forests in a kind of mail system that Thomas had developed. "If they hear that Jamous has won before they arrive, have them turn back."

She stared at him for a moment, then turned to leave.

"I'm sorry, Mikil. I know what Jamous means to you, but I need you here."

She paused, and then left without another word.

Thomas motioned after her with his head. "Go with her, William. Suzan, organize a sweep of the forest perimeter. Let's be sure there isn't another Horde army lurking."

They both left.

"You really think the Horde would try something like that?" Rachelle asked.

"I wouldn't have thought so a month ago, but they're getting smart about the way they attack. Martyn is changing them."

"So then, we're agreed," Ciphus said. The elder stroked his long gray beard. He was one of the older Council members, seventy. Bathing in Elyon's waters didn't stop the aging process. "The Gathering will proceed as planned in five days."

"Yes."

"Regardless of the Southern Forest's fate."

"You think they may fall?" Thomas asked.

"No. Have any of our forests fallen? But if one does, then all the more reason for the Gathering."

"I suppose so."

Thomas looked at his wife. She was only a few years younger than he was, but she looked half his battle-worn age. There was no doubt in his mind but that she would make an incredible commander. But she was also a mother. And she was his wife. The thought of exposing her to death on the battlefield made him sick.

He walked to her and touched his hand to her cheek. "Have I told you lately how beautiful you are?" he asked. He leaned over and kissed her full on the lips while the others watched silently. Romance had become their religion, and they practiced it daily. When a person wandered into the desert and neglected swimming in Elyon's water, their memory of the colored forest and the love that Elyon had shown them in the old lake also dimmed. But here in the forest, lingering memories had prompted Ciphus and the Council to develop rituals determined to cherish those memories. The Great Romance consisted of rules and celebrations and traditions meant to keep the people from straying. The way that a husband or wife expressed love for his or her spouse was a part of that romance.

Rachelle winked. "Your love for me makes my face shine," she said. He kissed her again.

"Ciphus, what can you tell me of the Books of Histories?" he asked, turning from Rachelle. "They say that the Books still exist. Have you heard of them?"

"We don't need the Books of Histories. We have the lakes."

"Of course. But do you believe they exist?"

Ciphus stared at him past bushy brows. "They aren't books anyone wants," he said. "They were hidden from us a long time ago for good reason."

"I didn't know you were so averse to the Books," Thomas said. "I'm simply asking if you know anything about them."

"This sudden interest in the histories again. You were consumed with them before," Rachelle said. "It's the dreams, isn't it?"

"It's not like you might think, Rachelle, but yes. Nothing's changed there. When I awoke in Bangkok, only a night had passed!" He walked to the rail and gazed at the celebration, now in full swing. "I know it sounds ludicrous, but we may have a very serious problem." He turned to her. "They need me."

"What is Bangkok?" Ciphus asked.

"The world in his dreams," Rachelle said. "When he dreams, he believes that he goes to another place, that he's living in the ancient histories, before the Great Deception. He thinks that he can stop the virus that led to the times of tribulation. You see why the rhambutan is so important, Thomas? Once—only *once*—you sleep without the fruit and your mind is whisked away. Ludicrous!"

"This is why you're interested in the Books of Histories?" Ciphus asked. "To save a dream world?"

Thomas clutched the wound on his shoulder. Suzan had bandaged it with herbs and a broad leaf. A swim in the lake would do it some good, but the deep cut would take some time to heal.

"You see this wound? It didn't come from the Horde. It came from the world in my dreams."

"But surely that world isn't real," the elder said. "Is it?"

"Weren't you listening earlier when I told you about the black powder? I don't know how real it is, but this cut is real enough."

"Then Elyon is using your mind to help us," Ciphus said. "But if you're suggesting that the dreams he's using are real, that's an entirely different matter."

"Call it what you will, Ciphus. My shoulder hurts just the same."

"Please, Thomas." Rachelle drew her hand over his hair. "For all you know the Horde cut you and you just don't remember. Yes? Fascination with the histories pushed Tanis into the black forest to begin with."

"No. I won't have that on my head. His preoccupation was there before I began to dream. Tanis made his own choice."

She removed her hand. "And now you'll make yours," she said. "I will *not* have you dreaming again."

"And what if not dreaming threatens my own life? We are dying there! The virus will kill me. They depend on me, but just as much, my very existence here may depend on my ability to stop the virus there!"

"No, I can't listen to this. Of course they depend on you. Without you they don't exist to begin with!"

"You're willing to risk my life?"

"The last time you dreamed, we all died."

They faced off, romance quickly forgotten. He understood her aversion. What was it she had said? *I will not have you loving another woman in your dreams while I am suckling your child.* Something similar. She was still jealous of Monique.

"These dreams sound like so much nonsense to me," Ciphus said. "I would agree with Rachelle. There is no benefit in dreaming if you lose your mind in them. But if you want to know about the Books of Histories, then you'll have to speak to the old man, Jeremiah of Southern. He is here, I believe."

Jeremiah of Southern? The old man who'd once been a Scab? He was one of very few who had come in and bathed in the lake of his own will. Much of what Thomas knew of the Desert Dwellers he'd learned from the old man. But he'd never mentioned the Books of Histories.

"He's here now?"

The Elder nodded. "For the Gathering."

"Thomas."

He faced Rachelle. She was giving him one of those looks that he adored her for, a fiery glare that threatened without casting any suspicion on her love.

"Please tell me that because you love me you will eat ten rhambutan fruits right now and forget this nonsense forever," she said.

"Ten?" He chuckled. "You want me sick? I would groan all night. That's how you welcome your mighty warrior home?"

Slowly a smile curved her lips.

"Then one fruit. And I promise to chase it down with a kiss that will make your mind spin."

"Now that's tempting," he said. He reached for her hand. "Would you like to dance?"

She took it and spun into him.

"I don't mean to interrupt lovers, but there is another matter," Ciphus said.

"There's always another matter," Thomas said. "What is it?"

"The challenge."

He knew already where the elder was going. "Justin?"

"Yes. We cannot allow his heresy to spread further. As is required, three elders have called for an inquiry before the people as is allowed by law. Do you concur?"

"He insulted my authority once. It would seem natural that I would agree."

"But do you?"

Thomas caught Rachelle's glance. She'd once told him that Justin was harmless and that going on about him only strengthened his popularity. He'd agreed at the time. Although he might not say so in front of Mikil and the others, Thomas still carried respect for the man. He was undoubtedly the best soldier Thomas had ever commanded, which might be one reason Mikil disliked him so much.

On the other hand, there could be no denying the man's flagrant heresy. Peace with the Horde. What utter nonsense.

"Is he really that dangerous?" he asked, more for Rachelle's sake than his. "His popularity is so great. A challenge carries serious consequences."

"But his offense is growing. We believe the best way to deal with him is now, to make an example of any such treasonous talk."

"If he wins your challenge?"

"Then he is permitted to remain, of course. If he refuses to change his doctrine and loses, he will be banished as the law requires."

"Fine." Thomas turned to leave. This was hardly his concern.

"You know that if the people can't decide, then it comes down to a fight in the arena," Ciphus said.

Thomas faced the elder. "And?"

"We would like you to defend the Council if Justin must be fought."

"Me?"

"It only seems natural, as you say. Justin has turned his back on the Great Romance, and he's turned his back on you, his commander. Anyone other than you and the people might think you have no stomach for it. Our challenge will be weak on that face alone. We would like you to agree to the fight if the people are undecided."

"It's pointless, this fight business," Rachelle said. "How can you fight Justin? He served at your side for five years. He saved your life more than once. Does he pose a danger to you?"

"In hand-to-hand? Please, my love, he learned what he knows from me."

"And he learned it well, from what I've heard."

"He hasn't fought in a battle for several years. And he may have saved my life, but he also turned his back on me, not to mention, as Ciphus so rightly says, the Great Romance. Elyon himself. What will the people think if I abandoned even one of our pillars of faith? Besides, there will be no fight."

He faced Ciphus. "I accept."

10

THE HORDE set fire to the Southern Forest at night, after three days of pitched battle. Never before had they done this, partially because the Forest Guard rarely let them close enough to have such an opportunity. But that was before Martyn. They'd ignited the trees with flaming arrows from the desert two hundred yards away from the perimeter. Not only were they using fire, they had made bows.

It had taken Jamous and his remaining men four hours to subdue the flames. By Elyon's grace the Horde hadn't started another fire, and the Forest Guard had managed an hour of sleep.

Jamous stood on a hill overlooking the charred forest. Beyond lay a flat white desert, and just now in the growing light he could see the gathered Horde army. Ten thousand, far fewer than what they'd started with. But he'd lost six hundred men, four hundred in a major offensive just before dusk last evening. Another two hundred were wounded. That left him only two hundred able-bodied warriors.

He'd never seen the Desert Dwellers engage in battle so effectively. They seemed to swing their swords more skillfully and their march seemed more purposeful. They used flanking maneuvers and they withdrew when overpowered. He hadn't actually seen the general they called Martyn, but he could only assume that was who led this army.

Word had come of the great victory at the Natalga Gap, and his men had cheered. But the reality of the situation here was working on Jamous's mind like a burrowing tick. One more major push from the Horde and his men would be overrun.

Behind them not three miles lay a village. It was the second largest village of the seven, twenty thousand souls in all. Jamous had been sent to escort these devout followers of Elyon to the annual Gathering when a patrol had run into the Horde army.

The villagers had voted to stay and wait for the Desert Dwellers' sound defeat, which they were sure would be imminent, rather than cross the desert without protection.

Until yesterday it had seemed like a good plan. Now they were in a terrible situation. If they fled now, the Horde would likely burn the entire forest or, worse, catch them from behind and destroy them. If they stayed and fought, they might be able to hold the army off until the three hundred warriors whom Thomas had sent arrived, but his men were tired and worn.

He crouched on a stump and mulled his options. A thin fog coiled through the trees. Behind him, seven of his personal guard talked quietly around a smoldering fire, heating water for an herbal tea. Two of them were wounded, one where the fire had burned the skin from his calf, and another whose left hand had been crushed by the blunt end of a sickle. They would ignore their pain, because they knew that Thomas of Hunter would do the same.

He looked down at the red feather tied to his elbow and thought of Mikil. He'd plucked two feathers from a macaw and given her one to wear. When he returned home this time, he would ask for her hand. There was no one he loved or respected more than Mikil. And what would she do?

Jamous frowned. They would fight, he decided. They would fight because they were the Forest Guard.

The men had grown silent behind him. He spoke without turning, indicating the desert as he did so.

"Markus, we will hit them on their northern flank with twenty archers. The rest will follow me from the meadow on the south, where they least expect it."

Markus didn't respond.

"Markus." He turned.

His men were staring at three men who'd ridden into camp. The one who led them rode a white horse that snorted and pawed at the soft earth. He wore a beige tunic with a studded brass belt and a hood that covered his head in a manner not unlike the Scabs. Not true battle dress. A scabbard hung on his saddle.

Jamous stood and faced the camp. His men seemed oddly captivated by the sight. Why? All three looked like lost woodsmen, strong, healthy, the kind who might make good warriors with enough training, but they certainly had nothing that would set them apart.

And then the leader lifted his emerald eyes to Jamous.

Justin of Southern.

The mighty warrior who'd defied Thomas by turning down the general's greatest honor now spent his days wandering the forests with his apprentices, a self-appointed prophet spreading illogical ideas that turned the Great Romance on its head. He'd once been very popular, but his demanding ways were proving too much for many, even for some of the pliable fools who followed him diligently.

Still, this man before him threatened the very fabric of the Great Romance with his heresy, and his rhetoric was growing stronger, they said. Mikil had once told Jamous that if she ever met Justin again, she wouldn't hesitate to withdraw her sword and slay him where he stood. She suspected that he had been manipulated by the druids from the deep desert. If the Horde were the enemy from without, men like Justin, who decried the Great Romance and spoke of turning the forest over to the Desert Dwellers, were the enemy from within.

The fact that Justin had turned down his promotion to general and resigned from the Forest Guard two years ago when Thomas needed him most didn't help.

Jamous spit to one side, a habit he'd picked up from Mikil. "Markus, tell this man to leave our camp if he wishes to live." He walked for his bedroll. "We have war to wage."

"You are the one they call Jamous."

The man's voice was soft and low. Confident. The voice of a leader. It was no wonder he'd bewitched so many. It was well known that the Horde's druids bewitched their own with slippery tongues and black magic.

"And you are the one they call Justin," Jamous said. "What of it? You're in the way here."

"How can I be in the way of my own forest?"

Jamous refused to look at the man. "I am here to save your forest. Markus, mount your horse and muster the men. Make sure everyone has bathed. We may have a long day ahead. Stephen, pull out twenty archers and meet me in the lower camp."

His men hesitated.

He whirled. "Markus!"

Justin had dismounted. He possessed the audacity to defy Jamous and approach the fire, where he stood now, hood withdrawn to reveal shoulder-length brown hair. He had the face of a warrior gone soft. All had known of his skill as a soldier before his defection from the Guard. But the lines of experience were softened by his brilliant green eyes.

"The Desert Dwellers will destroy you today," Justin said, reaching a hand out to the fire. He looked over. "If you attack them, they will run over what remains of your army, burn the forest, and slaughter all of my people."

"*Your* people? The people of this forest are alive *because* of my army," Jamous said.

"Yes. They have been indebted to you for many years. But today the Horde is too strong and will crush what's left of your army like they crushed this man's hand yesterday."

He pointed to Stephen, who had taken the sickle.

"You abandoned the army. What would you know of war?" Jamous asked.

"I wage a new kind of war."

"On whose behalf? The Scabs?"

Justin faced the desert. "How much blood will you spill?"

"As much as Elyon decides."

Justin looked surprised. "Elyon? And who made the Scabs? I believe Elyon did."

"Are you saying that Elyon did *not* lead us against the Horde?"

"No. He did. But aren't you really the same as the Horde without the lake? So then if I was to take the water from you and shove you out into the desert, we'd be cutting you to pieces instead of them. Isn't that right?"

"You're saying that I am one of them? Or maybe you're suggesting that *you* are."

Justin smiled. "What I'm really saying is that the Horde lurks in all of us. The disease that cripples. The rot, if you like. Why not go after the disease?"

"They don't want a cure." Jamous grabbed the horn on his saddle and swung up without using the stirrup. "The only cure fit for the Horde is the one Elyon has given us. Our swords."

"If you insist on attacking, maybe you should let me lead your men. We'd have a much better chance of victory." He winked. "Not that you're bad, not at all. I've been watching you since you came, and you're really very, very good. One of the best. There's always Thomas, of course, but I think you're the best I've seen in some time."

"And yet you insult me?"

"Not at all. It's just that I am very good myself. I think I could win this war, and I think I could do it without losing a single man."

Justin had a strange quality about him. He said things that would ordinarily bring out the fight in Jamous, but he said them with such perfect sincerity and in such a noncombative way that Jamous was momentarily tempted to smack him on the back as he would a good friend and say, "You're on, mate."

"That's the most arrogant thing I've ever heard."

"So then I take it you're going to battle without me," Justin said.

Jamous turned his horse. "Markus, now!"

"Then at least agree to this," Justin said. "If I can rid you of this Horde army on my own, ride with me in a victory march through the Elyon Valley to the east of the village."

Jamous's men had started to mount, but they stopped. Justin's companions hadn't moved from their horses. Nothing about this wild proposal seemed to surprise them.

Any hint of play had vanished from Justin's eyes. He stared directly at Jamous again, commanding. Demanding.

"Agreed," Jamous said, interested more in dismissing the man than taking any challenge from him seriously.

Justin held his eyes for a long while. Then, as if time was short, he walked to his horse, threw himself into the saddle, reined it around, and left without so much as a glance.

Jamous turned away. "Stephen, archers. Hurry, before the light is full."

———

Justin led Ronin and Arvyl through the trees at a gallop. They could hardly keep up, and he didn't push his mount as he often would when riding alone. There were others beside Ronin and Arvyl—thousands who would cry out his name in the right circumstances, but his popularity had waned as of late. They were a fickle people, given to the sentiments of the day.

He only hoped that he still had enough. His agreement with Martyn depended at least partially on his ability to deliver a crowd as planned.

Living as an outcast had extracted its price. At times he could hardly weather the pain. It was one thing to enter society as an orphan, as he had; it was another to be openly rejected as he was so often now.

At times he wasn't sure why Elyon didn't take his sword to the lot of them. Their Great Romance was no romance of Elyon at all.

Now their fate was in his hands. If they only knew the truth, they might kill him now, before he had the chance to do what was needed.

"Justin! Wait," Ronin called from behind.

They'd come to a grove of fruit trees. Justin pulled up. "Breakfast, my friends?"

"Sir, what do you have in mind? You can't take on the whole Horde army single-handedly!"

Still at a trot, Justin slid a pearl-handled sword from its scabbard, leaned far forward, flipped the blade over his head in a movement that approximated a figure eight, and then reined his horse in.

One, two, three large red fruits dropped from the tree. He caught each in turn and hurled one each to Ronin and Arvyl. "Ha!"

He bit deeply into the sweet nectar. Juice ran down his chin and he shoved his sword home into its scabbard. The fruit he would miss.

Ronin grinned and took a bite of his fruit. "Seriously."

Justin's horse stamped. Slowly the smile faded from his face. He looked off at the forest. "I am serious, Ronin. When I've said that leveling the desert with a single word is a matter of the heart, not the sword, you weren't listening?"

"Of course I was listening. But this isn't a campfire session with a dozen hopeless souls looking for a hero. This is the Horde army."

"You doubt me?"

"Please, Justin. Sir. After what we have seen?"

"And what have you seen?"

"I have seen you lead a thousand warriors through the Samyrian desert plain with twenty thousand Horde before us and twenty thousand behind. I have seen you take on a hundred of the enemy single-handedly and walk away unscathed. I have heard you speak to the desert and to the trees and I have seen them listen. Why do you question my confidence in you?"

Justin looked into his eyes.

"You are the greatest warrior in all the land," Ronin continued. "Greater I believe than even Thomas of Hunter. But no man can possibly go against ten thousand warriors alone. I'm not doubting; I'm asking what you really mean by this."

Justin held him in his gaze, then slowly smiled. "If I ever had a brother, Ronin, I would pray he would be exactly like you."

It was the highest honor one man could give another. In truth Ronin did doubt Justin, even by asking, but now he was wordless.

Ronin dipped his head. "I am your servant."

"No, Ronin. You are my apprentice."

Billy and Lucy watched the three warriors from behind their berry bush, barely breathing. In their hands they gripped wooden swords they had carved only yesterday. Lucy's sword wasn't as sharp or as sword-looking as Billy's because she had a hard time carving with her bad hand. It was good enough to wedge the wood against her leg, but otherwise the shriveled lump of flesh was good only for pointing or clubbing Billy over the head when he got too annoying.

It had been Billy's idea to sneak out of the village while it was still dark and join the battle—or at least take a peek.

His friend had tried to convince Billy that it was too dangerous, that nine-year-old children had no business even looking at the evil Horde, much less thinking they could fight them. Lucy hadn't thought they would actually come, but then Billy had awakened her and she'd followed, whispering her objections most of the way.

Now she was staring at the three warriors on their horses, and her heart was hammering loud enough to scare the birds.

"That's . . . that's him!" Billy whispered.

Lucy withdrew into the bush. They would be heard!

Billy looked at her, eyes wide. "That's Justin of Southern!"

Lucy was too terrified to tell him to shut up. Of course it wasn't Justin of Southern. He wasn't dressed like a warrior. She wasn't even sure that Justin even existed. They'd heard all the stories, but that didn't mean anyone lived who could really do all those things.

"I swear it's him!" Billy whispered. "He killed a hundred thousand Scabs with one hand."

Lucy leaned forward and took another peek. They were like the magical Roshuim of Elyon that her father said would one day strike down the Horde.

<hr />

"And what about you, Arvyl?" Justin asked. "What do you make of—"

He stopped midsentence. Ronin followed his gaze and saw that two children, a boy and a girl, crouched at the edge of the clearing, peering past a berry bush at the three warriors.

They were looking at Justin, of course. They always looked at Justin. Children were always captivated by him. These two looked like twins, blond hair and big eyes, about ten, far too young to have wandered so far from home at a time like this.

Then again, he hardly blamed their curiosity. When had such a battle come so close to them?

Justin had already slipped into another world, Ronin thought with a single glance. Children did this to him. He was no longer the warrior. He was their father, no matter who the children were. His eyes sparkled and his face lit up. At times Ronin wondered if Justin wouldn't trade his life to become a child again, to swing in the trees and roll in the meadows.

This love for children confused Ronin more than any other trait of Justin's. Some said that Justin was a druid. And it was commonly known that druids could deceive the innocent with a few soft words. Ronin had a difficult time separating Justin's effect on children from the speculation that he wasn't who he seemed.

"Hello there," Justin said.

Both children ducked behind the bush.

Justin slid from his horse and hurried toward the bush. "No, no, please come out. Come out, I need your advice." He stopped and knelt on one knee.

"My advice?" the boy asked, poking his head up.

A hand gripped his shirt and pulled him back. The girl wasn't so brave.

"Your advice. It's about today's battle."

They whispered urgently, then finally came out, the boy boldly, the girl cautiously. Ronin saw that they each carried a wooden sword. The girl was shorter and her left hand was bent backward at an odd angle. Deformed.

Justin's eyes lowered to the girl's hand, then up to her face. For a moment he seemed trapped by the sight. A bird sang in the tree above them.

"My name is Justin, and I . . ." He sat down and crossed his legs in one movement. "What are your names?"

"Billy and Lucy," the boy said.

"Well, Billy and Lucy, you are two of the bravest children I have ever known."

The boy's eyes brightened.

"And the most beautiful," he said.

The girl shifted on her feet.

"My friends here, Ronin and Arvyl, aren't convinced that I can single-handedly bring the Horde to its knees. I have to decide, and I think that you might be able to give me some direction. Look in my eyes and tell me. What do you think? Should I take on the Horde?"

Billy looked at Ronin, at a loss. The girl answered first.

"Yes," she said.

"Yes," the boy said. "Of course."

"Yes! You hear that, Ronin? Give me ten warriors who believe like these two and I would bring the entire Horde to its knees. Come here, Billy. I would like to shake the hand of the man who told me what grown men could not."

Justin stretched out his hand and Billy took it, beaming. Justin ruffled the boy's hair and whispered something that Ronin couldn't hear. But both of the children laughed.

"Lucy, come and let me kiss the hand of the most beautiful maiden in all the land."

She stepped forward and offered her good hand.

"Not that one. The other."

Her smile softened. Slowly she lowered her sword. Now both hands hung limp at her sides. Justin held her eyes.

"Don't be afraid," he said very quietly.

She lifted her crippled hand and Justin took it in both of his. He leaned over and kissed it lightly. Then he leaned forward and whispered into her ear.

To be perfectly honest, Lucy was terrified by Justin. But it wasn't a fearful terrified as much as a nervous terrified. She wasn't sure whether she should trust him or not. His eyes said yes and his smile said yes, but there was something about him that made her knees knock.

When he took her hand and kissed it, she knew he could feel her shaking. Then he leaned forward and whispered into her ear.

"You are very brave, Lucy." His voice was soft and it ran through her body like a glass of warm milk. "If I were a king, I would wish that you were my daughter. A princess."

He kissed her forehead.

She wasn't sure why, but tears came to her eyes. It wasn't because of what he had said, or because he'd kissed her cheek. It was the power in his voice. Like magic. She felt like a princess swept off her feet by the greatest prince in all the land, just like in the stories.

Only it wasn't the beautiful princess the prince had chosen. It was her, the one with the stub for a hand.

She tried her best to keep from crying, but it was very hard, and she suddenly felt awkward standing in front of Billy like this.

Justin winked at her and stood, still holding her own hand. He put his other hand on Billy's shoulder. "I want you both to go home as fast as you can. Tell the people that the Horde will be defeated today. We will march through the Elyon Valley at noon, victors. Can I count on you?"

They both nodded.

He released them both and turned back to where his horse waited. "If only we could all be children again," he said.

Then he swung into his saddle and galloped across the small clearing. Justin pulled up at the trees and spun his horse back.

If Lucy wasn't mistaken, she could see tears on his face. "If only you could all be children again."

Then he rode into the trees.

"Watch our flank!" Jamous thundered. "Keep them to the front!"

Markus drove his horse directly into a pocket of Horde warriors and pulled up just as one took a wide swipe with his sickle. Markus threw his torso backward, flat on the horse's rump. The sickle whistled through the air above. He brought his sword up with his body, severing the Scab's arm at the shoulder.

Jamous used his bow, sending an arrow through the back of the warrior bearing down on Markus from behind. The attacker roared in pain and dropped his sword.

"Back! Back!" Jamous cried.

It was their fourth attack that morning, and the strategy was working exactly as Jamous had designed it to. If they kept beating away at the flanks, their superior speed would keep the slower army from outmaneuvering them for position to the rear. They were like wolves tearing at the legs of a bear, always just out of reach of its slashing claws, just close enough to take small bites at will.

The forest lay a hundred yards to their rear. Jamous glanced back.

No, two hundred. That far?

Farther.

He spun around and stood in his stirrups, surveying the battlefield. A chill defied the hot sun and washed down his back. They were too far out!

"Back to the forest!" he screamed.

Even as he did, he saw the wide swath of Horde slicing in from the east, cutting them off.

He glanced to the west. The enemy ran too far to cut through their lines there. He spun to the west. An endless sea of Horde.

Panic swelled, then receded. There was a way out. There was always a way out.

"Center line!" he cried. "Center line!"

His men fell in behind him for running retreat. When the Horde moved to intercept, they would break off in a dozen directions to scatter them. But always they would move in the direction he first took them.

His horse reared high and Jamous looked desperately for that direction.

"They're cutting us off!" Markus yelled. "Jamous—"

He knew then what the enemy had done. The bear had suffered the wolves' attacks with patience, snarling and swiping as it always did. But today it had slowly, methodically drawn the wolves farther and farther into the desert, far enough so they wouldn't see the flanking maneuver. Too far to outrun it.

The Horde army closed in a hundred yards behind them. At the center a warrior held high their crest, the serpentine Shataiki bat. They were trapped.

The Scabs nearest him suddenly fell back a hundred yards and joined the main army. His men had clustered to his right. Their horses snorted and stamped, worn from battle. No one demanded that he do something. There was little they could do.

Except charge.

The Horde line between them and the forest was their only real option.

But it was already fifty yards wide, too many Scabs to cut through with fewer than two hundred men.

Still, it was their only option. An image of Mikil flashed through his mind. They would say that he had fought like no man had ever fought, and she would carry his body to the funeral pyre.

The Scab army had stopped now. The desert had fallen silent. They seemed content to let Jamous make the first move. They would simply adjust their noose in whichever direction he took them. The Horde army was learning.

Martyn.

Jamous faced his men, who'd formed a line facing the forest. "There's only one way," he said.

"Straight at them," Markus said.

"Elyon's strength."

"Elyon's strength."

Maybe a few of them could cut through the wall to warn the village.

"Spread the word. On my mark, straight ahead. If you make it, evacuate the village. They will be burning."

Had it really come down to this? One last suicide run?

"You're a good man, Jamous," Markus said.

"And you, Markus. And you." They looked at each other. Jamous lifted his sword.

"Rider! Behind!" The call came from down the line.

Jamous twisted in his saddle. A lone rider raced across the desert from the east, half a mile distant. Dust rose in his wake.

Jamous spun his horse. "Steady."

The rider was headed neither for them nor for the Desert Dwellers. He approached halfway between their position and the Horde army. A white horse.

The sound of the pounding hoofs reached Jamous. He fixed his eyes on this one horse, thundering in from the desert like a blinded runner who'd gotten lost and was determined to deliver his message to the supreme commander at any cost.

It was Justin of Southern.

The man still wasn't in proper battle dress. His hood flew behind him with loose locks. He rode on the balls of his feet as if he'd been born in that saddle. And in his right hand hung a sword, low and easy so that it looked like it might touch the sand at any moment.

Jamous swallowed. This warrior had fought and won more battles than any living man except for Thomas himself. Although Jamous had never fought with him, they'd all heard of his exploits before he'd left the Guard.

Justin suddenly veered toward the Horde army, leaned low on the far side of his horse, and lowered his sword into the sand. Still running full speed, he carved a line on the desert for a hundred yards before righting himself and pulling his mount to a stop.

The white stallion reared and dropped back around.

Justin galloped back, not once glancing at either army. The front ranks of the Horde shifted but held steady. He reined tight at the center of the line that he'd drawn and faced the Horde.

The armies grew perfectly still.

For several long seconds Justin stared ahead, his back to Jamous.

"What's he—"

Jamous lifted a hand to quiet Markus.

Justin swung his leg off his saddle and dropped to the ground. He walked up to the line and stopped. Then he deliberately stepped over the line and walked forward, sword dragging in the sand by his side. They could hear the soft crunch of sand under his feet. A horse down the line snorted.

He was only a hundred feet from the main Horde army when he stopped again. This time he thrust his sword into the sand and took three steps back.

His voice rang out across the desert. "I request to speak with the general named Martyn!"

"What does he think he's doing? He's surrendering?"

"I don't know, Markus. We're still alive."

"We can't surrender! The Horde takes no prisoners."

"I think he aims to make peace."

"Peace with them is treason against Elyon!" Markus spit.

Jamous glanced at the army to their rear. "Send one runner wide, to their eastern flank."

"Now?"

"Yes. Let's see if they let him pass."

Markus issued the order.

Justin still faced the army, waiting. A rider broke from Jamous's line and sprinted east, in much the same manner as Justin had. The Scabs made no move to stop him.

"They're letting him go."

"Good. Let's see if—"

"Now they're stopping him."

The Scabs were closing the eastern flank. The rider pulled up and headed back.

Jamous swore. "Well then, let's see how far treason gets us."

As if on cue, the Horde army parted directly ahead. A lone general on a horse, wearing the black sash of his rank, rode slowly out to Justin. Martyn. Jamous could make out his bland Scab face beneath the hood, but not his features. He stopped ten feet from Justin's sword.

The soft rumbling of their voices carried across the desert, but Jamous couldn't make out their words. Still they talked. Five minutes. Ten.

The general Martyn suddenly slid from his horse, met Justin at the sword in the sand, and clasped Justin's hands in the traditional forest greeting.

"What?"

"Hold your tongue, Markus. If we live to fight another day, we will drag him through his treason."

The general mounted, rode back to his men, and disappeared. A long horn blasted from the front line.

"Now what?"

Justin leaped into his saddle, spun his horse, and sprinted straight toward them. He'd come within twenty feet without slowing before it occurred to Jamous that he wasn't going to.

He cursed and jerked his horse to the left.

He could see the mischievous glint in Justin's emerald eyes as he blasted through the line and galloped toward the waiting Horde. Long before he met them, the Scab army parted and withdrew, first east and west, and then south like a receding tide on either side.

Justin pulled up at the tree line.

Jamous glanced back once, then kicked his horse. "Ride!"

It wasn't until he was halfway to Justin that Jamous remembered his agreement. The man had indeed rid him of the Horde, hadn't he? Yes. Not by any means he'd imagined—not by any means he even understood—but he had. And for that at least, Justin was victor.

Today the people would honor him.

11

HE'S STILL sleeping?" Phil Grant asked.

The frumpy doctor pushed the door to his lab open. "Like a baby. I insist that you let me study him further. This is highly unusual, you understand? I've never seen it."

"Can you unlock his dreams with more work?"

"I don't know what I can unlock, but I'm happy to try. Whatever's happening in that mind of his must be scrutinized. Must."

"I'm not sure how much time we have for your musts," Grant said. "We'll see."

Kara walked in ahead of the two men. It struck her as odd that only two weeks ago she'd lived a quiet life as a nurse in Denver. Yet here she was, being traipsed about by the director of the CIA and a world-renowned cognitive psychologist, who were both looking to her brother for answers to perhaps the single greatest crisis that the United States had ever faced. That the world had ever faced.

Thomas lay in a maroon recliner, lights low, while an orchestral version of "Killing Me Softly" whispered through ceiling speakers. She'd spent the afternoon putting their affairs in order: rent on their Denver apartment, insurance bills, a long call to Mother, who'd been climbing the walls with all the news about Thomas's kidnapping of Monique. Depending on what happened in the next day or so, Kara thought she might fly to New York for a visit. The prospect of never seeing her mother again wasn't sitting well. The scientists were all talking as though the virus wouldn't wreak havoc for another eighteen days, but really it could be less. Seventeen. Sixteen. The models were only so accurate. There was every possibility that they all had less than three weeks to live.

"So he's been sleeping for three hours without dreaming?"

Dr. Myles Bancroft walked to the monitor and tapped it lightly. "Let me put it this way. If he is dreaming, it's not like any dream I've ever seen. No rapid eye movement. No perceptual brain activity, no fluctuation in facial temperature. He's in deep sleep, but his dreams are quiet."

"So the whole notion of recording his dream patterns and feeding them back . . ."

"Is a nonstarter," the psychologist finished.

Grant shook his head. "He looks so . . . ordinary."

"He's far from ordinary," Kara said.

"Evidently. It's just hard to imagine that the fate of the world is hung up somewhere in this mind. We know that he discovered the Raison Strain—the idea that he has the antivirus hidden in that mind somewhere is a bit unnerving, considering that he's never had a day of medical training in his life."

"Which is why you *must* let me spend more time with him," Bancroft repeated.

They stared at him in silence.

"Wake him," Kara said.

Bancroft shook Thomas gently. "Wake up, lad."

Thomas's eyes blinked open. Funny how she rarely thought of him as Tom anymore. He was Thomas now. It suited him better.

"Welcome to the land of the living," the doctor said. "How do you feel?"

He sat up. Wiped at his eyes. "How long have I been asleep?"

"Three hours."

Thomas looked around the lab. Three hours. It felt like more.

"What happened?" Kara asked.

They were staring at him expectantly. "Did it work?" he asked.

"That's what we were wondering," Bancroft said.

"I don't know. Did you record my dreams?"

"Did you dream?"

"I don't know, did I? Or am I dreaming now?"

Kara sighed. "Please, Thomas."

"Okay, then yes, of course I dreamed. I returned to the forest with my army after destroying the Horde—the black powder worked wonders—met with the Council, then fell asleep after joining the celebration with Rachelle."

He slid his feet to the floor and stood. "And I'm dreaming now, which means I didn't eat the fruit. She'll have my hide."

"Who'll have your hide?" Grant asked.

"His wife. Rachelle," Kara said.

The director looked at her with a raised brow.

"And I asked about the Books of Histories," Thomas said. "I know the man who may be able to tell me where to find them."

"But you don't remember anything more about the antivirus," Grant pressed.

"No. Your little experiment failed, remember? You can't stimulate my memory banks because you can't record the brain signatures associated with my dreams because I'm not dreaming. That pretty much summarizes it, doesn't it, Doctor?"

"Perhaps, yes. Fascinating. We could be on the verge of a whole new world of understanding here."

Phil Grant shook his head. "Okay, Gains is right. From this point forward we've got to keep this dream-talk to a minimum. We keep the story straight and simple. You have a gift. You're seeing things that haven't happened yet. That's hard enough to buy, but at least there's precedent for it. In the light of our situation, enough people will at least give a prophet a chance. But the rest of this—your wife, Rochel or whatever her name is, your war council, the Horde, the fruit you didn't eat—all of it, strictly off-limits to anyone except me and Gains."

"You want to pitch me as some kind of mystical prophet?" Thomas said. "I'm not as optimistic as you. It'll do nothing for my leverage in the international community. Outside of this room I'm simply a person who may know more about the situation at hand than anyone else in this government because of my association with Monique. I was the last one to speak to her before she was taken. I'm the only one who has engaged the terrorists, and I'm the only one who has accurately anticipated their next move. Considering all of that, I am a man who should be taken very seriously. Judging the rather . . . lukewarm reception I got from the others in the meeting today, I think that might make more sense."

"I won't disagree," Grant said. "Are you anticipating the need for leverage in the international community?"

Thomas walked past him, his sense of urgency swelling. "Who knows? One way or another we've got to beat this thing. I can't believe the Books of Histories still exist! If I can get to them . . ."

He stopped. "I have to know something." Thomas faced them, eyes wide. "I have to know if this cut on my shoulder came from Carlos or from the Horde. In my dreams, that is."

They stared at him without offering any bold statements of support.

"From Carlos," Kara finally said.

"But you didn't see him cut me, right? I was already bleeding when you came into the room. No, I really need to know. They're insisting that the Horde cut me."

"How . . . can you prove it either way?"

"Yes. Cut me." He stuck out his arm. "Make a small incision and I'll see if I have it when I wake up."

All three blinked.

"Just give me the knife then."

Bancroft stepped to a drawer, opened it, and withdrew scissors. "Well, I have these—"

"You're not serious, are you?" Grant demanded.

Thomas took the scissors and drew their sharp tip along his forearm. He had to understand the rules of engagement. "Just a small scratch. For me. I have to know." He winced and handed the scissors back.

"You're suggesting that more than what's in your mind is transferred between realities?" the doctor asked.

"Of course," he said. "I'm there and I'm here. Physically. That's more than knowledge or skills. My wounds show up in both realities. My blood.

Life. Nothing else. My mind and my life. On the other hand, my aging doesn't show here. I'm younger here."

"This . . . this is absolutely incredible," the doctor said.

Thomas faced Grant. "So what's our status?"

The director took awhile to answer. "Well . . . the president's directed FEMA to direct all of its resources to work with the Centers for Disease Control, and he's brought in the World Health Organization. They've now confirmed the virus in thirty-two airports."

"What about the search for Monique? The rest may be pointless unless we find her."

"We're working on it. The governments of Britain, Germany, France, Thailand, Indonesia, Brazil . . . a dozen others are pulling out the stops."

"Switzerland?"

"Naturally. I may not be able to predict a virus, or battle the Horde, but I do know how to look for fugitives in the real world."

"Svensson's gone deep, into a hole somewhere that he prepared a long time ago. One that no one will think to look in. Like the one outside of Bangkok."

"Which you found how?"

Thomas glanced at Kara.

"Could you do that again?" she asked. "The world's changed, but that doesn't mean Rachelle isn't somehow connected to Monique, right?"

Thomas didn't respond. What if he was wrong? He was still Thomas Hunter, the failed writer from Denver. What right did he have advising the CIA? The stakes were astronomical.

On the other hand, he had been right more than once. And he had battled the Horde successfully for fifteen years. That earned him something, as the president had said.

"Will someone please explain?" Grant asked.

Kara faced him. "Rachelle, Thomas's dream-wife, inadvertently led him to Monique the first time. She seemed to know where Monique was being kept. But she became jealous of Monique, because she realized that Thomas was falling in love with her here. So she refused to help him again. It's why he agreed not to dream for fifteen years."

"I must be given more time," Bancroft murmured. "You're in love with two different women, one from each reality?"

"That's a stretch," Thomas said.

It was a thing that Thomas had been trying to squash ever since he'd awakened from the fifteen-year dream, but it lingered there in the back of his mind. It seemed absurd that he would have any feelings for Monique at all. Yes, they'd faced death together, and she'd kissed him as a matter of her own survival. He did find her fiery spirit attractive, and her face refused to budge from his mind's eye. But maybe Rachelle's jealousy was what triggered his romantic feelings for Monique in the first place. Maybe he wouldn't have started to fall for her if Rachelle hadn't suggested that he *was* falling for her.

Now, after fifteen years with Rachelle, any romantic notions he might once have felt for Monique had vanished.

"The whole thing is more than a stretch," Grant said, "starting with your prediction of the Raison Strain. But these are now facts, aren't they? So you get to your Books of Histories and you get to Rachelle and you convince her to help us here. Meaning you sleep and you dream."

He shook his head and started for the door. "With any luck you'll have something more sensible to tell the president when you meet with him tomorrow."

❈

They'd moved her again. Where, she had no clue.

Monique de Raison stared at the monitor, mind taxed, eyes burning.

It had been less than twenty-four hours since they'd put a sack over her head for the second time in as many days and led her into a car, then onto an airplane. The flight had lasted several hours—she could be anywhere. Hawaii, China, Argentina, Germany. She might have been able to figure out the region by any stray conversation she overheard, but they'd stuffed wax in her ears and taped them. She couldn't even determine the temperature or humidity, because they'd landed during a rainstorm that had wet her hood before she'd been shoved into another car and brought here.

A man of German or Swiss descent whom she'd never met before had pulled the bag off her head and unplugged her ears. He'd left her in this room without speaking.

Another laboratory. Blinding white. A small lab, maybe twenty by twenty, but crammed with the latest equipment. A Field Emission Electron Microscope, a Siemens, stood along one wall. The microscope could effectively examine wet samples as well as specimens treated with liquid nitrogen. State of the art. Next to it, a long table arrayed with test tubes and a Beckman Coulter Counter.

In the corner, a mattress, and in an adjoining room without a door, a toilet and a sink.

The room was constructed of cinder blocks, like the others. On second look, she was sure that whoever had built the other two labs she'd been in had also built this one. How many did they have? And each had been carefully supplied with everything a geneticist or a virologist would need.

She'd curled up on the mattress, dressed in the pale blue slacks and matching blouse they'd given her before the trip, and cried. She knew that she should be strong. That Svensson surely wouldn't actually release the virus as he'd threatened to. That if he did, she might be the only one who could stop it. But the chance of the back door she'd engineered surviving the mutation was terribly small. They had to be bluffing.

Still, she'd cried.

A man in a white smock with red hair and bifocals had entered the room twenty minutes later carrying a brown snakeskin briefcase. "Are you okay?" He actually looked surprised at her condition. "Goodness, what have they done to you? You're Monique de Raison, right? *The* Monique de Raison."

She stood and pushed her bangs from her eyes. A scientist. Her hope surged. Was he a friend?

"Yes," she said.

Only a few days earlier she might have slapped this man for his gawking. Now she felt small. Too small.

A glint sparkled in the man's eyes. "We have a wager. We have a wager."

He motioned to the door. "Who will find it first, you or us." He leaned forward as if what he was about to say was to be kept secret. "I am the only one betting on you."

He was slightly mad, she thought.

"None of us will find it," she said. "Do you realize what's happening?"

"Of course I do. The first to isolate the antivirus will be paid fifty *million* dollars, and the whole team will be paid ten million each. But there are eleven teams, so Petrov—"

She slapped him then. His glasses spun across the room. "He's going to release the virus, you idiot!"

He stared at her. "He already has."

Then he set the case on the floor, walked to his glasses, returned them to his face. "Everything you need is in the case," he said. "You will see all of our work in real-time calculations, and we will see yours."

He headed for the door.

"Please, I'm sorry!" She hurried after him. "You have to help me!"

But he closed the door and was gone.

That was over an hour ago. Now Monique stared at a dizzying string of numbers and tried desperately to focus.

He hasn't released the virus, Monique. The chances of finding an antivirus in time are too low. It would be suicide!

But he'd kidnapped her, hadn't he? He knew he would eventually be caught and would spend the balance of his life in prison. What did he have to lose?

And Thomas . . .

Her mind was swallowed by her two encounters with the American. His harebrained kidnapping of her. He had tied her to the air conditioner in the Paradise Hotel while he slept, while he took his dream-trip to retrieve information that he could not possibly know. The attack by Carlos. She'd seen Thomas shot, and yet he'd survived and come for her again. She'd kissed him. She'd done it to distract whoever was watching, but she'd also done it because he had risked his life for her, and she felt desperate for him to save her. He was her savior.

She didn't know if her irresponsible feelings for him were motivated by his character or by her own despair. Her emotions were hardly trustworthy in a time like this.

Was he still alive?

You have to focus, Monique. They will come for you again. Father will have the whole world looking for you.

She took a deep breath and reapplied her concentration. A model of her own Raison Vaccine filled one corner of the screen. Below it, a model of the Raison Strain, a mutation that had survived after the vaccine had been subjected to intense heat for two hours, exactly as Thomas had predicted. She'd analyzed a simulation of the actual mutation a hundred times over the past hour and saw how it had worked. This was a freak of nature far more complex than anything a geneticist could have come up with on his own.

Ironically, her own genetic engineering, designed to keep the vaccine viable for long periods without contacting any host or moisture, had allowed the inert vaccine to mutate in such adverse conditions.

As far as she could see, there were only two ways in which an antivirus could be developed with any kind of speed—meaning weeks instead of months or years.

The first would be for her to identify the signature she had engineered into her vaccine to turn it off, as it were. She'd developed a simple way to introduce an airborne agent into the vicinity of the vaccine—a virus that would essentially neutralize the vaccine by inserting its own DNA into the mix and rendering the vaccine impotent. It was her personal signature as much as a deterrent to foul play or theft.

If she could find the specific gene she'd engineered, and *if* it had survived the mutation, then introducing the virus she'd already developed to neutralize the vaccine *might* also render the Raison Strain impotent. *If, if,* and *might* being the key words.

She knew the signature like she knew her best friend. The problem now was how to find it in this mangled mess called the Raison Strain.

The only other way to unravel an antivirus in such short order was to chance upon the right gene manipulations. But ten thousand lab technicians could coordinate their efforts for sixty days and not strike the right combination.

Svensson knew something, or he wouldn't risk so much on a long shot. Surely he understood that her signature might not have survived, or that it might not work on the mutated vaccine.

Monique moved the cursor over the key below the diagram of the Strain and brought up a window of its DNA. She would search for her key first.

She slammed her fist on the black Formica desktop. Glass tubes rattled in a tray. She swore through gritted teeth. "This can't be happening!"

"I'm afraid it is."

Svensson! She spun in her chair. The old goat stood in the doorway, smiling patiently, leaning on a white cane.

He moved into the room, dragging his leg, eyes glimmering with self-satisfaction.

"Sorry to leave you alone so long, but I've been a bit preoccupied. The last couple days have been quite eventful."

Monique stood and held the desk to hide a tremble in her hand. The man wore a black jacket, white shirt, no tie. His dark hair was parted in the middle and slicked back with cream. Blue veins stood out on his knuckles.

"What's going on?" she asked, as evenly as possible.

"What isn't?" He closed the door. "But that's unfair. You have no idea how exciting the world has become in the last forty-eight hours, because you've been hard at work trying to save it."

"How can I work if you move me every twelve hours?"

"We're on an Indonesian island, in a mountain called Cyclops. Quite safe here. Don't worry, it will be home for at least three days. Have you made any progress?"

"With what? You've given us an impossible task."

The old man's smile didn't soften, but his eyes glazed. He studied her for an inordinate amount of time.

"You're not as motivated as I'd hoped." He walked toward her. "Please insert this disk," he said, withdrawing a CD-ROM from his breast pocket. "And please don't think of assaulting me. If you think I can't slit your belly open with the flip of my wrist, you're a fool."

She took the disk and slid it into the computer's DVD tray. It retracted.

"The rest of the world has had the benefit of what you're going to see for three days now. I want to make sure you understand everything."

A single virus shell popped onto the screen and she recognized it immediately. The Raison Strain. A clock showed real time at the bottom of the picture.

"Yes, a most efficient mercenary. But you haven't seen what it can actually do."

"This is a simulation," she said. "Anyone can create a cartoon."

"I assure you, not a single piece of hypothetical data has been used for this 'cartoon,' as you call it. I'll leave it for you to analyze later."

She watched as the virus entered a human lung and immediately went to work on the cells of the alveoli. She knew how it would work, penetrating the cells with its own DNA and ultimately rupturing the cells. Soon thousands of virus-infected cells were streaming through the body's network of veins and arteries, searching out new organs. Even so, with this microscopic damage, no symptoms would be evident.

The clock at the bottom sped up and began ticking off hours, then days. It slowed at sixteen. The infected cells had reached a critical mass and were producing symptoms. Their assault on the body's organs resulted in massive internal hemorrhaging and quick failure within two more days.

Like an acid, the virus had eaten the host from the inside out.

"Nasty little beast," Svensson said. "There's more."

Monique had seen a thousand superbug simulations. She'd participated in autopsies of Ebola victims. She had seen and studied as many viruses as any other living person. But she'd never seen such a ravaging animal, not one that was so contagious, so systemic, and so innocuous before reaching maturity and consuming its host like so many piranha.

Monique cleared her throat.

The next frame showed a map of the world. Twelve red dots lit up. New York, Washington, Bangkok, and on, tiny fires popping to life.

"Forgive the melodrama, but there really is no other way to show what the naked eye cannot see."

By the end of day one, the number of cities had reached twenty-four.

"Our initial deposit. Everything else is the virus's own doing."

Lines spread over the map, showing air-traffic routes. The lights spread. By the beginning of day three, half the map was solid red.

Now the simulation changed to show the spread of the virus from one host to another. Monique knew the facts well enough: One sneeze contained as many as ten million germs traveling at up to one hundred miles per hour. With this virus, the time between a person acquiring the germ and becoming contagious was a mere four hours. Even assuming each contagious agent infected only a hundred per day, the numbers grew exponentially. By day nine the number had reached six billion.

Svensson reached forward and pressed the space bar. The simulation froze.

"That brings us up to date."

At first she didn't understand. Up to date, meaning what?

"Give or take a few hours," he said.

"You're saying you've actually done it?"

"As promised. And I will admit that not all of the infected cities represent saturation. The red light means the virus is currently airborne, sweeping through that city. We calculate that it will take two weeks for global saturation."

He pulled out a small vial of amber liquid. Uncorked the lid. Sniffed the opening. "Odorless."

She knew the whole truth then. It was hard to grasp, even with his simulations. Computer models and theories and pictures were one thing, but to imagine that what she was seeing had actually happened . . .

He could be lying about all of it, forcing her to slave on an antivirus so that with it he could blackmail the world.

"You need more convincing, I can see." He pressed the intercom button on the phone. "Bring him down." He picked up a clean slide.

Maybe he really had done it.

"This is crazy. The United States would come unglued if—"

"The United States *is* coming unglued!" he shouted. "Every nation with anything resembling a military is coming unglued. The people don't know yet, but the governments have been scrambling for two days already. The CDC has already verified the virus in over fifty of its cities."

The door opened, and a bound man wearing a green shirt and a black bag over his head stumbled in. Carlos entered and shut the door.

Svensson withdrew a scalpel from his pocket and walked to the man. "We picked him up in a Paris nightclub. We have no idea who he is, although he looks like he might be a visitor from the Mediterranean. Perhaps Greek. His mouth is taped, so don't bother asking him any questions. The chances of him being infected are pretty good, considering where he was spending his time, wouldn't you agree?"

Without waiting for an answer, Svensson slashed the man across his chest. The man jerked back and moaned behind his gag. Svensson whipped the slide along the seeping line of blood that darkened the green shirt.

He walked toward the electron microscope, snapped it on, and slipped the slide into place.

"Look for yourself," he said, stepping back.

The man had fallen to his knees, shirt now soaked red.

Monique's head swam.

Svensson walked to the man, pulled out a pistol, and shot him in the head. His victim dropped to the floor.

The Swiss shoved the gun at the microscope. "Look!"

Ears ringing, pulse pounding, Monique walked to the monitor. She worked the familiar instrument without thinking what she was doing. It took too long to focus because she couldn't control her hands. They were shaking and seemed to have forgotten just what to do.

But when she finally found a patch on the slide that cooperated with the intense magnification, she could hardly miss the foreign bodies swimming through the man's blood.

She blinked and increased the magnification. Behind her the room was silent. Just her, breathing through her nostrils. This was it. This was the Raison Strain.

She straightened.

"No more games, Monique. There's no way to stop the spread of the virus. Without an antivirus we will all die. It really is that simple. We know that you engineer a back door into your vaccines. We need you to identify this back door, verify that it hasn't mutated with the vaccine, and then create the virus that will turn the Raison Strain off. I won't lie to you; I'm not telling you everything—you're clever enough to figure that out. But I am telling you what you need to know to play your part in helping humanity survive."

She faced him, suddenly cold. "I don't think you know what you've done."

"Oh, we do. And I, like you, am only playing my part. Everyone must play his part or the game will indeed end badly. But don't think any of this has escaped our calculation. We've anticipated everything."

He glanced at Carlos. "There is the matter of the pesky American, of course. But we're dealing with him. He may not die so easily, but we have other means. I doubt a soul alive understands the breadth of our power."

Thomas was still alive.

She glanced at the crumpled body on the floor. He was dead, but Thomas was alive. A sliver of hope.

"We need the key," Svensson said.

"I'll do my best."

"How long?"

"If it survived the mutation, three days. Maybe two."

Svensson smiled. "Perfect. Now I have a plane to catch. They will take good care of you. You are very important to us, Monique. We'll need brilliant minds when this is over. Please try to think positively."

⸺

"This is an outrage!"

Three of the four men in the room looked at Armand Fortier with shock in their eyes.

"Is it, Jean?" Fortier stood and faced France's leading men: the premier, Boisverte, who had just objected; President Gaetan, who was a weasel and would ultimately capitulate; Du Braeck, the minister of defense, who was the most valuable to Fortier; and the head of the secret police, the Sûreté,

Chombarde, who was the only one without round eyes at the moment. Each had been intentionally selected; each was now faced with the decision to live for tomorrow or die tonight, though they didn't understand it in those terms. Not yet.

"Be careful what you say," Fortier said.

"You can't do this!"

"I already have."

As minister of foreign affairs, Fortier had convinced Henri Gaetan to call this emergency session to address Valborg Svensson's recent ultimatum. Fortier had critical information relevant to the virus, he told Gaetan, and suggested that the leaders meet at the Château Triomphe in the Right Bank.

The private conference room beneath the ancient two-story retreat was the perfect setting for new beginnings. Lamps mounted on the stone walls cast an amber light across the plush furnishings. It was more like a private living room than a conference room: tall leather wing chairs budding with brass buttons, a large fireplace licked by greedy flames, a crystal chandelier over the brass coffee table, a fully stocked bar.

And most importantly, heavy walls. Very heavy walls.

Armand Fortier was a thick man. Thick eyebrows, thick wrists, thick lips. His mind, he would say, was sharp enough to cut any woman down to size in a matter of seconds. They never knew what to do with such an assertive statement, but it generally put them in a defensive mind-set so that when he did dominate them, they were not quite so submissive.

It was his only vice.

That and power.

He knew that he could have muscled his way into the presidency long ago, but he wasn't interested in France—the scrutiny leveled at such an office would have worked against him. His appointment as the minister of foreign affairs, however, put him in the perfect position to achieve his true aspirations.

Henri Gaetan was a tall, thin man with deep-set eyes and a jaw line as sharp as Fortier's mind. "What are you saying, Armand? That you work for Valborg Svensson?"

"No."

Fortier had first recruited Svensson fifteen years ago to conduct a much simpler operation: untraceable arms deals with several interested nations, which involved biological weapons research in exchange for lucrative contracts. The deals had earned him billions. The money had fueled Svensson's pharmaceutical empire, with strings attached, naturally.

Fortier hadn't grasped the true potential of the right biological weapon until he watched one of those nations discreetly use an agent of Svensson's against the Americans. The incident had forever altered the course of Fortier's life.

"Then how is this possible?" the president demanded. "You're suggesting that we give in to his demands—"

"No. I'm suggesting that you give in to my demands."

"So he works for you," said Chombarde.

"Gentlemen, perhaps you don't truly understand what has happened. Let me clarify. Half of our citizens are going to work and feeding their children and attending school and doing whatever else they do in this wonderful republic of ours today without the slightest notion that they have been infected with a virus that will overtake every last soul on this planet within two weeks. It is called the Raison Strain, and it will sit quietly for the next eighteen days before it begins its killing. Then it will kill very quickly. There is no cure. There is no way to *find* a cure. There is no way to stop the virus. There is only one antivirus, and I control it. Is there any part of this explanation that escapes any of you?"

"But what you're suggesting is morally reprehensible!" the premier said.

Only the minister of defense, Georges Du Braeck, hadn't spoken. He seemed ambivalent. This was good. Fortier would need Du Braeck's cooperation more than any of the others.

"No sir. Embracing death is morally reprehensible. I'm offering your only escape from that most certain death. Very few men in this world will be given the kind of opportunity I'm giving you tonight."

For a few moments no one spoke.

The president pushed himself to standing and faced Fortier at ten feet. "You're underestimating the world's nuclear powers. You expect them to just load up their aircraft carriers and their merchant fleets and float their entire nuclear arsenals to France because we demand it? They will *launch* them first!"

It was the same objection other heads of much smaller states had voiced when he'd first suggested the plan a decade ago. Fortier smiled at the pompous pole of a man.

"Do you take me for a fool, Henri? You think I have spent less time making calculations in the last ten years than you have after only a few minutes? Please sit down."

There was a tremble in Henri Gaetan's hands. He reached back for a grip on the chair and sat slowly.

"Good. They will object, naturally, but you underestimate the human drive for self-preservation. In the end, when faced with a choice between the bloody death of twenty million innocent children and their military, they will choose their children. We will make sure that the choice is understood in those terms. The British, the Russians, the Germans . . . All will choose to live and fight another day. As I hope you will."

The nature of his threat against each of them personally was starting to sink in, he thought.

"Let me phrase it this way: In fewer than eighteen days, the balance of power on this planet will have shifted dramatically. The course is set; the outcome is inevitable. We have chosen France to host the world's new superpower. As the leaders of France, you have two choices. You can facilitate this shift in global power and live as a part of the leadership you've all secretly wanted for so many years, or you can deny me and die with the rest."

Now they surely understood.

The minister of defense sat with legs crossed, glowing like any good Stalinist faced with such an ultimatum. He finally spoke. "May I ask a few questions?"

"Please."

"There is no physical way for the United States, let alone the rest of the world, to ship all of its nuclear weapons in fourteen days. They have to be evacuated from launching points and armament caches, shipped to the East Coast, loaded on ships, and sailed across the Atlantic."

"Naturally. The list we have given them includes all of their ICBMs, all long-range missiles, most of their navy, including their submarines, and most of their air force, much of which can be flown. The United States will have to take extraordinary measures, but we're demanding nothing of them or anyone else that can't be done. As for the British, India, Pakistan, and Israel, we are demanding their entire nuclear arsenals."

"China and Russia?"

"China. Let's just say that China will not be a problem. They have no love for the United States. China has agreed already and will begin shipments tomorrow in exchange for certain favors. They will be an example for others to follow. Russia is a different story, but we have several critical elements in alignment. Although they will sound off their objections, they will comply."

"Then we have allies."

"In a manner of speaking."

The revelation delivered a long moment of silence. "The Americans are still the greatest threat," said Gaetan. "Assuming the Americans do agree, how can France accommodate all of this"—the president drew his hand through the air—"this massive amount of hardware? We don't have the people or the space."

"Destroy it," the defense minister said.

"Very good, Du Braeck. Superiority is measured in ratios, not sums, yes? Ten to one is better than a thousand to five hundred. We will sink more than half of the military hardware we receive. Think of this as forced disarmament. History may even smile on us."

"Which is why you've chosen the deep water near the Brest naval base."

"Among other reasons."

"And how can we protect ourselves against an assault during this transition of power?" the defense minister asked.

Fortier had expected these questions and possessed answers so detailed that he could never begin to explain everything at this meeting. Inventories of hardware, possible troop movement, preemptive strikes, political will— every possibility had been considered at great length. Tonight his only task was to win the trust of these four men.

"Fourteen days is enough time to ship arms, not deploy troops. Any immediate long-range attack would come by air. Thanks to the Russians, we will have the threat of retaliation to deter any such attack. The only other immediate threat would come from our neighbors, primarily England. We will be at our weakest for the next three days, until we can reposition our forces to repel a ground attack and take on reinforcements from the Chinese. But the world will be in a political tailspin—confusion will buy us the time we need."

"Unless they learn who is responsible now."

"They will have to assume that the French government is being forced. Besides that, they have no guarantee that an attack would secure the antivirus. The antivirus won't be held up in a vial in our parliament for all the world to see. Only I will know where it is."

"Why France?"

"Please, Georges. Wasn't it Hitler who said that he who controls France controls Europe, and he who controls Europe controls the world? He was right. If there were a more strategic country, I would take my leave and go now. France is and always will be the center of the world."

The president had crossed his legs; the head of the *Sûreté* had stopped blinking; the minister of defense was virtually glowing. They were softening.

Only Prime Minister Boisverte still glared.

"Let me give you an example of how this is going to play out, gentlemen. Jean, would you come here?"

The defiant prime minister just stared at him.

He motioned him. "Please. Stand over here. I insist."

The man still hesitated. He was hard to the bones.

"Then where you are will do." Fortier reached into his jacket and pulled out a silenced 9 mm pistol. He pointed the gun at the prime minister and pulled the trigger. The slug punched through the chair just above his shoulder.

The prime minister's eyes bulged.

"You see, this is what we have done. We've fired a warning shot across their bow. Right now they aren't certain of our will to carry through. But soon enough"—he shifted the pistol and shot the man through his forehead—"they will be."

The prime minister slumped in his chair.

"Don't think of this as a threat, Henri. Jean would have died in eighteen days anyway. We all will unless we do exactly what I have said. Does anyone doubt that?"

The remaining three men looked at him with a calm that pleasantly surprised Fortier.

Fortier slipped the gun back into his pocket and straightened his jacket. "If I die, the antivirus would be lost. The world would die. But I have no intention of dying. I invite you to join me with similar intentions."

"Naturally," Georges said.

Fortier glanced at the president. "Henri?"

"Yes."

"Chombarde?"

The head of the *Sûreté* dipped his head. "Of course."

"And how do we proceed?" the president asked.

Fortier walked around his chair and sat.

"As for the members of the military, the National Assembly, and the Senate, who must know, our explanation is simple: A new demand has come from Svensson. He has chosen our naval base in Brest to accommodate his demands. France will agree with the understanding that we are luring Svensson into our own web. A bluff. Voices of opposition will begin to disappear within the week. I anticipate we will have to call for martial law to protect against any insurgence or riots at week's end. By then we will have most of the world in a vise, and the French people will know that their only hope for survival lies in our hands."

"My dear, my dear," the president muttered. "We are really doing this."

"Yes. We are."

Fortier reached for a stack of folders on the table at his elbow. "We don't have the time to work through all of our individual challenges, so I've taken the liberty of doing it for you. We will need to adjust as we go, of course." He handed each a folder. "Think of this as a game of high-stakes poker. I expect you will each hold your cards close to the chest."

They took the folders and flipped them open. A sense of purpose had settled on the room. Henri Gaetan glanced at the slumped body of the prime minister.

"He's taken an emergency trip to the south, Henri."

The president nodded.

"Thomas Hunter," Chombarde said, lifting the top page from his folder. "The man who kidnapped Monique de Raison."

"Yes. He is . . . a unique man who's stumbled into our way. He may know more than we need him to know. Use whatever force is necessary to bring him, alive if possible. You will coordinate your efforts with Carlos Missirian. Consider Hunter your highest priority."

"Securing a man in the United States could be a challenge at a time like this."

"You won't have to. I am certain that he will come to us, if not to France, then to where we have the woman."

A beat.

"There are 577 members in the Assembly," the president said. "You have listed 97 who could be a problem. I think there may be more."

They reviewed and on occasion adjusted the plans deep into the night. Objections were overcome, new arguments cast and dismissed, strategies fortified. A sense of purpose and perhaps a little destiny slowly overtook all of them with growing certainty.

After all, they had little choice.

The die had been cast.

France had always been destined to save the world, and in the end that's exactly what they were doing. They were saving the world from its own demise.

They left the room six hours later.

Prime Minister Jean Boisverte left in a body bag.

12

THOMAS JERKED awake. He tumbled out of bed and searched the room. It was still dark outside. Rachelle slept on their bed. Two thoughts drummed through his mind, drowning out the simple reality of this room, this bed, these sheets, this bark floor under his bare feet.

First, the realities he was experiencing were unquestionably linked, perhaps in more ways than he ever could have guessed, and both of those realities were at risk.

Second, he knew what he must do now, immediately and at all costs. He must convince Rachelle to help him find Monique, and then he must find the Books of Histories.

But the image of his wife sleeping unexpectedly dampened his enthusiasm to solicit her help. So sweet and lost in sleep. Her hair fell across her face, and he was tempted to brush it free.

Her arm was smeared with blood. The sheet was red where her arm had rested.

His pulse surged. She was bleeding? Yes, a small cut on her upper arm—he hadn't noticed it last evening in all the excitement of his return. She hadn't mentioned it either. But was all this blood from such a small cut?

He glanced at his own forearm and remembered: He'd cut himself in the laboratory of Dr. Myles Bancroft. Yes, of course, he'd been sleeping here when that had happened, and he'd bled here, exactly as he feared he might.

His forearm had rubbed Rachelle's arm. The blood was half his. Half hers.

The realization only fueled his urgency. If he couldn't stop the virus, he would undoubtedly die. They might all die!

Then what? He hurried to the window and peered out. The air was quiet—an hour before sunrise. The thought of waking Rachelle to persuade her to forget everything she'd said about his dreams struck him as a futile task. She would be furious with him for dreaming again. And why would she think his cut was anything but an accident?

The wise man, on the other hand, might understand. Jeremiah.

Thomas pulled his tunic on quietly, strapped his boots to his feet, and slipped into the cool morning air.

Ciphus lived in the large house nearest the lake, a privilege he insisted on as keeper of the faith. He wasn't pleased to be awakened so early, but as soon as he saw that it was Thomas, his mood improved.

"For a religious man, you drink far too much ale," Thomas said.

The man grunted. "For a warrior, you don't sleep enough."

"And now you're making no sense. Warriors aren't meant to sleep their lives away. Where can I find Jeremiah of Southern?"

"The old man? In the guesthouse. It's still night though."

"Which guesthouse?"

"The one Anastasia oversees, I think."

Thomas nodded. "Thank you, man. Get back to sleep."

"Thomas—"

But he departed before the elder could voice any further objections.

It took him ten minutes to locate Jeremiah's bedroom and wake him. The old man swung his legs to the floor and sat up in the waning moonlight.

"What is it? Who are you?"

"Shh, it's me, old man. Thomas."

"Thomas? Thomas of Hunter?"

"Yes. Keep your voice down; I don't want to wake the others. These houses have thin walls."

But the old man couldn't hold back his enthusiasm. He stood and clasped Thomas's arms. "Here, sit on my bed. I'll get us a drink."

"No, no. Sit back down, please. I have an urgent question."

Thomas eased the old man down and sat next to him.

"How can I host such an honored guest without offering him a drink?"

"You have offered me a drink. But I didn't come for your hospitality. And I am the one who should honor you."

"Nonsense—"

"I came about the Books of Histories," Thomas said.

Silence came over Jeremiah.

"I have heard that you may know some things about the Books of Histories. Where they might be and if they can be read. Do you?"

The old man hesitated. "The Books of Histories?" His voice sounded thin and strained.

"You must tell me what you know."

"Why do you want to know about the Books?"

"Why shouldn't I want to know?" Thomas asked.

"I didn't say you shouldn't. I only asked why."

"Because I want to know what happened in the histories."

"This is a sudden desire? Why not ten years ago?"

"It's never occurred to me that they could be useful."

"And did it ever occur to you that they are missing for a reason?"

"Please, Jeremiah."

The old man hesitated again. "Yes. Well, I've never seen them. And I fear they have a power that isn't meant for any man."

Thomas clasped Jeremiah's arm. "Where are they?"

"It is possible they are with the Horde."

Thomas stood. Of course! Jeremiah had been with the Horde before bathing in the lake.

"You know this with certainty?"

"No. As I said, I've never seen them. But I have heard it said that the Books of Histories follow Qurong into battle."

"Qurong has them? Can . . . can he read them?"

"I don't think so, no. I'm not sure *you* could read them."

"But surely someone can read them. You."

"Me?" Jeremiah chuckled. "I don't know. They may not even exist, for all we know. It was all hearsay, you know."

"But you believe they do," Thomas said.

The first rays of dawn glinted in Jeremiah's eyes. "Yes."

So the old man had known all along that they existed with the Horde, and yet he had never offered this information. Thomas understood: The Books of Histories had long ago been taken from Elyon's people and committed to an oral history for some reason. If it made good sense so long ago, then surely it made good sense now. Hadn't Tanis, as Rachelle so aptly pointed out, been led down the wrong path by his fascination with their knowledge? Perhaps Jeremiah was right. The Books of Histories were not meant for man.

Still, Thomas needed them.

"I'm going after them, Jeremiah. Believe me when I say that our very survival may depend on the Books."

Jeremiah stood shakily. "That would mean going after Qurong!"

"Yes, and Qurong is with the army that we defeated in the Natalga Gap. They're in the desert west of here, licking their wounds." Thomas stepped quickly to the window. Daylight had begun to dim the moon.

"You've told me where the commander's tent lies—in the center, always. Isn't that right?" he asked, turning.

"Yes, where he is surrounded by his army. You'd have to be one of them to get anywhere near—"

The old man's eyes went wide. He walked forward, face stricken. "Don't do this! Why? Why would you risk the life of our greatest warrior for a few old books that may not exist?"

"Because if I don't find them, I may die." He looked away. "We may all die."

———— ❧ ————

Rachelle sat at the table as if in a dream.

Knowing that it was in fact a dream.

Knowing just as well that it was no more a dream than the love she had for Thomas. Or didn't have for Thomas. The thoughts confused her.

The dream was vivid as dreams went. She was working desperately over the table, seeking a solution to a terrible problem, hoping that the solution would present itself at any moment, sure that if it didn't come, life as she knew it would end. Not just in this small room, mind you, but all over the world.

This was where the generalities ended and the specifics began.

The white table, for example. Smooth. White. *Formica.*

The box on the table. *A computer.* Powerful enough to crunch a million bits of information every thousandth of a second.

The mouse at her fingertips, gliding on a black foam pad. The equation on the monitor, the Raison Strain, a mutation of her own creation. The laboratory with its electron microscope and the other instruments to her right. This was all as familiar as her own name.

Monique de Raison.

No. Her real name was Rachelle, and she wasn't really familiar with anything in this room, least of all the woman who bore the name Monique de Raison.

Or was she?

The monitor went black for a moment. In it she saw Monique's reflection. *Her* reflection. Dark hair, dark eyes, high cheekbones, small lips.

It was almost as if she *was* Monique.

Monique de Raison, world-renowned geneticist, hidden away in a mountain named Cyclops on an Indonesian island by Valborg Svensson, who had released the Raison Strain in twenty-four cities around the world.

Whoever searched for her would probably never find her. Not even Thomas Hunter, the man who'd risked his life twice for her.

Monique had some feelings for Thomas, but not the same as Rachelle had for him.

She stared at the screen and dragged her pointer over the bottom corner of the model. One last time she lifted the sheet of paper covered with a hundred penciled calculations. Yes, this was it. It had to be. She set the page down and withdrew her hand.

Something bit her finger and she jerked her hand back. *Paper cut.* She ignored it and stared at the screen.

"Please, please," she whispered. "Please be here."

She clicked the mouse button. A formula popped into a small box on the monitor.

She let out a sob, a huge sigh of relief, and leaned back into her chair.

Her code was intact. The key was here and, by all appearances, unaffected by the mutation. So then, the virus she engineered to disable these genes might also work!

Another thought tempered her elation. When Svensson had what he wanted, he would kill her. For a brief moment she considered not telling Svensson how close she was. But she couldn't hold back information that might save countless lives, regardless of who used that information.

Then again, she might not be close at all. He hadn't told her everything. There was something—

"Mother. Mother, wake up."

Rachelle bolted up in bed.

"Thomas?"

Her son stood in the doorway. "He's not here. Did he go out on the patrols?"

Rachelle threw the covering off and stood. "No. No, he should be here."

"Well, his armor's gone. And his sword."

She looked at the rack where his leathers and scabbard usually hung. It stood in the corner, empty like a skeleton. Maybe with all of the people arriving for the Gathering, he'd gone out to check on his patrols.

"I asked in the village," Samuel said. "No one knows where he is."

She pulled back and closed the canvas drape that acted as their door. She quickly traded her bed clothes for a soft fitted leather blouse laced with crossing ties in the back. In her closet hung over a dozen colorful dresses and skirts, primarily for the celebrations. She grabbed a tan leather skirt and cinched it tight with rolled rope ties. Six pairs of moccasins, some decorative, some very utilitarian, lay side by side under her dresses. She scooped up the first pair.

All of this she did without thought. Her mind was still in her dream. With each passing moment it seemed to dim, like a distant memory. Even so, parts of this memory screamed through her mind like a flight of startled macaws.

She'd entered Thomas's dream world.

She'd been there, in a laboratory hidden in a mountain named Cyclops with—or was it as?—Monique, doing and understanding things that she had no knowledge of. And if Monique had found this key of hers, she might be killed before Thomas ever found her.

Her heart pounded. She had to tell Thomas!

Rachelle crossed to the table, snatched up the braided bronze bracelet Thomas had made for her, and slid it up her arm, above the elbow where—

She saw the blood on her arm, a dark red smear that had dried. Her cut? It must have been aggravated and broken open during the night.

The sheets were stained as well.

In her eagerness to find Thomas, she considered ignoring it for the moment. No, she couldn't walk around with blood on her arm. She ran to the kitchen basin, lowered it under the reed, and released the gravity-drawn water by lifting a small lever that stopped the flow.

"Marie? Samuel?"

No response. They were out of the house.

The water stung her right index finger. She examined it. Another tiny cut.

Paper cut. This was from her dreams! Her mouth suddenly felt desert dry.

A thought crashed into her mind. Exactly how she was connected to Monique she didn't know, but she was, and this cut proved it. Thomas had been emphatic: If he died in that world, he would also die in this one. Perhaps whatever happened to Monique could very well happen to her! If this Svensson killed her, for example, they both might die.

She had to reach Thomas before he dreamed again so that he could rescue her!

Rachelle ran into the road, looked both ways through several hundred pedestrians who loitered along the wide causeway, and then ran toward the lake. Ciphus would know. If not, then Mikil or William.

"Good morning, Rachelle!"

It was Cassandra, one of the elder's wives. She wore a wreath of white flowers in her braided hair, and she'd applied the purple juice from mulberries above her eyes. The mood of the annual Gathering was spreading in spite of the unexpected Horde threats.

"Cassandra, have you seen Mikil?"

"She's on patrol, I think. You don't know? I thought Thomas went with them?"

Rachelle ran without further salutation. It was unlike Thomas to leave without telling her. Was there trouble?

She raced around the corner of Ciphus's house and pulled up, panting. The elder was in a huddle with Alexander, two other elders, and an old man she immediately recognized as the one who'd come in from the desert. Jeremiah of Southern. The one who knew about the Books of Histories.

Their conversation stalled.

"He's gone?" she demanded.

No one responded.

Rachelle leaped to the porch. "Where? He's on patrol?"

"A patrol," Ciphus said, shifting. "Yes, it's a patrol. Yes, he's gone—"

"Stop being so secretive," she snapped. "It's not a patrol or he would have told me." She looked at Jeremiah. "He's gone after them. Hasn't he? You told him where he might find the Books and he's gone after them. Tell me it isn't so!"

Jeremiah dipped his head. "Yes. Forgive me. I tried to stop him, but he insisted."

"Of course he insisted. Thomas always insists. Does that mean you had to tell him?" At the moment she was of a mind to knock these old men's heads together.

"Where has he gone? I have to tell him something."

Ciphus shoved his stool back and stood. "Please, Rachelle. Even if we knew where he was, you couldn't go after him. They left early on fast horses. They're halfway to the desert by now."

"Which desert?"

"Well . . . the big desert outside the forest. You cannot follow. I forbid it."

"You're in no position to forbid me from finding my husband."

"You're a mother with—"

"I have more skill than half of the warriors in our Guard, and you know it. I trained half of them in Marduk! Now you will either tell me where he's gone or I will track him myself."

"What is it, child?" Jeremiah asked gently. "What do you have for him?"

She hesitated, wondering how much Thomas had told the man.

"I have information that might save both of our lives," she said.

Jeremiah glanced at Ciphus, who offered no direction. "He's gone to the Natalga Gap with two of his lieutenants and seven warriors."

"And what will he find there?"

"The leader of the Horde, in the desert beyond the Gap. But you mustn't go, Rachelle. His decision to go after these books may lead to tragedy as it is."

"Besides," Alexander said, "we can't afford to send more of our force on yet another crazed mission."

"This has to do with these dreams of his?" Ciphus asked.

"They may not be dreams after all," Rachelle said, and she was surprised to hear the words come from her mouth.

"You as well?"

She ignored the question. "I have information that I believe may save my husband's life. If any of you would even consider holding me back, then his death will be on your hands."

Her overstatement held them in silence.

"If you have any other information that would help me, please, now is not the time to be coy."

"How dare you manipulate us!" Ciphus cried. "If there is any man who can survive this fool's errand, it is Thomas. But we can't have his woman chasing him into the desert four days before the Gathering!"

Rachelle stepped off the porch and turned her back on them. Now her determination to track Thomas down was motivated as much by these men's insults as by her own realization that her husband had been right about his dreams.

"Rachelle."

She turned and faced Jeremiah, who'd walked to the end of the porch.

"They will be due west of the Gap," he said. "I beg you, child, don't go." He paused, then continued with resignation. "Take extra water. As much as your horse can carry. I know it will slow you down, but the disease will slow you down even more."

The tremble in the old man's voice put her on edge.

"He means to become one of them," Jeremiah said. "He means to enter their camp."

Rachelle could not dare believe what she had just heard.

And then she knew it was true. It was exactly what Thomas would do if he knew, if he absolutely *knew*, that both realities were real.

Rachelle sprinted for the stables.

Dear Elyon, give me strength.

───

They were nine of his best, including William and Mikil. With himself, ten.

The three extra canteens of water they each carried weighed them down more than Thomas would have liked. It was a dangerous game that he was playing, and he couldn't risk being caught without the cleansing water.

They had ridden hard all day and now entered the same canyon their black powder had blasted thirty-six hours earlier. The stench rose from thousands of dead buried beneath the rubble and strewn on the desert floor.

They rode the Forest Guard's palest horses. Thomas's steed snorted and pawed at the sand. He urged the horse on and it moved forward reluctantly.

"Hard to believe that we did all this," William said.

"Don't think it's the end of them," Mikil said. "There's no end to them."

Thomas pulled a scarf over his nose and led the warriors into the rocks. The horses carried them through the canyon, past the burlap-cloaked bodies of their fallen enemy. He'd seen his share of dead, but the magnitude of this slaughter made him nauseated.

It was said that the Horde cared less for the lives of their men than the lives of their horses. Any Scab who defied his leader was summarily punished without trial. They favored the breaking of bones to flogging or other forms of punishment. It wasn't unusual to find a Scab soldier with numerous bones broken left to die on the hot desert sand without having shed a drop of blood. Public executions involved drowning the offender in pools of gray water, a prospect that instilled more fear in the Scabs than any other threat of death.

The Horde's terror of water had to be motivated by more than the pain that accompanied cleansing in the lakes, Thomas thought, *though he wasn't sure what.*

He waited until they had passed the front lines of the dead before stopping by a group of several prone bodies. He dismounted, stripped the hooded robe off a Scab buzzing with flies, and shook it in the air. He coughed and threw the cloak over the rump of his horse.

"Let's go, all of you," he said. "Dress."

William grunted and dismounted. "I never would have guessed I'd ever stoop so low as to dress in a whore's clothes." He dutifully began to strip one of the bodies. The rest found cloaks and donned them, muttering curses, not of objection, but of offense. The stench couldn't be washed from the burlap.

Thomas retrieved a warrior's sword and knife. Studded boots. Shin guards. These were new additions, he noted. The hardened, cured leather was uncharacteristic of the Desert Dwellers. The painful condition of their skin tempered their use of armor, but these shin guards had been layered with a soft cloth to minimize the friction.

"They're learning," he said. "Their technology isn't that far behind our own."

"They don't have black powder," Mikil said. "Ask me and I'll say they're finished. Give me three months and I'll have new defenses built around every forest. They don't stand a chance."

Thomas pulled the robe he'd liberated over his head and strapped on the foreign dagger.

"Until they do have black powder," he said, stuffing his own gear behind a boulder. "Have you considered what they could do to the forest if they had explosives? Besides, I'm not sure we have three months. They're growing brave and they're fighting with more intelligence. We're running out of warriors."

"Then what would you suggest?" Mikil asked. "Treason?"

She was speaking of the incident in the Southern Forest. A runner had arrived just before their departure and reported on the Southern Forest's victory over the Horde.

Only it wasn't Jamous who'd driven the Scabs away. He'd lost over half of his men in a hopeless battle in which he was outflanked and surrounded—a rare and deadly position to be caught in.

No, it was Justin, the runner said with a glint in his eye. He'd single-handedly struck terror into the Horde without one swipe of his blade. He'd negotiated a withdrawal with none other than the great general, Martyn himself.

The entire Southern Forest had sung Justin's praises in the Elyon Valley for three hours. Justin had spoken to them of a new way, and they had listened as if he were a prophet, the runner said. Then Justin had disappeared into the forest with his small band.

"Have I once suggested yielding to the Horde in any way?" Thomas asked. "I'll die waiting for the prophecy's fulfillment if I have to. Don't question my loyalty. One stray warrior is the least of our concerns at the moment. We'll have time enough for that at the Gathering."

He'd told her about the challenge and the Council's request that he defend it, should it come down to a fight.

"You're right," she said. "I meant no disrespect."

Thomas mounted and brought his horse around. "We ride in silence. Pull your hoods over your heads."

They headed out of the canyon, dressed as a band of Desert Dwellers, following the Horde's deep tracks.

The sun set slowly behind the cliffs, leaving the group in deep shadows. They soon emerged from the rock formations and headed due west toward a dimming horizon.

Thomas's explanation of the mission had been simple. He'd learned the Horde had a terrible weakness: They rode into battle with the superstitious belief that their religious relics would give them victory. If a small band of Forest Guard could penetrate the Horde camp and steal the relics, they might deal a terrible blow. He had also learned that at this very moment, Qurong, who'd certainly commanded the army they'd just defeated, carried those relics with him. The relics were the Books of Histories. Who would go with him to deal such a blow to the Horde?

All nine had immediately agreed.

At this very moment, he was lying in a hotel room not ten blocks from the capitol building in Washington, D.C., sleeping. A hundred government agencies were burning the midnight oil, trying to make sense of the threat that had stood the world on its end. Sleep was undoubtedly the furthest thing from their minds. They were busy trying to decide who should know and who should not, which family members they could warn without leaking the word that might send a panic through the nation. They were thinking of ways to isolate and quarantine and survive.

But not Thomas Hunter. He understood one thing very few others could. If there was a solution to Svensson's threat, it might very well lie in his sleep.

In his dreams.

They first saw the sea of fires four hours later, pinpricks of smoking light from oil torches several miles beyond the dune they had crested. Wood was scarce, but the black liquid that seeped from the sand in distant reserves met their needs as well or better than wood. Thomas had never seen the oil reserves, but the Forest Guard frequently confiscated barrels of the stuff from fallen armies and hauled it off as spoil.

They drew up side by side, ten wide, looking west. For several seconds they sat atop the dune in total silence. Even what was left of the army was daunting.

"You are certain about this, Thomas?" William said.

"No. But I am certain that our options are growing thin." He sounded far more confident than he felt.

"I should come with you," Mikil said.

"We stick to the plan," he said. "William and I go alone."

They knew the reasons. First there was the matter of their skin. All but Thomas and William had bathed in the lake before leaving. Then there was Mikil: Horde women didn't normally travel with the armies. Even if her skin turned, entering could be dangerous for her, despite her claim that she could look as much a man in burlap as any of them.

"How is your skin, William?"

His lieutenant pulled up his sleeve. "Itching."

Thomas dismounted, pulled out a bag of ash, and tossed it to him. "Face, arms, and legs. Don't be stingy."

"You're sure this will fool them?" Mikil asked.

"I mixed the ash with some of the sulfur we used for the black powder. It's the scent as much as the—"

"Ugh! This is horrid!" William gasped, nose turned from the bag. He coughed. "They'll smell us coming a mile away!"

"Not if we smell like them. It's their dogs that worry me the most. And our eyes."

Mikil stared into his eyes. "They're paling already. In this light you should be fine. And honestly, in this light with enough of that rotten ash on my skin, I could pass as easily as you."

Thomas ignored her persistence.

Ten minutes later he and William had powdered their skin gray, checked their gear to be sure none of it would be associated with the Guard, and remounted. The others remained on foot.

"Okay." Thomas took a deep breath and blew it out slowly. "Here we go. Look for the fire, Mikil, just as we planned. If you see one of their tents suddenly go up in flames, send the rest in for us on horse, fast and low. Bring our horses. Whatever you do, don't forget to keep your hoods on. And you might want to throw some ash on your face for good measure."

"Send the rest? Lead them, you mean."

"Send them. I need someone to lead the Guard in the event it all goes badly."

She glared at him and set her jaw. "I think you should reconsider going in."

"We go with the plan. As always."

"And as always you refuse any voice of caution. I'm looking at the camp and I'm watching my general about to throw himself into this pack of wolves and I'm starting to wonder why."

"For the same reason we've had all day," he said. "Jamous nearly lost his life yesterday, and we the day before. The Horde is gaining strength, and unless we do something to cripple them, not only Jamous, but all of us along with our children, will die."

Mikil crossed her arms and squatted.

"Let's go," William said. "I want to get out of there before daylight."

"The people need you," Thomas told Mikil softly.

"No, the people need you, Thomas."

She frowned. It was hopeless.

"Elyon's strength," Thomas said.

"Elyon's strength," the others muttered. Mikil said nothing. She would snap out of her brooding mood soon enough, but at the moment he let her make her statement.

Thomas clucked his tongue and eased his horse down the slope.

—∞∞∞—

"Perhaps we should stop here for the night," Suzan said, staring out at the black desert.

"How can we? I didn't come all this way to wait for him. I could have waited for him at the village."

Rachelle kicked her horse into a trot. They'd ridden hard most of the day and picked their way through the body-strewn canyon in the last hour. She'd seen her share of battlefields, but this one had been terrifying.

Suzan drew abreast. "We can't be sure they even went out—there are too many tracks for me to know."

"I know my husband; he went out. If he left the village without so much as a whisper to me, trust me, he's on a mission. He won't stop for darkness. And you're the best tracker in the Guard, aren't you? Then track."

"Even if we do catch them, what advantage is tonight over tomorrow?"

"I told you, I have information that may save his life. He's going for the Books of Histories because of his dreams, Suzan. He may say it's to give the Guard an advantage, and I'm not saying it wouldn't, but there's more to the story. I have to reach him before he dreams so that he can find me."

"Find you?"

She shouldn't have said so much.

"Before he dreams."

"We're risking our necks over another dream?"

"His dream of black powder saved us all. You were there."

Any further explanation would be futile. Thomas himself hadn't been able to satisfy her, neither fifteen years ago nor last night. She pressed her thumb against the forefinger that had been cut in her own dream. There were two worlds, and each affected the other. With each passing mile, her conviction had grown. With each recollection of Thomas's dreams fifteen years earlier, her understanding had broadened, though she had no clue how it was happening, much less why.

But she could not ignore the pain in her finger.

Forgive me, Thomas. Forgive me, my love.

"It still makes no sense to me," Suzan said, searching the ground for tracks.

"And it may never make sense to you. But I'm willing to stake my life on it. I don't want my husband to die, and unless we reach him, he might."

"Thomas doesn't die easily."

"The virus doesn't care who dies easily."

⸺◦∞◦⸺

They approached the Horde camp from the northeast, over a small rise that fell into a broad flat valley, with a light breeze in their faces.

Thomas lay on his belly next to William and studied the camp. Tens of thousands of torches on stakes lit the desert night with a surreal orange glow. A giant circular blob of lights spread across the sand. Their tents were square, roughly ten by ten, woven from a coarse thread made from the stalks of desert wheat. The stalks were pounded flat and rolled into long strands that the Horde used for everything from their clothing to bindings.

"There!" William pointed to their right. A huge tent rose above the others south of center. "That's it."

"And it's a good half mile past the perimeter," Thomas said quietly.

They'd left their horses staked behind them where they would be hidden by the dune. The Guard had never attempted to infiltrate a camp before. Thomas was banking on a minimal perimeter guard as a result. He and William would go on foot and hopefully slip in unnoticed.

"That's a lot of Horde," William said.

"A whole lot."

William eased his sword a few inches out of its scabbard. "You ever swung a Scab sword before?"

"Once or twice. The blades aren't as sharp as ours."

"The thought of killing a few with their own weapons is appealing."

"Put it away. The last thing I want is a fight. Tonight we are thieves."

His lieutenant shoved the sword home.

"Remember, don't speak unless directly questioned. No eye contact. Keep your hood as far over your face as possible. Walk with pain."

"I *do* have pain," William said. "The cursed disease is killing me already. You said it won't affect the mind for a while. How long?"

"If we get out before morning, we'll be fine."

"We should have brought the water. Their dogs would never know the difference."

"We don't know that. And if we are taken, the water would incriminate us. They can smell it, trust me."

"You have any idea what the Books look like?" William asked.

"Books. Books are books. Maybe scrolls similar to the ones we use, or the flat kind from long ago. If we find them, we'll know. Ready?"

"Always."

They stood.

Deep breath.

"Let's go."

Thomas and William walked as naturally as they could, careful to use the slightly slower step that the rot forced upon the Desert Dwellers. A ring of torches planted every fifty paces ran the camp's circumference.

There was no perimeter guard.

"Stay in the shadows until we enter the main path that leads to the center," Thomas whispered.

"Right up the middle?"

"We're Scabs. We would walk right up the middle."

The stench was nearly unbearable, if anything, stronger than the powder they'd applied. No dogs were barking yet. So far, so good.

Thomas wiped the sweat from his palms, momentarily touched the hilt of the sword hanging from his waist, and walked past the first torch, through a gap between two tents, and into the main camp.

The retarded pace was nearly unbearable. Everything in Thomas urged him to run. He had twice the speed of any of these diseased thugs, and he could probably race straight up the middle, snatch the Books, and fly to the desert before they knew what had happened.

He squashed the impulse. *Slow. Slow, Thomas.*

"Torvil, you ungracious piece of meat," a gruff voice said from the tent to his right. He glanced. A Scab stepped past the flap and glared at him. "Your brother is dying in here and you're looking for women where there are none?"

For a moment Thomas was frozen by indecision. He'd spoken to Scabs before; he'd even spoken at length to their supreme leader's daughter, Chelise.

"Answer me!" the Scab snorted.

He decided. He walked straight on and turned only partially so as not to expose his entire face.

"You're as blind as the bats who cursed you. Am I Torvil? And I would be so lucky to find a woman in this stinking place."

He turned and moved on. The man cursed and stepped back into the tent.

"Easy," William whispered. "That was too much."

"It's how they would speak."

The Scabs had retired for the night, but hundreds still loitered. Most of the tents had their flaps tied open, baring all to any prying eye. The camp where he'd met Chelise had been strewn with woven rugs dyed in purple and red hues. Not so here. No children, no women that he could see.

They passed a group of four men seated cross-legged around a small, smoky fire burning in a basin of oil-soaked sand. The flames warmed a tin pot full of the white, pasty starch they called sago. Made from the roots of desert wheat. Thomas had tasted the bland starch once and announced to his men that it was like eating dirt without all the flavor.

All four Scabs had their hoods withdrawn. By the light of fire and moon, these did not look like fearless suicidal warriors sworn to slaughter the women and children of the forests. In fact, they looked very much like his own people.

One of them raised light gray eyes to Thomas, who averted his stare.

It took Thomas and William fifteen minutes to reach the camp's center. Twice they had been noticed; twice they had passed without incident. But Thomas knew that getting into the camp in the dead of night wouldn't be their challenge. Finding the Books and getting them out would be.

The large central tent was actually a complex of about five tents, each guarded. From what he could determine, they'd come at the complex from the rear.

The canvas glowed a dull orange from the torches ablaze inside. The sheer size of the tents, the soldiers who guarded them, and the use of color collectively boasted of Qurong's importance. Horde dyes came from brightly colored desert rocks ground into a powder. The dye had been applied to the tent's canvas in large barbed patterns.

"This way."

Thomas veered into an open passage behind the complex. He pulled William into the shadows and spoke in a whisper. "What do you think?"

"Swords," William said.

"No fight!"

"Then make yourself invisible. There are too many guards. Even if we get inside, we'll meet others there."

"You're too quick with the sword. We'll go in as guards. They wear the light sash around their chests, you saw?"

"You think we can kill two without being seen? Impossible."

"Not if we take them from the inside."

William glanced at the tent's floor seam. "We have no idea what or who's inside."

"Then, and only then, we will use our swords." Thomas whipped out his dagger. "Check the front."

William stepped to the edge of the tent and peered around. He returned, sword now drawn. "Clear."

"We do this quickly."

They understood that surprise and speed would be their only allies if the room was occupied. They dropped to their knees, and Thomas ran the blade quickly along the base of the tent with a long ripping slash that he prayed would go unheard.

He jerked the canvas up and William rolled inside. Thomas dove after him.

They came up in a room lit by a flickering torch flame. Three forms lay to their left, and William leaped for one that was rising. These were clearly the servants' quarters. But the cry of a servant could kill them as easily as any sword.

William reached the servant before he could turn to see what the disturbance was. He clamped his hand around the Scab's face and brought the sword up to his neck.

"No!" Thomas whispered. "Alive!"

Keeping hold of the startled servant, William stepped toward the others, smashed the butt of his knife down on the back of the sleeping man's head, and then repeated the same blow on the third.

The Scab in William's arms began to struggle.

"She'll wake the whole tent," William objected. "I should kill her!"

A woman? Thomas grabbed her hair and brought his own dagger up to her throat. "A sound and you die," he whispered. "We're not here to kill, you understand? But we will if we have to."

Her eyes were like moons, wide and gray with terror.

"Do you understand?"

She nodded vigorously.

"Then tell me what I want to know. No one knows that you saw us. I'll knock you out so that no one can accuse you of betrayal."

Her face wrinkled with fear.

"You would rather have me kill you? Be sensible and you'll be fine. A bump on the head is all."

She didn't look persuaded, but neither did she make any sound.

"The Books of Histories," Thomas said. "You know them?"

Thomas felt a moment's pity for the woman. She was too horrified to think, much less speak. He released her hair.

"Let her go."

"Sir, I advise against it."

"You see? He advises against it," Thomas said to the woman. "That's because he thinks you'll scream. But I think better of you. I believe that you're nothing more than a frightened girl who wants to live. If you scream, we'll have to kill half the people in this tent, including Qurong himself. Cooperate and we may kill no one." He pressed the blade against her skin.

"Will you cooperate?"

She nodded.

"Release her."

"Sir—"

"Do it."

William slowly let his hand off her mouth. Her lips trembled but she made no sound.

"Good. You'll find that I'm a man of my word. You may ask Chelise, the daughter of Qurong, about me. She knows me as Roland. Now tell me. Do you know of the Books?"

She nodded.

"And are they in these tents?"

Nothing.

"I swear, woman, if you insist on—"

"Yes," she whispered.

Yes? Yes, of course he'd come for precisely this, but to hear her say that the Books of Histories, those ancient writings of such mythic power, were here at this very moment . . . It was more than he'd dared truly believe.

"Where?"

"They are sacred! I can't . . . I would be killed for telling you. The Great One allows no one to see them! Please, please I beg you—"

"Keep your voice down!" he hissed. They were running out of time. At any moment someone would come bursting in.

Thomas lowered his blade. "Fine then. Kill her, William."

"No, please!" She fell to her knees and gripped his robe. "I'll tell you. They are in the second tent, in the room behind the Great One's bedchamber."

Thomas raised his hand to William. He dropped to one knee and scratched an image of the complex into the sand. "Show me."

She showed him with a trembling finger.

"Is there any way into this room besides through the bedchamber?"

"No. The walls are strung with a . . . a . . . metal . . ."

"A metal mesh?"

"Yes, yes, a metal mesh."

"Are there guards in these rooms here?" He pointed to the adjoining rooms.

"I don't know. I swear, I don't—"

"Okay. Then lie down and I will spare your life."

She didn't move.

"It will be one knock on the head and you'll have your excuse along with the others. Don't be irrational!"

She lay in her bed and William hit her.

"Now what?" William asked, standing from the unconscious form.

"The Books are here."

"I heard. They are also in a virtual vault."

"I heard."

Thomas faced the flap leading from the room. Apparently no alarm had been raised.

"As you said, we don't have all night," William said.

"Let me think."

He had to find more information. They now knew that the Books not only existed, but lay less than thirty yards from where he stood. The find gripped him in a way he hadn't expected. There was no telling how valuable the Books might be. In the other world, certainly, but even here! The Roush had certainly gone out of their way to conceal them. How had Qurong managed to lay his hands on them in the first place?

"Sir—"

Thomas walked to the wall, where several robes hung. He stripped off his own.

"What are you doing?"

"I'm becoming a servant. Their robes aren't as light as the warriors'."

William followed suit. They pulled on the new robes and stuffed the old under the servant's blanket. They would need those again.

"Wait here. I'm going find out more."

"What? I can't—"

"Wait here! Do nothing. Stay alive. If I'm not back in half an hour, then find me. If you can't find me, get back to the camp."

"Sir—"

"No questions, William."

He straightened his robe, pulled the hood over his head, and walked from the room.

———❧———

The tents were really one large tent after all. Nothing less than a portable castle. Purple and red drapes hung on most walls, and dyed carpets ran across the ground. Bronze statues of winged serpents with ruby eyes seemed to occupy every corner. Otherwise, the halls were deserted.

Thomas walked like a Scab in the direction the servant had shown him. The only sign of life came from a steady murmur of discussion that grew as he approached Qurong's quarters.

Thomas entered the hall leading to the royal chambers and stopped. A single carpet bearing a black image of the serpentine Shataiki bat whom they worshiped filled the wall. To his left, a heavy turquoise curtain separated him from the voices. To his right, another curtain cloaked silence.

Thomas ignored the thumping of his heart and moved to the right. He eased the cloth aside, found the room empty, and slipped in.

A long mat set with bronze goblets and a tall chalice sat in the center of what could only be Qurong's dining room. What Thomas called furniture was sparse among the Desert Dwellers—they lacked the wood—but their ingenuity was evident. Large stuffed cushions, each emblazoned with the serpentine crest, sat around the mat. At the room's four corners, flames licked the still air, casting light on no less than twenty swords and sickles and clubs and every conceivable Horde weapon, all of which hung from the far wall.

A large reed barrel stood in the corner to his right. He hurried over and peered in. Stagnant desert water. The water ran near the surface in pockets where the Desert Dwellers grew their wheat and dug their shallow wells. It was no wonder they preferred to drink it mixed with wheat and fermented as wine or beer.

He wasn't here to drink their putrid water.

Thomas checked the hall and found it clear. He was halfway through the entryway when the drape into the opposite room moved.

He retreated and eased the flap down.

"A drink, general?"

"Why not?"

Thomas ran for the only cover the room offered. The barrel. He slid behind, dropped to his knees, and held his breath.

The flap opened. *Whooshed* closed.

"A good day, sir. A good day indeed."

"And it's only beginning."

Beer splashed from the chalice into a goblet. Then another. Thomas eased as far into the shadow as he dared without touching the tent wall.

"To my most honored general," a smooth voice said. No one but Qurong would refer to any general as *my general.*

"Martyn, general of generals."

Qurong and Martyn! Bronze struck bronze. They drank.

"To our supreme ruler, who will soon rule over all the forests," the general said.

The goblets clinked again.

Thomas let the air escape his lungs and breathed carefully. He slipped his hand under his cloak and touched the dagger. Now! He should take them both now; it wouldn't be an impossible task. In three steps he could reach them and send them both to Hades.

"I tell you, the brilliance of the plan is in its boldness," Qurong said. "They may suspect, but with our forces at their doorstep, they will be forced to believe. We'll speak about peace and they will listen because they must. By the time we work the betrayal with him, it will be too late."

What was this? A thread of sweat leaked down Thomas's neck. He moved his head for a glimpse of the men. Qurong wore a white robe without a hood. A large bronze pendant of the Shataiki hung from his neck. But it was the man's head that held Thomas's attention. Unlike most of the Horde, he wore his hair long, matted and rolled in dreadlocks. And his face looked oddly familiar.

Thomas shook off the feeling.

The general wore a hooded robe with a black sash. His back was turned.

"Here's to peace then," Martyn said.

Qurong chuckled. "Yes, of course. Peace."

They drank again.

Qurong dropped his goblet and let out a satisfied sigh. "It is late and I think the pleasure of my wife beckons me. Round the inner council at daybreak. Not a word to the rest, my friend. Not a word."

The general dipped his head. "Good evening."

Qurong turned to go.

Thomas forced his hand to still. A betrayal? He could kill them both now, but doing so might raise the alarm. He would never get to the Books. And Qurong might assume that their plan had been overheard. He and William could just as easily slit the leader's throat as he slept later.

Qurong drew aside the drape and was gone.

But the general remained. Imagine, taking out Martyn! It was almost worth the risk of discovery.

The general coughed, set his goblet down with care, and turned to leave. It was in his turning that he must have seen something, because he suddenly stopped and looked toward Thomas's corner.

Silence gripped the room. Thomas closed his hand around the dagger. If killing Martyn ruined their plans, then doing so took priority over the Books. They could always—

"Hello?"

Thomas held still.

The general took two steps toward the barrel and stopped.

Now, Thomas! Now!

No, not now. There was still a chance the general would turn away. Taking the man from the side or back would reduce his chances of crying out.

For a long moment, neither moved. The general sighed and turned around.

Thomas rose and hurled the dagger in one smooth motion. If the mighty general even heard the *whoosh* of the knife, he showed no sign of it. The blade flashed in rotation, once, twice, then buried itself in the base of the man's neck, severing his spinal cord before the man had time to react.

Like a sack of rocks cut loose from the rafters, the man collapsed.

Thomas reached him in three long strides and covered the general's mouth with his hand. But the man wouldn't be raising any alarm.

Thomas jerked his knife out and wiped the blood on his robe. A trickle of blood ran down the man's neck. One, two spots on the floor.

Thomas hauled the man to the barrel, hoisted him up, and eased him into the water. Their mighty general would be discovered drowned in a barrel of water like a common criminal.

Thomas found William where he'd left him, standing in the corner, barely visible from the doorway.

"Well?"

"We have to wait. Their fearless leader is with his wife," Thomas said.

"You found the bedchamber?"

"I think so. But like I said, he's busy. We'll give him some time."

"We don't *have* time! The sun will be rising."

"We have time. Their mighty general, Martyn, on the other hand, does not have time. If I'm not mistaken, I just killed him."

Their wait lasted less than thirty minutes. Either Qurong's allusion to his wife was for the benefit of his general, or he'd forgone pleasure for the sake of sleep; no sound other than a soft steady snore reached Thomas's ears when he and William listened at what they assumed to be Qurong's bedchamber.

Thomas pulled back the drape and peered into the room. A single torch lit what looked like a reception room. One guard sat in the corner, head hung between his legs.

Thomas lifted a finger to his lips and pointed at the guard. William nodded.

Thomas tiptoed to a curtain on the opposite end of the room, eyes on the guard. William hurried to the guard. A dull thump and the Scab sagged, unconscious. With any luck, the guard would never confess to being overpowered by intruders. He was a guard after all, not a servant, and guards who let thieves sneak up on their Great One surely deserved to be drowned in a barrel.

Thomas peeled back the curtain. The bedchamber. Complete with one fearless leader spread out, facedown, snoring on a thick bed of pillows. His wife lay curled next to him.

They entered the bedchamber, closed the flap, and let their eyes adjust. A dull glow from both the adjacent hall and the reception room behind them reached past the thin walls.

If the servant girl hadn't misled them, Qurong kept the Books of Histories in the chamber behind his bed. Thomas saw the drape. Even in the dim light Thomas could see the cords of metal woven into the walls all around the bedroom. Qurong clearly had gone to great lengths to keep anyone from slicing their way in.

Thomas eased across the room, dagger drawn. He resisted a terrible impulse to slit the leader's throat where he lay next to his wife. First the Books. If there were no Books, he might need Qurong to lead him to them. If they found the Books, he would kill the leader on the way out.

He reached an unsteady hand out and pulled the drape aside.

Open.

Thomas slipped in, followed by William.

The room was small, dim. Musty. Tall bronze candlesticks stood on the floor in a semicircle, unlit. Above them on the wall, a large, forged serpentine bat. And beneath the bat, surrounded by the candlesticks, two trunks.

Thomas's heart could hardly beat any harder, but somehow it managed exactly that. The trunks were the kind the Horde commonly used to carry valuables—tightly thatched reed, hardened with mortar. But these trunks were banded by bronze straps. And the lids were each stamped with the Shataiki crest.

If the Books were in these two trunks, the Desert Dwellers had embraced them as part of their own evolving religion. The Books had come from Elyon long before the Shataiki had been released to destroy the land. And yet Qurong was blending these two icons, which stood in unequivocal contrast with each other. It was like putting Teeleh next to a gift from Elyon and saying that they were the same.

It was the deception of Teeleh himself, Thomas thought. Teeleh had always wanted to be Elyon, and now he would make sure that in the minds of these Scabs, he was. He would claim history. History was his. He was the Creator.

Blasphemy.

Thomas knelt on one knee, put his fingers under the lid's lip, and pulled up. It refused to budge.

William was already running his thumb along the lip. "Here," he whispered. Leather ties bound rings on both the lid and the trunk.

He quickly sawed at the leather. It parted with a soft snap. They glanced at each other, held stares for a moment. Still nothing but soft snoring from the leader's chamber.

They pulled up on the lid together. It parted from the trunk with a soft scrape.

The problem with being caught in this room was that there was only one way out. There would be no quick escape through a cut in the wall. In essence they were in their own small prison.

They tilted the lid toward the rear together, and as soon as the leading edge cleared the trunk, Thomas knew they had struck gold.

Books.

He lifted quickly. Too quickly. The lid slipped from Thomas's fingers and thumped to the floor. It struck one of the candlesticks, which teetered and started to fall.

Thomas dove for the bronze pole. Caught it. They froze. The snores continued. They set the lid down, sweating profusely now.

The Books of Histories were leather bound. Very, very old. They were smaller than he'd imagined, roughly an inch thick and maybe nine inches long. He estimated there were fifty in this trunk alone.

He lowered his hand and smudged the thin layer of dust that covered one of the Books. Clearly they hadn't been read in a long time. No surprise there; he wondered if any of the Horde could even read. Even among the Forest People, only a few still read. The oral traditions sufficed for the most part.

The book came up heavy for its size. Its title was embossed in corroded foil of some kind: *The Stories of History.* He opened the cover. An intricate cursive script crossed the page. And the next. The same writing from his dreams. English.

Plain English. Yet the daughter of Qurong had said the Books were indecipherable. So the Horde couldn't read then. Unless there was something unique about these books.

He set the book down and lifted another. Same title. Down in the trunk all the other Books he could see bore the same inscription, although some had subtitles as well. He lay the book he held on the floor.

"It's them." William barely whispered.

Thomas nodded. It was most definitely them, and there were many. Too many for Thomas and William to take.

He motioned to the other trunk. They cut the leather thong and pried its lid clear. It too was full of books. They eased the lid back down.

"We'll have to come back," Thomas whispered.

"They'll know we were here! You killed Martyn."

Not necessarily. That could be the work of a disgruntled soldier, Thomas thought. On the other hand, they had cut the leather fasteners on the trunks. They would need to be retied.

They could take a few with them, perhaps one that made reference to—

Qurong coughed in the adjoining room.

He froze. There was simply no time to rummage through the trunks now. They would have to come back with more help and haul them off whole.

Sounds of stirring from the bedroom sent Thomas into action. He motioned with his hands and William quickly understood. It took them longer than Thomas hoped working in silence, but finally both lids were secure. He snatched up the single book he'd withdrawn and stood to examine the trunks. Good enough.

They waited for a long stretch of silence, then slipped past Qurong, ignoring the impulse to finish him. Only after he had the Books. He couldn't risk a full-scale lockdown on the camp due to Qurong's death. With any luck at all, no one would know the bedchamber had been violated. They stole back to the servant's quarters, switched back into the cloaks they'd worn, and squeezed through the cut in the canvas wall.

"Remember, walk slowly," Thomas said.

"I'm not sure I *could* walk fast. My skin is killing me."

The Horde slumbered. If anyone even saw the two on their midnight walk through the middle of camp, they didn't show themselves. Twenty minutes later Thomas and William left the tents behind them and hurried out into the dark desert.

———⌘———

"Then we go now!" Mikil said. "We have an hour before the sun will rise. And if they're sleeping, what does it matter if our skin has or hasn't changed? I say we go in and kill the lot of them!"

"Let me wash first," William said, standing. "I'd rather take a sword across my belly than put up with this cursed disease."

Thomas looked at his lieutenant. Neither of them had washed yet—the possibility of returning before the sun rose had delayed their decision.

"Wash," he said.

"Thank you."

William marched to his horse, stripped off his garments, hurled them to one side with a muttered curse, and began to splash water on his chest. He winced as the water touched his skin—after only two days the disease wasn't advanced enough for water to cause undue pain, but he clearly felt it.

"We're losing time, Thomas," Mikil said. "If we're going to go, we have to go now."

She was still furious at having been left out. Thomas could see it in her eyes. She still couldn't understand why they hadn't just slit Qurong's throat while he lay sleeping.

He lifted the book they'd retrieved and opened the cover once again. The first page was blank. The second page was blank.

The entire book, *blank!*

Not a single mark on any of its pages. How could this be? The first book he'd picked up had writing, but this one, the one he hadn't looked in, was empty.

They had to get the other books. Mikil wanted to kill Qurong, but they couldn't do that until they knew more. And until they had both trunks.

He slapped the book closed. "It's too risky. We'll wait and go in tomorrow night."

"You can't last until tomorrow night!" Mikil said. "Another day and you'll lose your mind to the disease. I don't like this, not at all."

"Then I'll bathe and go in tomorrow with the ash, like you. We can't rush into this. The opportunity may never come again. How often does Qurong come so close to our forests? And this plan of his troubles me. We have to think! By the accounts from the Southern Forest, Martyn was courting peace. It may be in our best interests to play along with this plan of theirs without letting on that we know." He stood and walked toward his horse. "There are too many questions. We wait until tomorrow night."

"What if they move tomorrow? And the Gathering is in three days— we can't stay out here forever."

"Then we follow them. The Gathering will wait. Enough!"

A horse snorted in the night. Not one of their horses.

Thomas instinctively dropped and rolled.

"Thomas?"

He pushed himself to one knee. *Rachelle?*

"Thomas!"

She rode into camp, slipped from her horse, and ran to him.

"Thomas, thank Elyon!"

———— ∞ ————

Rachelle knew it was Thomas, but his condition stopped her halfway across the sand. Even in the dark she could see he was covered by what looked like gray ash, and his eyes were pale, nearly white. She'd seen the rot, of course. It wasn't uncommon for members of the tribe to gray when they delayed bathing for one reason or another. She'd even felt the onset of the disease a few times herself.

But here in the desert, with the odor of sulfur so strong and his face nearly white, the disease took her by surprise.

"Are . . . are you okay?"

He stared at her, dumbfounded. "We had to go in dressed like one of them," he said. "I haven't bathed. Why are you here?"

His men and Mikil stood around a small circle of bedrolls on the sand. No fire—a clean camp. Their horses stood in a clump beside Thomas. William was only half dressed and was wiping his body down with water. His skin was a mix of clear pink and pasty white.

"How could you do this without telling me?" she demanded. "You haven't bathed since leaving? You've lost your mind!"

He said nothing.

No matter, he was safe; that's what she cared about. She ran back to her horse, pulled out a leather bag full of lake water, and threw it to him.

"Wash. Hurry. We have to talk. Alone."

"What's happened?"

"I'll tell you, but you'll have to wash first. I'm not kissing any man who smells like the dead."

He washed the disease clear, and Suzan told the Guard about their journey. But when Thomas demanded to know why they had taken such a risk, she only glanced at Rachelle.

Thomas jerked a tunic from his saddlebag, snapped it once to clear the dust, pulled it on, and faced the others.

"Excuse us for a moment."

He took her elbow and led her away. "I'm sorry, my love," he said in a hushed tone. "Please forgive me, but I had to come and I couldn't worry you."

He still smelled. A spit bath would never compare to a swim in the lake. "Running off wouldn't worry me?" she asked.

"I'm sorry, but—"

"Don't ever do that again. Ever!" She took a deep breath. "I know why you came. I talked to the old man, Jeremiah. Did you find them?"

"You know I came for the Books?"

"And I'm guessing that you didn't take the fruit last night as I thought we had agreed you would."

"You don't understand; I had to dream."

Rachelle stopped and glanced back at their small camp. Then she looked into his eyes and swept a strand of hair from his face. "I dreamed last night, Thomas."

"You always dream."

"I dreamed of the histories."

He searched her face urgently. "You're sure?"

"Sure enough to chase you halfway across the desert."

"But . . . how is that possible? You've never dreamed of the histories! You're absolutely sure? Because you may have dreamed of something that felt like the histories, or you may have dreamed that you were like me, dreaming about the histories."

"No. I know it was the histories because I was doing things that I have no business knowing how to do. I was in a place called a laboratory, working on a virus called the Raison Strain."

She'd rehearsed this a hundred times in the last twelve hours, but telling him now brought a lump to her throat and a tremble to her voice.

"You were a scientist? You were actually there, *working* on the virus?"

"Not only was I there, but I had a name. I shared the mind of a woman named Monique de Raison. For all I know, I was her."

His body tensed. "You . . . how's that possible?"

"Stop asking that. I don't know how it's possible! Nothing makes sense to me, any more than it ever made sense to you. But I know without question that I was there. In the histories, I shared the mind of Monique de Raison. Look, I have a cut on my finger that proves it. She . . . I . . . I was handling a piece of white parchment . . . no, it was called paper. The edge of the paper cut my finger."

She lifted her finger for him, but there wasn't enough light to see the tiny cut.

"You could have cut yourself here and imagined that you were cutting yourself in a place called a laboratory working on the virus that I've spoken of many times."

"You have to believe me, Thomas! Just like you wanted me to believe you. I was there. I saw the . . . computer. Did you ever talk to me about a device called a computer that computes in a way we can't even imagine here? No, you didn't. Or a micro . . ." She couldn't remember all the names or details; they'd grown fuzzy with each passing hour. "A device that looks into very small things. How could I know that?"

His eyes were wide. He ran his hand through his hair and paced. "This is incredible! You think that you're actually her? But you look different there than here."

"I don't know how it works. I felt like I was her, but also separate. I shared her experiences, her knowledge."

"I'm Thomas in both realities, but I look the same in both. You don't look like Monique."

"You're exactly the same person?"

"Yes. No, I'm younger there. Only twenty-five I think."

"The details get fuzzy the longer you're here," she said.

He suddenly stopped his pacing, looked directly at her, and kissed her on the mouth. "Thank you! Thank you, thank you."

She couldn't help her shallow grin. Here they stood, in the middle of the desert with the Horde not a few miles away, kissing because they had this connection with their dreams.

"Have you dreamed again?" he asked.

Her smile faded. "On my horse, I slept, yes."

"And?"

"And I dreamed of the Gathering."

"But not of Monique. Something must have happened for you to dream that one time." He rubbed his temples. "Something . . . does she know?"

"Monique?"

"When I dream, I'm conscious of myself in the other reality. I know that at this very moment, while I'm awake here, I'm also asleep in a hotel in a place near Washington, D.C. Do you know, is Monique sleeping now?"

Rachelle had no idea. She shrugged. "I don't think she knows about me, or at least she doesn't think of me. Or I should say that she didn't think of me when I was . . . looking through her eyes."

"Perhaps because she hasn't dreamed of you. You know she exists, but she doesn't know *you* exist!"

He was far more excited about his conclusion than she was. "I don't find that comforting," Rachelle said.

"Why not? The point is, you *know*! You have no idea what this means to me, Rachelle. We're somehow bound together in both realities. I'm not the only one anymore. Do you know how many times I've been tempted to think I've lost my mind?"

"So now your lunacy has spread to me. What a delightful prospect. And I don't think we *are* bound together in both realities, as you call them. Not the way I understand bonding." She lowered her voice. "Do you love Monique?"

He blinked. "No. Why?"

"You should!"

Thomas stared at her.

"I mean, if I *am* Monique, then you have to love me."

"But we don't know if you are Monique."

"No. But at the least, she and I are connected."

"Yes."

Rachelle lifted her cut finger. "And what happens to her happens to me."

"It would seem that way."

"A man—Swenson?—this man . . . he will kill Monique."

Thomas didn't say anything for a moment, as though a real understanding of what she was saying had begun to reach him. Then he gently wrapped his hand around Rachelle's and lifted her finger to his lips. He kissed her cut. "Dreams can't kill you, my love." Thomas's hand was shaking.

"You don't need to pretend. You know it better than I do. You told me the same thing yourself fifteen years ago. You said it again last night. If we die in the histories, we may very well die here. I don't understand it. I'm not sure I want to understand it, but it's true."

"I won't let you die!"

She took a step closer to Thomas so that her body touched his. "Then you must dream, husband. You must stop the virus, because we know from the histories that the virus kills most of them, and I doubt very much that this Swenson has any intention of letting Monique live."

"Then you think I can change the histories?"

She looked into his eyes. "If you can't . . . if we can't, then we both may die. There and here. And if we die here, what will become of the forests? What will become of our children? You must rescue Monique. Because you love me, you must rescue Monique."

Thomas looked stricken.

"I have to get the rest of the Books of Histories! Now, before the Horde moves."

"No. You must dream. I know where Monique is being held."

13

THE OVAL Office. More power flowed from this room than any other room in the world, but watching the hubbub of activity while waiting for his audience with President Blair, Thomas wondered if that power might have short-circuited.

He didn't know precisely who knew about the Raison Strain, but the urgency on their faces betrayed the panicked disposition of half a dozen other visitors who'd evidently demanded and received appointments with the world's highest office.

Some were undoubtedly secretaries or aides in the cabinet itself; others had to represent fires the president felt obligated to put out—opposition leaders threatening to go public, concerned lawmakers with good intentions that would ruin the country, et cetera, et cetera.

If this was the kind of panic that disturbed these stately halls, what was the scene in other governments? From what Thomas could overhear, the governments of the western nations were all but caving in already, only two days into the crisis.

Thomas was seated on the gold sofa with his feet on the presidential seal, facing the president, who sat on an identical couch directly across from him. Phil Grant sat on the couch next to the president. To his right Ron Kreet, chief of staff, and Clarice Morton, who'd come to Thomas's rescue in the meeting yesterday, sat in the green-and-gold armchairs by the fireplace. A painting of George Washington eyed them from its frame between them. Robert Blair, Phil Grant, and Ron Kreet all wore ties. Clarice wore a plum business suit. Thomas had opted for the same black slacks and white shirt he'd worn yesterday—at the moment, they were the only clothes he owned that had any real dress to them, although he doubted it mattered much to this president.

"You're sure about this, Thomas?" the president said.

"I'm as sure as I can be about anything, Mr. President. I know it still sounds like a stretch to you, but this is how I learned about the virus in the first place."

"You're saying that you found the Books of Histories—these history books that may tell us what happens next—but more importantly, you know where they're keeping Monique de Raison."

"Yes."

The president looked at Kreet, who lifted an eyebrow as if to say, *Your call, not mine.*

Thomas had awakened early and spent the first hour trying to track down Gains or Grant—actually anyone who could respond to this new information he'd retrieved from his dreams. Both had stayed up late and were finally asleep, he learned. By the time he convinced Grant's assistant to patch him through, it was almost nine in the morning.

Three minutes later he had both Grant and Gains on a conference call. He had new information, and when he told them what it was, they'd pulled whatever strings needed pulling to move the meeting with the president up.

He'd convinced Kara to take an early flight to New York. Their mother needed her children in a time like this, but Thomas couldn't leave Washington. Not now.

It was eleven, and he'd just made his case to the most powerful man alive. Monique was being held in a mountain called Cyclops, he said.

"So you're saying that your wife, this wife in your dreams, is somehow connected to Monique de Raison. Is that right?" Clarice said.

He sensed that she wanted to believe him. Maybe a part of her did believe him. But the twinkle in her eyes betrayed more than a little doubt.

He looked at the president. "Mr. President, permission to be blunt, Sir."

"Of course."

A woman dressed in a black suit slipped in and whispered something in the president's ear.

"When?"

"In the last two minutes."

He turned to the CIA director. "Phil, I think you're needed. We just received word from the French. Find out what's going on and get back in here as soon as you have the picture."

"I knew it," Grant muttered. "Those sons of . . ." He left the office with the lady in black.

"The French?" Kreet said. "We were right?"

"Don't know." President Blair looked at Thomas. "Five of their leaders including the president and the prime minister were seen walking into an unscheduled meeting yesterday. Only four came out. Some are saying that President Henri Gaetan is no longer who he was yesterday."

"A coup?"

"That's a bit premature," Kreet said. "But it wouldn't surprise us if elements of the French government weren't somehow connected to Svensson."

The president stood and walked to his desk, one hand in his pocket. He rapped the top of his desk, sat against it, and folded his arms.

"Okay, Thomas. Fire away. Tell me why I should listen to you."

"Honestly, I'm not saying that you should. Two weeks ago I was trying to pay rent by holding down a job at the Java Hut in Denver."

"That's not what I need. Why should I listen to you?"

Thomas hesitated. He stood and walked around the couch.

"I'm the only one here who's seeing both sides of history. As the only person seeing both sides of history, there's a good chance that I'm also the only one who can *change* that history. I don't know that as a fact, but I'm fairly confident it's true. If I can't change history, then billions of people, including you, will soon be dead."

The chief of staff raised an eyebrow.

"These are the facts," Thomas said. "And the more time I spend justifying myself, the less time I have to change history."

His delivery seemed to have taken the president off guard. He stared at Thomas silently.

It did sound awfully arrogant, Thomas thought. With his own people, as the supreme commander of the Forest Guard, this kind of presentation would be expected. But here he was still the kid from Denver who had flipped out. At least to some. He only hoped the president wasn't among them.

A slight grin nudged Robert Blair's mouth. "Now that's what I call spunk. I pray to God you're wrong about all of this, but I have to agree that in a strange way you actually make sense."

"Then I'll tell you more, if you like."

"I'm all ears."

Thomas walked to a painting of Abraham Lincoln and faced them again. "I'm sure your people have considered this already, but I've had more time than most of them to think this through. Clearly, it's just a matter of time before the rest of the world discovers what's happening. You can't hide the kind of arms movement Svensson is demanding from the press for long. When they do learn of it, the world will begin to fracture. There's no telling what kind of chaos will ensue. Pressure to comply with Svensson's demands will become astronomical. So will pressure to launch a preemptive strike. Both will end badly."

"And exactly what scenario won't end badly?" the president asked. "You may have given this a lot of thought, son, but I'm not sure you can appreciate the full complexity of the situation."

"Then tell me."

Kreet cleared his throat. "Excuse me, but I really don't think this is the best use of—"

The president held up his hand. "It's okay, Ron. I want him to hear this."

He turned to Thomas. "For starters, short of invoking emergency powers, I don't run this country alone. It's a republic, remember? I can't just do what I want to."

"You can and you have to. Invoke emergency powers."

"I may. In the meantime, the virus has cropped up in over a hundred of our cities. The CDC and the World Health Organization are up to their eyeballs in data they can't begin to unravel in any amount of reasonable time. Apart from this premonition of yours called Cyclops, we have no clue where Svensson's hiding out, assuming he's the person we should be looking for. Dwight Olsen's opposition is already circling the wagons. Knowing him, he'll find a way to blame this whole mess on me and bog down my emergency powers. There are already rumblings of a preemptive nuclear strike, and I think Dwight might reverse himself on this one. If we go down, we go down fighting. You know the drill, and I'm not sure I disagree. Even if we give in to these ridiculous demands of this New Allegiance of theirs, we have no guarantee that they'll give us the antivirus."

"They won't. Which is why you can't give in."

"You know this from these books?"

"If I were their strategist and you were the Horde—if you were my enemy—I wouldn't give you the antivirus. The instruments of battle have changed, but not the minds behind them. It also explains why over half the world's population is wiped out by the virus according to the histories. They plan to give out the antivirus selectively, regardless of any promise to the contrary. I'm quite sure you're not at the top of their list of favorite people."

Clarice stood and crossed the floor. There were now three on the gold carpet—only Kreet remained in his chair. "So you insist we don't give in to their demands, and you insist we don't wage war, assuming we ever pin down a target. What, then?"

The president acknowledged her question with a nod and looked at Thomas evenly.

"I doubt very much any conventional solution will change anything. They would have been tried in the histories and failed. My solution requires you to believe me. I understand that's the challenge here, but in the end you'll find it's the only way."

"Be more specific, Thomas," the president said. "What exactly are you suggesting?"

"First, believe me when I say I know where Monique is. She is your key to securing the antivirus. Second, do whatever is necessary to prevent both nuclear war and the international community's capitulation to Svensson's demands. Bluff if you have to. Start the nuclear weapons on their way. Withhold enough weapons for a credible threat, and if we have no solution when the weapons actually reach their destination—"

"You sound like you know that destination," the president said.

"If I were them, I would choose a European country, for a list of reasons I could give you if you want. France would be ideal."

The president frowned. "Continue."

"If we still have no solution by the time the weapons reach their destination, then pull back. You'll have to persuade other nuclear powers that are closer to France, if I'm right, like England and Israel, to actually send their weapons. If they don't at least appear to cooperate, then we'll have a nuclear war on our hands, and more than the virus will kill people by the millions."

Robert Blair glanced at Ron Kreet. The chief of staff turned his head skeptically. "Israel won't go for it."

"Which is why you begin building the coalition immediately, starting with Israel," Thomas said. "I mean today. You have to commit to this now."

"I still don't hear a plan, Thomas," Clarice said.

Thomas looked at all three. They were lost, he realized. Not that he wasn't, but he did have a slight advantage.

"My plan is for you to delay them by all possible means of trickery and diplomacy and hope that *I* can find a way to stop them."

For a long time they were either too embarrassed or too impressed to respond. Surely the former.

"Let me take a team to Cyclops," he said. "If I'm right, we'll find her. If I'm wrong, I can still relay information from the Books of Histories back to you when I get my hands on them. My remaining here is pointless."

"Even if we do send a team," Kreet said, "I don't see how you're qualified to lead our Rangers. How far do you expect us to go with this . . . dreaming of yours?"

"I think he may be on to something," the president said. "Finish."

"Maybe I could show you something," Thomas said, walking to the center of the room. He glanced at the ceiling. "If you check, you'll find that I have no acrobatics training. I did learn martial arts in the Philippines, but trust me, I could never move like I've learned to move in my dreams while leading the Guard. Stand back."

They glanced at each other, then cautiously stepped back.

Thomas took a single step and launched himself into the air, flipped through one and a half rotations with a full twist, landed on his hands, and held the stand for a count of three before reversing the entire move.

They stared at him, gawking like schoolchildren who had just seen a magic show.

"Maybe one more," Thomas said, "just so you're sure. Pick up that letter opener"—he nodded at a brass blade on the desk—"and throw it at me. As hard as you can."

"No, it's quite all right." The president looked a little embarrassed. "I'd hate to miss and stick the wall."

"I won't let you."

"You've made your point."

"Go ahead, Bob," Clarice said. She eyed Thomas with a new kind of interest. "Why not?"

"Just hurl it at you?"

"As hard as you possibly can. Trust me, there's no way you can hurt me with it. This isn't a ten-foot sickle or a bronze sword. It's hardly a toy."

The president picked up the letter opener, glanced at a grinning Clarice, and hurled the blade. Blair had been an athlete and this blade wasn't traveling slowly.

Thomas caught it by its hilt, an inch from his chest. He held it steady.

"You see, the skills I learn in my dreams are real." He tossed the letter opener back. "The information I learn is as real. I need to lead the team because there's a possibility I may be the only one alive who can get to Monique. I should be on my way already."

The door opened. Phil Grant entered, face drawn.

"We have twenty-four hours to show movement of our arms. The destination is now the Brest naval base in northern France. The government claims they are cooperating with Svensson only because they have no choice. All communications to the matter must be held in strictest confidence. The media must not be alerted. They are working on a solution, but until they come up with one, they insist we must cooperate. In a nutshell that's it."

"They're lying," Thomas said. The others looked at him.

The president faced his chief of staff. "Ron?"

"They probably are lying. But it really doesn't matter either way. Even if Svensson is holding hands with Gaetan himself, we can't very well drop nukes on France, can we?"

The president walked around his desk and dropped into his chair. "Okay, Thomas. I'm authorizing the removal and transportation of the weapons they've demanded. I have a meeting with the joint chiefs in an hour. Until someone offers a reasonable argument to the contrary, we do it your way."

He set his elbows on the desk and nervously tapped his fingers together. "Not a word about any of this dream stuff to anyone. Clear? That includes you, Thomas. No more tricks. You go on assignment from this office and you go with my clearance; that's all anyone needs to know."

"Agreed," Thomas said.

"Phil, get him a clearance. I want him in Fort Bragg by chopper as soon as possible. I'll make sure they give you whatever you need. It's a long haul to Indonesia—make the plans you need in the air if you have to. And if you're right about Svensson being in Cyclops, I just may turn the White House over to you." He winked.

Thomas extended his hand. "I wouldn't know what to do with the White House. Thank you for your confidence, Mr. President."

Robert Blair took his hand. "I'm not sure I'm offering any confidence. As you pointed out, we're just a little short on alternatives at the moment. I just got off the phone with the Israeli prime minister. Their cabinet has already met with the opposition. The hard-liners are insisting the only way they'll deliver any of their weapons is on the end of a missile. He's not inclined to disagree."

"Then you have to convince them that any nuclear exchange would be suicide," Thomas said.

"In their minds, disarming would be suicide. Submitting has landed them in a world of hurt before—they're not going to be easy, and frankly I'm not sure they should be. I doubt Svensson has any plans of giving the Israelis the antivirus, regardless of what they do."

"If the virus doesn't finish us off, a war just might," Thomas said. "A leak to the press might do the same. But then you already know that."

"Unfortunately. We're spinning a story about an outbreak of the Raison Strain on an island near Java. It'll make enough noise to distract anything for a few days. The other governments involved understand the critical nature of keeping this under wraps. But there's no way to hide this for long. Not with so many people involved. Keeping Olsen in line will be a full-time job in itself."

The president drew a deep breath and let it out, eyes closed.

"Let's pray you're right about Monique."

———— ∞∞∞ ————

Thomas changed back into clothing he felt more comfortable wearing—cargo pants, Vans, and a black button-down shirt. Phil Grant sent three assistants along who had marching orders to coordinate whatever intelligence Thomas needed. He asked for and received a ream of data on the target area, which he'd already gone over once with the CIA. He browsed through the thick folder again.

He knew of the Indonesian island called Papua through a friend of his in Manila, David Lunlow, who attended Faith Academy. David had grown up on the remote island, the son of missionaries. At the time it was called Irian Jaya, but had recently changed its name to Papua because of some misguided political notion that doing so might further its quest for independence from Indonesia.

Papua was unique among the hundreds of Indonesian Islands. The largest, by far. The least populated, and mostly by tribes, scattered across mountains and swamps and coastal regions that had swallowed countless explorers over the centuries. More than seven hundred languages were spoken on the island. Largest city, Jayapura. Fifty miles down the coast, a small airport was attached to a sprawling community of misfits and adventurers. It wasn't unlike the Old West. There was a strong expatriate community whose primary purpose was to give the downtrodden and lost seekers new direction. Missionaries.

It was there, a fifteen-minute Jeep haul from Sentani, that Cyclops waited.

Thomas studied the maps and satellite images of the jungle-covered mountain. How Svensson had ever managed to build a lab in such a remote, inaccessible place, Thomas could hardly guess, but the strategy of it made perfect sense. There was no true military or police threat within a thousand miles. There were no villages or known inhabitants above the base of the mountain. A helicopter approach from the far side would go virtually unnoticed except by the odd bushman, who had no reason to report such a thing and no one to report it to.

Thomas set the map down and stared through a portal at a long stretch of clouds below them. Serene, oblivious. From thirty thousand feet up, the idea that a virus was ravaging the earth below seemed preposterous.

"Sir? Do you need anything else?" She was CIA and her name was Becky Masters.

"No. Thank you."

He returned his attention to the data on his lap, and slowly he began to draw up plans.

They landed and led him into a briefing room two hours later. The Ranger team that he would accompany was commanded by a Captain Keith Johnson, a dark-skinned man dressed in black dungarees who looked like he could take the head off any man with a word or two. He snapped off a salute and called Thomas "sir," but his skittering eyes betrayed him.

Thomas stuck out his hand. "Good to meet you, Captain."

The man took his hand with some hesitation. There were about twenty others in the room, all clean-cut, a far cry from his Forest Guard. But he'd seen enough of the Discovery Channel to know that these men could do serious damage in most situations.

"Men, I'd like you to meet Mr. Hunter. He's been given carte blanche on this mission. Please remember who signs your paychecks." Meaning, *You work for the government, so even if this bozo looks like someone off a movie set, follow orders,* Thomas thought.

"Thank you," Thomas said.

The captain sat without acknowledging him. A map of Papua and Cyclops was already on the overhead projector as he'd requested. He scanned the room.

"I know you've been given the general parameters of the mission, but let me add a few details." He walked to the map and ran through his plan to approach six primary points on the mountain that he and two CIA map readers thought Svensson might have used.

The mission was to rescue Monique de Raison, not to take out the lab or to kill Svensson or any other lab technician who might be at the location. On the contrary, keeping these targets alive was crucial. No explosives could be used. Nothing that might endanger the integrity of the data held in the lab or by those who worked there.

"I have to catch some sleep on the flight," he said, "but we'll have plenty of time to rehearse the rest over the Pacific. Captain, you may want to suggest some modifications. You know your men best, and you'll be leading your men, not me."

None of them, not even the captain, moved a muscle. *They don't know how to respond to me,* Thomas thought. No blame. He wasn't the kind of person people know how to take. These fighters would do what they'd been trained to do, starting with following orders, but in this situation he needed more.

He couldn't keep doing these stupid tricks for doubters. *Look, fellers, look at what I can do.* Soon enough, word would get out and his reputation would speak for itself, but at the moment these fighters had no benefit of the knowledge they should have, given the situation. They didn't know the fate of billions could rest on their shoulders. They didn't know about the virus. They didn't know that the man who stood before them was from a different world. In a manner of speaking.

Thomas walked across the room, studying them. The president had said no tricks. Well, this wasn't really a trick. He stopped near Johnson.

"You look like you might have some reservations, Captain."

Johnson didn't commit either way.

"Okay. So then let's get this out of the way so we can do what we have to do." He walked down the aisle and started to unbutton his shirt.

"I'm smaller than most of you. I'm not Special Forces. I have no rank. I'm not even part of the military. So then who am I?"

He slipped the last button free.

"I'm someone who's willing to take on the captain and any five of you right here, right now, with an absolute promise that I will do each one of you some very serious bodily damage."

He turned at the end of the aisle and headed back up, eying them.

"I don't want to sound arrogant; I just don't have the time it typically takes to win the kind of respect needed for a mission like this one. Do I have any takers?"

Nothing. A few awkward smirks.

He peeled his shirt down to his waist and faced them at the front again. Although normal aging and other physical events didn't transfer between his two realities, blood did. And wounds. And the direct effects of those wounds. Kara had examined them, awed by the graphic change to his body, literally overnight. Twenty-three scars.

He saw them take in the numerous Horde scars that marked his chest. A few of the smirks changed to admiration. Some wanted to try him; he could see it in their eyes, an encouraging sign. If things got hairy, he would depend on these more than the others. He continued before they could speak.

"Good. We wouldn't want to bloody the walls of this room anyway. The reason I've been selected by the president of the United States to lead this mission is because no one else alive qualifies in the same way I do for reasons you'll never know. But believe this: The success or failure of this mission will send shock waves around the world. We *must* succeed, and for that you *must* trust me. Understood? Captain?"

⸺◦∞◦⸺

Seven hours later, Thomas was on a night flight across the Pacific with Captain Johnson and his team and enough high-tech hardware to sink a small yacht. The transport was a Globemaster C-17, flying at mach point seven, loaded with electronic surveillance equipment. Their flight would last ten hours with three in-flight refuelings.

They still weren't sure what to make of him—big words and a few scars didn't amount to a hill of beans when you got right down to it. And honestly, he wasn't sure about them. What he wouldn't give for Mikil or William at his side.

They would soon find out just who was who.

Thomas reclined in the seat farthest to the back and let the soft roar of the engines lull him into sleep. Into dreams.

14

QURONG STORMED into the dining room, ignoring the pain that flared through his flesh. "Show me his body!"

They'd already pulled the general from the keg of water and laid him on the floor. For a moment Qurong panicked. He'd been with the general just last night, before he'd been killed. The only comfort in this terrible murder was the discovery that a knife, not the water, had ended his life.

"Who did this?" he screamed. "Who!"

The flap snapped open and Woref, head of military intelligence, walked in. "It was the Forest Guard," he said.

Under any other circumstance, Qurong would have dismissed the claim. The very idea that the Forest Guard had been in his own camp was outrageous. But Woref made the claim as if reporting on a well-known fact.

Still, he couldn't digest it. "How?"

"We've taken a confession from one of the servants. Two of them entered through the wall in their quarters. She said that they came for the Books of Histories."

The revelation drained blood from his face. Not because he cared so much for the symbolic relics, although he did, but because of where the Books were kept. His religion was one thing; his life was another altogether.

Qurong strode for his bedchamber.

"There's more, sir." Woref followed him. "We have just received word from a scout that there is a small camp of Forest Guard just three miles to the east."

So then it was true. He walked through the atrium. "Drown the guard on duty last night," he snapped.

The two chests sat where they always did, encircled by the six candle-sticks. "Open it," he told Woref.

Few had ever entered the small room, and he doubted that Woref had ever been here. But he knew the trunks well enough; he'd been responsible for their construction nearly ten years ago. The rest of the Books—thousands of them—were in hiding, but he kept these two trunks with him at all times for the aura of mystery they lent him, if not for any tangible power.

None of them could read the Books—they seemed to be written in a language that none of his people could read. Rumor had it that the Forest People could read the words easily enough, but this was the wagging of stupid tongues. How could the Forest People read what none of them had set eyes on?

"The leather has been cut," Woref said, inspecting the straps on either side. "They were in here."

The moment they opened the lid, Qurong knew that someone had been in his bedchamber. The dust on the Books was smeared.

Qurong swept the curtain aside and walked out. Air. He needed more air.

"But they didn't kill me."

"Then they were only after the Books," Woref said.

"And plan to return now that they know we have them?"

"But why would they come after these relics when they could have . . ." Woref didn't finish the thought.

"It's Thomas," Qurong said. Yes, of course it was! Only Thomas would place such value on the Books.

"We have the tenth division south of the—"

"How many of the Guard are in this camp?"

"A dozen. No more."

"Send word immediately. To the tenth division south of the canyons. Tell them to cut off any escape. How long before they could be in place?"

"They have to move a thousand men. Two hours."

"Then in two hours we move in. With any luck we may actually have that dog in a noose."

"And if it is Thomas, would killing him now jeopardize the capture of the forests?" Woref asked.

He ignored Woref's question. There was no secret about the general's interest in securing the forests. Woref was to be given Qurong's daughter, Chelise, in marriage upon the completion of that task. All had their prizes waiting, and Woref's would be the object of his unrequited obsession. But Qurong was no longer quite sure about the wisdom of his agreement to turn Chelise over to this beast.

Qurong walked to a basin of morst, a powdery white mixture of starch and ground limestone, dipped his fingers in, and patted his face. The stuff provided some comfort by drying any sweat on the skin's surface. Any kind of moisture, including sweat, increased the pain.

"How long before the main army from the Southern Forest reaches us?" Qurong asked.

"Today. Perhaps hours. Maybe we should wait until he gets here."

"Is he issuing the orders now? He may have come up with this plan, but as I was last aware, I am still in charge."

"Yes, of course, your excellence. Forgive me."

"If we can kill Thomas, the Forest People will be even less likely to learn of our plans. They still don't know about the fourth army on the far side of their forest. Their firebombs will only go so far against four hundred thousand men."

"They do have other capable leaders. Mikil. William. And they may know more than we think they know."

"None of them compares to Thomas! You will see, without him they are lost. Send the word: Cut them off! Have the rest of our men begin to break camp as if we are leaving for the deep desert. I swear, if Thomas of Hunter is among them, he will not live out this day."

⸺◦✸◦⸺

A gentle word on the wind woke him. Thomas was falling asleep on the transport plane, but he was also waking, here in the desert, with these words in his ear.

"They're moving."

Thomas sat up. Mikil squatted on one leg.

"It's not a war assembly—they're packing the horses. My guess is back into the desert."

Thomas scrambled up, hurried to the top of the dune, took the eyeglass from William, and peered down. They couldn't see the whole camp; the back end was hidden by a slight rise in the desert. But as far as he could see, the Scabs were slowly loading down their carts and horses.

Rachelle ran up the slope. "Thomas!"

He rolled on his back and sat up. "Did you dream?"

She glanced at William as if to say, *Not here.*

"William, tell the others to prepare to follow the army into the desert," Thomas ordered.

"Sir—"

"How can you possibly go after them now?" Rachelle demanded. "The Gathering is in two days!"

"We have to get the Books!"

She glanced at William again.

"William, tell the others."

"She's right. If we follow them out for a day, it will add another day to our journey home. We'll miss the Gathering."

"Not at the rate these slugs travel. And I think Elyon will understand us missing the Gathering if we are busy destroying his enemies."

"We're stealing books, not destroying the enemy," William said.

"We will destroy the enemy with the Books, you muscle-head!"

"How?"

"Just tell them."

William ran down the dune.

"What happened?" Rachelle asked.

"Did you dream?" he demanded.

"No. Not about the histories. But you did. What happened?"

He stood. "You were right; there is a mountain called Cyclops in Indonesia. Something happened that allowed you to dream."

"Then you're going after Monique?"

"We're on our way now."

"Then let the Books of Histories go. It's too dangerous! You can stop the virus with Monique's help."

"And what if we can't rescue Monique? What if she can't stop the virus? The Books may be able to tell us what we need to know to stop Svensson! The rest can't understand that, but you have to."

She started back down the dune, and he hurried to catch her.

"Rachelle, please, listen to me. You have to go back. I'll send two of my men with Suzan to take you safely—"

"And why should I go if you're out here risking your neck in the desert?"

"Because if anything happens to you out here, Monique might die! Don't you see? We can't risk any harm coming to you. And what about our children?"

"And what about you, Thomas? What happens to Monique or me or the forest or the earth if something happens to you? Our children are in good hands; don't patronize me."

He caught her arm and pulled her around. "Listen to me!"

She swallowed and gazed over his shoulder at the horizon.

"I love you more than life itself," he said. "For fifteen years I've been fighting off these beasts. Nothing will happen to me now, I swear it. Not here. It's there that worries me. We have to stop the virus, and for that we need the Books of Histories."

Her eyes were paling. She'd bathed last night, but only with a rag and some water from the canteens.

"Please, my love. I beg you."

She sighed and closed her eyes.

"You know that I'm right," he said.

"Okay. But promise me you won't let the disease take you."

"Leave your extra water."

"I will."

They stood in silence. The others were casting curious glances up the dune.

Rachelle leaned forward and kissed him lightly on the cheek. "Please come back in time for the Gathering."

"I will."

She turned and walked toward her horse.

———∞∞∞———

Thomas lay on the crest of the dune, watching with the other seven who'd remained behind. Their horses waited behind them, impatient in the rising heat. They'd scavenged as much water as they dared from the four who'd left two hours earlier, enough to keep them for two more days if they were careful. William and Suzan had gone back with Rachelle.

"Is it just my imagination, or are they moving slowly?" Mikil asked.

"They're Scabs. What do you expect?" someone said.

"If they cut out half of all that baggage, they could move twice as fast," she said. "It's no wonder they march so slow."

Thomas scanned the horizon. A tall hill rose to their right. Far beyond this hill lay the Southern Forest, where Jamous had been delivered by Justin, who brokered a peace with the Scabs.

The words he'd heard the night before ran through his mind. *We'll speak about peace and they will listen because they must,* Qurong had said. *By the time we work the betrayal with him, it will be too late.*

Who was *him*? Martyn? No, Qurong had been speaking to the general, who was now dead. Perhaps Justin, but Thomas couldn't accept that. His former lieutenant may have gone off the deep end, but he would never conspire against his own people.

Or would he?

"Sir, there's some movement."

He refocused down the hill. A line of horses had emerged over the distant rise and were headed toward them.

Then another.

Not just two lines of horses. A division, at least, riding at a gallop toward them. Thomas felt his muscles tighten.

"Sir . . ."

"They know," he said. "They know we're here!"

"Then we leave," Mikil said. "We can outrun them without a sweat."

"And the Books?"

"I think that the Books are, for the moment, history," she said. "No pun intended."

"Sir, behind!"

The voice had come from the Guard at the end of the line. Thomas whipped around. Another line of horses was just now edging over the dunes to the east, between them and the forest. A thousand, at least.

It was a trap.

Thomas plunged down the hill. "To the north, hurry!"

He reached his horse first, grabbed the pommel, and kicked the steed before his seat touched the saddle. "Hiyaa!"

The animal bolted. Behind him the other horses snorted and pounded sand.

The army on their left marched into clear view now, a long line that stretched farther than he'd first thought. While he and his men had been watching the breaking camp, the Horde had circled behind. Or worse, this army had been camped to the east or south and had been summoned.

They were now flanked on the east and the west. Surely the Horde knew that they would simply ride north out of the trap. Unless—

He saw the warriors directly ahead. How many? Too many to count, cutting off their escape.

Thomas pulled back on his reins, pitching his horse into a steep rear. Three of his men thundered past him.

"Back!"

They saw the Horde and pulled up.

Thomas jerked his horse around. "South!"

But he'd just laid into the wind when he saw what he feared he would see. The dunes to the south swelled with yet another division.

He veered to his left and plowed up the same dune they'd first hidden behind. There was no sense running blind. He had to see what was happening, and for that he needed elevation.

They brought their horses to stomping fits atop the dune. From here their predicament became abundantly clear. Scabs pounded toward them from every direction. Thomas turned his horse, looking for a break in their ranks, but each time he saw one, it closed.

They had been outwitted by Qurong.

Thomas took quick stock. He'd been in too many close scrapes to panic, too many close battles to consider defeat. But he'd never been eight against so many.

There was no way to fight their way out. Mikil had drawn her sword, but this wasn't a matter of swords. They'd been beaten by a mind, and now they could only win with their own.

These thoughts came over Thomas like a single pounding wave.

But the thoughts that mattered—the ones suggesting a sane course of action—didn't follow in its wake. The sea had gone silent.

Not even his dreams could help now. They could knock him out and he could dream, and they could wake him up in a matter of seconds, but to what end?

Rachelle's words of warning spoke tenderly in his ear. She hadn't used a sweet voice, but now any thought of Rachelle could only be tender.

I am so sorry, my love.

He touched the book that he'd strapped tightly to his waist under his tunic. Maybe he could use it as leverage. Buy time. To what end, he had no clue, but he had to do something. Thomas yanked the book out and thrust it over his head. He stood in his stirrups and screamed at the sky.

"The Books of Histories! I have a Book of History!"

The Horde did not seem impressed. Of course, they hadn't heard him yet.

He released the reins, stood tall with knees tight against the horse, and galloped in a small circle around his men, right hand lifted high with the book between his fingers.

"I have the Books! I have a Book of History!" he cried.

When the circle of warriors reached the dunes surrounding his, they pulled up. Five thousand at least, seated on sweating horses in a huge circle many deep. The sand had turned into men. Scabs.

Perhaps their hesitation was simply a matter of who was willing to die and who wanted to live. They knew that the first few to reach the Forest

Guard would die. Maybe hundreds before they overpowered Thomas of Hunter and his warriors.

They would overpower him, of course. Not one soul who had the scene in their eye could doubt the final outcome.

He yelled at them at the top of his voice. "My name is Thomas of Hunter, and I have the Books of Histories, which your leader Qurong reveres! I dare any man to test my powers!"

Over a hundred horses stepped from the ranks and slowly approached. They bore the red sash of the assassins, the ones who'd sworn to give their lives for Thomas's at a moment's notice. It was said among the Guard that most of them were surviving relatives of men slain in battle.

"It's not working," Mikil said.

"Steady," Thomas muttered. "We can take these."

"These, but there are too many!"

"Steady!"

But his own heart ignored the command and raced ahead of its usually calm rhythm.

The sound of a lone horn cut through the air. The ring of horses pulled up. The horn came again, long and high. Thomas looked for the source. South.

There, atop the tallest hill, stood two riders on pale horses. The one on the left was a Scab. Thomas could see that much from this distance, but nothing more.

The other rider, telling from his tunic, was a Forest Dweller.

"It's him!" Mikil said.

"It's who?"

"Justin." She spit.

Another long horn blast. There was a third man, Thomas saw, seated on a horse just behind the Scab. It was he who blew the horn.

The Forest Dweller suddenly plunged down the hill toward the encroaching Horde. They began to part for his passage. The Horde frequently communicated with various horns, and this blast must have indicated sanctuary of some kind.

The rider rode hard through the Scabs without looking at them. He was still a hundred yards away, in the thick of the Horde army, when Thomas confirmed Mikil's guess. He could never mistake the man's fluid, forward-leaning riding style.

This was indeed Justin of Southern.

Justin rode up the dune and reined to a stop fifteen yards away. For a long moment, he just looked at them. Mikil scowled on Thomas's right. The rest of his men held their places behind him.

"Hello, Thomas," Justin said. "It's been awhile."

"Two years."

"Yes, two years. You look good."

"Actually, I could use a swim in the lake," Thomas said.

Justin chuckled. "Couldn't we all?"

"Including these friends of yours?" Thomas asked.

Justin looked around at the Scab army. "Especially them. Never can get used to the smell."

"I think the smell might be coming from your skin as well as theirs," Mikil said.

Justin stared at her with those piecing green eyes of his. He looked freshly bathed.

"I see you've gotten yourself in a bit of trouble here," he finally said.

Thomas frowned. "Perceptive."

"We don't need your help," Mikil said.

"Mikil!"

Justin smiled. "Maybe you should consider changing your approach. I mean, I love the spirit of it. I'm tempted to join you and fight it out."

There was a twinkle in his eyes that inspired confidence. This was one of the reasons Thomas had selected him to be his second two years ago.

"Have you, by any chance, noticed how large the Horde's armies are these days?" Justin asked.

"We've always been outnumbered."

"Yes, we have. But this isn't a war you're going to win, Thomas. Not this way. Not with the sword."

"With what. A smile?"

"With love."

"We do love, Justin. We love our wives and children by sending these monsters to Hades where they came from."

"I wasn't aware they came from hell," Justin said. "I was always under the assumption that they were created by Elyon. Like you."

"And so were the Shataiki. Are you suggesting we take them to bed as well?"

"Most of you already have," Justin said. "I fear the bats have left the trees and taken up residence in your hearts."

Mikil wasn't one to tolerate such sacrilege, but Thomas had made his will clear, and so she spoke to him, not Justin. "Sir, we can't sit here and listen to this poison. He's riding with them."

"Yes, Mikil, I know how much these words sting such a religious person as yourself." They all knew that she was religious only when it served her. She bathed and followed the rituals, of course, but she would rather plot a battle than swim in the lake any day.

She harumphed.

"There's a saying," Justin said. "For every one head the Horde cuts off, cut off ten of theirs, isn't that it? The scales of justice as it were. The time will come when you'll break bread with a Scab, Thomas."

Someone coughed behind Thomas. Clearly Justin was delusional. Even Thomas couldn't resist a small smile.

"Mikil has a point. Did you come down here to give us a hand, or are you more interested in converting us to your new religion?"

"Religion? The problem with the Great Romance is that it's become a religion. You see what happens when you listen to the bats? They ruin everything. First the colored forest and now the lakes."

Heat spread down Thomas's neck. Speaking against the Great Romance was blasphemy! "You've said enough. Help us or leave."

Justin lowered his eyes to the book in Thomas's hand. "The Books of Histories. The worst and the best of man. The power to create and the power to destroy. Whatever you do, don't lose it. In the wrong hands it could cause a bit of trouble."

"It's empty."

Justin nodded once, slowly. "Take care, Thomas. I'll see you at the Gathering."

Then he turned his horse and galloped past the Scabs, back up the tall dune where he pulled up next to the Desert Dweller.

A long horn blasted once, twice. The call to retreat. At first none of the Horde moved. The assassins seemed confused, and a murmur rumbled over the sand.

The horn blasted twice again, with more force.

The price for disobeying an order such as this was immediate execution for any Scab. They withdrew en masse, in the same directions they'd come from.

Thomas watched, dumbstruck as the desert emptied.

Then they were gone. All of them.

Their salvation had come so fast, with so little fanfare, that it hardly felt real.

He twisted in his saddle to look at Justin.

The hill was bare.

Mikil spit. "I could kill that—"

"Silence! Not another word, Mikil. Your life has just been spared."

"At what cost?"

He didn't have an answer.

15

CYCLOPS.

Stealth was out of the question. They didn't have a week to sweep the jungle in search of a tunnel that might lead into the mountain. What they did have was infrared technology that would electronically strip Cyclops of enough foliage to reveal any suspicious anomalies, such as heat.

They'd landed the tactical C-17 at the Sentani airport, refueled, and immediately climbed back into the skies to take on the mountain looming over the coast. The forecast was fair, the winds were down, and the team had slept well on the flight over the Pacific.

Even so, Thomas couldn't shake his anxiety. What if he was wrong? What if Rachelle had been mistaken?

And another piece of information now complicated things: He'd failed to retrieve the Books of Histories in his dream. Qurong still possessed them all except for the one book with blank pages. The only useful information he had from his dreams was Rachelle's claim that Monique was here, in this mountain.

The transporter flew low, scanning the trees, covering the backside of the mountain in long sweeps. Captain Keith Johnson approached him from the cockpit looking like something out of a comic book with all of his camouflaged equipment: a helmet with a communications rig that allowed him to view the proximity of each of four team leaders through a visor that hovered over his right eye. Parachute. Jungle pack. Two grenades. A green-handled knife with a shiny blade that Mikil might trade her best horse for.

The rest looked the same. Only Thomas was dressed down. Camouflaged jumpsuit, knife, radio, an assault rifle he had no intention of using, and a parachute he had no choice but to use. Buddy jump.

"Just completed the first full sweep," the captain said, dropping to one knee. "Nothing yet. You sure we shouldn't cover the other side?"

"No, this side."

"Then the operator wants to go lower. But you know anyone down there's going to hear us. This thing sounds like a stampede flying over."

Thomas removed his helmet and ran his fingers through damp hair. "You have an alternative?"

They'd been through a dozen scenarios on the flight over. Thomas had offered his thoughts, but when it came to electronic surveillance, he was clearly out of their league. He'd deferred to them.

"No. Not with your time constraints. But I gotta tell you, if they're down there, they're all eyes."

"I'm not sure we don't want them to find us. If we're lucky, we'll force their hand. They can't leave without exposing themselves."

The captain eyed him, then nodded. "I don't mind saying that we're hanging our rear ends out pretty far. This wouldn't be my first choice."

"I realize the danger, Captain, but if it makes you feel any better, the president might put the entire 101st Airborne in these same shoes if he thought it would speed Monique de Raison's recovery. Let's take her down."

⸺✺⸺

The decision to use the French secret police to deal with Hunter had been Armand Fortier's call. The head of the *Sûreté* had called Carlos directly. They were putting over three hundred agents on the case, each with the order to return Hunter to France immediately or, thus failing, to kill him. They'd already activated a wide network of informants in the United States and learned that the man had flown to Fort Bragg and then disappeared.

Three possibilities, Carlos thought. *One, he was still at Fort Bragg, keeping a very low profile. Two, he was on his way to France to deal directly with Fortier. Or three, he was on his way here, to Indonesia.*

Carlos peered through the binoculars at the approaching transporter and knew that he'd made the right call. No doubt Hunter was in that plane.

The man now unnerved him in a way not even Svensson could. Three times Hunter had miraculously slipped out of his grasp. No, not entirely correct: Twice he had been mortally wounded and then apparently healed, and once he'd slipped from his grasp—the last time.

It wasn't just his nine lives. Hunter seemed to know things that he had no business knowing.

True, it was from the man's dreams that they had supposedly first isolated the Raison Strain. But if Carlos was right, the man was still learning things from his dreams. The plane that now approached, undoubtedly with infrared scanners, was proof enough. He'd elected to let the French track Hunter in the United States while he returned here, where he was sure the man would eventually come. He would come for Monique.

"How many times?" Svensson's voice crackled on the radio.

Carlos keyed his mike. "Seven. They're coming in lower this time."

Static.

"How did they find us?"

"As I said. He knew about the virus, he knew about the antivirus, now he knows where we are. He's a ghost."

"Then it's time to bring your ghost in for a talk. You don't think a crash will kill him?"

"I don't. The rest maybe, but not Hunter."

"Then bring them down. No other survivors."

"We'll evacuate?"

"Tonight, by dark. Fortier wants this man in France."

"Understood."

Carlos stepped from the shielded netting that had kept his heat signature to a minimum, shouldered the modified Stinger launcher, and armed the missile. A direct hit would cut the transporter in half. He wasn't certain that Hunter would survive, of course, but it was a gamble he was gladly willing, even eager, to take. More than a small part of him wanted to be wrong about Hunter's impossible gift. Better for him to die.

He waited for the plane to turn at the far end of the valley and head back toward him. Svensson had dug into the mountain at its center, and the plane was now approaching him at eye level. They would see him this time. He would have one good shot.

It was all that he needed.

———

"Contact bearing, two-nine-zero."

Thomas heard the electronics operator above the aircraft's din. He twisted and looked out of his window.

"Contact, one—"

"Incoming! Incoming!"

The warning came from the cockpit, and Thomas immediately saw the streaking missile through the window.

He was right then. Monique was here.

He was also staring death head-on.

He grabbed the rail by his seat. The C-17 rolled sharply away from the incoming missile.

"Countermeasures, deployed." The pilot's voice was drowned out by the sudden roar of the four Pratt and Whitney engines as the jet pitched up and groaned for altitude.

"It's gonna hit!" someone yelled.

For a brief moment panic fired the eyes of twenty men who'd faced death before but not in these circumstances. This fight could be over before it started.

Whomp!

The fuselage imploded with a huge flash of fire just behind the cockpit. A ball of heat rolled back through the cabin, hot enough to burn bared skin.

Thomas got his head down before the heat hit him. A roar swallowed him. Hot air. Then cool air. Someone was screaming.

It all happened so quickly that he didn't have to react. He knew they'd been hit by a missile, but he had no understanding of what that meant.

His eyes sprang open. The C-17 floated lazily to his right, cut into three pieces just in front of the wings and at the tail. The middle section was still under full power and now roared past the nose and tail sections.

Thomas was suspended in the air, still strapped to his seat. He didn't seem to be falling, not yet. He'd been thrown from the aircraft, maybe through the exposed tail, and now floated free.

But the trees were less than three thousand feet below him, and this buoyancy wouldn't last more than—

It occurred to him that he was already falling. Like a rock.

Panic immobilized him for a full three count. Thunder to his right jerked him out of it. An oily tower of fire rose from where the main fuselage slammed into the valley under full power. No one could have possibly survived an impact like that.

Thomas twisted in his seat, but the chair just turned with him. He grabbed the harness release, flipped it open, and rolled to his right, fighting his instinct to stay in the relative safety of the metal frame.

Two thousand feet.

The chair caught wind and flipped past him. Now he was free-falling without a seat. He'd jumped from a bungee tower once, but he'd never even worn a parachute before today, much less made a jump.

The nose and tail sections plowed through trees on the opposite mountain slope. No explosions.

One thousand feet.

He grabbed the rip cord and jerked. With a pop the chute deployed, streamed skyward, and snapped open. The harness tugged at him. He gasped, sucked in a lungful of blasting air. His helmet had flown off at some point.

The green canopy rushed up to his feet. Something cracked loudly, and at first he thought it might be his leg, but a branch was crashing down beside him. He'd broken a branch off.

Leaves obscured his view of the ground. The moment his boots struck a solid surface below him, he rolled hard. Too hard. He slammed into a thick tree and collapsed by its long exposed roots, winded and barely aware.

Birds screeched. A macaw. No, a year bird; he'd know the distinctive call anywhere. The long-beaked black bird was sitting atop one of the trees nearby, protesting this sudden intrusion.

I'm alive.

He groaned and forced a breath. Moved his legs. They seemed to be in one piece. What if he was actually unconscious and back in the desert?

He pushed himself up. Slowly his head cleared. The foliage was a mix of reed grass and bushes, thanks to a creek that gurgled thirty yards off. A huge fallen log rested on the bank to his right.

Thomas stood, released the parachute harness, and quickly checked his bones. Bruised, but otherwise intact. His only weapon was the bowie knife strapped to his waist.

Smoke boiled to the sky several miles up the valley. He grabbed the radio at his hip, twisted the volume switch.

"Come in, come in. Anybody, come in."

The speaker hissed. He tried again, got nothing. The transmitter could be dead. But from what he'd seen, he thought it was more likely that the people on the other end were dead. His gut turned. Maybe a few had survived by getting clear like he had, although he couldn't remember seeing any other falling bodies.

Thomas turned, ran up the riverbank, vaulted the log, and landed ankle-deep in sucking mud.

Slow down, slow down. Think!

He scanned the jungle again. If he remembered right, the missile had been fired from a point halfway up the eastern slope. He had to get to the C-17 wreckage. Survivors. A weapon. Radio. Anything that might help him. And before nightfall if he could. He didn't have the same body as Thomas of Hunter in the desert, but he had the same mind, right? He'd been in worse situations. He'd been in one far worse, a hundred Horde assassins within striking distance of his throat, just last night.

Thomas cut back into the jungle, where the canopy shielded the sun and slowed the undergrowth, and headed for the boiling smoke several miles up-valley. His mission took precedence over any survivors, regardless of how inhumane that felt. His purpose here was to find Monique at any cost, even if that cost included the death of twenty soldiers.

He gritted his teeth and grunted.

Several times he resisted the temptation to cut to his right and angle for the source of the missile. But he ran on. They'd surely seen his parachute deploy. They would be ready for him this time.

And this time he wouldn't bounce back from a bullet to his head. He needed more than a knife.

Carlos lifted the radio. "How far?"

"A hundred meters. Running up the river," the voice said softly. "Take the shot?"

"Only if you know you can hit him below the neck. Are you sure it's him?"

A pause.

"It's him."

"Remember, I need him alive." A tranquilizer dart could kill if it hit a man in the head.

Carlos waited. They'd tracked Hunter since his landing, three miles down the valley. Four others had survived the crash: two in similar manner as Hunter, two others broken and bleeding but alive near the crash site. Their survival had been temporary.

If his man didn't take the shot now, they would take him at the wreckage. Better now. The last thing Carlos needed was another of Hunter's escapes.

"Status?"

It was Svensson on the other radio.

Carlos keyed the transmitter. "We have him in our sights."

"So he did survive."

"Yes."

"He's healthy?"

"Yes."

"Keep him that way."

Come out here and keep him healthy yourself, you impossible sloth. Of course he would keep him healthy. As long as the man didn't try anything.

"Target down," his other radio crackled.

He waited, sure that a reversal would immediately follow the report. *Target back up and running.*

But no such report came.

"He's still down?"

"Down."

"Handcuffs tight. And I suggest you hurry. He may not be down for long."

———

Monique lay on the mattress only half-aware. She'd dreamed of thunder. A loud peal from the crashing skies announcing the end of the world. The people cried out to a huge face in the clouds, which presumably belonged to God. They begged for a hero to save them all from this terrible and unfair turn of events. They wanted a fix. So God had pity. He pointed to a woman with long dark hair named Monique. This was the one who'd first made the Raison Vaccine. This was the one who could now tame it.

Monique opened her eyes and took a deep breath. But there was a problem. Svensson now owned her fix.

The deadbolt slid open and the door creaked.

She closed her eyes. The only thing worse than being trapped in this white room was having to face Svensson or the man from the Mediterranean who smelled like a bar of scented soap. Carlos.

Several sets of feet walked in. Something thudded softly on the concrete floor. What was that? She dared not look now.

The boots left and the door was once again bolted shut from the outside.

Monique waited as long as she could before opening her eyes. She moved her head. There in the middle of the floor lay a body with its face down and turned away from her. Camouflaged jumper and muddy black boots. Hands cuffed behind. Dark hair.

She sat up. Thomas?

It looked like it could be him, but he was dressed wrong.

She hurried across the room and walked around the man. Yes, it was a man—his forearms were too well muscled for a woman. Then she saw his face.

Thomas.

A hundred thoughts raced through her mind. *He'd come for her. He knew where to find her. He had come as a soldier. Were there others?*

To see a man unconscious and handcuffed at her feet would normally turn her stomach, but today was not normal, and today the sight of a friend filled her desperate world with so much joy that she suddenly thought she was going to cry.

She knelt and nudged his shoulder. "Thomas?" she whispered.

He was breathing steadily.

She shook him hard. "Thomas!"

His cheek was pressed against the clean floor, bunching his lips. A day's growth of stubble darkened his face. His wavy hair was tangled and knotted.

"Thomas!"

This time he moved, but only barely before settling back into oblivion.

She stood and stared at his prone body. What kind of man was he really? Her thoughts had been drawn to Thomas Hunter a hundred times in the ten days since he'd first burst into her world and kidnapped her for her own safety. To save the world, he'd said. An absurd suggestion to any person not thoroughly intoxicated.

Now she knew differently. He was special. He knew things he couldn't possibly know, and he made a habit of risking his life to defend that knowledge.

And on a more personal level, to defend her. Save her.

Monique glanced up at the security camera. They were watching, of course. And listening.

She walked to the sink, dipped a beaker into the basin of water (the mountain provided no running water, at least not in her quarters), slipped the hand towel from its rack, and returned to him. She wet the towel and gently wiped his face and neck.

"Wake up," she whispered. "Come on, Thomas, please, we need you awake."

She squeezed more water on his head, his face, his shoulders, and she shook him again. He closed his mouth, swallowed. Finally his eyes fluttered open.

"It's me, Monique."

His eyes turned up to her face, widened, and then squeezed shut with furrowed brow. He groaned and struggled to rise.

She grabbed his handcuffed arm and pulled him, but it didn't seem to help much. He struggled to get his knees under him and his seat in the air. She wasn't sure how to help him—he was awkward yet determined on his own. Finally he managed to bring his head up and sit back on his haunches, eyes closed.

"Are you okay?" she asked. It was a dumb question.

"They shot me," he said.

"You're wounded?" Where? She hadn't seen any blood!

"No. They drugged me."

He just rolled his neck and swallowed.

"You should lie down. Here, let me help you."

"I just got up."

"I have a mattress."

"We don't have time. As soon as they think the drugs have worn off, they'll come for me. We have to talk now. Can you get these handcuffs off?"

She looked at them. "How?"

"Never mind. Man, my head feels like . . ."

His eyes suddenly widened.

"What?" she demanded.

"I didn't dream!"

The dreams again. She wasn't sure what to make of them anymore, but they were certainly more than mere dreams.

"You were drugged," she said. "Maybe that affected you."

He spoke as if he actually was in a dream. "It's the first time I haven't dreamed in two weeks. I mean from this side anyway. There I stopped dreaming for fifteen years by taking the rhambutan fruit."

He was handcuffed and on his knees in a white dungeon, and the world was dying of a virus bearing her name, and he was talking about a fruit.

"Rhambutan," she echoed.

"And we think that you might be connected to Rachelle," he said.

"Rachelle."

He stared at her for a long moment. Then he turned away and whispered under his breath. "Man, oh man. This is crazy."

She didn't know why he thought she would be connected to Rachelle, and for the moment it really didn't matter—he was clearly given to fantasy. What did matter, on the other hand, was the fact that Thomas was the only one who seemed to be able to find her. She glanced at the camera again. They had to be careful.

"They're listening. Sit by my bed with your back to the opposite wall."

He seemed to understand. She helped him across the room and he sat heavily, cross-legged, facing her mattress.

"If we talk quietly, they may not hear us," she said, easing herself onto the mattress.

"Closer," he said.

She scooted closer, so that their knees were nearly touching.

"How did you find me?" she asked.

He stared at her, then past her. "First the virus. It's been released."

"I . . . I know," she said. "How bad is it?"

"Bad. Twenty-four gateway airports. It's spreading unchecked."

"They haven't closed the airports?"

"Won't slow the virus enough to justify the panic." His voice was clearer now—the drug was wearing off quickly. "When I left Washington, only the affected governments were even aware that the virus existed. But they can't keep it quiet for long. The whole world's going to wake up to it one of these days."

She swore softly in French. "I can't believe this happened! We took every precaution. It wasn't just heating the vaccine to a precise heat; it was holding it there for two hours. One hour and fifty minutes or two hours and ten minutes, and the mutation doesn't hold."

"It's not your fault."

"Maybe not, but you do know that my vaccine was actually a virus that—"

"Yes, I know all about your vaccine actually being a virus; you told me that in Bangkok. And it was a brilliant solution to some very big problems. If anyone is to blame here, it's me. I was the one who told the world how your vaccine could be changed into the virus it's become."

"Through your dreams."

"Yes. Where you're connected to Rachelle."

She didn't want to talk to him about these dreams right now. He'd looked at her strangely each time he'd claimed that she was connected to Rachelle.

She refocused the discussion, keeping her voice to a whisper. "Do they know who's behind this? Do they know where we are?"

"The French are involved. Or at least some rogue elements in the French government. That's the prevailing theory. Svensson's not on his own—he's the man behind the virus, but there's a lot more to this than the virus. They call themselves the New Allegiance, and they're demanding huge caches of nuclear arms from all the nuclear countries in exchange for the antivirus."

"They'll never agree!"

"They are already," he said. "China and Russia. The United States is preparing to comply." He blinked and she wondered how true that was. "Others. Israel may be a problem, but with enough pressure they'll probably go along. The prospect of whole populations dying off in a matter of weeks trumps any other logic. This all comes down to the antivirus."

"What about my father? Is the company looking for a way?"

"Your father is screaming bloody murder in Bangkok, but apart from trying to find an antivirus, there's not a lot he can do. Everyone's looking for a way—another reason to delay telling the public. If they do find a way to stop the virus, panic will never have a chance to gain momentum."

"They have leads, then."

"No. Not that I've heard. Not besides you."

"You mean the back door."

"I'm guessing that's why Svensson took you in the first place. Did your key survive the mutation?"

Someone had obviously filled him in. "Yes. And I think I may be able to create a virus that will render the Raison Strain impotent. Hopefully."

He exhaled and closed his eyes. "Thank God."

"Unfortunately, I'm here. And now so are you."

"Did you give it to Svensson? And what do you mean *hopefully*?"

"Hopefully, as in I haven't actually tried it yet. I gave it to them twenty-four hours ago."

"Can you tell me what this virus-killer looks like?"

She knew what he was asking. If they were separated, or if he escaped but not she, he could carry the information to the outside world. But the antivirus in her mind was far too complex for anyone without an education in genetics to remember, much less understand.

"I don't think so."

"You don't think so because you don't know how to or because it's too complicated?"

"I would need to write it down."

"Then write it down."

"It is."

"Where?"

"By the computer." She glanced over his shoulder at the work station. "I would much rather you just take me out of here."

"Trust me, I'm not going anywhere without you. I'd never hear the end of it."

"From whom?"

"From Rachelle," he said.

⚉

Thomas's head slowly cleared. The handcuffs bit deep—there was nothing he could do about them. They had to get out with the antivirus, but there was nothing he could do about that at the moment either. The only thing he *could* do anything about right now was Monique.

He looked into her brown eyes and wondered if Rachelle really was in there somewhere, now, at this very moment. Honestly, looking at Monique now, he wasn't sure that she was Rachelle.

He glanced at Monique's right forefinger. The cut was there, exactly like Rachelle's. He looked into her eyes again. The last time he'd seen Monique was in Thailand last week. But that was fifteen years ago, before he'd married Rachelle. Odd.

Monique's full understanding of the situation might have critical and practical value, however. If they became separated and Monique knew that she could connect with Rachelle, she might find a way to do what Rachelle had done. She might be able to dream as Rachelle if need be.

Thomas considered this as he stared into her eyes.

Monique broke off the stare. "Who's Rachelle?"

Both women shared the same fiery spirit. The same sharp nose. But as far as he could see, that was where the similarities ended.

"Thomas?"

"Rachelle?"

"Yes, Rachelle," Monique said.

"Sorry. Well, you know how I've told you about my dreams. How I learned about the Raison Strain from the Books of Histories in my dreams."

"How could I forget?"

"Exactly. Every time I fall asleep, I wake up in another reality with people and . . . and everything. I'm married there."

"Rachelle is your wife," she said.

She knew! "You remember?"

She stared at him, and for a moment he thought she did remember. "Remember what?"

Why had he said that? "I don't know exactly how it works, but Rachelle dreamed she was you. She told me where to find you."

He paused. "You might be Rachelle. I . . . we don't know."

Monique stood. Thomas couldn't tell if she was offended or just startled. "And what on earth brought you to that conclusion?"

"You have a paper cut on your right forefinger. I know that because Rachelle woke up with a paper cut on her right forefinger. If you and Rachelle are not the same, at least Rachelle is sharing your experiences."

Monique lifted her finger and glanced at a tiny red mark. Then she lowered her hand and slowly looked to Thomas.

"Your wife's in danger."

The door bolt slammed open. Monique's eyes widened and shifted over his shoulder.

Mike Orear had been sure that Theresa was overreacting. She had taken the full brunt of the virus's threat head-on and come away reeling. He didn't doubt any of her facts. It was true, a man named Valborg Svensson had released a virus that had mutated from the Raison Vaccine. The virus was undoubtedly very dangerous and would kill millions, maybe billions, unless it was stopped.

But it would be stopped.

The world didn't just end because some group of deviants got their hands on a vial of germs. His life wouldn't end just because Svensson or whoever was pushing his buttons wanted some nukes. Things just didn't work like that.

That was three days ago, T minus eighteen, give or take a few days if they believed the models at the CDC. Now it was T minus fifteen, and Mike Orear was converting to Theresa's religion of fear.

He sat in his office and studied the spread of legal-pad notes in front of him. They all screamed the same thing, and he knew what they were screaming, but he knew there was a mistake here somewhere. Had to be. Just had to be.

He'd talked to Theresa a dozen times in the last three days, and each time he'd asked if anyone had made any progress on an antivirus, expecting that eventually she would respond in the affirmative. She would say one of the labs in Hong Kong or Switzerland or at UCLA had made a breakthrough.

But she didn't. On the contrary, the labs working on the problem were learning just how unlikely finding any antivirus in less than two months would be.

News about a highly virulent outbreak of a mutated viral vaccine, dubbed the Raison Strain, on a small island south of Java had hit the wires yesterday morning, and the wires were burning hot. The population of the island was roughly two hundred thousand, but there was no airport, and the ferries to and from had been suspended. The island was isolated, and the virus contained. No other shipments of the vaccine had been released.

Given the nature of the virus, the World Health Organization, together with the Centers for Disease Control, had put up unrestricted funds and massive rewards for an antivirus that would save the two hundred thousand people who would otherwise die in less than three weeks. Contracts were being bought out by the government to free up all of the major labs across the country. The healthcare community had gone nearly ballistic.

A red herring, Mike thought, *a red herring for sure.* And even then the networks were reporting a watered-down version of the story. They understood the threat of panic and they were playing ball.

But they didn't know the half of it, Mike thought. Not even a hundredth of it. How could a threat of this magnitude not leak to the press? How many other newsagents were sitting in their offices right now, thinking the same thought? Maybe they were all afraid to run outside and declare to the world that the sky was about to fall. The story was too big. Too unbelievable.

He stood and walked to the mirror on his wall. Opened his mouth and looked at his gums. Stretched his cheeks and peered around his eyeballs. There was no indication at all that he was infected with a killer virus. But he was. He'd given Theresa a blood sample just to be sure, and it had come back positive. He didn't know if he'd caught it from her or from someone else that day, but according to her report, he was a dead man walking.

Mike returned to his desk and stared at his notes. He'd spent most of the last two days scouring the electronic highways and making discreet phone calls in his attempt to piece this puzzle together, and now that it was together, he wasn't sure his effort had been a good idea.

Fact: The president had gone underground for the last four days. The official word was that, due to health concerns, he'd canceled three fund-raising dinners and an alternative-energy lobbying trip to Alaska. He was having some polyps on his colon checked out—routine stuff, they said. He had even gone to the hospital on two occasions. Maybe there was some truth to the polyps story.

Fact: The Russian premier had canceled a trip to the Ukraine due to pressing matters connected with Russia's energy crisis. Another good cover. But Russia's entire naval fleet had also been recalled and was now converging on several major ports. For what purpose?

Fact: No fewer than eighty-four military transport columns had been spotted headed east in the last two days alone. The rails were no exception. There was a lot of military hardware headed to the East Coast. Nothing that would spark a wave of concern to anyone who didn't see the whole picture, but surely some of the officers in charge suspected something, especially if they married this movement of arms with the steady repositioning of navy vessels headed to various eastern seaports.

Fact: The French government had gone virtually AWOL. Two sessions of the National Assembly had been canceled, and a number of papers were asking some troubling questions about the sudden departure of their prime minister, supposedly on an unscheduled vacation. To make matters even more interesting, the bulk of the French army had been called to its northern border for what they called emergency exercises.

Fact: The highest offices in England, Thailand, Australia, Brazil, Germany, Japan, and India, plus another six nations, had gone oddly silent over the past three days.

These were five of twenty-seven facts that Mike had painstakingly compiled over the past forty-eight hours. And they all said that the most powerful people in the world were as concerned with something as Theresa was with this Raison Strain. Maybe more so.

And why had he compiled all of this information? Because Mike knew he couldn't keep his mouth shut for long. When he did open his mouth and let the world know what was really happening while they went about daily life as if all was just peachy, he would have to substantiate his claims with his own data, not data that pointed to Theresa. He felt bound to certain rules, even if the world was in a countdown.

"This is nuts," he mumbled.

Yesterday he'd dropped the finance anchor, Peter Martinson, at the airport for a flight to New York. "Hypothetical question," Mike had said.

"Shoot."

"Let's say you had some information that you knew would affect the markets tomorrow. Say you knew the markets were going to crash, for example. You have an obligation to report it?"

Peter chuckled. "Depends on the source. Insider trading? Off-limits."

"Okay then, let's say you knew that a comet was going to wipe out Earth, but you were sworn to secrecy by the president of the United States because he didn't want to start a panic."

"Then you go out in a flame of glory, spilling your guts to the world just before dying with the rest."

He'd forced a small laugh and changed the subject. Peter had prodded him once but then let it go. He left promising to return with the definitive word on whether the market was going to crash in the next week or so.

A knock sounded on Mike's door. He shuffled the papers together. "Come in."

Nancy Rodriguez, his coanchor on their late-afternoon show, *What Matters*, poked her head in. "You going down to the meeting?"

He'd forgotten that the news director had called the meeting to review a new evening lineup. "Go ahead. I'll be right down."

She pulled the door closed.

He stuffed the papers in his right-hand drawer. *Why was he going to a meeting about a new lineup anyway? Why wasn't he back in North Dakota visiting his parents and friends? Why wasn't he bungee jumping at Six Flags or buying a Jaguar or stuffing lobster down his mouth? Or better still, why wasn't he down at the church confessing to the priest?* The thought stopped him.

A slow wave of heat spread over his head and down his back. This was really happening, wasn't it? It wasn't just a story. It was his life. Everyone's life.

How could he not tell them?

⸱⸱⸱⸰⸱⸱⸱

The door opened. "I'll try to get you the paper," Monique whispered. She was speaking about the antivirus.

Thomas twisted. Carlos walked into the room, followed by a man Thomas hadn't yet met. He was tall and walked slowly with a white cane, favoring his right leg. His black hair was greased back. Svensson. He'd seen pictures in Bangkok.

The Swiss looked like he was smothering a temptation to gloat. Carlos, on the other hand, looked more grim.

The man from Cypress pulled the chair from the desk to the middle of the room, walked up to Thomas, grabbed his handcuffs, and hauled him up. Thomas stood and staggered backward before his shoulder joints were unreasonably strained.

"Sit," Carlos ordered, pointing four fingers at the chair. His fingernails were long but neatly manicured. He smelled like European soap.

Thomas walked to the chair and sat. Carlos herded Monique to the sink, where he handcuffed her to the towel rack. Why?

Svensson moved around Thomas slowly. "So this is the man who has given us both the world and a world of trouble. I must say, young man, you look younger than your pictures."

Thomas stared at Monique. He could take care of the old man—even with handcuffs it would hardly be a challenge. But Carlos was another matter. Carlos walked behind him and made the thought pointless by quickly securing his ankles to the chair legs with duct tape.

"I understand you have a few skills that make you quite valuable," Svensson said. "You found us; Armand regards that with some fascination. He wants you in France. But I have some questions of my own to ask first, and I'm afraid I'm going to have to insist that you answer them."

"You need both of us alive until the end," Thomas said.

The scientist chuckled. "Is that so?"

"Only a fool would eliminate the two people who first made this all possible with information they alone had."

Svensson stopped circling. "Perhaps. But I now have that information. At some point your usefulness becomes a matter of history."

"Maybe. But when?" Thomas asked. "When does the virus mutate again? What kind of antivirus will be needed then? Only we know the answers, and even then, we don't know all of them yet. Armand is right."

He didn't know who Armand was, but he assumed it was a person Svensson worked for.

"There will be no more mutations," Svensson said easily. "But I'm happy to announce the formulation of the first antivirus." He pulled a small syringe filled with a clear fluid from his blazer. Now his gloating did spread to his mouth. "And I thought it would be appropriate for both of you to see the fruit of your labor."

He slapped the crux of his left arm with two fingers, removed the plastic shield from the needle with his teeth, and clenched his fist. He found a blue vein in his arm and pushed the needle into it. Two seconds and the liquid was in his bloodstream. He jerked the syringe out and put it into his jacket pocket.

"You see. I am now the only person alive who won't die. That will change shortly, of course, but not before I extract my price. Thank you, both of you, for your service."

He waited as if expecting an answer.

"Carlos."

Monique saw the long stainless-steel needle before Thomas did, and the bottom of her stomach seemed to fall out. Carlos stepped up to Thomas and let the point hover over his shoulder.

"Penetrating the flesh isn't so painful," Svensson said. "But when he tries to push the needle through your bones, it will be."

"What are you thinking?" Monique cried.

All three looked back to where she stood by the sink.

Svensson was the one who answered. "Loftier thoughts than you, I'm sure. Please try to control yourself."

They hadn't even started on him yet and already her eyes were blurry from tears. She clenched her teeth and tried to still the trembling in her hands.

"It's okay, Monique," Thomas said. "Don't be afraid. I've seen how this ends."

She doubted that he had. He was only trying to confuse them and ease her mind.

"Then let's start with this knowledge of yours," Svensson said. "How did you find us?"

"I talked to a large white bat in my dreams. He told me that you were in a mountain named Cyclops."

Svensson regarded him with a frown. Glanced at Carlos.

The man from Cypress pushed the needle into Thomas's shoulder about a centimeter.

Thomas closed his eyes. "There are books in my dreams called the Books of Histories. They've recorded everything that has happened here. That's how I first learned about the virus."

"History books? I'm sure there are. Then tell me what happens next."

Thomas hesitated. He opened his eyes and looked directly at Monique. She could hardly stand to watch him with that needle sticking out of his arm.

"Over half the world dies from the Raison Strain," Thomas said. "You get your weapons. The times of the Great Tribulation begin."

He kept his eyes on hers. *They were speaking to each other in this strange way,* she thought. She wouldn't look at his arm. She would look only into his eyes, to give him strength.

"Yes, of course, but I was referring to the next few days, not weeks. It doesn't require any precognition to guess how this will end. I want to know how we will get there. Or more to the point, what the Americans will do in the next few days."

He thought about the demand. "I don't know."

"I think you do. We know you've met with the president. Tell me what his plans are."

Monique felt her chest tighten. This wasn't about his dreams. They wouldn't stop until they knew what had passed between Thomas and Robert Blair.

"They didn't tell me what their plans were."

Svensson glanced at Carlos again.

"You want me to make something up?" Thomas said. "I told you, I don't know what the United States will do."

"And I don't believe you."

Carlos pushed and the needle slid in easily before abruptly stopping at the bone. Thomas closed his eyes, but he couldn't hide the tremble that overtook his cheeks.

Carlos leaned on the needle.

Thomas groaned. His body suddenly relaxed and slumped. He'd passed out! Thank God, he'd passed out.

Carlos grunted and withdrew the needle.

"Just a little aggressive, are we?" Svensson said, eying the man.

"I would have expected more from him," Carlos said.

"He still has drugs in his system."

Svensson walked over to the computer, ripped the cord from the wall. He picked up Monique's notes and the pencils she'd used earlier. Satisfied that he'd confiscated her basic tools, he moved toward the door.

"We'll have plenty of time later. I want them ready to move by nightfall."

16

A LOUD bang jerked Thomas from sleep. He cried out and was rolling from the bed before he rightly knew where he was.

The floor greeted him hard, pounding the scream from his lungs.

"Thomas!"

He was in his own house. Rachelle had slammed through the swinging door.

"What is it?" She dropped by his side and helped him to his feet. "Are you okay?"

"Sorry, I just . . ."

"What's this?" She touched his shoulder, where a small trickle of blood ran down his arm. "What's happening?"

"Nothing. It's just a scratch. Nothing." He wiped the blood away, images of this nothing bright in his mind. Carlos had shoved a needle into his arm. The pain had been unbearable. But he had to think it through before telling Rachelle.

He shook the dream from his head and reacquired his sense of this reality.

They'd returned from the desert last night, and one of his men had blurted out the details of how Justin had saved their hides in the desert. The news spread throughout the village like fire.

They were only a day away from the Gathering, and the population had swelled to nearly a hundred thousand, including the large group from the Southern Forest. The air was full of celebration.

He'd slept late.

"What time is it?"

"I'm not sure I believe you. What happened?"

"I'll tell you. But you came in here in an awful hurry. What's going on?"

She seemed to remember why she'd flown in. "They're calling for you. In the Valley of Tuhan. We have to hurry."

"Who's calling for me?"

"The Council. The people. Justin's coming. There's been word all morning; he's coming through the Valley of Tuhan. Half the village is gathered there to receive him already."

"To *receive* him? Whose idea is this? The valley isn't for magicians and politicians!"

She rested her finger on his lips. "Yes, I know, the valley is for mighty warriors. And any man who saves the life of my husband must be a mighty warrior."

"Then it was *your* idea?"

"No. It was rather spontaneous, I think. Dress, dress. We have to go."

"Why do the people want me there?"

"Someone suggested you might want to thank him."

Thomas was bent, strapping his boot, and he nearly fell over at the suggestion.

"Thank him? Who is he, our new king?"

"To hear the people from the Southern Forest, you might think so. Are you jealous? He's harmless."

"Harmless? He's the man I may fight at the challenge tomorrow!"

"Even if there is a fight, you have the option of banishment."

"The Council will want his death. This is the price for disregard of Elyon's love. If he's found guilty, they'll want his death."

"And banishment is death! A living death."

"The Council—"

"The Council is mad with jealousy!" Rachelle said. "Stop this talk. There will be no fight anyway. The people love him!"

"I can't go to the Valley of Tuhan and pay him homage. It would look ridiculous."

"To whom? Your Guard? They're as jealous as the Council. It would look petty if you don't pay a man who saved your life the appropriate respect."

"But the Valley of Tuhan? That's not for every soldier who saves their commander's life. We've only used the valley several times."

"Well, it's being used today, and you *will* come."

He finished dressing and strapped the Book of History to his waist with a broad band of canvas. Rachelle had examined the book upon their return and declared it useless. Yes, he knew, but he wouldn't be separated from it. It might play a role in his mission yet.

They left the house. Evidence of the Gathering was everywhere. White tuhan flowers he liked to call lilies covered the streets; lavender puroon garlands hung from every door. People were dressed for the celebration— light-colored tunics accessorized with hair flowers and bronze bracelets and tin headbands. Not a person they passed didn't acknowledge Thomas with a kind word or a head dipped in respect. Each of their villages had been saved by his Forest Guard numerous times.

He returned each kind word with another. Although the village was brimming with people, it wasn't as crowded as he would have expected the day before the annual Gathering. The people had gone to the valley. The Council would be furious.

They left through the main gate and walked a well-worn path that led directly to the Valley of Tuhan, roughly a mile from the outskirts.

Rachelle glanced back to make sure they were alone.

"So, now tell me. What happened?"

The dream.

"We found Monique."

Her eyes grew round. "I knew it!" She skipped once like a child in her enthusiasm. "It's all true. I told you to believe me, Thomas. That I was there in that white room." She threw her arms around his neck and kissed him on the lips, nearly knocking him off the trail.

"I did believe you," he said. "As I recall, it was you who didn't believe me once upon a time."

"But that was before. So you rescued me?"

"No."

"No?"

"I'm working on it."

"Tell me everything."

He told her. Everything except for the torture.

"So you not only failed to rescue Monique, but now we're both in the dungeon," Rachelle said when he'd finished. She stopped, eyes wide. "This is terrible news. We're in mortal danger!"

"We've always been in danger."

"Not like this."

"The virus presents more of a danger than this. At least we know that the antivirus now exists, and I'm in the vicinity of the people who have it. Maybe I can find a way out."

"We're both in the dungeon, for goodness' sake! We'll be killed, both of us."

He took her hand and they walked on. "That's not going to happen." He looked at the forest. The sound of a distant celebration whispered on the wind.

Thomas sighed. "All around us people are preparing for a celebration and we're talking about being tortured in a dungeon—"

"Tortured? What do you mean tortured?"

"The whole thing. It's torture. Svensson's torturing us with this imprisonment of his."

She seemed satisfied by his quick recovery.

"If you and I live in both worlds, isn't it possible that we all live in both worlds?" she asked.

"I've thought about it. But we may only be sharing the dreams and realities of people in the other world."

"Either way, who is Qurong there? And who is Svensson here? If we could find Svensson here and kill him, wouldn't he die there?"

"We need Svensson alive. He has the antivirus. These are delicate matters, Rachelle. We can't just start killing people."

He challenged her theory on another front.

"Besides, if everyone there also lived here, we would have a much larger population."

"Then maybe we're only part of them. There could be other realities."

"Even then, why aren't people just falling over dead here when they die there from an accident or something?"

"Maybe they aren't truly connected unless they know. We know because of the dreams, but others don't. Perhaps the realities can't be breached without understanding."

"Then how did I first breach these realities?"

She shrugged. "It's only a theory."

Interesting thoughts. And she'd had them on the fly.

She was grinning. "You see the power of a woman's thoughts."

"I think I'm the only gateway between these realities. Blood, knowledge, and skills are the only things that are transferable, and I'm the only gateway."

"Yet I went."

The reason why came to Thomas suddenly and clearly. "You were cut with me. And you were bleeding. Both of us were."

"And maybe this is all nonsense," she said.

"It may be."

───── ⊶⊷⊶ ─────

The valley of Tuhan had never seen so many people at once, not even after the Winter Campaign, when the nearest forests had come together to honor Thomas.

They first heard the crowd a hundred yards from the valley, a soft murmur of voices that grew with each step. When Thomas and Rachelle finally rounded the last bend in the forest and faced the broad green valley of grass, the murmur became a steady roar.

Thomas stopped, speechless. The valley looked like a large oblong bowl that gently sloped to a flat base. White lilylike flowers called tuhans grew along the banks of a small creek that ran the length of the valley, thus its name, the Valley of Tuhan. A wide path had been worn beside the creek.

But it was the crowd that stopped Thomas. They weren't cheering. They were waiting on the slopes on either side, talking excitedly, thirty thousand at least, dressed in white tunics with flowers in their hair. So many! He knew Justin's popularity had never been as great as it was now. His victory at the Southern Forest and the incident yesterday in the desert had catapulted him to the status of hero overnight. The beat had always been there, of course, but now the fickle crowds had taken up their drums and joined the parade, ready to march en masse.

"Thomas! It's Thomas of Hunter!" someone cried.

Thomas dipped his head at the man who spoke, Peter of Southern, one of the elders from the Southern Forest. Peter hurried over. The news that Thomas had arrived spread down the valley; thousands of heads turned; a cry swelled.

Thomas of Hunter.

He smiled and lifted a hand to the people while looking for any sign of Ciphus or the Council.

"You should be at the front, Thomas," Peter said. "Hurry, he'll be here soon."

"I can see well enough—"

"No, no, we have a place reserved." He took Thomas's arm and pulled him. "Come. Rachelle, come."

A chant had started and they called his name as was the custom. "Hunter, Hunter, Hunter, Hunter." Thirty thousand voices strong.

With their eyes on him and their voices crying his name, he had little choice but to follow Peter of Southern down the slope, where the crowd had parted for him, to the valley floor, where the children had been jumping and dancing only a moment ago. Now they stilled and stared in awe at the great warrior whose name was being chanted.

Peter led him to the front row.

"Thank you, Peter."

The elder left.

His son and daughter, Samuel and Marie, worked their way toward him from the left, glowing with pride but trying not to be too obvious about it. He winked at them and smiled.

The chant hadn't eased. *Hunter, Hunter, Hunter, Hunter.* He lifted his hand and acknowledged the crowd again. They waited on the slopes, natural bleachers. The seventy-yard swath down the middle of the valley was the parade route, and not a soul ventured out to disturb the grass. This was the custom. The path Justin would ride down split the valley in two, only thirty yards from where they stood.

A small girl, maybe nine or ten years of age, with a small white lily in her hair, stared at him with huge brown eyes, ten feet away. *In her shock at being so close to this legend, she'd forgotten how to chant,* Thomas thought. He smiled at her and dipped his head.

Her round mouth split into a wide smile. One of her teeth was missing, he saw. Maybe she was younger than nine.

"She's adorable," Rachelle said, next to him. She'd seen her staring.

Still the crowd chanted his name.

No one gave the signal. No bright light appeared in the sky to signal any change. And yet everything changed in the space of two chants. It was *Hunter, Hunt—* and then silence.

The profound, ringing silence seemed louder to Thomas than the roar that preceded it.

He glanced across the valley and saw that every head had turned to his left. There, where the trees ended and the grass began, stood a white horse. And on the horse sat a man dressed in a white sleeveless tunic.

Justin of Southern had arrived.

Two warriors in traditional battle dress were mounted side by side behind him. *Justin and his merry men,* Thomas thought.

For a long moment that seemed to stretch beyond itself, Justin sat perfectly still. He wore a wreath of white flowers on his head. Bands made of brass were wrapped around his biceps and forearms, and his boots were bound high, battle style. A knife was strapped to his calf and a black-handled sword hung in a red scabbard behind him. He sat in the saddle with the confidence of a battle-hardened warrior, but he looked more like a prince than a soldier.

His eyes searched the crowd, lingered on Thomas for a moment, and then moved on. Still not a sound.

His horse pawed the ground once and stepped into the valley.

A roar shook the ground, an eruption of raw energy bottled in the throats of thirty thousand people. Fists were thrown to the air and mouths were stretched in passion. Their thunder seemed to fuel itself, and when Thomas was sure it had reached its peak, the roar swelled.

They were three miles from the village, but there wasn't a doubt in Thomas's mind that the shutters of every house there were at this very moment rattling. How many of these people were shouting because the others were shouting? How many were willing to celebrate, regardless of the object of that celebration? Apparently, most.

He glanced at Rachelle, who beamed and shouted, caught up in the moment. He smiled. Why not? Every warrior deserved honor, and Justin of Southern, though perhaps deserving of other considerations as well, had certainly earned some honor. Let the Council sweat in their robes. Today was Justin's day.

Thomas lifted his fist in a salute.

Slowly, with deliberate pronounced steps, Justin rode his horse into the valley. He stared straight ahead without acknowledging the crowd. His men marched abreast thirty paces behind.

Now the chant began. The thunder formed a word that roared from the throats of every man, woman, and child in the valley, perhaps beyond . . .

. . . *Justin, Justin, Justin, Justin* . . .

. . . until it sounded like pounding detonations that exploded with each roar of his name.

Justin! Justin! Justin! Justin!

Thomas had never seen such a display of worship for one man before. The fact that Justin accepted the praise without so much as a modest grin only seemed to justify their adoration. It was as if he knew that he deserved no less and was willing to accept it.

The air reverberated with their cries. The leaves of the trees along the creek trembled. Thomas felt the sound reach into his belly and shake his heart.

Justin! Justin! Justin! Justin!

Justin rode halfway into the valley and stopped his horse. Then he stood tall in his stirrups, threw his fists to the sky, lifted his head, and began to scream something.

At first they couldn't hear his words for the roar, but as soon as the people figured out that he was saying something, they began to quiet. Now Justin's cry rose above the din. He was screaming a name. He was bellowing a name at the sky.

Elyon's name.

A chill washed over Thomas. Justin was claiming the authority of the Creator. And this, knowing full well that a challenge had been cast against him. The Council would rage. If Justin wasn't innocent, then he was as devious and manipulating as they came.

Justin cried the name of his Maker, eyes clenched, face twisted, as one who was torn between gratitude and terrible fear. The valley stilled with uncertainty.

With one last unrelenting cry that exhausted every ounce of his breath, Justin screamed the name. *Elllllyyyyonnnnnn!*

Then he settled back in his saddle and slowly faced Thomas.

"I salute you, Thomas of Hunter," he called.

Thomas dipped his head. But he couldn't go so far as to salute the man in return, not with the challenge at hand.

Justin dipped his head in return. He looked at the people, first the far side, turning his horse for a full view, then Thomas's side. His stallion stepped nervously under him. He seemed to be looking for someone.

The children, Thomas thought. *He was looking at the children.*

He spun his horse back around and gazed at the far side again. Then to Thomas's side again, green eyes searching, searching.

Forty feet from where Thomas stood, a young girl stepped out of the crowd, walked a few paces into the meadow, and stopped. Her hair was blond, past her shoulders. Her arms were limp by her sides. One of her hands was shriveled to a stump. She trembled from head to foot and tears ran down her cheeks.

Thomas's first thought was that her mother should call this poor child back immediately. The traditions of the valley were clear enough: No one ever approached any warrior honored on their march. It was a time of order and respect, not chaos.

But then he saw that Justin was staring directly at this child. Surely he hadn't been searching for her.

A small bushy-haired boy stepped out and stopped just behind the girl.

To Thomas's amazement, he saw that tears were on Justin's cheeks. He ignored the gathered throng and exchanged a long stare with this young girl.

"He knows her," Rachelle whispered.

Justin suddenly slid off his horse and faced the girl. Then he dropped to one knee and spread his arms wide.

She ran for him, weeping audibly now. Her white tunic swished around her small legs, and the flowers in her hair fell to the ground as she ran.

The girl collided with Justin in the middle of the field. His arms wrapped around her and he held her tight. A lump rose in Thomas's throat.

The girl showed Justin her hands, which he kissed. He stood and led her ten paces from the horses, where the entire valley could see clearly. He whispered something in her ear and then walked on while she stood still. What was he doing?

Justin swept the crowds with a steady gaze.

"I tell you on this day, that the greatest warriors among you are the children," he cried out for all to hear. "It is with ones like these that you will wage a new kind of war."

He faced the girl, who was beaming from ear to ear now. A twinkle brightened Justin's eyes. He stretched his hand out to her.

"I present to you my princess. Lucy!"

It was impossible to tell if this show was a deception or completely sincere. As either, it was a brilliant performance.

Justin took the white wreath from his head, placed it gently on her head, and stepped back. He settled to one knee, put one hand over his breast, and raised the other to the crowd.

A cry erupted spontaneously.

Thomas thought the girl's face might split in two if she beamed any brighter. Beside him, Rachelle was dabbing her eyes.

Justin motioned excitedly for the boy, who now ran for them.

"And my prince, Billy!"

He swept the boy from his feet and spun him around. Then he led both of the children back to his horse, swung into the saddle, and hoisted them up, Lucy behind and Billy in front. He gave the reins to the boy and nudged the horse.

The thunder began again, now with chants of Lucy and Billy mingled in. Justin took time to acknowledge the crowd now. To look at him riding with such confidence and being so worshiped, one would think he had been a king from the ancient stories instead of a forest vagabond who'd abandoned the Guard and now spoke of treason.

When Justin finally reached the far side of the valley, he set the children down and disappeared into the trees.

—⊗⊘⊗—

"Now do you think there will be a fight at tomorrow's challenge?" Rachelle asked. The din had died and the valley was emptying.

"Justin is either a man who deserves this praise or a man who deserves to die," Thomas said, "in which case he's much more dangerous than I ever could have guessed."

"And who do you think he is?"

Thomas stared at the trees that had swallowed Justin. Was his the face of deception or the face of grace? It hardly mattered in the end, because either way it was definitely the face of treason. Any man who brokered peace with the sons of Shataiki could not be a man who followed Elyon.

"Thomas, you're drifting on me again."

"I think he's a very dangerous man. But we'll let the people decide tomorrow."

"It sounds to me like they've already decided."

"That's because you haven't heard the others yet. Not everyone was here."

17

PRESIDENT ROBERT Blair hadn't slept in twenty-four hours. The air was charged with panic. No one was happy. They were all out of their league, every last one of them. They bore titles like president of the United States and secretary of defense and director of the Central Intelligence Agency, but inside they were all just men and women on the shore, facing a massive tidal wave that blocked their view of the horizon. There was no running; there was no fighting; there was only bracing.

Not true. There was God. It was out of their hands in the hands of God—a scary thought considering his complete lack of understanding in such matters.

And there was Thomas Hunter.

Senate majority leader Dwight Olsen slammed his palm on the table, round face red. "Send them!" He glared at the president. "For Pete's sake, we're running out of time. Give them what they ask for. We have the technology, we can rebuild, we can start over, but we need some breathing space. If you think the American people would condone this game of poker . . ."

He stopped short. *Not thinking too clearly,* the president thought. But then none of them were.

"I *am* thinking of sending the missiles, Dwight. Fully armed and on a collision course with Paris. Israel may beat us to it." He'd already authorized the shipments, but considering Olsen's arrogance, he withheld the revelation for the moment.

"Then you and Benjamin would defy what the Russians, the Chinese, even England is doing. Maybe they have more sense—"

"Shut up!"

Easy, Robert.

"Just shut up and listen to me. You're not thinking this through very clearly. The Russians are complying with Paris because they are in *bed* with Paris. So are the Chinese—we have to assume that based on the intelligence I just laid out to you. Arthur, on the other hand, has convinced our British counterparts to comply with Paris on *my* word that we would not ultimately do so. We will ship our missiles as a sign of good faith, but I'll die before I hand over one pistol to those maniacs so that they can turn around and fire it back at us."

"We have their word—"

"They have no intention of keeping their word!"

"You can't know that," Olsen said.

"They're terrorists, for crying out loud!"

"If either you or Israel does anything stupid, like try a preemptive strike, you'll send us all to our graves based on an assumption that is more likely wrong than right."

The president looked at Graham Meyers. His secretary of defense was listening patiently as were the others. Now Meyers came to his defense.

"Israel won't try that. Our intelligence—"

"Cut the intelligence nonsense," Olsen said. "Who? What intelligence?"

Meyers glanced at the president and Blair dipped his head. *Go ahead, Grant, spill the beans. We're past cat and mouse with this idiot.*

"The same intelligence that located Valborg Svensson," he said.

Olsen blinked. "Svensson. You found him," he said in a doubtful tone.

"Yes, Dwight. We found him," the president said. "They shot down a C-17 that was making a low pass over his compound roughly eight hours ago."

"Where?"

"Indonesia. Furthermore, we received a communiqué two hours ago from the French. They claim they have incontrovertible evidence that Svensson has an antivirus in his possession. Evidently they wondered if we were sure on that point."

Olsen's collar was stained dark with sweat. "And what's being done?"

"The pilot reported their situation before the plane went down. We don't know who survived. Three beacons were activated when their parachutes deployed, but there's been no word since, so we're assuming the worst. A squadron of stealth fighters and three C-17s took off from the Hickam base in Hawaii seven hours ago. An hour ago we dropped forty Navy Seals on the spot where our people believe the Stinger that took down our plane was fired from. This is the kind of intelligence we're talking about."

"So there's a chance we may find Svensson with the antivirus."

"A chance, yes."

"And how did your people find Svensson so easily?"

Blair hesitated, and then decided to finish what he'd started.

"Thomas Hunter," he said. "I'm sure you remember Thomas. The psychic, I think you called him. The communiqué from France also claimed that the New Allegiance had Thomas Hunter in custody and that any further attempts at military action would cost both him and Monique their lives."

The Senate majority leader was taken completely off guard by the revelation.

"Okay, so you have a psychic in your intelligence circles. And I take it this psychic has told you that the United Sates won't receive the antivirus in time. And now you're going to base your entire strategy on this revelation of his. Have you considered the basic logic that if they administer the antivirus to France, the United States is only a seven-hour flight away? It doesn't matter who they give the antivirus to; our scientists can copy it from any carrier."

They'd discussed the scenario already, and there were ways that Svensson could still keep the United States from acquiring and duplicating any antivirus in time. But Thomas had insisted that the United States would not receive the antivirus. In light of his recent success, Blair was prone to believe him.

"Maybe. I'll take it under advisement. Our hope is to avoid getting to that point."

"God knows I hope we can. But if you play hardball with the French on this, I'm going to bring this whole nation down around your ears."

"I'll take that under advisement as well. If our current mission fails, the arms will ship on schedule. I won't do anything rash; you have my word. Only as a very last resort. But don't expect me to roll over yet. Give me at least that much, for heaven's sake. If you really think these guys are going to let us live to fight another day, you're not seeing what I see."

"Well, we always did live in different worlds, didn't we? I hope you can keep the Israelis calm."

"Calm, no. They're climbing the walls behind closed doors over there. But I do have Benjamin's word that they will make a show of compliance, at least for the time being. You do understand that they will not go down without a fight, don't you, Dwight?"

"Fools." Olsen stood to leave. "Meanwhile our country's totally in the dark out there. We have to tell them soon. I can promise you they will be enraged for not being told sooner."

"I would have thought you would count that politically expedient, Dwight."

The man gave him a parting glare, and Blair was sure the man had already considered his political future in all of this. It was perhaps the only reason he hadn't already run to the press.

"Keep this quiet," the president said.

Dwight Olsen turned. "I'll give you two days. If I like what I see, I may play ball. If not, no promises."

"You leak this and I'll have you arrested."

"On what grounds?"

"Treason. Leaking sensitive military operations is an actionable offense. We have a virus, but we also have a military action under way."

It was more bluff than actionable, but Blair didn't care.

"Sir." Intercom.

"Yes?"

"Report in from Hawaii."

He caught Olsen's eyes. It was the mission.

The secretary of defense glanced up, eyes wide. "Send it in, Bill."

Ten seconds later Graham Meyers had a red folder in his hands. His eyes scanned the report. Olsen had quietly stepped back into the room.

The president loosened his already sloppy tie. "Well, spit it out, for crying out loud."

"The mission successfully located and entered a large complex on the backside of Cyclops. No casualties. The complex was abandoned."

"What?"

"Abandoned within the last several hours. They're gathering some computers now, but the hard drives have been removed. The place is clean." Grant looked up. "There's evidence to suggest at least one soldier was in one of the rooms. Buttons from one of our uniforms."

"Hunter."

The room was silent.

"They can't be far," someone said.

The president pushed back his chair and stood. "Find him!"

18

THE CELEBRATION had gone late into the night, as was always the case during the three days the Forest People held their annual Gathering. Music and dancing and plays and food, too much food. And drink, of course. Fruit wines and berry ales mostly. Anything and everything that even hinted at their memories of the Great Romance in the colored forest.

The opening ceremonies were held with each tribe marching down the avenue that led to the lake, led by the elders from that tribe. Ciphus led the largest entourage from the Middle Forest, followed by the other forests by their location, from north to south.

Twenty thousand torches burned around the lake as Ciphus recited their creeds and reminded them all why they must adhere to the very fabric of the Great Romance without the slightest deviation, as Elyon would surely have it. Their religion was a simple one, with only six laws at the heart, but the other laws, the ones the Council had refined over the years to assist in following the six, had to be given the same weight, he said. The way to love Elyon was to give yourself completely to his ways, without the slightest compromise.

Thomas had collapsed in bed late, slept with heavy dreams of torture, and awakened with two parallel preoccupations.

The first was this business of finding out who Carlos might be in this reality, if indeed such a thing was even possible, as Rachelle had suggested in passing. A thin thread, to be sure, but following it was the only way he could think of to escape the dungeon with Monique.

The second was the challenge, which was to be held that afternoon. Other than posting notice of it, the Council had been wisely silent about Justin. Still, it had been the talk of the village all morning.

Some wondered why an inquiry was even necessary—the doctrines of Justin weren't so different from any they had followed all these years. He talked about love. Wasn't the Great Romance all about love? Yes, his teachings of peace with the Horde were very difficult to follow, but now he was talking love. Perhaps he'd changed.

Others wondered why Justin wasn't simply banished out of hand—his teachings were clearly an affront to all that was sacred about the Great Romance, *beginning* with his talk of peace. How could anyone make peace with the enemies of Elyon? And his teachings were difficult only because they worked against the Great Romance, they said.

The amphitheater where the challenge would be held was large enough to hold twenty-five thousand adults, which was nearly adequate as only adults could attend. The rest would have to find places in the forest above the large bowl-like structure on the west side of the lake.

The stone slabs that acted as benches on terraced earth were nearly full shortly after noon. By the time the sun hung halfway down the western sky, there was no longer empty space to stand, much less sit.

Thomas sat with Rachelle and his lieutenants in one of the gazebos overlooking the spectacle.

"I should be tracking the Horde into the desert," Thomas muttered.

"Don't think that you won't be called on to do your part here," Mikil said. "When it's finished, we'll go after the Horde and I'll be the first by your side."

She stood next to Jamous. They'd announced their plans for marriage at the celebration last evening. To their right, William scanned the crowd.

Rachelle put her hand on Thomas's arm. She alone understood his dilemma here.

"Even if there is a fight, I won't kill him, Mikil," he said. "Banishment, but not death."

"Fine. Banishment is better than giving him the freedom to poison the minds of our children," she said.

He took a calming breath. "I have to go after the Books of Histories again."

"And this time I will enter the tent," Mikil said. "The rest of this Gathering I can do without. We deal with Justin and then we leave to find your books. And Jamous will come with us."

Jamous kissed her on the lips. "As long as I am with you, I could cross the desert."

"Always," she said.

"Always," he repeated, and they kissed again.

The crowd suddenly hushed.

"They're coming."

Thomas walked to the railing and looked down on the amphitheater. Ciphus was walking down the long slope in his long white ceremonial robe. Behind him, the other six members of the Council. They approached a large platform in the middle of the field. Seven large torches burned in a semicircle around eight tall wooden stools. A stand held a bowl of water between them.

They walked in silence to seven of the stools. The eighth remained empty. If Justin won the inquiry, he would be allowed to sit with the Council in a show of their acceptance of him. Since the Council had cast the inquiry, they were not obligated to accept his doctrine, but in time, even it might be incorporated in the Great Romance.

The members climbed onto their stools and faced a similar, smaller platform with a single stool twenty yards from their own.

"Where is Justin?" Mikil whispered.

Ciphus lifted a hand for silence, though no gesture was needed—no one was moving, much less speaking. If Thomas were to cough, the whole arena would likely hear him.

"The Council will issue its challenge of the philosophies of Justin of Southern in this the tenth annual Gathering of all Forest People," Ciphus cried. His voice rang loud and clear.

"Justin of Southern, we call you forth."

The Council turned back toward the slope down which they had walked. At the crest of the slope, seven large trees marked the only entrance to the amphitheater.

No one appeared.

"He's going to default," Mikil said. "He knows that he's wrong and he's—"

"Who is that?" William asked.

A villager was walking from one of the lower seats. Instead of wearing the more popular short tunic, he was dressed in a longer, hooded beige one. And he wore the boots of a soldier.

"That's him," Jamous said.

The Council still hadn't seen him. The man walked to the lone stool, seated himself, and pulled back his hood.

"Justin of Southern accepts your challenge," he said loudly.

The Council spun as one. Murmurs ran through the amphitheater. A few chuckles.

"He's daring; I'll give him that," Mikil said.

Thomas could practically see the steam coming from Ciphus's ears.

The elder held up his hand for silence, and this time it was required. He walked to the bowl, dipped his hands into the water, and dabbed them dry on a small towel. Behind him the other members took their seats.

Ciphus paced the leading edge of the platform and pulled at his beard. "It is precisely this kind of trickery that I fear has deceived you, my friend," he said, just loudly enough to be heard.

"I have no desire to confuse the important questions you will ask," Justin said. "It is what we say today, not how we look, that will win or lose the hearts of the people."

Ciphus hesitated, then addressed the people. "Then hear what I have to say. The man we see seated before us today is a mighty warrior who has favored the forests with many victories in his time. He is the kind of man who loves children and who marches like a true hero and accepts praise with graciousness. Each of these we all know. For each of these I owe a debt of gratitude to Justin of Southern." He dipped his head at Justin. "Thank you."

Justin returned the bow.

Ciphus was no fool, Thomas thought.

"Nevertheless, it is said that this man has also spread the poison of blasphemy against Elyon throughout the Southern Forest in these past two years. Our task today is only to determine if this is true. We judge not the man, but his doctrine. And as with any challenge, you, the people, will be the judge of the matter when we have concluded our arguments. So then, judge well."

On Thomas's left, murmuring broke out, voices of dissent already. These must be those of the Southern Forest, Justin's strongest supporters. Where were the two men who had entered the Valley of Tuhan with Justin? Ronin and Arvyl, if Jamous had told him correctly. Their voices were in the crowd, surely, but not on the floor as Thomas might have expected. On the other hand, it was like Justin to fight his own battles and defend his own philosophies. He'd probably forbidden them from interfering.

"Silence!"

They hushed again.

"It won't take long. A very simple matter in fact. I think that for this inquiry we could have the children vote and end up with a clear, just verdict. The matter is this."

Ciphus turned to Justin.

"Is it or is it not true that the Horde is truly the enemy of Elyon?"

"It is true," Justin said.

"Correct, we all know this. So then, is it or is it not true that to conspire with the enemy of Elyon is to conspire against Elyon himself?"

"It is true."

"Yes, of course. We all know this as well. So then, is it or is it not true that you advocate creating a bond with the Horde by negotiating peace?"

"It is true."

A gasp flushed through the arena. Shocked mutterings rose from the left and admonishments to let them finish from the right. Ciphus again silenced the crowd with his hand. He measured Justin carefully, undoubtedly thinking that he was plotting some of his trickery.

"You do realize that to conspire with the Horde has always been treasonous to us? We don't compromise with the enemy of Elyon, according to the word of Elyon himself. We subscribe to the boy's prophecy, that Elyon will provide a way to rid the world of this scourge that's upon us. Yet you seem to want to make peace with it. Isn't this blasphemous?"

"Blasphemous, yes," Justin said.

The man had no sense, Thomas thought. With those words he'd conscripted himself to banishment.

"The question is," Justin continued, "blasphemous against what? Against your Great Romance, or against Elyon himself?"

Ciphus was shocked by this assertion. "And you think there is a difference?"

"There is a great difference. Not in spirit, but in form. To make peace with the Horde may defile your Great Romance, but it does not blaspheme Elyon. Elyon would make peace with every man, woman, and child on this world, even though his enemies are found everywhere, even here in this very place."

Silence. The people seemed too stunned to speak. *He'd cut his own throat,* Thomas thought. What he said had a freshness to it, perhaps an idea that he might entertain if he were a theologian. But Justin had decried all that was sacred except Elyon himself. By questioning the Great Romance, he might as well have included Elyon as well.

"You say that we are Elyon's enemy?" There was a tremble in Ciphus's voice.

"Do you love your lake and your trees and your flowers, or do you love Elyon? Would you die for these, or would you die for Elyon? You are no different than the Horde. If you would die for Elyon, perhaps you should die for the Horde. They are his, after all."

"You would have us die for the Horde?" Ciphus cried, red faced. "Die for the enemy of Elyon, whom we have sworn to destroy!"

"If need be, yes."

"You speak treason against Elyon!" Ciphus pointed a trembling finger at Justin. "You are a son of the Shataiki!"

Order abandoned the amphitheater with that one word: *Shataiki.* Cries of outrage ripped through the air, met head-on with cries of objection that Ciphus could say such a thing against this prophet. This Justin of Southern. If they would only let the man explain himself, they would understand, they cried.

Any ambivalence Thomas had felt toward this hearing left him. How could any man who'd served under him dare suggest they die for the Horde? Die in battle defending Elyon's lakes, yes. Die protecting the forest and their children *from* the Horde, yes. Die upholding the Great Romance in the face of an enemy who'd sworn to wipe Elyon's name from the face of the earth, yes.

But die *for* the Horde? Broker peace so that they might be free to work their deceit?

Never!

"How can he say that?" Rachelle asked beside him. "Did he just suggest we lie down and die for the Horde?"

"What did I tell you?" Mikil said. "We should have killed him yesterday when we had the chance."

"If we'd killed him yesterday, we'd be dead today," Thomas said.

"Better dead than indebted to this traitor."

The arena was a mess of riotous noise. Ciphus made no attempt to stop them. He walked to the bowl of water and dipped his hands in once again. He was done, Thomas realized.

The elder conferred with the other Council members one by one.

Justin sat calmly. He made no attempt to explain himself. He seemed satisfied despite having put up no real defense at all. Maybe he wanted a fight.

Ciphus finally raised both hands and, after a few moments, quieted the crowd enough for him to be heard.

"I have made my challenge to this heresy, and now you will decide this man's fate. Should we embrace his teaching or send him away from us, never to return? Or should we put his fate in Elyon's hands through a fight to the death? Search your hearts and let your decision be heard."

Thomas prayed the vote would be clear. Despite his aversion to what Justin had said, he wanted no part in a fight. Not that he feared Justin's sword, but the thought of being dragged down in support of the Council didn't sit well with him either.

On the other hand, there would be a kind of justice in asserting himself over his former lieutenant in one final match before sending him to live with the Horde. Either way, Ciphus would not get his death.

"It's over," he said quietly.

"Then you weren't in the valley yesterday," Rachelle said.

Ciphus lowered his right hand. "If you say this man speaks blasphemy, let your voice be heard!"

A thunderous roar shook the gazebo. Enough. Surely enough.

Ciphus let the cry run on until he was satisfied, then silenced them.

"And if you say we should accept this man's teaching and make peace with the Horde, then let your voice be heard."

The Southern Forest dwellers had strong lungs, because the cry was loud. And it swelled with as much thunder as the first cry. Or was it less? The distinction was not enough for Ciphus to call it.

Thomas's heart rose into his throat. No one outside this gazebo knew that he would defend the Council in a fight. And there would be a fight. No matter how deaf Ciphus wanted to be at this moment, he could not call this a clear decision. The rules were plain—there could be no doubt.

Ciphus lowered both hands and the people quieted. They all knew what was coming. For a long time the elder just stood still, perhaps taken aback that the crowd was so divided.

"Then we will place the fate of this man in Elyon's hands," he said loudly. "I call to the floor our defender, Thomas of Hunter."

The crowd gasped. Or at least half of it gasped. The southern half, which had decided to claim Justin as their own since he'd delivered their forest a week earlier. They clearly couldn't see him fighting their Justin.

The other half began to chant his name.

Rachelle's eyes were dark with fear.

He kissed her cheek. "I taught him; remember that."

He climbed over the railing, and the people made a way for him down through the bleachers. He gripped his sword at his side and vaulted over the short wall that separated the field from the seats. The walk to the main platform seemed long with all the cheering and with Justin drilling him with a stare.

He stood before Ciphus, who shut down the crowd.

"I request you, Thomas of Hunter, supreme commander of the Forest

Guard, to defend our truth against this blasphemy in a fight to the death. Do you accept?"

"I will. But I will seek banishment, not death, for Justin."

"That is my choice to make, not yours," Ciphus said.

Thomas had never heard of such a thing.

"I understood that it was my choice," he said.

"Then you misunderstand the rules. The Council made this rule and now you must abide by it. It will be a fight to the death. The price for this sin is death. I am not willing to consider the living death."

Thomas thought a moment. It was true that the law required death of anyone who defied Elyon. Banishment was a kind of death, a living death, as Ciphus called it. But now, forced to consider it, he realized there could be a problem with banishing Justin. What if he entered the Horde and gained power under Qurong? What if he then led their armies against the forest? Perhaps death was the wiser choice, though not what he desired.

"Then I accept." He dipped his head.

"Swords!" Ciphus cried.

A Council member lifted two heavy bronze swords from the floor by his stool and set them on the stage.

"Choose your sword," Ciphus said.

Thomas glanced at Justin. The warrior watched him with mild interest now. Did the man have a death wish?

Thomas picked up the swords, one in each hand, and walked toward Justin. "Do you have a preference?"

"No."

Thomas flipped both swords into the air. They turned lazily in unison and stuck into the boards on either side of Justin.

"I insist," Thomas said. "I don't want it said that I beat Justin of Southern by picking the better sword."

The crowd reacted with a rumble of approval.

Justin kept his eyes on Thomas without looking at the swords. He stepped forward, yanked out the one to his right. "Neither would I," he said, tossing the weapon so that its blade pierced the earth at Thomas's feet.

Another rumble of approval.

"Fight!" Ciphus yelled. "Fight to the death!"

Thomas plucked the sword out and swung it twice for feel. It was a standard Guard weapon, well balanced and heavy enough to sever a head with one swipe.

Justin put his hand on the sword and waited. Enough of this posturing. The sooner they ended the fight, the better. To know a man in a match of this kind meant watching his eyes. And Thomas didn't like what he saw in Justin's eyes. They were too full of life to cut so easily from his shoulders. The man was full of beguiling influence that unnerved him.

He skipped to his left and leaped to the platform, ten feet from Justin. He briefly wondered if the man was simply going to die without a fight, because he hardly shifted.

Thomas lunged and brought the sword around with enough force to cut the man in half.

At the last moment, Justin pulled his sword up and deflected the blow. A horrendous clash filled the arena. It was exactly what Thomas had expected. In the moment when Justin was blocking his blow, he reached out with his left hand and tapped the man on the cheek.

It was a move he'd taught them all as a bit of a joke once. Mikil dubbed it "The Cheek." What Thomas didn't expect was the hand that shot out from Justin at precisely the same moment. It tapped his cheek.

The crowd roared and Thomas thought he could hear Mikil's cry of approval above the din.

He couldn't help but smile. Good. Very good. Justin smirked. Winked.

Then they went a full round, gripping their swords with both hands. Clash and counterclash, jabbing, sparring, thrusting, moving around the platform—fundamental swordplay to loosen the joints and feel out the opponent. Nothing about the way Justin fought surprised Thomas. He reacted precisely the way Mikil or William or any of his other lieutenants would to each of his attacks.

And he was sure that nothing he did surprised Justin either. That would come later.

They began to add a few of the Marduk moves, feigning, bobbing,

weaving, rolling—off the stage to the field, then along one side of the platform and around the perimeter. Back on top of the stage.

"You're a good man, Thomas," Justin said too softly for the crowd to
hear. "I always liked you. And I still do, very much."

Their swords clanged again.

"You've kept up your skills, I see," Thomas said. "Killing a few of your
Horde friends on the side, are we?"

Justin blocked a blow, and they faced each other in a momentary
stall.

"You have no idea what you've gotten yourself into. Be careful."

Thomas sprinted four steps. It was a classical approach to a vault, but
Thomas didn't vault. He planted his sword as if to flip over it, but instead
of going high he swung low.

Justin had already lifted his sword to ward off the expected jab that
would come when Thomas catapulted himself over his head. But now
Thomas was closer to Justin's ankles. It would end here, when he took
Justin from his feet and followed with his blade.

Thomas swung around his sword, feet first, bracing for the impact of
his shin against Justin's calves.

But suddenly Justin's calves weren't there. At the last moment he'd seen
the reversal, and although he was completely off balance, he'd managed to
launch himself into a backflip. A high somersault off the edge of the platform. Then around in almost perfect form.

He landed on the field, feet spread and hands on his sword, ready for
anything.

Thomas saw it all while he swung through his empty kick, and he used
his momentum to pivot all the way around into a back handspring, off the
platform, into what was called a back-whip.

The full aerial roundhouse move forced an opponent to guard against
a lethal heel to his face, but then morphed into a pirouette, one full rotation to bring the sword, not the feet, around with blazing speed.

Thomas executed the move perfectly. Justin misjudged it. But he threw
himself backward in time to catch the blade as a glancing blow skipped off
his chest.

Instead of continuing into a back handspring, he dropped to his back and rolled in the direction opposite the one in which Thomas's momentum carried him.

Smart. Very smart. If he'd gone for the back handspring, as most warriors certainly would, Thomas could have carried his own momentum into another direct attack before the man had fully recovered.

The crowd knew it too. Their cries had fallen to silence.

Justin came to his feet in a ready stance, eyes blazing with amusement.

"You should have accepted my promotion two years ago instead of losing your head to the desert," Thomas said. "You're a better warrior than the others."

"Am I?" Justin straightened, as if this revelation took him off guard. He tossed his sword on the dirt. "Then let me fight you without a sword. The coming battle won't be won with the sword."

Thomas stepped forward, sword extended. "Pick up your sword, you fool."

"And what, kill you?"

Thomas brought his blade to Justin's neck. The man made no attempt to stop him.

"Kill him!" Ciphus screamed. "To the death!"

"He wants me to kill you."

"If you can," Justin said.

"I can. But I won't."

They were speaking low. "You deceive the people into thinking there can be peace when at this very moment the Horde is planning a betrayal," Thomas said.

Justin blinked.

"Pick up your sword!" Thomas yelled for all to hear.

Justin slowly stepped back and to his left. But he ignored his sword and dropped his hands to his sides, stared at Thomas.

Thomas had given the man from Southern enough latitude; now his antics were infuriating. Thomas attacked. He covered the ground between them in three long strides and swung his sword full strength. The blade would cut the man in two without knowing it had hit anything.

But Justin wasn't there for the sword to hit. Thomas saw the man rolling back to his right, snatching up his sword, and too late he knew that he had been lulled into overcommitting himself to this blow he was already halfway through.

His own words in training screamed through his mind. Never over-commit in close combat!

Yet in anger, he had. He could have killed the man. Now the man might kill him.

With a slower opponent, his error wouldn't have mattered. But Justin moved as fast as he did. His blow came from behind, the broadside of his sword hitting Thomas squarely on the back.

He landed hard. There was grass in his hands. Both hands. He'd lost his sword.

He threw himself to the right, rolling to his back. A blade pressed against his neck and a knee dropped into his solar plexus. Justin kneeled over him, green eyes blazing, and Thomas knew that he was finished.

The breath seemed to have been sucked from the arena along with his own. He stared into his old lieutenant's eyes and saw a fierce fire.

Then the man sprang up, backed away, and tossed his sword high into the air. It twirled in the afternoon sun and fell on its side with a dull thump, twenty yards away.

He strode toward the Council and stopped in front of their platform. "Your challenger has been defeated. Elyon has spoken."

"The match is to the death," Ciphus said.

"I will not kill him for your sin."

"Then Elyon has not spoken," the elder said quietly. "The only reason you are alive now is because Thomas failed to finish. You were defeated first."

"Was I?"

"This isn't over," Ciphus ground out.

"Live!" someone from the crowd shouted. "Let Thomas live!"

A chant began. "Live, live, live, live!"

Thomas pushed himself to his feet, mind spinning. He'd been defeated by Justin in fair combat.

Ciphus clearly wasn't up to defying the people under such ambiguous circumstances. He let them chant.

Justin turned to the crowd. "I will let him live!" he shouted.

The chant settled and died.

He paced slowly, studying the people. "I will show you now, since I have earned the right, the true way to peace." Now he was walking toward the slope that rose to the trees at the entrance. "At this very moment the Horde is conspiring to crush you with an army that will make the battles to the south and west seem like childish skirmishes."

How could Justin know this? And yet Thomas knew that he did. They had to get word to the scouts—search the farthest perimeter.

He spun toward the gazebo, saw Mikil, and motioned for her to make it so. She and William disappeared.

Justin spread his hands out to calm the confused crowd. "Silence! There is only one way to meet this enemy. It is the way of peace, and today I will deliver this peace to you."

He stopped and motioned to the trees. For a moment, nothing. And then a hooded man stepped out.

A Scab!

Wearing the sash of a general.

Justin had smuggled a general from the Horde into the forest. Ten thousand voices cried out. The rest of the crowd gaped in stunned silence.

The tall, hooded man walked quickly, and Justin met him halfway up the slope. They clasped hands and dipped their heads in greeting. Justin faced the arena and spread his arm in a manner of introduction.

"I bring to you the man with whom I will negotiate peace between the Desert Dwellers and the Forest People." He paused.

"The mighty general of the Horde, Martyn!"

Martyn! Was it possible? Then who had he killed in Qurong's tent?

Thomas glanced back at the gazebo. It was already empty. His Guard would not allow this man to leave the village alive. Not now, with this revelation that the Horde was gathering on their exposed flank.

Thomas snatched his sword and ran for the slope. The day had seen enough showmanship. He couldn't kill Justin now, but this general was another matter.

"I have given him my word that you would not kill him," Justin said. "His armies are close now and could swarm the forest and wage a battle that would turn the valleys red with blood. But if Elyon's children all die, then who would be victor?"

The revelation that the Horde was on their doorstep seemed to have tempered the crowd's nerve. The people were actually listening. Thomas saw William and several of the Guard emerge from the trees at the top of the slope behind Justin. Rachelle was with them.

What was she doing? She had no business with them.

He shoved the thought aside and walked toward Justin and the Scab. The Guard moved down the hill to cut off any possible escape.

Justin stepped up to meet him. "Thomas, I beg you to hear me. I have proven my loyalty to you. Now you must allow me this!"

"You are wrong. He has betrayal in his blood!"

They were both weaponless as far as he could see. Thomas's men edged down the slope, swords drawn.

Thomas rushed at the general. Justin seized his arm. "Thomas! You don't know who he is!"

Martyn backed up.

Thomas could see the Scab's white eyes peering from the shadows of his hood. The rare circle tattooed over the man's right eye marked him as a druid, confirming the rumors.

"You think my sword can't draw the blood of the man who has slaughtered ten thousand of my men?" He directed his challenge to Martyn. "Will your magic protect you from a cold blade?"

His men were now only a few paces behind the Scab. Martyn sensed them, glanced back, and stopped. Thomas tore his arm free from Justin's grip and covered the last few steps. He thrust his sword into the bottom of the general's hood and held him at point.

He flicked the blade. Martyn didn't respond to the small cut on his neck. Red blood seeped from the surface wound.

"You think he won't bleed the way my men have bled? I say we send him back to his Horde in pieces."

Justin ran past Thomas, grabbed the general's hood, and yanked it back.

Martyn's face was ashen. A curving scar ran down his right cheek. He blinked pale eyes in the sudden light. He was hardly human, and yet he was fully human. But there was more.

Thomas knew this man.

His heart crashed in his chest.

Johan.

He yanked his sword back.

Johan? And the scar . . . Why did this scar surprise him?

"Johan," Justin said.

Thomas saw Rachelle over the man's shoulder. She was at the crest and she'd heard the words.

"Johan?" she said.

Then she was running. Down the slope. She raced around the general and stared at his exposed face.

"Johan? It's . . . it's you?"

The general showed no emotion at the sight of his sister. His mind had been taken by the disease, Thomas knew. He hadn't been killed in battle as they'd all assumed. He'd been lost to the desert and become a Scab three years ago. It was why the Horde's strategies had become so effective. They were being led by one of the old Forest Guard who had lost his mind to their disease.

Rachelle reached out to him, but he withdrew. She stared at him, grieved. Horrified.

"You must let us go," Justin said. "It's the only way."

William edged closer. "Sir, he's diseased. We can't let him—"

"Then wash him!" Rachelle cried.

"You can't force a man to bathe," Thomas said. "He is what he chooses to be."

"He will bathe! Tell them, Johan. You will wash this curse from your skin. You'll swim in the lake."

His eyes widened with a momentary flash of fear. "If it is peace you want, I can give you peace." Thomas recognized the voice, but barely. It was now deeper. Pained. "Otherwise we bring a curse you have never known to this forest."

William grabbed the man's cloak and drew back his sword. "Enough of this!"

"Let him go!" Thomas ordered.

"Sir—"

"Release him!"

William let the robe go and stepped back.

"I will not kill my own brother!"

His Guard would never agree to the terms of any peace Justin and Martyn drew up, but a truce might stall the Horde long enough for the Guard to prepare if truly there was an army in the plains.

Behind them, Ciphus was silent. Why?

Thomas faced Justin. "Take him. Broker your peace, but don't expect me and my men to go along with it. If we see a single Scab within sight of the forest, we will hunt you both down and drain your blood."

Rachelle gripped his arm. She was trembling.

Martyn replaced his hood and turned. William wouldn't move.

"Let them go, William." Then louder. "These two have my personal word of safe passage from our forest. The man who touches them will face me."

His men parted.

Justin and Martyn, the mighty general of the Horde whose name was also Johan, walked up the slope into the trees and vanished.

19

THOMAS STARED at the man he now knew had masterminded the virus. A thick Frenchman with fat fingers and greasy black hair who looked like he could stand in the face of a hurricane without batting an eye.

This was Armand Fortier.

They had been sedated, Monique told him. Within an hour of him passing out, they'd both been given shots. Men were dismantling the laboratory. They were going to be moved; she got that much from one of them. But to where she didn't know.

Then *she'd* passed out. Neither of them knew how much time had passed since then.

They'd awakened here, in this windowless stone room with a pool table and a fireplace. They were both handcuffed with impossibly tight cuffs, seated in wooden chairs, facing the Frenchman and, behind him, Carlos. Monique was still dressed in her pale blue slacks and blouse, and Thomas still wore the camouflaged jumpsuit.

Thomas had tried to deduce their possible location, but he had no memory of being moved, and there was nothing in this room that couldn't be found anywhere in the world. For all he knew they'd been out for two days. If he was right, the reason he'd dreamed at all was because he hadn't been drugged for that first hour after Carlos had tortured him.

That first hour, he'd dreamed of the inquiry where he'd fought Justin and discovered that Martyn was Johan . . .

"Just so you know, the Americans did try to rescue you," Fortier said. He seemed to find the fact interesting. "And I know from a very reliable source that they were after more than the antivirus. They want you. Everybody seems to want Thomas Hunter and Monique de Raison."

His eyes moved to Monique. "You have this solution in your head. You'd think I would just kill you and eliminate the risk of them finding you. Fortunately for you, I have reasons to keep you alive."

His eyes shifted back to Thomas. "You, on the other hand, are an enigma. You know things you should not. You gave us the Raison Strain, and then you inadvertently gave us the antivirus, both sides of this most useful weapon. But it doesn't stop there. You continue to know things. Where we are. What we will do next, perhaps. What should I do with you?"

Thomas's mind returned to the dream of Justin's challenge.

Johan. The man who'd led the Horde against them so effectively had been Johan. And Johan had a scar on his cheek. Thomas had watched the duo walk into the woods to broker peace with Qurong, a peace that was somehow entwined with betrayal.

The crowd had erupted in fierce debate. Thomas had returned to his Guard, and the Council had joined them to berate his decision to give Johan safe passage from the forest. But how could he kill Johan? And hadn't Justin won the inquiry? They had no right to undermine him now.

The festivities that night had been more dissension than celebration—a strange mix of exuberance by those who believed that Justin was indeed destined to deliver them from the Horde with this peace of his, and animosity by those who argued vehemently against any such treasonous betrayal of Elyon.

Thomas had finally collapsed into a fitful sleep.

"What are you thinking?" Fortier asked.

Thomas focused on the thick Frenchman. He had no doubt that this man would succeed with his virus. The Books of Histories said he would. And, as it was turning out, changing history wasn't as easy as he'd once hoped. Impossible, maybe. All of this—his discovery of the virus in the first place, his attempts to derail Svensson, and now this encounter with Fortier—might very well be written in the Books of Histories. Imagine that: *Thomas Hunter's attempt to rescue Monique de Raison at Cyclops failed when the transport he was flying in was shot down . . .* If he'd been successful in retrieving the Books from Qurong's tent, he could have read the details of his own life! But it seemed that the path of history was continuing exactly as it had been recorded, and he knew its final destination if not the precise course it would take.

The question now was *when*. When would they finally kill him? When would Monique die? When would the antivirus actually be released to the chosen few? When would the rest die their hideous diseased death?

"They searched for you with nearly a hundred aircraft loaded with enough electronic equipment to power Paris for a week," Fortier was saying. "It was quite a spectacle, not all at once or to one region, of course. In circles and to airports throughout the South Pacific. They blocked the air-traffic routes between Indonesia and France. To be quite honest, we barely made it out."

His lips twisted in a small grin. "We wouldn't have if I hadn't foreseen exactly this possibility. You see, you're not the only one who can see the future. Oh, your sight might be different from mine based on this . . . this gift rather than solid deductive reasoning, but I can promise you that I have seen the future, and I like what I see. Do you?"

"No," Thomas said. "I don't."

"Very good. You still have your voice. And you're honest, which is more than I can say for myself."

He turned away.

"I need to know something, Thomas. I know that you know the answer, because I have ears inside your government. I know the president has no intention of actually delivering the weapons that are just now entering the Atlantic. What I don't know is how far the president will carry his bluff. I need to know when to take the appropriate action. We are now fully prepared for a nuclear exchange, you must know. Knowing if and when they might attack would be helpful."

"He won't fire nuclear weapons," Thomas said.

"No? Maybe you don't know your president as well as I do. We anticipate it. Any knowledge you give me won't change the outcome of this chess match; it will only determine how many people must die to facilitate that outcome."

Fortier glanced at his watch. "We are going public in France in three days. Over a hundred less-progressive members of the government will meet untimely ends between now and then. A Chinese delegation is waiting for a meeting with President Gaetan in his office, and I've been asked to join them. Evidently news of the altercations with you in Indonesia have leaked and are causing a stir. The Australians are threatening to go public and must be calmed. One of our own commanders is asking the wrong questions. I am a busy man, Thomas. I have to leave. We'll talk again tomorrow. I hope your memory serves you better then."

He regarded Monique, dipped his head barely, and left the room.

Thomas's mind spun with the details that the Frenchman had just given him. The world was indeed rushing to its well-known end. While he was off dreaming about the Gathering and how it could possibly be that the great general Martyn was really Johan, complete with scarred—

Thomas stopped. He stared at Carlos, who had crossed the room and opened a door that led into darkness.

He turned in profile to Thomas. The scar. Right cheek. Curved like a half moon, exactly as he remembered Johan's.

"Let's go," the man said. "Don't make me drag you."

No, Carlos wouldn't want to drag them. It would mean getting too close—an opportunity for Thomas to do something. The man knew to play things safe.

But none of this interested Thomas at the moment.

The scar.

What if Rachelle was right about how the realities worked? Thomas might be the only true gateway between the realities, but if someone was aware of both realities, then both realities had potential to affect that person. For instance, now that Rachelle believed in both realities, if Monique was cut, Rachelle would also wake up with a cut. And if Monique was killed, Rachelle would also die. Would Monique die if Rachelle did? Thomas hadn't convinced Monique to believe yet. Nor had Monique ever come into contact with Thomas's blood.

The link between the realities was belief? Or Thomas's blood?

Perhaps both. It did make a strange kind of sense. Life and blood and skills and knowledge were all transferable between realities—he'd already experienced that much. Proven it. But why?

Belief.

If someone with even the slightest belief came into contact with Thomas's blood, then their belief would be enough to connect them to his reality with him. It would explain everything! And it wouldn't require that Rachelle and Monique be one and the same.

It was as good a working theory as he'd come up with yet.

"Now. Please," Carlos said, indicating the room.

There was still a hole in his theory. Primarily, why he was Thomas in both realities, why he didn't share this experience with someone else.

Thomas stood. "I have something to say," he said. "Can you get the Frenchman?"

Carlos studied him. "You'll have to wait."

"What I have to say he will want to hear before he meets with the Chinese."

"Then tell me."

"It has to do with how I knew where you were keeping Monique. You knew I'd come, didn't you?" Thomas walked forward a few paces and stopped ten feet from the man. Behind him, Monique kept her seat.

"You could have tracked me down in Washington, but you chose to go to Indonesia and wait for me there, because you knew that I would know," Thomas continued. "Am I right?"

"What does this have to do with the Chinese?"

"Actually, it's not tied directly to the Chinese per se. I just said he should know this before he meets with them."

"And this is?"

"That I am going to escape before he meets with them."

Thomas didn't have any such knowledge, but he needed the man's full attention, and this was the first step.

"Then it would have been a wasted call," Carlos said. "I have no intention of letting you escape. This isn't a useful discussion."

"I didn't say you were going to let us escape. But our escape will involve you. I know this because you're not like them. You're a deeply religious man who follows the will of Allah, and I know you well. Much better than you think I might. We've met before."

Carlos shifted. "If you know me so well, then you know that I'm not easily swayed by a fool who speaks in riddles."

"No, you aren't. But you have been swayed. Deceived. I know that without a doubt. Do you think that Svensson and Fortier have any intention of allowing Islam to thrive after they gain power? Religion is their enemy. They may set up their own, they may even call it Islam, but it won't be the Islam you know. One of the first to die will be you. You know too much. You're much too powerful. You are the worst kind of enemy—they know that. You must as well."

He didn't respond.

"You're not curious as to *how* we met before?" Thomas asked.

"We haven't."

"You don't have the memory of it yet. We've met in the other reality. The one with the Books of Histories. There your name is Johan, and you are the brother of my wife. You're also a great general who has caused me and my Forest Guard more than our share of grief."

Carlos apparently found neither humor nor persuasion in the claim. "The only reason you're alive is because of your witchcraft," he said. "If you cross me again, I will kill you. I see that you're not healing so well these days." He glanced at the bruises and cuts the handcuffs had worn into Thomas's wrists. "I think you will die easily enough. Give me a reason and I will test the theory now."

"My gift is from witchcraft? Or because I'm a servant of El—of God? I'll admit, I haven't followed him in this reality, but I really haven't had a chance, and that's changing. Listen to yourself. You're marked for death *because* of your belief in the one you call God! You serve two demons who kill for their own gain. You think they will let you live?"

He blinked.

"What if I could prove it to you? Brother."

"Don't be absurd."

"But you do believe that I know things I shouldn't," Thomas said. "That's why you waited for me in Indonesia. You knew I would show up. I say that you too believe in a reality where there's more than meets the eye."

Thomas could see the light in his eyes. As a Muslim, such a belief would be natural to him.

———∞∞∞———

Carlos was tempted to shoot the man then. If Svensson and Fortier weren't so taken by Hunter's strange gift, he would defy them and kill the man here.

"Your name is Johan and we are destined to be brothers," Thomas said.

His mind ached with this nonsensical revelation. Who'd ever heard of such nonsense?

His mother had. She was a practicing Sufi mystic.

The Prophet, Mohammed, had.

Hunter might be misinterpreting his visions, but he might very well have seen others in his dreams. Maybe even him. Carlos. The man's claims enraged him.

On the other hand, Thomas was smart enough to try something exactly like this to distract him. Handcuffed, the man hardly had a prayer of reaching him, much less escaping from him. But Carlos wouldn't underestimate him.

"I'll consider what you've said. Now if you will please—"

"Then I'll prove it," Thomas said. "I'll cut Johan on the neck without touching you."

The words triggered an alarm in Carlos. Heat spread down his neck.

"Do you believe I can do that? Do you believe that if I'm healed in the other reality, I will be healed in this one? Or that if I die there, I will die here? Do you remember shooting me, Carlos? Still, I'm alive. You live in the other reality with me too, and I've just had a confrontation with you at the Gathering. I cut your neck with my sword."

"Don't be ridiculous! Stop this at once!" But Carlos's mind reared with fear. He had heard the mystics speak like this. The Christians. He'd heard some claim belief that if a man would only open his eyes he could see another world. And a small part of him did believe. Always had.

"Do you believe, Carlos? Of course you do. You always have."

At first, Carlos mistook the sensation in his neck for the rage that filled his veins. But his neck was burning. His flesh was stinging as if it had been cut. It couldn't possibly be true, yet he knew that it was.

He lifted his left hand to his neck.

⸺⸺⸺

Thomas watched with surprise as the skin on Carlos's neck suddenly began to bleed, precisely as it would if he'd just taken a blade to it.

He hadn't just cut Carlos. But enough of Carlos believed his story about Johan to cause the rift in the realities. One of these two worlds might be a dream, but at the moment it didn't matter. At the moment Carlos was bleeding because Johan was still bleeding!

The man lifted his hand to his neck, felt the small wound, pulled his fingers away bloody. His eyes stared in confounded fascination.

Thomas moved then. Two steps and he left the ground. His foot struck Carlos before the man could tear his eyes free from his hand.

The man hadn't even braced for the impact. He crumbled like a chain that had been cut from the ceiling.

Thomas landed on both feet and spun around. Monique was staring, stunned by the developments. Then she was running for him.

"Quick! He has the keys in his right pocket!" Her words piled on top of each other. "I saw them; he has them in his pocket!"

Thomas squatted by the man and felt behind him for the pocket, dug the keys out, and stood. "Back up to me. Hurry!"

They freed themselves in a matter of seconds. Monique's wrists were bleeding because of the cuffs as well. She ignored the cuts. "Now what?"

"You're okay?"

"I'm free; that's better than I've been for two weeks."

"Okay, stay close," Thomas said.

She was staring at Carlos, who lay unconscious, bleeding from a slight wound on his neck. "What just happened?"

"Later. Hurry."

The hallway was empty. They ran to the staircase at the end and were about to climb when Thomas changed his mind. Sunlight poured through a three-foot window directly ahead and above. The latch was unlocked.

He redirected her toward it, pulled himself up, opened the window, and swung into the window well outside. He glanced over the top, saw no guard, and turned back for Monique.

"Jump. I'll pull you up," he whispered.

She caught his hand and he plucked her easily from the floor, wincing with the thought of the pain she must feel in her torn wrists. She struggled a bit to get her knees up on the ledge, but soon they crouched in the window well, window firmly closed behind them. Less than three minutes had passed since Carlos hit the floor.

Monique poked her head up for a look. "We're in the country," she whispered. "A farm."

Thomas saw several large barns and a driveway that disappeared into the forest. This building was covered by old stonework. The sun was already dipping toward the western horizon.

Carlos would wake up soon. They had to put some distance between them and this farm.

"Okay. We go straight for the forest." Thomas studied the closest trees. "Once we run, we don't stop. Can you do that?"

"I can run."

He glanced around one last time. Clear.

Thomas leaped from the window well, pulled Monique up, and ran for the forest, making sure she stayed close. The crunch of twigs and dried leaves welcomed them into the protective trees.

Thomas glanced back. No alarm. Not yet.

———

Mike Orear guided Theresa Sumner by the arm toward the CDC parking lot. She'd ignored his phone calls for the last twenty-four hours, presumably because she was out of town. But by the looks of the bags under her eyes, he wouldn't be surprised to learn that she'd been holed up here, working on the virus.

He'd driven out to her house last night. No luck. It was eight the next morning before he'd finally driven here.

"Mike, you've made your point. And the answer is no. You can't go public. Not yet." She pulled her arm away.

"Twenty-four hours, Theresa. This isn't about you and me anymore. I made a promise, but I wasn't thinking clearly. You tell whoever needs to know that they have twenty-four hours to come clean, or I'm putting the story on the air."

She reached her white SUV and pulled up, face brave but dog tired. "Then you might as well join the terrorists, because you'll hurt as many people as they will."

"Don't be naive. Are you telling me that if I don't run the story, more people will live?"

She didn't answer. Of course not, the answer was no, because if the virus was real, they were all dead anyway. And this virus *was* as real as she'd said. Real as milk or bread or gasoline. He'd gone from incredulity to a state of constant horror over this impending sickness that was growing in his body at this very moment.

"Which means that you're not making any progress," he said. He turned away. "Great. All the more reason to break this open."

"Are you glad that you know?" she asked. "Has the quality of your life improved because I dragged you into this?"

The last five days had been a living hell. He looked away.

"Exactly," she said. "You want to draw the rest of the world into the same kind of miserable knowledge? You think it'll help us deal with the problem? You think it'll bring us one minute closer to an antivirus or a vaccine? Not a chance. If anything, it slows us down. We'll be dealing with a whole new set of problems."

"You can't just *not* tell people that they're going to die. I don't care how much you want to protect them; it's their lives we're talking about. The president is still holding firm on all this?"

She crossed her arms and sighed. "His advisers are split. But I promise you, the moment the people know, this country shuts down. What am I supposed to do if I can't get a line out to the labs in Europe? Thought about that? Why would the employees at AT&T go to work if they knew they only had thirteen days to live?"

"Because there's a chance we'll all live if they keep the lines open, that's why."

"That would be a lie. You'd just be replacing one lie for another," she said.

"What? Now there's *no* chance we can survive this?"

"Not that I see. We have thirteen *days*, Mike. The closer we look at this thing, the more we realize what a monster it really is."

"I can't accept that. Someone has to be making progress somewhere. This is the twenty-first century, not the Middle Ages."

"Well, it just so happens that DNA is no respecter of centuries. We're all just groping around in the dark."

"You know the word will get out soon anyway. I'm surprised the rest of the press hasn't pieced this together already."

She took a deep breath. "It's only been a week. Patterns take time to recognize unless you know what you're looking for. The military knows what to look for, but they've been told what to expect under various cover stories."

"But for how long? This is insane!"

"Of course it's insane! The whole thing is insane!"

He put his hand on the hood of her Durango. Cold. She'd been here for a while. Maybe all night. Or longer.

"Our story about the quarantined island south of Java is starting to fall apart," she said. "A number of people made it off the island before they shut it down. The press over there is wondering how far it's spread. So are half the labs working with us."

"My point exactly. There's no way they can hold this in. We should have every lab in the world working around the clock on this—"

"We do have practically every lab in the world working around the clock on this!"

"We should have the whole military out, looking for these terrorists—"

"They've got every intelligence agency with anything to offer on it already. But please, these guys have the antivirus—we can't just send a toma-hawk cruise missile after them."

"We know where they are?"

She didn't answer, which meant she either did know or had a very good idea.

"It's France, isn't it?"

No answer.

"Finally, an excuse to nuke France."

"I think there may be some takers."

"Surely not the government proper."

"No. I don't know anything else, Mike." She held up a hand. "No more. I'm wasting time out here." She started back.

"People need to make things right," he said. "With their children. With God. Twenty-four hours, Theresa. I won't implicate you."

She looked back at him. "Do whatever you have to do, Mike. Just think long and hard before you do it."

"Where are we going?" Monique panted.

Thomas scanned the meadow that lay ahead of them. Beyond it, a hazy horizon. "Away from Carlos. Do you have any idea where we are?"

"I would say up north. Maybe outside of Paris."

"The *Sûreté* will be scouring the country for us as soon as Carlos sends word," he said. "We have to get to a phone that has service to the United States. The airports will be too dangerous. What about the English Channel?"

"If we could find a way to the Channel without being tracked down. Why not Paris?"

She was French and would pass easily. He might stand out.

"You know Paris well?"

"Well enough to get lost in the crowd."

"We have three days before they go public. When that happens, they'll have to declare martial law. Public transportation may be shut down. We have to get you out of the country before then."

"Then Paris is our best bet. I would say it lies to the west."

"Why?"

"The horizon isn't as clear to the west. Smog."

He considered her reasoning. "Okay, west."

They ran west for nearly two hours before the sun began to dip past the western horizon. They'd encountered several farm buildings, which they skirted after a quick look, but still no paved roads. The problem with using a farm phone was that the *Sûreté* would undoubtedly track any overseas calls originating from this part of the country, a simple task when there couldn't be more than a few hundred in a hundred square miles out here. A pay phone in a place frequented by tourists would be much safer.

The problem with finding such a place was simply that Thomas and Monique were running blind. Not only were they losing light, but they still weren't sure where they were.

They ran on, torn between taking the time to find the right direction and keeping distance between them and any pursuit Carlos gave. Twice Thomas cut back on their own path, struck out due south for several hundred yards, and then continued west again.

Thomas's mind grappled with other issues as they ran. The wound he'd inflicted on Carlos's neck. He had been right: Knowledge and belief of the realities opened a link between them. Not a gateway, mind you—neither Carlos nor Johan had awakened as the other. Not that he knew of, anyway. But some kind of cause-and-effect relationship had been triggered between them. Those who believed in both realities saw the transferable effects in both realities. Blood, knowledge, skills.

You bleed in one; you bleed in the other.

Surely Monique would believe after seeing what had happened to Carlos. With Thomas's prompting, she would likely believe that she was connected to Rachelle. But was this a good thing?

And if he killed Johan, would Carlos die here? Perhaps.

Allowing Johan to live had been the right decision; he was sure of it. Now that he knew the link with Carlos, he would have to reconsider. But how could he kill Rachelle's brother?

And there was another matter that bothered him, something he was having difficulty placing. His memory had been clouded with these dreams, and he couldn't quite say why, but there was a problem with Justin of Southern.

The warrior had defeated him soundly and revealed his intentions of brokering a peace, while the Horde was plotting their final defeat. Mikil had sent out two groups of scouts, but none had yet reported any grave threat. Thomas had reinforced the Guard on each side of the forest, but otherwise he could do nothing except wait while Justin—

He pulled up.

Monique stopped. "What?"

"Nothing." He ran on.

But there was something. There were Qurong's words—the ones he'd overheard in the Horde camp. He could hear them now.

"I tell you, the brilliance of the plan is in its boldness," Qurong had said. "They may suspect, but with our forces at their doorstep, they will be forced to believe. We'll speak about peace and they will listen because they must. By the time we work the betrayal with him, it will be too late."

By the time we work the betrayal with *him*, it will be too late.

Who was "him"? When Thomas learned he hadn't killed Martyn— that the man Qurong had been speaking to *wasn't* Martyn—he'd assumed that "him" had to be Martyn. The thought had passed through his mind as Justin led Martyn from the amphitheater. It was partly why he had no intention of believing in any peace those two brokered. His Guard would be ready.

But what if "him" was Justin of Southern?

Of course! Who better to betray than a hero among the people, a mighty warrior who'd ridden like a king through the Valley of Tuhan and defeated the commander of the Guard in hand-to-hand combat?

It was a trap! Justin must have an alliance with Martyn already. He'd negotiated the Scabs' withdrawal from the Southern Forest. Then he'd ridden back to the main Horde camp with Martyn and arrived in time to save Thomas and his band in a show of good faith. The man atop the hill overlooking Thomas and his men had been *Martyn.*

It all made perfect sense! The battle at the Southern Forest, Qurong's words in the tent, Justin's saving Thomas in the desert, Justin's victory in the challenge, and now this unveiling of Martyn as Johan. Even the march through the Valley of Tuhan.

And it was all to this end. A trap. A betrayal.

What if the betrayal ended in the slaughter of their village? The death of the children? The death of Rachelle? Would Monique die? What if he was killed by the Horde? He was needed here.

Thomas would not be fooled by their betrayal. He would hold the line and refuse any peace offered by Johan and Justin. It would end in a terrible battle, perhaps, but—

Another thought struck him. What if he used this knowledge against the Horde? What if he created a reversal of his own, one that might avoid war altogether? His own peace on his own terms.

Thomas stopped again, heart pounding with an eagerness to dream again. He had to return and deal with Justin's betrayal!

Ahead, at the edge of a clearing, lay a small stone quarry. The lights of a farm cottage glowed several hundred miles down in the valley.

"What now?" Monique demanded, panting.

"It's almost dark. We don't know how far we have to go or where we're really going, for that matter. We have to stop for the night."

"What if he catches up to us?"

"I don't think Carlos will expect us to stop for the night—he'll go on to the city or he'll search the barns and the towns." He nodded at the farm lights ahead.

She looked around. "You want us to stop here?"

He jogged over to the quarry. The ground fell twenty feet, like a bowl. Several huge boulders lay at the bottom.

"We can lay down some branches or straw."

He thought she might protest. But after a moment she agreed. "Okay."

Ten minutes later they had covered the ground with grass and propped several large leafy branches against the largest rock to form a rough lean-to.

Thomas sat on a boulder near the lean-to, strung too tight to even think about sleep. But that was just it—he had to sleep now. He was desperate to sleep. To dream. To stop Justin before the betrayal could destroy both worlds.

"Thomas?"

He looked at Monique, who leaned on the boulder next to him.

"We'll be okay," he said.

"I think you're too optimistic."

"How can I not be optimistic? Three days ago I persuaded the president of the United States that my dreams were real, and he sent me on a fool's mission to find you. It cost some men their lives, but I *did* find you. Now we're free, on our way back to the world with information that will change history."

She looked away, clearly unconvinced. "We're in France. Unless I missed something back there, the people who're doing this have control over France. And you do understand that I have no evidence that the information I have will actually create the antivirus, don't you?"

"Svensson has the antivirus. We watched him inoculate himself."

"But I don't know if what he used is based on the information I gave him."

"Fortier all but said it was yours."

"Why did they keep me separate from the others?"

They sat in silence. Under other circumstances it might have been an uncomfortable silence, but now, on the eve of the world's destruction, with pretension long gone, it was only silence.

"So you really do believe all of this," Monique said.

She meant his dreams. "Yes."

"How is it possible?"

"You didn't have too much trouble believing that I got information from my dreams. That's information out of thin air. Why not more?"

"There's a far cry between dreaming up information and cutting someone's neck without touching him," she said.

"I was also shot dead in the hotel right in front of you."

She paused. "It goes against everything I've ever believed."

He shrugged. "Then you've believed in the wrong things. And if it's any consolation, so have I. When you live it like I have, it begins to feel quite real. Even natural. I'm not saying I understand. I'm not saying that I'm even meant to understand it."

She looked at the sky. "You think about God in all of this?"

"I don't have a good history with religion, despite my father being a chaplain. Maybe that's *because* my father was a chaplain. For the first couple weeks of these dreams, even though I had some incredible dreams of encountering God in the emerald lake, I kept it all in its own little box, reserved for the unexplained. There was the colored forest with its version of God, and there was this Earth, each in its own set of dreams. On this Earth God doesn't exist, I believed. I wasn't ready to think differently."

"And now?"

"Now the reality of Elyon is feeling very compelling again. In my dreams, I mean. For a long time after the Shataiki invaded the colored forest, battle was more real to me than Elyon. I've been commander of the Guard, fighting wars and spilling blood for fifteen years, and not once has anyone reported seeing a black bat or hearing a single word from Elyon. We call our religion the Great Romance, but really it feels more like a list of rules than anything similar to the Great Romance we once had. But now I think the knowledge of Elyon is starting to work its way into me again—in both realities. Make any sense? If Elyon's real there, surely God must be real here."

"It might explain your dreams," she said.

Another long silence.

"I'm still not ready to believe that I'm connected to a woman named Rachelle who is conveniently married to you," she said.

He sighed. "It may be best that you don't believe it. Because if you are connected to her, then anything that happens to Rachelle may also happen to you."

"You mean if Rachelle gets cut, I get cut? Like Carlos?"

"Rachelle has already experienced that very thing. We can't allow anything to happen to you."

"Because it will affect Rachelle as well."

Thomas sighed and leaned back against the boulder.

"Is Rachelle in danger of being killed?"

"As a matter of fact, yes. We all are."

"Then I suppose you'd better dream and save the world."

By her tone he knew that she was frustrated with these ideas of dreams, but he didn't have the energy to win her over now. He decided to give her one parting thought.

"I just may. But I think I'll have to go after Justin to do that."

She didn't ask who Justin was.

The moon was bright and the night cold when they finally agreed that they should sleep. The lean-to was meant to hide them from any prying eyes in the sky, and Thomas insisted they both sleep under the leafy branches.

Despite their initial attempts at modesty, they both accepted the fact that comfort and warmth were more important at the moment than forcing themselves into positions that would keep them up half the night. They lay shoulder to shoulder, arm to arm in the dark and began to drift off.

Thomas was almost asleep when he felt her hand rest on his. His eyes opened. At first he wondered if she was touching his hand in her sleep. He should ease his arm away.

But he couldn't. Not after what he'd put her through.

It took him another fifteen minutes to begin drifting again. They fell asleep like that, wrist to wrist.

———

Carlos covered the ground in a steady, fast walk. The moon was high enough to light his way, which made the going easier than during the first hour of darkness, before the moon rose.

He traveled alone because this issue of Thomas Hunter had become a very personal matter, and also because he knew he could deal with the problem without ever revealing the full truth of what had happened in the house.

In his hand he held a receiver that accepted a signal from the woman. They'd sewn the transmitter into her waistband a week earlier—no reason not to keep very close tabs on such a valuable asset. If and when she discarded the slacks, he would have a problem, but until she reached a town, she wouldn't have the opportunity. And based on their course, that wouldn't happen before morning.

They had stopped. Even at this pace he would reach them in a matter of hours.

He lifted his hand and touched his neck again. The blood had dried; the cut was hardly more than a scratch. But the manner in which he'd received it played heavily on his mind.

As did what Thomas had said about his own demise after his usefulness had expired. He'd considered the possibility that Fortier would simply dispose of him once the man had what he wanted—there were never guarantees with men like Fortier.

But Carlos wasn't a man without his own plans. This development with Hunter could actually play into his hands. For one, it gave him a perfect reason to kill Hunter once and for all. But it could also ensure his own value until he had the opportunity to take out both Svensson and Fortier. He would tell them that before dying Hunter had confessed something new from these histories of his, a major coup attempt immediately following the transition of power to Fortier. They would keep him alive at least long enough to head off the coup.

Hunter would make no such claim, of course, but there was some truth in the statement. There would be a coup attempt.

Muslims, not a godless Frenchman, would end up the winners in this war of Allah's.

Fortier wasn't the only man who knew how to think.

20

THOMAS GASPED in his sleep and was instantly awake. He jerked up.
Black. Silent.

He blinked and strained for sight. The walls slowly came into focus.
Monique was in the bed beside him, breathing steadily.

No, not Monique. Rachelle, who'd cried herself to sleep last night after
learning the truth about her brother, Johan.

An ache ran up his forearm and he felt his wrist. Bruised and cut.
Yes, of course—the handcuffs they'd placed on him were too tight and
had bit into his skin. There had been blood on his wrists. He had bled
here as well.

The events of both worlds crashed in on him. He'd escaped with
Monique and was sleeping under a boulder in the quarry, desperate to
dream so that he could come back here and deal with the betrayal.

He swung his feet out of bed, grabbed his boots and clothes, and
sneaked into the main room without waking Rachelle. Leaving her alone
without a word for the second time in a week struck him as possibly cruel.
Yet he didn't dare wake her and run the risk of her interfering with such a
perfect plan. What he had in mind had a ring of lunacy to it, and Rachelle
would undoubtedly hear that ring and call it out.

Mikil, on the other hand, would jump at the chance.

He dressed quickly, slung his sword over his shoulder, and slipped into
the cool morning air. The overcrowded village was still lost in deep dreams
of the day's unusual events and the evening's high-pitched celebrations.
They'd roasted a hundred goats along the shores of the lake as was the custom on the second night. The dances had gone late, and the talk of Justin
and Martyn had gone later.

The warrior from Southern was defended as vigorously by some as he was chastised by others. The idea of peace with the Horde, regardless of the circumstances, was offensive to most. Even Justin's supporters agreed on one thing: If the Horde did march on the forest, it would probably mean that Justin had betrayed them. But not to worry—their hero of the Southern Forest would never betray them. When he said he would broker peace, he had only true peace in mind.

Why Thomas hadn't realized earlier the truth of Qurong's words, he didn't know. Perhaps because his dreaming had confused his mind one too many times. Maybe because he was so taken aback by Martyn's true identity that he couldn't keep his thoughts objective. Either way, he was sure that if he told the counsel what the Horde leader had said in that tent, they would rally an army to head off Justin and Martyn's plan for "peace."

He found Mikil in deep sleep and woke her with a gentle shake. She bounded out of bed, sword in hand.

"It's me!" he whispered.

"Thomas?"

"Yes. Hurry, we have business."

"The scouts have reported in?" She rushed to the window and peered past the shutters.

"No. No word. Hurry."

"Then what?"

"I'll tell you on the way. Meet me at the stables."

He ran for the Guard stables at the edge of the village and was there when she caught up to him.

"Where are we going?"

"Shh, keep quiet. What would you say if I told you that Justin might have betrayal in mind?"

"I would say this is old news. You've learned something new?"

He opened the stable gate. "Saddle up. I'll explain when we're clear."

They walked their horses past the main village entrance, then mounted and rode into the forest.

"Tell me," she demanded, glancing back. "What is it?"

"I dreamed."

"That again. Fine. What did you dream?"

"I dreamed of what I overheard in Qurong's tent." He told her again, word for word, and explained his logic.

She kicked her horse, surged ahead, and then turned it back. "I knew it! He'll be the end of the forest! How many times did I warn you?"

She was right. His silence was confession enough.

"We have to stop this!" she said.

"Why do you think we're on horses before dawn? We ride to the eastern desert, where Qurong last camped. If I'm right, he will still be there, maybe even closer."

"What, you plan on the two of us taking on the whole army?"

"I think our scouts will find that Justin was right: The Horde has gathered in larger numbers than we've guessed. For all we know they have an army to the west, waiting until our preoccupation with the east bares our flank. That would be Martyn's kind of strategy."

"Then you're thinking of negotiation? That's the same plan Justin has! No, Thomas. No peace!"

"I'm thinking that Martyn will listen to another proposal. One that will turn the tables completely."

———⚬⚬⚬———

The sun was hot.

Monique opened her eyes. Sun?

Light streamed through shutters, exposing a thousand particles of lazily floating dust.

Where am I?

I am home.

Who am I?

You are Monique.

She pushed herself to her elbow and blinked. She wasn't entirely herself. Or she was *completely* herself. *Rachelle.*

She lifted her hand and moved her fingers. She was Monique, and she knew that she had to be dreaming while sleeping under the boulder next to Thomas, but she also knew that she was experiencing much more than just a dream. Amazing. This was how Thomas felt when he woke.

She'd dreamed of Thomas's other world because she was holding his hand while she slept? And she was dreaming as Rachelle because she believed that she was connected to Rachelle? It was about belief, Thomas had said. She was sharing Rachelle's life.

Does this mean it's all true? Everything Thomas said is true?

She knew the answer immediately, because as Rachelle she knew this reality was as real as France or Bangkok. What else did Rachelle know?

My husband's name is Thomas. And I have children.

She twisted to his side of the bed. "Thomas!"

But Thomas was gone. Of course, he always woke early. She knew that too. She knew that he was only home one out of every two days because he was the commander of the Guard, a mighty warrior and hero whose name was practically revered in all of the forests.

Her husband, a mighty warrior.

She knew that he had fought Justin yesterday and lost. And she knew that the Horde general, Martyn, was her own brother, Johan.

Rachelle swallowed and set her feet on the floor. This was how Thomas had first felt, waking up in the black forest fifteen years earlier. He'd tried to make her understand, but only now could she. Only he'd awakened without any memory because of his fall.

He'd fallen in the black forest and as a result began dreaming of the histories. This was the reality; that was the dream. She was sure of it. At least at this moment she was sure of it.

Her wrists hurt. The handcuffs. They'd drawn blood, and Thomas said that blood was special. They'd fallen asleep, hand in hand, her wrist touching his. It was why Monique was dreaming of Rachelle at this very moment. It was how she had dreamed of Monique before. She'd cut her shoulder on the door and it had bled in her sleep next to Thomas. A connection had been made in their blood.

Her children . . .

She threw off the blanket, donned a long-sleeved blouse to hide her wrists, and hurried from the room. She found Marie exactly where she expected to find her, digging through the fruit basket for a choice nectar.

"Hi, Mother." Her daughter yawned. "Papa's gone."

"Yes. Your brother's still sleeping?"

"That's all he does anymore."

"He's a growing boy."

She hurried to his room. Yes, indeed, there lay Samuel, arm hanging over the edge of his bed, lost to dreams of fighting the Horde with a sword as tall as he. She walked over and kissed the back of his head.

She was living a second life! In an instant she'd become a whole new person. She could smell Tuhan blossoms. Someone was cooking meat. Laughter drifted in from outside. Everything felt new. This was the time of the annual Gathering when the streets would be full of dancing and stories and the drinking of ale. And she was a magnificent dancer, wasn't she? Yes, of course she was. One of the best.

Her heart was having a hard time keeping up. She understood why Thomas was so persuaded. She had to find Thomas and tell him about this immediately!

Marie had found a large yellow nanka, and its juice ran down her chin.

"Don't be a pig, Marie. Wipe your chin." She looked at the living room. *Her* living room. Thomas's second sword, which normally leaned in the corner, was gone. Odd.

"Do you know where Papa went?" she asked Marie.

"No. He left early. Before the sun was up. I heard him."

Rachelle froze. His words to her in France echoed through her mind. *I'll have to go after Justin to do that,* he'd said.

After Justin?

He'd gone after Justin! Justin was with Martyn. They would be with the Horde. For the second time this week, he'd left her sleeping while he sneaked off on some harebrained mission that only a man as stubborn as Thomas could take beyond mere fantasy.

Justin and Martyn had gone east, according to the scouts. East toward Qurong's army.

She hurried to the bedroom and completed dressing. If Justin was with

Martyn, then he was also with Johan. Did Thomas mean that he was going after her brother?

What if he meant to kill Johan, thinking that in doing so he would kill Carlos? But he couldn't do that. Johan was her brother! They'd all lost family to the Horde fifteen years ago, when Tanis was deceived, but they dealt with it as part of a great tragedy. The thought of losing her own brother to her husband's sword now brought a small panic to her chest.

She had to stop him! And even if he hadn't gone to kill Johan, she had to tell him that she now knew. She was Rachelle. She was Monique! Without a doubt, they were connected.

She wrapped her wrists and managed to make the bandage look like bands with brass accents. The first major task was to get out of the village alone without casting suspicion on her intent. She couldn't walk too fast to Anna's, and when she asked the older mother if she would watch over Marie and Samuel for the day while she went out to gather a special treat for Thomas, she had to sound natural.

Andrew, who oversaw the common stables, would ask questions about why she was taking one of the stallions, but she'd simply tell him that she was in the mood for a wild ride. The Gathering inspired the women as well as the men.

Samuel had dragged himself from sleep by the time she returned with Anna's blessing. She hugged both children, told them to mind their Aunt Anna, and promised to be back by nightfall. If she wasn't back, not to worry, she and Papa had some preparations they had to attend to.

A full hour after waking, Rachelle left behind the last of the curious well-wishers who'd inquired where she was headed on such a magnificent animal. She led the horse through the gates, threw her leg over the saddle, and rode east.

The first hour seemed to last only minutes. With Monique everything felt new and fresh, as if experienced for the first time, which was the case in Monique's mind. The French woman had surely never imagined feeling so powerful, such an accomplished rider, so full of passion as Rachelle was now.

So invigorated was she in fact that she half hoped that one of the Horde would jump out from behind a tree so she could kick him back to where he belonged. Twice she very nearly dismounted to try a few flips. But her thoughts of finding Thomas kept her on the run.

One hour became two and then three and then five. The forest flew by and her mind flew with it. With each passing mile, her eagerness to find Thomas increased. She now knew that he had indeed come this way—his stallion's tracks, which she could read like her own palm, marked the mud at nearly every turn. He'd passed with Mikil. At least he had the sense to bring his best warrior.

She considered the potential danger ahead, but whatever danger her husband had submitted himself to wasn't too much for her. The fate of worlds was at hand, and she had her role to play.

She reached the edge of the forest late in the afternoon and pulled up. The sky and the desert were both blood red this time of day. She'd left the village about two hours after Thomas and had followed his tracks up to this point. If she rode hard, she might reach the place where—

Her heart suddenly rose into her throat. The Horde camp was there, on the horizon, just visible against the red sand. They'd moved closer.

Much closer.

Did they plan to attack? She felt immobilized by panic. The camp seemed larger than she remembered. Nearly double in size. This could only be a gathering for war! Thomas had gone down to them?

She studied his tracks. They went straight on and turned down the canyon. There were two well-traveled paths down to the desert, and Thomas had taken this one. He'd seen the Horde camp and continued. Then she would as well.

Rachelle prodded her horse.

The black stallion had taken only two steps when something struck her broadside.

She gasped and looked down. A stick protruded from her side. The shaft of an arrow. Pain screamed through her body.

Another arrow smacked into her shoulder, and a third into her thigh. She saw the Scabs near the tree line now, a party of five or six. They had bows! She didn't know—

The next arrow hit Rachelle in the back. She kicked the horse into a startled gallop. To her left! She had to get away from them!

There were arrows sticking from her body. Arrows! Panic crowded her mind.

The stallion plunged down a narrow path, over the canyon's lip.

Three more arrows whipped by her head and she ducked. The pain from the others rode up and down her back and leg in waves now.

"Hiyaa!" The path was steep and the horse slipped on the stones but caught itself and leaped over a boulder that suddenly blocked their way. Then around a bend.

Would the Scabs follow?

They were yelling above her now. Laughing.

She reached the sandy bottom and pointed the horse up the first narrow canyon to her right. Hoofs clacked along the stone high above. They were giving chase along the top of the canyon. She pulled the horse close to the left wall and leaned low, wincing with the pain. Terrible pain through her gut.

She was shot. Four arrows—two in her body, one in her leg, one in her arm. She had to hide and then find help.

Should she try to remove the arrows?

We're going to die.

No, no, she couldn't die! Rachelle couldn't die! Not now!

The horse slowed to a trot. Voices echoed, but they seemed to have fallen back. The rocky canyons were like a maze—it was no wonder they had opted to ride along the plateau. But if she worked her way further in, away from the walls near the forest, they would have a difficult time finding her.

Rachelle cut into a side wash, then through a small gap that fed into a long basin. The voices sounded distant now, but her mind wasn't as clear as it had been. Maybe she wasn't hearing as well. She gave the horse its head and examined the arrow in her leg. If she left it in, the movement of the horse might cause the tip to work its way farther in. If she pulled it out, it would bleed badly.

She moaned. The arrow in her side was worse. It had sunk in deep.

Through her internal organs. Even if she could extract it without passing out, she would risk terrible internal bleeding. She could feel the stalk of the one in her back.

It was horrible! She had ridden after her husband like a fool and now would die out here in the canyons, alone!

She didn't know how long she rode, or where the horse took her. Only that her strength steadily faded. The Scabs had lost her, but she didn't know if they were waiting along the edge for her to return, so she kept the horse walking.

You have to find help. You have to go back into the forest and hope for help. She stopped and looked around, but her vision was blurred, and she knew that she would never find the forest in this waning light.

In fact, if she was right, she was at the edge of the desert now, where the canyons gave way to miles of sand. How far had she traveled? If she just kept riding, she might find herself even farther from where she needed to go. And she couldn't keep riding with the arrows in her. The slightest movement shot spikes of pain along her leg and up her spine.

She had to rest. She had to get off the horse and lie down. But she was afraid that if she tried to dismount, she might faint.

"Elyon, help me," Rachelle whispered. "Dear God, don't let me die."

But she knew she would.

21

THOMAS AND Mikil sat across a reed table from Martyn in an open tent that some of the general's aides had erected for their leader after he'd agreed to talk to Thomas. The stench of Scab was almost too much to bear.

The fact that the Horde had nearly doubled in size and moved closer to the forest was an ominous sign, all the more reason for Thomas to approach Martyn.

They'd ridden in waving a white flag—Thomas's idea. No one had ever used a white flag, to his recollection, but the sign was understood quickly enough, and the camp's perimeter guard had held them off at a hundred paces while they checked with their leaders. Another general had finally come out, heard that Thomas of Hunter requested an audience with Martyn, and relayed the question.

"Tell Martyn that Thomas of Hunter requests a meeting with Johan," Thomas said to the general.

"You mean Justin of Southern?"

"No, not with Justin. With Johan. That is the name I know him by. Johan."

Half an hour later they had their meeting.

Johan was clearly there under his stinking, flaking skin. Older now, late twenties. Paint his eyes green and his skin flesh-colored, and no one who'd known the boy could possibly mistake him. The round circle of the druids was shaded on his forehead.

But he moved and spoke like a completely different man. His eyes shifted warily and he kept his movements short to minimize the pain from his disease. Like all of the Horde, he didn't think of the rot as a disease. His mind was sharp, but he'd been swallowed by lies that had long ago

persuaded him that this was the way all good men should look and move
and feel. Pain was natural. The smell of rotting flesh was more a scent of
wholesome humanity than a stench.

Johan looked down at Thomas and wrinkled his nose. "The lakes do
that to you?"

"Do what?"

"Give you that terrible smell."

"I suppose so. And your skin is no less offensive to us. You hated the
smell yourself, three years ago. Where's Justin?"

Johan hesitated. "He left an hour ago."

"Will he be back?"

"Yes."

"Will you agree to peace with him?"

"That is clearly his intent."

"Is it yours?"

"You tell me; is it?"

The man was talking in riddles. He needed to speak with Johan
candidly.

"What I have to say is for your ears only," he said. "Send your men
away and I will send my lieutenant away."

"Sir—"

He held up his hand to Mikil. She wouldn't question him further in
public.

"Surely you don't fear me," Thomas said. "You're my wife's brother."

"Leave," Johan said to the four warriors behind him.

They hesitated, then backed out. Thomas looked at Mikil who glared
disapprovingly, then left. Both parties walked off about fifty paces in opposite directions, then stopped to watch from the open desert.

"Johan," Thomas said. "You don't remember your real name, do you?"

"You mean the name I had as a child. Every boy grows up. Or are all
Forest People still children?"

"Is there any of Johan left in you?"

"Only the man."

"And why is it that one of my soldiers can kill five of yours?"

Johan's eye twitched. "Because my men are only just now learning to fight you. I know your ways. Our skills will soon surpass yours."

"You are teaching them new tricks, aren't you? But think back, Johan. Before you lost your way in the desert. You were much stronger than you are now. The skin condition, it's a disease."

The man just held his gaze.

"How did you get lost?"

"Is this why you called me out? To talk about a time when we played with toy swords?"

Johan's mind was as scaled as his flesh, Thomas thought. He wondered if Rachelle could break through his deception.

"No. I've come because I know more than I should." He had to be careful. "I overheard a discussion in your leader's tent several nights ago when I killed the general. I hope you won't hold his death against me."

"The general you killed was a good friend of mine."

"Then please accept my condolences. Either way, I now know that you're conspiring with Justin and Qurong against the Forest People. You will offer them peace, and in the face of overwhelming odds, you think Justin will persuade our people to accept your offer. But you intend to betray us once you have won our trust."

Thomas let the statement stand. Johan made no comment. It was impossible to read his face, shrouded by the dark hood and scaled as it was.

"I'm curious, what will Justin receive for his betrayal?"

"That's none of your concern."

"How long have you been planning this?"

"Long enough."

"I should have known. You're both originally from our forest. First you go missing three years ago, and then you conveniently show up as a general who knows our ways. A year later Justin refuses my appointment and begins to preach his peace. All the while you two are plotting the overthrow of the forest. For all I know you hatched the plan with Justin in the Southern Forest and then chose the life of a Scab. He's been seeding doubt while you've been building your army to take advantage of that doubt. Was it his idea or yours? Will you make Justin supreme leader of the Horde?"

Johan—Martyn, the druid general—stared at him for a long time. But he refused to answer.

"Still, you must be worried about the toll a battle in the forest would have on your army or you'd just march on us now, without any attempt at betrayal," Thomas said. "Betrayal is your equalizer. You hope to catch us with our guard down."

"Is that right? Well, if you know this, our plan is foiled."

Such a quick admission? But Johan didn't have the tone of a defeated man.

"Not necessarily. We each have a problem. Mine is Justin; yours is Qurong. I think that Justin may have enough power to compromise our will for battle."

Johan hesitated. "A surprisingly candid admission."

"I'm not here to play games. Even with your betrayal, the battle would be fierce. Many of your men would die. Most."

"A possibility. And what is my problem?"

"Your problem is Qurong. He will fight this battle even knowing his betrayal has been compromised. In the end, the forest will be red with blood and you will have few people left to govern."

"Isn't that the way it is? War?"

"No." Thomas lowered his voice. It had taken Mikil most of the ride through the forest to embrace the wisdom of what he was about to propose.

"There can never be a true peace between our people; neither of us can accept it. But there can be a truce." He tapped his finger on the table. "Now."

"As Justin has proposed. A truce."

"He's proposed a peace that will end in more bloodshed than anyone can imagine, most of it Horde blood. The only way I see out of this quagmire is for the brother of my wife, Johan, to lead the Horde instead of Qurong. You may have become a man, but will you kill your own sister?"

"I could have you killed for such words," Johan said. He glanced at his men. Clearly he wasn't excited about the mention of treason against his leader.

"You're suggesting a revolt against Qurong, the man who is my father."

"He's not your father."

"His name was Tanis, and I've always seen him as my father."

Tanis. *Tanis?* The firstborn of all men. A father figure to the people of the colored forest. Qurong was Tanis! Thomas felt his chest constrict. He took this in with alarm, though he hoped none showed.

"If you think your armies can survive the explosives we have for them, you're sadly mistaken. Surely you heard about the fate of your Scabs in the canyons. If it's more death you want, tell Qurong to march now, tonight! But I can promise you, for every one of my Guard you kill, our gunpowder will rip the head off a hundred of yours."

It was all a bluff; they had no explosives. But by Johan's slight reaction, Thomas thought it had at least created some confusion.

He continued quickly. "I will ensure your safe passage into the forest with Qurong and Justin. Bring a thousand of your best warriors if you like. Before the people, you will expose the betrayal of Justin and Qurong, and I will swear that what you say is the truth. We will condemn Qurong to death. You will step into the vacancy."

Slowly a smile nudged Johan's mouth. "You are the son of the Shataiki, aren't you?"

"That would be Qurong, the firstborn who brought this sickness upon us in the first place."

"And Justin?"

Thomas shrugged. "He will be discredited. Banished."

"I may kill him?"

The question struck Thomas as strange. "Why?"

"His loyalty to Qurong would be a problem for me."

Thomas hesitated. "Do what you must."

"You think I'm foolish enough to walk into a trap with only a thousand of my men at my side? Qurong will never agree to this."

"He will if I agree to stay here as a guarantee of his safety." It was the most troublesome element of the plan for Mikil. But Thomas had convinced her that the world was at stake. Without some kind of compromise, there would be a bloodbath. Qurong would attack. The forest would be burned. They might kill most of the Horde army, but in the end they wouldn't have their wives or children to justify such a terrible victory.

"Your plan is treasonous," Johan finally said. "I'm not a man who will entertain treason."

"My plan will save your people. And mine. I am the husband of your sister. I beg you, consider your heritage and help me build a truce. With Qurong there is only war. Teeleh has bound him hand and heart. I believe that in your heart there is still room for Rachelle and your own people."

Johan looked at him and finally stood. "Wait here." He walked out into the desert and faced the distant dunes. For a long time he stood with his back to Thomas. Then he walked slowly back into camp.

Mikil ran into the tent. "Well?"

"I don't know."

"Is he considering it?"

"I think."

"I still don't like it. What's to keep a stray soldier with a sickle from taking off your head?"

"I will insist on protection. The last time I checked, I could handle a stray maniac with a single sickle. Besides, you'll have Qurong at the tip of your sword."

She nodded thoughtfully. "Then they don't take you into custody until Qurong is in the forest, under our Guard's watch."

"Of course. Here he comes."

She retreated, eying the approaching general with skepticism.

Johan swept his robe aside and sat down. "I don't care what you say; you are a son of the Shataiki," he said. "But I like your plan. My conditions are as follows: As a sign of good faith, you will not only stay, as you have offered, but you will pull the army on your perimeter back to the center of the forest. I don't want you waging war while I am inside."

Thomas considered the request. Qurong would be their guarantee. As long as Mikil had their leader, they would never attack.

"Agreed."

"My other condition is that you allow me to conduct Qurong's execution as a show of my new authority over my people. It is a language they will understand."

"Understood."

Martyn, general of the Horde whose name was once Johan, dipped his head. "Then we have an agreement."

———∞———

They spent another half hour refining details before Thomas and his lone aide mounted and rode away from the camp. His second—Mikil, she was called—would leave for the forest tonight after dark. Qurong, Martyn, Justin, and a thousand warriors would follow the next morning. They would enter the forest in exchange for Thomas, who would then be taken into custody by the Horde army.

Qurong and Thomas would entrust their lives to each other.

The entourage would arrive at the lake in the evening with full assurance that Mikil had set the stage. If she hadn't done so satisfactorily, Qurong and Martyn would retreat. If they were ambushed by the Guard, Thomas would also die. And of course, vice versa.

So it was planned. So it was agreed.

Martyn stared toward the west, where he could just see the distant forest in the twilight. Qurong stood beside him, frowning.

"So they suspect nothing?"

"Nothing. He honestly thinks I would betray you. They are children, as I once was."

"And Justin will agree?"

"Justin will agree. He knows what he's doing."

Qurong grunted and turned back to the camp. "As will they all, soon enough."

22

DARKNESS SWALLOWED the desert. The moon rose and cast an eerie glow over the rising dunes. How many hours had passed? The sun would surely rise soon—she had to hang on until then. That's what Rachelle kept telling herself. If she could just make it to morning, the light would bring new hope.

But now a new problem presented itself: She hadn't bathed for a full day and a half, since the night of the celebration, and her skin was beginning to burn. The pain beneath her skin was now nearly as bad as the dull ache of her wounds.

She lay on one side, feeling the disease slowly eat at her skin, afraid to close her eyes, afraid sleep would take her life, afraid someone might find her and kill her, afraid that she might never see Thomas or Samuel or Marie again. How would they cope without a loving wife and a knowing mother?

They would be lost without her. She didn't think of herself in any inflated way; it was simply a fact. Thomas needed her like he needed water. Samuel and Marie had friends who'd lost their fathers to war, but not their mothers.

She'd managed to crawl off her horse without losing consciousness. The stallion waited patiently, twenty paces away. She wasn't sure whether she wished it would go and find help, or stay in case she needed it to ride out, although she couldn't imagine either actually happening.

She faded in and out of a semblance of sleep. Oddly enough, she was quite sure that she was still asleep under the lean-to with Thomas in France. Perhaps this was all a dream. Was she bleeding from her leg and side there?

So much that she didn't understand.

The hours dragged on. No crickets here. No forest sounds. The silence of the desert was its own sound. It was cold, but that was good because it kept her from slipping into unconsciousness. She had to concentrate to keep from shivering, because shivering sent waves of pain through her back. Maybe she had a fever, because she couldn't remember it ever being—

Was that light? Rachelle stared at the barely graying horizon.

Already! The dawn was coming. She'd made it! Filled with an irrational hope, she moved her arm to sit up. Sharp pain sliced through her belly.

She closed her eyes and winced. Her whole body was going stiff. She couldn't get to her feet, much less to the horse. And when the sun was finished welcoming her to the land of the living, it would only burn her to a crisp. Hope fell to the pit of her stomach like a lead weight.

Her heart plodded on, but it felt slower now. Hardly like a heart at all. Like a horse walking through sand. A *shooshing* sound more than a thudding heart sound. For a moment she imagined herself on a horse, plodding out to the desert. She was hallucinating.

Rachelle cracked her eyes. Saw the horse. Plod, plod, *shoosh, shoosh.* Right toward her as if it were real and the means for her delivery.

That is a real horse, Rachelle.

Now she did hear her heart, and it was bolting in her chest. There, not twenty paces away, stood a pale horse. Its rider was throwing his leg over the saddle to dismount.

This was a Forest Dweller!

She jerked up. Pain filled her eyes with black specks, but she held on. "Hel . . . hello?"

"It's okay," the voice said. "Hold on!"

He—yes, it was a he—was hurrying to her. Thomas?

Her vision cleared and she saw him plainly for the first time. This was Justin of Southern!

Her strength gave way and she sank back down. Tears flooded her eyes, but they weren't from the pain.

Justin ran the last few steps and knelt by her side. His hand gently touched her forehead. "Just relax. Breathe. I'm so sorry, my dear. I came to find you as soon as I heard what the patrol had done, but it took me all night to follow your tracks through the canyons. You're a fighter, no doubt about that."

She didn't know what to say. She wasn't sure she even had the strength to speak intelligently. This was Justin. She wasn't even sure what to *think* about that. Tears were leaking down her cheeks, blurring her vision.

"Shh, shh. It's okay, Rachelle. I promise you it will be okay."

He knew her from when he was under Thomas's command. His hand touched the arrows, each one, as if he was checking to see whether they were too deep to pull.

"I'm dying," she stammered.

"No, I won't let you. But you're turning." He glanced over his shoulder. "Are you carrying water on your horse?"

She glanced at the skin on her arm. Gray. He must not be carrying any, or he'd have retrieved his own.

"Some," she said.

"Where is your horse?"

She looked past him. The horse had gone off?

It was suddenly all too much. There was no way. Even now, having been found, she knew that she could never survive the injuries she'd sustained. And the lake was too far. Her life was seeping from her by the moment.

She closed her eyes and let herself go. Sobs wracked her body. Not sorrow for herself, but for her children and for Thomas.

"Why are you crying?" he asked.

She sniffed and swallowed deep. She would die with her head high, not blubbering like a baby.

"Hear me, my child. I will not let you die today."

He was trying to console her, but she was lying here with arrows protruding from infected wounds, barely clinging to life; his words rang empty. Did he think she was a child to build her hopes on such empty words of promise?

"Don't lie to me," she said.

"No, I would never—"

"Don't lie to me!" she shouted. "I'm dying! And I'm dying because of *you.* He came out here because of your obsession with this impossible peace!" The words came out in a rush that left her breathless. Justin deserved no such tirade, and her anger was really directed at her circumstance more than him, but she didn't care. This was the man who'd defeated her husband in the inquiry. And, at least in part, she was dying now because of it!

Justin stood. Then stepped back. He stared at her, eyes round. She'd hurt him, surprised him. But she was too far gone with pain and dread over her own predicament to care. She rolled her head away from him and cried.

For a long time she stayed like that, and for a long time she didn't know what he was doing. A minute passed. Two. It occurred to her that he might have left. The thought terrified her.

She jerked her head around and looked for him.

He was gone!

But what was this? Someone else was there. A small boy was pacing in front of a large boulder twenty feet away. The boy was crying. His arms hung limp by his side and he was naked except for a loincloth.

Samuel? No, it wasn't Samuel. The sickness was taking her mind. The boy was weeping, beside himself. Sympathy spiked through her heart. But she knew this had to be a figment of her imagination. Yet the boy looked so real. His cries sounded terribly real.

The boy!

This was the boy!

She closed her eyes, opened them. The graying sky was blurry, and she blinked rapidly to clear her vision. The boy was gone.

Justin stood not ten feet away, with his back to her, hands on hips, head hung. Was this also a hallucination? She blinked again. No, this was Justin. But what she'd seen had unnerved her to the core. An image of Justin sweeping the little girl off her feet in the Valley of Tuhan ran through her mind.

The warrior lifted his head and stared at the cliffs. This was the man who had defeated Thomas in battle. Who seemed to be able to have his will with any opponent. It was no wonder that the women and children and fighters from the Southern Forest were so taken with Justin. He was an enigma.

And she'd yelled at him.

But why wasn't he helping her? "I'm sorry," she said. "But I'm going to die here. Please allow a dying woman her liberties."

"You're not going to die," he said softly. "I have too much riding on you to let you die."

She'd heard that before. Where had she heard that?

He faced her. "You think a few arrows and some torn flesh have much to do with death? I will take your pain away, Rachelle, but it is your heart that worries me."

"How can you take away my pain? My skin is gray and there are still arrows in my body. I'm dying and you're just standing there!"

"You're as stubborn as Thomas. Maybe more. And your memory is no better than his either."

He was talking nonsense. A shot of pain traveled through her bones, and she grimaced.

"I want you to listen to me very carefully, Rachelle." He knelt on one knee and clasped her hand in his. He was making no attempt to help her or tend to her wounds. He knew as well as she that there was nothing either of them could do.

"We have brokered a peace between the Desert Dwellers and the Forest People. Qurong will go with Johan and me to the village, where we will offer our terms for peace."

The Council would never accept any terms for peace; didn't Justin know that?

"Thomas will stay in the Desert Dweller's camp as a guarantee for safe passage. Mikil is with Qurong to ensure Thomas's safety. When the Council understands that a second army, twice the size of the one to the east, is camped on the other side of the forest, they will agree to peace. What happens then must happen for the boy. Do you understand? Because of the boy's promise."

"Thomas is in the Horde camp? They'll *kill* him!"

"Mikil will have Qurong and Johan in trade. It must happen this way. No matter what happens, remember that. No matter how terrible or at what cost." He paused. Then he put his other hand on her head, leaned over, and kissed her forehead. "When the time comes, remember these words and follow me. It will be a better way. Die with me. It will bring you life."

Rachelle closed her eyes. She wanted to scream. Her heart felt like it might break free from her chest, and she understood none of it. Not what he said nor her own emotions. "I don't want to die."

"Find Thomas. Your death will save him."

"I can't die!" she cried.

"They're waiting for me." Justin stood. "I must go." He strode to his horse and swung into the saddle. The steed snorted and stamped.

He was leaving her?

"I don't understand," she cried. "Don't leave me!"

"I have never left you. Never!" His eyes flashed with anger, then filled with tears. "We will be together soon and you will understand." He spurred his horse and the stallion galloped into the canyon.

She was too stunned to speak. He was leaving her?

"Remember me, Rachelle! Remember my water."

"Justin!" she screamed.

"Remember me!"

This time his voice echoed long as he pounded down the canyon. The echo of his last word, *me*, seemed to dip into laughter. A child's laughter.

A giggle. A boy's giggle that bubbled like a brook.

She caught her breath. She'd heard that sound before!

The laughter suddenly grew, as if it had taken a turn at the end of the canyon and decided to rush back toward her. Louder and louder, until it seemed to swallow her whole.

Something unseen hit her hard. She gasped. Her whole body jumped off the ground and then arched. She shook in the air for several seconds, then dropped hard back to the sand.

The sound of giggling was sucked back into the canyon, leaving only silence in its wake.

Rachelle sucked in a lungful of air and trembled. But it wasn't from fear. It wasn't from pain. It was from a strange power that lingered in her bones.

Her world momentarily faded.

Then with a flash it returned. What had . . . what had happened?

Monique was gone, for one thing. She'd probably woken.

Rachelle jerked up. No pain. She stared at her side, shocked. Where an arrow had protruded just moments ago, there was only a bloody hole in her tunic. She pulled the garment up and examined her flesh. Blood, but only blood. No wound.

And her skin had lost its gray pallor.

She scrambled to her feet and frantically grasped at the bloody spots. Not a single wound. In fact, she felt as refreshed and whole as if she'd slept the night in perfect peace. She lifted her head up and stared at the canyon.

Remember me.

A chill washed over her skull. They were the words that the boy had spoken to her so long ago before he'd run down the bank and disappeared into the lake. *Just remember me, Rachelle,* he'd said.

I have a lot riding on you.

She couldn't breathe. It was him! Justin was the boy! Only he wasn't a lamb or a lion or a boy now. He was a warrior and his name was Justin! How could she have missed it?

"Justin!" Her call came out like a squeak. She ran. She tore over the sand, desperate to catch him.

"Justin!" This time her cry echoed up the canyon. But he was gone.

Justin was the boy, and the boy was Elyon. Elyon had just touched her. Kissed her forehead! If she had known—

She groaned past a terrible ache that had filled her throat.

"Elyonnnn!"

She fell to her knees. Sobs wracked her body. Panic. Waves of heat that flushed her face. But there was nothing she could do. He'd been within a foot of her and she hadn't fallen to her knees to kiss his feet. She hadn't clung to his hand in desperation.

She'd yelled at him!

She gripped her head and cried long, silent wails that washed away her sense of time. Then slowly she began to come back to herself.

The boy had come back to them. She sniffed and struggled to her feet. Dawn had lightened the sky.

Their Creator had come back to them, and he was going to make peace with the Horde. It was the day of deliverance!

Find Thomas, Justin had said.

She spun and faced the sand dunes. She'd seen the camp to the east. Thomas was being held in the camp. It couldn't be more than a few hours away, even by foot.

She grabbed her tunic and ran into the desert, only briefly thinking about his other words. Your death will save him, Justin had said. But it meant nothing.

She was alive. Elyon had healed her.

23

THOMAS GAZED at the eastern horizon, where the sun was just now rising over the dunes. The lieutenant of the perimeter guard, Stephen, stood beside Thomas, holding the reins of his horse. Behind them, three hundred Forest Guard waited along the tree line. Ahead of them, the contingent from the Horde waited on their horses to make the exchange as agreed. Johan, Qurong, Justin. And behind them, a thousand Scab warriors.

They were about to make history in the desert. Odd to think that at this very moment he was doing nothing more spectacular in the other reality than sleeping next to Monique under a boulder in France, dreaming.

"I don't like it, sir," the lieutenant said. "You're just going to let them take you in shackles?"

"Not 'just,' Stephen. As long as you have Qurong and Martyn, I'm safe."

Thomas and Mikil had spent three hours covering every possible contingency before Mikil headed off to prepare the Guard and the Council for Qurong and Martyn's arrival as agreed. Only Mikil, Thomas, the Council, and Johan knew the truth of what was to happen.

Thomas had spent a fitful night waiting for daybreak. Not a wink of sleep. Despite his tone of confidence with Stephen, he was nervous.

"They have a thousand warriors; you have no one," the man said.

"Are you telling me you and your men can't deal with a thousand warriors in the forest, where they will be lost?"

"No, I'm not saying that. It just strikes me as disproportionate."

"I'm willing to take that chance. Remember, this is a mission of peace. Unless you hear differently from myself or Mikil, no harm to them."

"So Justin has done what he promised," the man said. "He's broker-ing peace and you're in agreement."

"Justin is brokering peace. For the moment I am in agreement."

"The Council will never accept."

"They will. You will see; they will."

Thomas left his lieutenant's side and walked toward the waiting con-tingent. The truth, of course, was that instead of brokering their peace in front of the Council, Johan would accuse Qurong of plotting betrayal with Justin. He would tell the congregation that Qurong and Justin were planning to ransack the forest as soon as the Guard had accepted peace. Mikil would step forward and tell the people that on her word, Thomas of Hunter concurred. Qurong would then be convicted and executed, and Justin's fate would be left up to the new leader of the Horde, Johan.

That was the plan. Thomas and Mikil had considered it a dozen times and agreed it would work. It would spare the forest a terrible battle. Just as importantly, they weren't conspiring with the Horde, which would be trea-son. No, they were conspiring against the Horde leader, Qurong, by using Johan—a Scab, yes, but also Johan. Enough of a technicality to assure the Council's approval, surely.

Gravel crunched under Thomas's feet as he walked. He was the only one not on a horse and armed. For all practical purposes, he was naked.

He reached the midpoint between the two small armies when Justin suddenly dismounted and walked out to meet him. There had been no mention of this, but Johan and Qurong didn't object, and so neither did Thomas.

Justin met him halfway. "Good morning, my brother." The warrior dipped his head.

"Good morning." Thomas returned his gesture.

For a moment they just looked at each other.

"So," Justin said, "it's come down to this after all."

"I guess it has. It's what you wanted, isn't it? Peace?"

"I told them that you would come."

The revelation caught Thomas off guard. "I'm not sure I understand."

"I knew it when I looked in your eyes at the challenge. You don't understand what's happening, but you want peace. You've always wanted peace. And this is the only way for peace, Thomas."

"How did you know that I would come?"

"You taught me to judge my enemy well. Call it a lucky guess." His eyes twinkled. "Johan refused to believe that you would offer yourself as a guarantee for Qurong's safety, but when I saw you ride in yesterday with Mikil, I knew we had won."

Justin had told Johan that he was going to offer an exchange? Johan had known? The general had smiled at the suggestion—perhaps because of Justin's accuracy in predicting it.

But Justin couldn't know the whole truth.

Thomas felt a pang of remorse for his offering up the man in exchange for Qurong's death. But it was the only way.

"Then you're a better tactician than I am," Thomas said, glancing at the Scabs. "If you know so much, tell me this: Will I be safe in their shackles?"

Justin hesitated. "Let's just say that I think you'll be safer in their shackles than I will be in the hands of my own Council."

He stretched out his hand. Thomas took it, and Justin bent to kiss his fingers. "Take courage, Thomas. We are almost home. I'll see you in the lake."

Then Justin turned and walked back to his line.

Thomas hesitated, wondering at this latest exchange. But the die had been cast. He walked to the boulder they'd agreed on and stood tall. Justin remounted and led the Horde contingent forward. As soon as Qurong was within slaying reach of the Forest Guard, a dozen Scabs rushed Thomas and fixed shackles on his wrists.

The Horde army vanished into the trees and Thomas was led away on a horse, hopelessly shackled.

24

MONIQUE BOLTED up, wide awake. Twigs hung in her face. She was in the forest? She'd been wounded by the Desert Dwellers and then Justin had healed her!

No. She was in France. Sleeping beside Thomas. It had been a dream.

A dream! She closed her mouth and swallowed, but her throat was parched and tacky. Beside her, Thomas slept soundly, chest rising and falling. Her hand was in his. She pulled it free and wiped the sweat from her face.

She'd dreamed that she was Rachelle, and yet she knew that it was more than a dream, because she knew that as Rachelle she'd dreamed of being Monique.

Monique stared past the leaves that made up the lean-to, stunned by this change in her perception of reality. She had shared Rachelle's life.

Her bladder was burning. Was it this that had awakened her or the trauma of her dream? Either way, she had to relieve herself. And when she returned, she would wake Thomas and tell him what had happened.

Monique slipped out of the lean-to as quietly as possible and stood. It was only then that she felt the damp spots on her leg. She looked down and saw that her clothes were wet.

Blood! She gasped involuntarily.

The arrows! She touched then pushed on the spots. No pain, no wounds. The dark splotches spread out from where the arrows had struck her. The bleeding hadn't been terrible because the arrows had stopped up the wounds.

Monique felt tremors overtake her body. It had really happened. This was beyond her. She swallowed and headed, weak-kneed, for the trees just beyond the quarry.

The moon had fallen into the horizon when Carlos stopped near the edge of the clearing and took stock of his situation. Through the trees, maybe three hundred meters down the valley, a farmhouse stood in darkness. He was approximately halfway between Melun and Paris, headed west toward the capital. It was midnight.

Thomas and Monique were somewhere within a hundred meters of him, to the southeast, according to the small screen in his palm. He studied the clearing ahead, careful not to expose himself beyond the tree line.

The quarry. Yes, of course, it would be a natural place to stop. Seventy paces ahead and to his left. They were in the quarry. Unless the woman had discovered the tracking device and discarded the transmitter.

Carlos slipped the receiver into his pocket and worked around the perimeter of the clearing, toward the quarry.

He heard a rustle and froze by a large pine. A rabbit?

The quarry lay just ahead, a depression in the ground that was partially overgrown with stubborn tufts of grass.

Carlos withdrew his pistol and chambered a round. He now wished he'd thought to bring the silencer—a gunshot might disturb whoever lived in the farmhouse, although the lay of the quarry would absorb much of the sound.

He stepped around the tree, crouched down, and walked toward the edge of the depression. Gravel scattered, knocked by his boot, and he stopped. He let the sound clear and then eased slowly forward.

The moment he saw the branches set against the boulder, he knew that he had found them. It would be different this time. He would either kill or be killed, and he was certain it would be the former.

Monique was standing by a log, ten meters into the forest, but her mind was still in another forest, in another world altogether.

Monique closed her eyes and clenched her jaw to clear her thoughts. *Reality, Monique. Back to reality.*

But that was the problem—the other *was* reality. The smells, the memories, the sights, the feelings in her heart. All of it!

She pulled the pale blue slacks completely off and hung them from a dead branch that jutted up from the fallen trunk. She could barely see by the starlight, and she didn't want her only clothes to end up with leaves or, worse, bugs in them.

She stood by the log dressed only in her muddied tennis shoes and a cotton blouse, which hung loosely past her underwear. She wouldn't remove her shoes, not with critters under the leaves.

The sound of skittering gravel reached her ears. She froze.

But it was nothing.

He could hear their breathing. Carlos crouched by the edge of the quarry and peered at the dark shadow beneath the branches they'd leaned against the boulder. On the left end, Hunter's boots. He would slip around to the right and put the first two bullets into Hunter's head before turning the gun on the woman. It would have to be quick. Best for both to die in their sleep.

They had what they needed from Monique. Fortier and Svensson might question the events, but they wouldn't second-guess his decision to kill them, despite their desire to keep her alive. They had chosen him for his ability to make such determinations, and they knew enough to leave security in his hands. If Carlos decided that Hunter had to die, then Hunter would die. End of issue. There was too much at stake to quibble over his judgment now. Killing them would ensure that what they knew would never leave France.

Carlos moved slowly, crouching to minimize his profile against the forest behind. Tumbling rocks were his primary concern. Stones clicked softly under his feet, but not enough to wake the average man.

Then again, Hunter wasn't the average man. But he was unarmed, and he was with a woman he would undoubtedly want to protect.

The moment the ground leveled, Carlos rushed in on the balls of his feet. Four long steps, quick pivot. The wedge of darkness beneath the branches opened up to him. He dropped to one knee, extended the nine millimeter's barrel to the head of the man he recognized as Thomas Hunter, and pulled the trigger.

Thunder crashed in his ears.

The body jerked.

There was no second body.

The revelation that the woman wasn't here stopped him short of pulling the trigger a second time. If not here, then where?

He quickly felt Hunter's neck for a pulse, found none, and ran around the boulder, gun still extended. Nothing. He rounded another boulder, but with each step his hope of finding her faded. She wasn't here.

He ran back to where Hunter lay and noted the ground beside his body. Small indentations in the earth confirmed that another body had rested here. No sign of the slacks with the tracking device. He felt for Hunter's pulse one last time, and satisfied that the man was very much dead, he stood and scanned the forest.

She had been here less than five minutes ago. He pulled out the receiver and turned it on. It took only a few seconds to acquire the signal. Directly ahead in the forest. Close. Very close.

Carlos began to run.

⸺⊗⊗⊗�⸺

The odor of sulfur hung low and thick over the Scab camp. It had taken them an hour to reach the huge army, and the sun was already hot on their backs. Twenty warriors rode on either side of Thomas as they approached the same spot where he'd negotiated his treachery with Johan less than twenty-four hours ago.

He'd bathed from a canteen last night, and he was now allowed one additional canteen, which now hung from his belt. He wouldn't drink it, but he would bathe if the meeting at the Council kept him more than a day. Justin would arrive in the evening. The Council would hear the matter, and the reversal would end in Qurong's death. By morning, Johan would be exchanged for Thomas at the forest perimeter. But if there was any delay, he might need the water.

In the meantime, he was consigned to spend the rest of the day and the night in this cursed—

Something hit his head.

He jerked upright and twisted in his saddle. Nothing. But his head was ringing as if a mallet had struck it. Pain spread down his spine. He began to lose focus.

He knew then that something had happened in the other reality. Carlos had found them. He'd been shot. In the head!

Thomas's world suddenly began to spin and darken. He felt himself falling from the horse. Heard his body thud into the ground.

His last thought was that his assumption had been right. If he died in one reality, he also died in the other.

Then everything went black.

⸺∞⸺

Monique had her thumbs hooked in her underwear when the still night exploded with a terrible *boom.*

She instinctively jerked. Behind her! A gunshot in the quarry! She spun, thumbs still hooked, heart pounding.

The trees blocked most of her view, but she peered under a branch by her head and saw in one horrifying moment what had happened. A dark figure stood up by the lean-to, then ran around the boulder, gun in hand.

Carlos! It had to be Carlos! He'd followed them. And he'd just shot . . .

Monique lifted her hand to her mouth and stifled a cry. Thomas!

She nearly ran for him, but she immediately knew that she couldn't— not with Carlos so close. He'd fired point-blank! No one could have survived that.

Monique stood frozen by horror. How could his life end like this? Would he come back? No, he'd told her that his dreams could no longer heal him! Or was that something she'd learned from her own dream? They were terrified that Thomas might be killed here, because they were sure it would mean that he would also die there.

Carlos ran back around the boulder, dropped to his knees, and was checking Thomas's pulse. This confirmed it. Thomas was dead.

Monique fought a nauseating wave of panic. She had to get away! Carlos had already searched the quarry for her . . . he'd assume she'd gone into the trees . . .

She ran then, on her toes, through the forest toward the distant farmhouse. The leaves crinkled under her feet. Too loud! She slid to a stop, turned to the quarry, saw that Carlos was still leaning into the shelter. He hadn't heard her.

She moved quickly, but as quietly as possible now.

Her slacks! No, no time to go back.

Monique was halfway around the quarry when she glimpsed Carlos through the limbs, running toward the section of forest she had occupied only a minute earlier. Had he seen her?

Run! Run, Monique, straight across the quarry, across the meadow to the farmhouse!

No, she shouldn't. In fact, she should do the opposite. She should stop. Monique slid behind a tree and breathed deep and slow to catch her breath. The night was quiet. No rustling of leaves or snapping of twigs from where she'd run. What was Carlos doing? Waiting?

She stood still for what seemed like an hour, though it couldn't have been more than a few minutes. Tears blurred her vision. The thought of Thomas lying there, bleeding on the ground, was enough to make her scream, and it took all of her strength to bury the emotion. She had to survive. Thomas had risked his life to bring her out. She had information the outside world desperately needed.

Monique tiptoed forward, picking her way over the leaves as carefully as possible. She remembered seeing that this strip of woods ended in a meadow to her left. The meadow ran directly to the farmhouse.

It took her only a minute of high-stepping to reach the grass. She stopped for a few seconds, heard no sound of pursuit, and entered the field. Maybe Carlos was waiting by the quarry, watching for her return. Ten steps out she felt the horror of her exposure. If Carlos was anywhere near this side of the forest, he would surely see her! But she'd committed herself.

She began to run. If the man behind had noticed her, there was nothing she could do now except run.

With every step she was terribly aware of the fact that she was leaving Thomas dead behind her. She tried to think of a way to get to him, bring him with her. Wasn't it possible that he was alive?

No, she had to reach safety. She had to survive, and then she had to reach England.

She hadn't noticed the Peugeot in the driveway until now; it was parked near the front of the farmhouse, out of sight of the quarry.

Could she?

Yes, she could. Assuming the keys were in it, she could take the car and explain to the owner later.

She approached it in a crouch. Tried the door. Open! She slid in and searched madly for keys. Visor. Passenger seat. Cup holder. Dash.

They were in the ignition. She twisted and looked out the rear window. Still no sign of pursuit. But if she started the car . . .

Monique gently pulled the door closed, heard the latch click. No lights—she couldn't dare use lights. The driveway was gray enough to see despite the lack of moonlight. She prayed the car had a decent muffler, fired the engine, pulled the stick into drive, and rolled over the dirt, holding her breath to help the silence.

She made two short turns before driving behind a hill. Still too close for lights. Still too close to rev the engine. He might hear or see, even at this distance. For all she knew, Carlos was sprinting across the meadow now. Over the hill to cut her off.

The moment she entered the trees she picked up her speed, but she dared not turn the lights on. Without them, she could hardly see. She drove at ten kilometers per hour for a kilometer. Then two. Still no one behind.

But that wasn't true. Thomas was behind. An image of his body filled her mind. Bleeding from the head. Dead.

She wiped her eyes to see the road.

After five kilometers, Monique turned on the lights and shoved the gas pedal to the floor.

25

DEPUTY SECRETARY Merton Gains adjusted the receiver to give his neck a break. He'd been on hold for ten minutes despite the assurances that the president would take his call immediately. Immediately had always meant a short wait, but ten minutes? This was the new meaning of immediately—the one that came after a week of beating their heads against this brick wall called the Raison Strain.

Gains always vaguely feared it would come down to something like this. It was why he'd introduced his bill to change the way vaccines were used in the United States. Of course, he'd never anticipated a crisis as widespread and terminal as this one, but the danger had always lurked out there. Now it had bitten them in the rear end without so much as a warning.

He'd seen Raison Strain simulations a dozen times. It grew quietly and then struck with a vengeance, rupturing cells in indiscriminate, systemic fashion. *It was precisely how the political fallout from the crisis would develop,* he thought.

At this very moment, a hundred governments were on the verge of ending the silence they'd managed so far. A thousand reporters were sniffing and starting to come up with questions no one could answer. The world's genetics labs were working overtime, and the thousands of scientists on the Raison Strain were murmuring already.

This didn't include the military personnel who had been involved in the massive movement of hardware to the eastern seaports. They'd been trained to keep their questions to themselves and their mouths firmly shut. But all told, over ten thousand people now directly engaged the Raison Strain, and most of those suspected that the new virus that had been restricted to a small island south of Java wasn't nearly so isolated as everyone was saying.

He'd taken a call yesterday from Mike Orear with CNN. The man was on to them. He didn't say how he'd uncovered his information, but he knew that terrorists had released a virus of some kind, and he threatened to break the story in twenty-four hours if the president didn't come clean. It was all Gains could do to hold the man back. He couldn't very well refuse to comment, and a flat denial might push Orear over the edge. Gains had threatened the man with a long list of national security violations, but in the end, it was apparent the man knew too much. Orear had finally agreed to hold off until Gains had spoken with the president.

That was twenty-four hours ago, and the president had seemed surprisingly ambivalent about the prospect of CNN breaking the story. When the news broke, it would boil over and swamp the world. God only knew to what end.

There was only one way to temper the news.

"Merton?" The president's voice took him off guard.

"Yes, hello, Mr. President. I, um . . . I just got off the phone with England, sir."

"I don't mean to push, but I'm late for a meeting with the World Health Organization."

"Yes, sir. I just got off the phone with Monique de Raison. She called me from Dover about twenty—"

"She's alive?"

"She evidently escaped from an undisclosed location in France. She managed to get across the English Channel."

"And Thomas?"

"He was killed during the escape."

The receiver hissed quietly.

"You're sure about this?"

"About which—"

"About Hunter! You're sure he's dead?"

"Monique seems quite sure."

Gains hadn't realized how much stock the president had put in Thomas, and hearing the admission in his tone brought surprising comfort. Amazing that certain things didn't change even in the face of crisis.

"Does she have it?" the president demanded.

"She thinks so. At least a very strong lead."

"Okay. I want her here now. Put her on the fastest plane we have out of our air base in Lakenheath. Use an F-16—use whatever we have that can make the flight. The British are aware of this?"

"I'm waiting for a callback."

"Callback? This isn't a time for callbacks! I want her here in four hours, you understand? And make sure that she's under a heavy guard the whole way. Send an air escort with her. Treat her like she's me. Clear?"

"Yes sir."

26

RACHELLE CRESTED the dune that overlooked the Horde camp when the sun was halfway up the eastern sky.

Find Thomas, Justin had said. The words had haunted Rachelle as she stumbled over the sand. *No matter how terrible,* he had said. What could possibly be so terrible?

She ran down the dune toward the Horde camp. In all truth her spirit soared. Yes, Thomas was in the Horde camp, their virtual prisoner, and yes, there was danger on every side—she could feel it like the sun on her back.

But she'd found Elyon! Justin was the boy; she was sure of it. He'd changed her skin from gray to flesh tone, and he'd healed her wounds with a single word. Elyon had come to save his people! She couldn't wait to tell Thomas.

She understood that Monique had made a connection with her. What Monique was doing now, she had no clue. Unlike Thomas, who seemed to have an awareness of both worlds at all times, her and Monique's connection was apparently sporadic and depended on Thomas.

Rachelle began to yell when she was still two hundred yards out, before anyone had seen her. Whatever happened, she couldn't risk them misunderstanding her intentions as hostile.

"Thomas! I need to see Thomas of Hunter!"

She must have screamed it a dozen times before the first soldiers appeared at the perimeter. And then there were a hundred of them, staring out at the strange sight. This unarmed woman screaming in from the desert, demanding to see Thomas of Hunter.

She pulled up panting, twenty paces from the line of ugly beasts.

"I've been sent to speak to Thomas of Hunter. It's urgent I see him."

They stared at her as if she'd lost her mind. And why would they ever agree to let her see him? Thomas was their insurance.

"What business do you have?" one of them demanded.

"I am here because my lord needs me," she said, remembering what Thomas had told her about the way the Horde women spoke of the men. Several seemed stunned by her request. Was something wrong with Thomas?

"I am here to ensure that nothing is wrong with him. I am sent by our Council to know that he's in good health."

The Scab who'd assumed charge scowled. "Be gone, you wench! Tell your commander that we don't accept spies."

Rachelle panicked. "Then Mikil will cut Qurong's throat!" she screamed.

That set them back.

"If you turn me back, I will go straight to them and tell them that you've betrayed them, and Qurong will die. If I don't return in good health myself, then the same will happen. So don't think of hurting me."

The leader, a general by his sash, studied her for a moment. "Wait here."

He backed away, conferred with several other warriors, sent one of them off with a message, then returned.

"Follow me."

She entered the camp surrounded by a small army. The smell was hardly tolerable, and so many shrouded eyes peering at her made her skin crawl. She tried to breathe in shallow pulls, but it only made her dizzy. So she breathed deeply and forced her mind from the stench.

No women that she could see. Naturally, the Horde didn't allow their women to fight. She couldn't bear to look the men in the eyes, but she refused to look any less than a warrior herself, so she walked tall and straight, praying that she would be directed at the next possible moment into a tent to see Thomas.

They led her to a large tent in the middle of the camp. If she was right, this was the royal tent where Thomas had found the Books of Histories.

A guard parted the front flaps and she stepped in. The general who met her was named Woref, if she understood the guards correctly. His eyes had the look of a snake, and his face looked as though it might crack if he tried to smile.

"Where's Thomas?"

"We did nothing to him. You should know this. His wounds are self-inflicted."

"What wounds? Take me to him!"

He dipped his head and led her down a hallway. The serpentine bat they worshiped was everywhere—decorative paintings on the walls, molded statues in the corners. Teeleh. *Elyon, protect me.* They entered a large room where a half-dozen guards stood at the ready. A long table was spread with an array of fruits and wines and cheeses.

But where—

A body lay on a cushion along one of the walls. The head was bloody.

Thomas? Yes, it was him; she recognized his tunic immediately. He was wounded!

Rachelle ran over to him, dropped to her knees, and stared in horror at a round hole the size of her finger in his head. Blood had run into his hair. Dried.

"Thomas?"

But he was dead. Dead! And by the looks of him, he had been dead for some time.

She couldn't breathe. It wasn't possible! No, this couldn't be happening! Justin had found her, and she had just been saved, and Samuel and Marie were still children, and . . .

What could have made this kind of wound? No weapon of this world.

Something had happened to Thomas in the other reality. She recalled that Monique had been sleeping next to him under the boulder. Carlos must have found them! Now Thomas was dead. But she was still alive!

The thoughts drummed through her head painfully. Her heart didn't feel like it was moving. And behind her the Scabs were staring.

She spun around. "Out! Get out!" she screamed. Her vision was clouded with the pain. "Leave!"

The general scowled but left her alone with the body.

Rachelle sank slowly to her knees, knowing precisely what she had to do. Elyon had told her to find Thomas, not this dead body. Justin had healed her from near death. He carried the power of the fruit in his hands, they said, because he *was* the power of the fruit.

TED DEKKER

And now she would use that same power.

She rested both hands on his cheeks. Her tears fell on his face. "Wake up, Thomas," she whispered. "Thomas, please."

But he didn't wake up.

Now her voice rose to a soft wail. "Please, please. Save him, Elyon. Wake him from the dead."

Waking from the dead isn't like healing.

"Yes, it is!" she shouted. "Wake up, Thomas! Wake up!"

But he still didn't wake up. There was still a hole in his forehead. He was still dead.

She kissed his cold lips and began to sob. What if Justin didn't know he was dead? No, that was impossible. "Wake up," she cried again, slapping his face. "Wake up!"

Justin had to know. He knew everything. They didn't know; they didn't even remember—

Remember me. Remember my water.

His water. She frantically grasped the canteen still hooked to Thomas's belt. Pulled it free from the clip. Spun off the cap.

She splashed some on his face before she'd really thought it through. The clear liquid ran over his lips and his eyes and filled the small wound on his forehead.

She dumped more on. "Please, please, please . . ."

Thomas's mouth suddenly jerked open.

Rachelle cried out and jumped back. The canteen flew from her hands.

Thomas gasped. The wound closed, as if his skin was formed of wax that had melted to fill itself in. She had seen nothing like it for fifteen years, when she chose Thomas by healing him of the deadly wounds he'd suffered in the black forest.

Thomas's eyes opened.

Rachelle lifted both hands to her lips to stifle a cry of joy. Then she threw her arms around him and buried her face in his throat.

"Get off me, get off me, you . . ."

He didn't know who she was! She lifted her head so that he could see her face. "It's me, Thomas!"

She kissed him on the lips. "Me. You remember my mouth if not my face."

"What . . . where are we?" He struggled up.

"Be quiet; they're outside," she whispered. "We're in the Horde camp."

He jumped to his feet. The blood was still on his face, but his wound was gone. She could hardly take her eyes off his forehead.

"You were dead," she said. "But Elyon's water healed you."

"His water heals again? I . . . how is that—"

"No, I don't think his water's changed. I think he just used it to heal you. Justin is the boy, Thomas."

He lifted a hand to his hair, felt the blood, looked at his fingers. "I was shot. But I didn't dream. I don't have any memory of a dream."

He closed his eyes and rubbed the back of his head. What was it like coming back to life? Hopefully he was putting the pieces of his memory back in place.

"What do you mean, Justin is the boy?"

"I mean he's him. Don't you see? The signs were all there. He's come—"

"He can't be Elyon. He grew up in the Southern Forest. He was a warrior under my command!"

They were whispering, but loudly.

"And who's to say that he's not Elyon? I saw him—"

"No! It's not possible! I know when I see—"

"Stop it, Thomas!"

He stared at her, mouth still open, ready to finish his statement of disbelief. He clamped his jaw shut.

She told him what had happened in the desert. She hurried through the events in a whisper, and when she was finished, he just looked at her, face white.

"And I just saved you with his power. How dare you question me?"

"But Elyon? I fought Elyon?"

"He's come to save us from ourselves, just like he said he would, when we didn't think it could get any worse."

"I . . ." He turned from her. "Oh my God. My dear, dear God, Elyon! I've betrayed him!"

"We all did. And he beat you handily."

"No, with Johan!"

She pulled him around by the arm. "What do you mean?"

"I mean I struck an agreement with Johan that would make Johan the king of the Horde."

"So—"

"So he insisted that he betray both Qurong and Justin. I . . . I agreed."

These words weren't making sense to her. How could anyone betray Justin now? "But once they know that Justin is Elyon, there won't be any such thing."

"It's already started! They are due to reach the forest late this afternoon and work the betrayal. Mikil has informed the Council. Johan intends to kill Justin."

It was suddenly clear to her. Qurong and Johan were influenced by the Shataiki. By Teeleh. They were being used as the creature's instrument against Justin. This wasn't only about the Forest People; it was about Justin!

"We have to stop them!"

Thomas looked around frantically. "How many are outside?"

As if in answer, the flap parted and the general Woref stepped inside. His eyes flashed at the sight of Thomas standing.

Her husband walked toward the man. "Which one of your men tried to kill me?" he demanded.

"None."

Thomas moved quickly. He leaped for the Scab's sword, yanked it free from its scabbard, and ran for the far wall. "Hurry!"

He swung the blade over his head and down, parting the wall from top to bottom, opening it to daylight. He ripped the cut wide and held the sword out to stop the general.

"You follow and you die," he said, and then stepped through the tear into the passageway between the tents. They had already started through the camp before the stunned general gave the alarm.

"The horses!" Thomas yelled, pointing to several that were tied to the side of the tent. They both swung onto a horse. Then they were galloping out of the camp, dodging Scab warriors taken completely off guard by the two horses.

No one tried to stop them—naturally, they'd probably been strictly instructed not to touch Thomas of Hunter. Only the general, and probably now his men, knew what was really happening. It might not have made a difference anyway. The horses outran any words of warning.

They galloped from the Horde's camp straight toward the distant forest.

"Can we make it?" she demanded.

He rode hard just ahead, leaning forward, face drawn.

"Thomas!"

"I don't know!" Thomas snapped. He slapped his horse, coaxing every last ounce of strength from its fresh legs. "Hiyaa!"

The general from whom Thomas and Rachelle had escaped stared out at the dunes that led to the forest. Woref, head of military intelligence, despised the Forest Guard perhaps more than he hated Qurong.

He played the loyal general, but under his pain, not a day went by that he didn't curse the father of the woman who would one day be his. Qurong had forbidden any man from marrying his daughter, Chelise, until the forests had fallen. It was the leader's way of motivating a dozen senior-ranking generals who vied for her hand. If the decision had been left to Woref, they would have burned the forests long ago, then killed every last woman and child who bathed in the lakes and feasted on their flesh for the victory. But Qurong seemed more interested in conquering and enslaving than killing.

"Do we give chase?" his aide asked.

"No," Woref said. They had planned for this contingency. As long as Thomas was delayed by four or more hours, he would be too late. The western army would march.

He glanced at the sun. "Prepare the men to march at nightfall. We are going into the forest."

By week's end, the daughter of Qurong, Chelise, would be his. And then he would look to become Qurong himself.

27

MONIQUE PEERED at the Washington skyline through the Suburban's tinted windows. The American people didn't know yet; that was her first shock. Most of them probably didn't even know that the Raison Strain even existed, much less that it had infected most of the world's population already.

America's Deputy Secretary of State Merton Gains was on his cell phone, talking in rapid-fire sentences with someone named Theresa Sumner from the CDC in Atlanta. Their plan was to debrief Monique here in Washington before getting her to a yet-undisclosed lab that was already working on the Raison Strain. She'd managed only an hour of dreamless sleep over the Atlantic, and her weariness was beginning to play with her mind—not a good thing, considering the task ahead of her.

The deputy secretary snapped his phone closed. "You sure you're okay?" he asked yet again.

"I'm tired. But otherwise I'm fine. Unless of course you're referring to the Raison Strain, in which case I'm sure that I'm dying like the rest of you."

"That's not what I meant."

She looked over his shoulder at a boy riding a blue bicycle with a fake engine down the sidewalk. His hands were free, and he was holding a soft drink.

"I still can't believe that no one knows."

"It'll break soon enough. Hopefully we'll have some good news to go along with the bad."

"My good news," she said.

"Your good news."

"Then let's hope probability is on our side."

"Where would you put the probability?"

She shrugged. "Sixty percent?"

He frowned, then flipped open his phone and placed another call, this one to someone who was evidently working on a report that Russia's leadership was fracturing.

Monique closed her eyes and let her mind slip back to Thomas. She'd asked about him the moment her feet hit the tarmac, but Gains only knew what she'd told him. No new word. They assumed he was dead.

As did she. The water no longer healed as it had in the hotel room in Bangkok. And even if there was a way to heal Thomas in the forest, he might not be healed here as he had been three times before.

Astounding that she was even thinking like this. She'd lived in Rachelle's skin for less than a day, and only in her dreams, but the experience had been so real that she couldn't deny the existence of Thomas's reality. She'd spent the last ten hours contemplating this strange phenomenon, and with each passing hour her conviction that Rachelle and Justin really did exist strengthened.

Which meant that Thomas had indeed been healed by Elyon's water after being shot on the hotel bed in Bangkok. That time he'd been in the vicinity of water, which healed him immediately, perhaps before he'd actually died. When Carlos had shot him in the head after his first rescue attempt, he'd actually been in the lake, and his healing had been instantaneous. He probably hadn't died either time.

But this time, he had really died. She'd watched Carlos check his pulse. There was no way the killer would have left him without being completely satisfied that he was dead. That meant Thomas would have died in the desert as well. Maybe the Horde had double-crossed him and killed him. Or maybe he'd just died. Even if Justin brought him back to life, there was no guarantee that he would come back to life here.

He was dead. He was really dead this time.

Monique swallowed a lump in her throat. If so, then she would make it well known that he had saved them all. Assuming her antivirus worked. Either way, he had saved her. Carlos would have killed her sooner or later. If not him, then the virus would have.

For that matter, it still might.

"There's something you should know," she said. "The man behind Svensson is the director of foreign affairs, Armand Fortier."

"You know that for a fact?" he asked, surprised. "We'd speculated, but I'm not sure we've confirmed anything."

"Thomas and I met with him. I'm also quite sure that he has someone on the inside over here. Someone who has access to your president."

She might as well have dropped a bomb. He just stared at her. It occurred to her that Fortier's mule could be this very man. She could be telling the wrong man the wrong things and never know the better of it.

"I could be mistaken," she said. "But he seemed to make that claim."

Merton Gains broke off his stare. "Dear God, what next?"

Mike Orear slipped into his chair behind the set of the show he co-anchored with Nancy Rodriguez and fixed his earpiece. Behind him large black letters spelled out the show's name, *What Matters.*

"Ready in five. You right?" Nancy asked.

"As rain."

He'd been in front of the camera too many times to count in his relatively short career, but never had he been so anxious to spill the beans. He'd delayed because of the State Department's adamant demand that he keep his mouth shut. It was non-news, they'd said. But none of that mattered any longer.

What did matter was that he'd awakened this morning with a rash under his arms and on his thighs, and although he succeeded in persuading himself that it had nothing to do with the Raison Strain, the rash reminded him just how real this non-news of his was.

This non-news that the world was dying of the Raison Strain without knowing it.

Windows peered into the studio from a second story above and behind the cameras. The show was directed by Marcy Rawlins, who was reviewing last-minute details with Joe Spencer behind the glass. Any breaking news or changes would come over their earpieces from that room.

"You okay?" Nancy asked.

"I'm fine. Let's roll."

"You look pale."

"I want to change things up a little. Lead with something off the schedule."

"Marcy clear this?"

"No. Trust me, she won't have to."

Nancy arched her brow. "Your skin, not mine."

"No, Nancy, you're wrong. It's your skin too. You'll see."

"What the heck is that—"

"Ten seconds." The program director's voice in their earpieces.

"What's that supposed to mean?" she repeated.

"You'll see."

"Three . . . two . . . one . . ." She gave the on-air signal.

Nancy was already smiling and opening the show. She ran down today's show highlights, none of which Mike heard. His mind was elsewhere.

There was a good reason he hadn't put the story through the normal news channels. Even breaking-news channels, for that matter. Fact was, Marcy probably would have jumped all over it, assuming she believed his sources at all.

But news of this kind would have to be cleared with the brass. Some of them would say that if true, any story of this magnitude should be broken by the president himself or, at the very least, someone with more seniority than Orear. They would hold it while they got up to speed. Might even spike it.

Mike wasn't going to take that chance. A week had passed, and signs that something very significant was in the air were everywhere, and none of his peers seemed to notice. If they did, they sure weren't connecting the dots.

Maybe he intended to do a bit of grandstanding, but not much. How could anyone accuse a condemned man of grandstanding, for heaven's sake? He was dying. They were all dying. That was news and that was that. Time to let the cat out of—

" . . . Mike."

Nancy was giving him that look of nonchalance that some of the best anchors had mastered. *I am a very significant force in the world of news, and the fact that I don't look like I'm swimming in it makes me even more important.*

He looked up into the camera. Wrong one. The one to their left, with the red light on.

"Ladies and gentlemen, I hope you're sitting down. The news I'm about to deliver is of the gravest kind."

He'd thought through his little speech a hundred times, but now it sounded trite and stupid. Delivering his bomb as if it were news lessened its importance. And yet it was that: news.

"Mike, what are you doing?" Marcy's voice in his ear.

He reached up and pulled out his earpiece.

"I . . . I'm not sure how to deliver this. It's not the kind of news any reporter knows how to report." From the corner of his eye he saw that Marcy had a phone to her ear. She slammed it down. The State Department had called? Or the attorney general. That was fast. One of their agents was undoubtedly watching his show.

He had to do this before the program director could pull the plug.

"CNN has learned that a new virus for which there is no known cure, which was previously thought to be isolated on a small island south of Java in the Indonesian islands, has spread far more widely than initially believed, perhaps to most of the world in fact. We have confirmed that the Raison Strain is widespread in the United States and has infected . . ."

So trite. So understated. So impossible to put into words.

" . . . most of us. If this report is correct, and we have it on very good sources that it is, the world is facing a very, very grave crisis."

Impossible or not, all of it had gone out live.

"This has come to us from the highest possible sources. It seems that our government has known for over a week and is making every possible effort to find a vaccine or an antivirus that would counter—"

The red light went off. He'd been pulled off the air.

Mike jerked his head to view the monitor that showed what viewers at home saw, which was at this moment a Lexus ad. The dozen or so technicians in the studio had frozen.

The door to the studio flew open and Marcy stood in the frame, white-faced.

"What was that?"

Mike stood.

"Was that . . ." Nancy pushed back her chair. "Where did you get that?"

"That was the truth, Marcy," he said. "And thank you for cutting to the Lexus ad. It drove the story home for our viewers. Kinda has the feel of the Gestapo jerking the plug, doesn't it?"

"I just got a call from the attorney general," Marcy snapped. "They're watching this. You're going to incite—"

"Of course they're watching this!" Mike yelled. "They're watching because they know that it's true and they know I've got the whole story. Get us backup, Marcy. Call whoever you have to; just get me backup."

"I can't do that! You can't just go on the air and tell the world that they're all about to die! Have you lost your mind?"

He walked straight toward her. "Fine. But if I walk out of this building, I go straight to Fox. Tell them that. You have about thirty seconds to make up your minds. Either way, the full story breaks today."

"Don't you dare threaten me! You're going back on the air, and you're going to tell them that you had no business saying what you did."

Her voice echoed through the room. She still didn't believe him, did she? She was either suffering a terminal case of denial or had lost her compass in the shock of hearing about the virus.

"You tell them, Marcy," he said quietly. A dozen sets of eyes stared at him. The Lexus advertisement had yielded to a Mountain Dew commercial.

The door behind Marcy burst open. "Who's manning the hotline?" This was Wally, the news director. His eyes took in Marcy, then moved to Mike standing on the main floor by the cameras instead of seated in his seat beside Nancy. "What in the blazes is going on down here?"

"You get back in that seat," Marcy said icily.

"I need a news break. Now! NBC is reporting that the French government has just declared martial law," Wally said. "We've confirmed it."

"Martial law?" Mike said. "Why?"

"To control the threat of a virus they claim has affected France."

"The Raison Strain?"

Wally obviously hadn't been watching Mike's little speech.

"How did you know that?"

28

MARTYN, COMMANDER of the Horde army under Qurong, stood beside his leader, facing Ciphus and the rest of the forest Council. Qurong was working his betrayal exactly as he'd planned so many months ago.

Thousands of the villagers had gathered in the amphitheater on short notice. The news that a thousand Scab warriors had entered the village from the backside with Justin had spread quickly. Now they filled the bleachers and peered down in silence to the proceedings on the ground beneath them.

Ciphus stood on the stage near the center, facing Qurong. Mikil and Justin were there on the left with a thousand of the Forest Guard to match his own warriors on the right. The fate of the world was riding on this play of Qurong's. So far everything had progressed precisely as he had anticipated. By morning, the forests would be theirs.

"Hear me, great Ciphus," Qurong said. "I have put my life in your hands to meet with you. Surely you will consider my proposal for a truce until we can work out a lasting peace between us."

This wasn't going as Ciphus had anticipated; that much was clear. Mikil had told the Council that Martyn would give up Qurong, but she'd been wrong.

The Council leader shifted his eyes to Martyn, perhaps expecting, wanting, the commander to step in as Thomas had proposed.

Ciphus cleared his throat. "Of course, we are always willing to listen. But you must realize that we have no basis for peace. You live in violation of Elyon's laws. The penalty for disobeying Elyon is death. Now you want us to deny Elyon his own law by making peace with the Horde? You deserve death, not peace."

This was the classic doctrine of the Forest People. Ciphus was opening the door for Martyn to spring his trap, to offer Qurong's life in exchange for peace. *Not so fast, you old goat.*

"How many of us will you kill to satisfy your God?" Qurong demanded.

"You live in death already!" Ciphus cried. "You would have us make an alliance with death? You have the whole desert; we have but seven small forests. I should ask you, why do you wage war against a small peaceful people?"

Qurong glanced at Martyn. They made no overt signal, but the message was clear. The supreme leader was going to proceed as planned.

"It is because we have no basis for trust between our people that we can't extend true peace," Qurong said. "You won't elevate us above dogs, and we see you for the snakes you really are."

A rumble hurried through the crowd. Ciphus held up a hand.

"You are right; we don't trust you. A dog will see a golden rod and think it has seen a snake. Your eyes are blinded by your rebellion against Elyon."

Qurong smiled, but he didn't take the bait to defend himself.

"Then I will offer you more than the words of a dog today," Qurong said. "I will show you and your people on this day that I am an honorable leader in my own way. If I do so, will you consider a truce between our people?"

Martyn studied the elder. *Come on, you wheezing old bat. You can only accept. I know you.*

Ciphus frowned and finally spoke quietly. "We would consider it."

"Then hear me, all of you," Qurong said. "I have two armies camped outside of your forest at this moment. The two hundred thousand warriors to the east you know of well enough. What you don't know is that we have a second army, twice as large, camped in the western desert."

This news was received by total silence. Perhaps they thought their Guard could deal with both armies. They were wrong for reasons beyond their understanding. In twenty-four hours, their Guard would be defeated.

"I am willing to commit my armies to a campaign that will destroy much of your forest and most of your warriors," Qurong said. "But my victory would not be certain unless I had an element of complete surprise. We both know this."

Here it was, then. Sweat stung Martyn's cracked skin, but he hardly noticed it.

"As a sign of goodwill, I will now show my hand in the hopes of winning your faith. We came here today with betrayal on our minds. We planned to offer you peace, and when you accepted that peace—when your Guard was compromised—we planned to bring the full force of our armies against you in one massive campaign."

The silence deepened, and Martyn was quite sure it was from shock now.

"But I will hold back for the sake of a peace accord!" shouted Qurong. "I have already told you about my army to the west. I have just now revealed my intentions and robbed myself of any victory. I see that peace is more valuable than victory."

Ciphus glanced at Martyn. He hadn't expected quite this. Mikil wasn't prepared for this either. She had the look of a dumb goat.

"Then what do you propose?" Ciphus demanded. "That we offer you peace because you have confessed your intent to ruin us? We are to believe that you've experienced some kind of wholesale conversion since entering our village? A man does not change so quickly. There can be no peace without the appropriate payment. You can't make peace with Elyon while living in your disease!"

"No. I realize that your laws have to be satisfied in order for there to be peace. As do our laws. I propose to meet the requirements of those laws."

"By confessing? It's not enough."

"By the death of the man who would lead us to war. I am not the one who concocted this scheme."

"Then who?"

"It was him." Qurong pointed his finger toward the Forest Guard. Toward Justin.

"Justin."

Confusion swept through the crowd.

"It was Justin who claimed our victory would be complete by offering peace!"

Justin looked at Martyn, expressionless. The people were yelling in such chaos that it was impossible to tell their reaction to this news. Ciphus shouted his silence at the crowd, and slowly they quieted enough for his voice to be heard.

"How dare you accuse one of our own in order to save yourself?" Ciphus said, voice shaking. Martyn wondered if he'd misjudged the man. Surely this emotion was for show.

The elder took a breath and continued, voice lower. "If what you say is true, then yes, we would consider your argument. But what corroboration is there that Justin planned any of this? You take us for fools?"

"I can corroborate!" Thomas's second yelled, stepping forward from the ranks of the Guard. Mikil. "And I can do so with Thomas of Hunter's authority. He is in the Horde camp now, guaranteeing the commander's safety with his own life so that Qurong can expose the truth of this betrayal. Justin is complicit in the plot against the Forest People!"

"What more could show my true intent?" Qurong said. "I give you your traitor and I consign myself to peace."

Ciphus crossed his arms into the sleeves of his robe and paced. "Intent? And what do intentions have to do with peace?"

"Then I will satisfy your own law. I will give you a death at my own expense."

Ciphus stopped his pacing.

"Death to the traitor!" a lone voice cried from the bleachers.

Dissension and argument exploded. But were they for or against Justin? Martyn couldn't tell.

"Your laws require death for defilement of Elyon's love," Qurong shouted. "If treason is not defilement, then what is? Furthermore, he has also waged war against the Desert Dwellers. Our law also requires his death. His death will satisfy both of our laws."

Ciphus seemed to be deep in thought, as if he hadn't considered this thought. He faced Justin.

"Step out."

Justin walked three paces and stopped.

"What do you say to this charge?"

A woman cried over the crowd. "Justin! No, Justin!"

A dozen voices joined. If Martyn wasn't mistaken, children's voices were mixed in. The sound was oddly unnerving.

"Silence!" Ciphus shouted.

They quieted.

"What do you say to these charges?" the elder demanded again.

"I say that I have fulfilled your laws, and I have bathed in the lakes, and I have loved all that Elyon loves."

"Have you conspired to betray the people of Elyon?"

Justin remained silent.

Justin hadn't conspired, but it wouldn't have mattered either way. Hearing the silence, Martyn knew they would win this war. In a day's time, he would defeat these Forest People without lifting a sword.

If they only knew.

It had been Justin's idea for Johan to enter the desert as Thomas had guessed. But now the culmination of their planning would end very differently than even Justin knew.

"Answer me!"

Justin spoke in a low voice—too quiet to be heard past the floor. "Have you become so blind, Ciphus, that you can't remember me?"

"What?"

"Has it been so long since we swam together?"

Ciphus had frozen like a tree. He was actually shaking. "Don't try your deceitful words on me. You're forgetting that I am the elder of Elyon's Council."

"Then you should know the answer to your question."

"Answer me or I'll condemn you myself! You lost the challenge yesterday, except for Thomas's failure to finish you. Perhaps this is the justice of Elyon now. What say you?"

The amphitheater had grown so quiet that Martyn thought he could hear Ciphus breathing. Justin looked up at the people. Martyn thought he was going to say something, but he remained silent. His eyes met Martyn's. The deep green eyes struck terror into his heart.

Justin lowered his head. If Martyn wasn't mistaken, the man was struggling to keep his desperation in check. What kind of warrior could cry before his accusers? When Justin lifted his head, his eyes swam in tears. But he held his head steady.

"Then condemn me," Justin said softly.

"And you realize that condemnation will mean death." The elder's voice was unsteady.

Justin didn't answer. He wouldn't walk the path that Ciphus set before him, but it was close enough. Ciphus lifted both fists and glared at the man below him.

"Answer me when I speak to you in this holy gathering!" the elder shouted. "Why do you insult the man whom Elyon has made your superior?"

Justin looked at the man but refused to speak.

Ciphus lifted both fists above his head. "Then for treason against the laws of Elyon and his people, I condemn you to death at the hands of your enemies!"

Wails cut the air. Shouts of approval. Cries of outrage. It all blended into a cacophony of confusion that Martyn knew would amount to nothing. There was no prevailing voice. No one would defy the sentence of the Council.

"Take him!" Ciphus shouted at Qurong.

"I will accept him on one condition," Qurong said. "He will die according to our laws. By the drowning. We will give him back to your God. Back to Elyon, in your lake."

Ciphus hadn't expected this. If he refused, Martyn had the appropriate contingency plans. The elder conferred with his Council, then turned to give his verdict.

"Agreed. Our Gathering ends tonight. You may deal with him then."

"No, it should be now, with your cooperation. Let his death be a seal for a truce between our armies. His blood will be on both of our hands."

Another short conference.

"Then let our peace be sealed with his blood," Ciphus said.

—◦◦◦—

Thomas and Rachelle came into sight of the village at sunset, winded and worn due to lack of sleep. The ride had been filled with long stretches of silence as the two retreated into their own thoughts. There was little to say after they'd exhausted the telling and retelling of Justin's healing touch and his words. *I have too much riding on you. Remember me.* They were the same as the boy's words.

They heard the first sign of trouble when they passed the gates, the unmistakable wail of mourning for the dead.

"Thomas? What is that?"

He urged his horse into a trot, past the main gate. The women were mourning a death. There had been a skirmish, and some of his Guard had been killed. Or there was news of a battle on the western perimeter. Or this was about Justin.

The sky was already dark gray, but the glow of torches cast an orange hue over the lake at the end of the main road. Lawns and doorways were vacant of the loitering so typical on crowded Gathering evenings. There was a man here and a woman there, but they avoided Thomas's eyes and shuffled with distraction.

A sudden cry of horrible agony echoed distant. Thomas's heart rose into his throat.

"Thomas!" Rachelle sounded frantic. She slapped her horse and galloped past him, straight for the lake.

"Rachelle!" He wasn't sure why he called her name. He kicked his horse, and together they thundered down the wide stone causeway that split the village in two.

They saw the crowd before they reached the end of the street. A sea of people stood on the shore with their backs to the village, staring toward the lake.

"You have to stop them!" Rachelle cried. "It's him!"

"Can you see him?"

They both brought their horses to a rearing halt where the road gave way to the beach. She stared over heads, her eyes wide and her face wrinkled with anguish.

Then Thomas saw what she was looking at. A square wooden tower had been erected to their left, by the shore. Beside the tower, a ring of Horde encircled two Scabs. The Council stood on one side; Qurong and Martyn stood on the other. In the center was a post, and on that post hung a man.

Justin.

One of the Scab's arms went back, then swung forward and struck Justin's ribs. *Crack!* One of his ribs broke with the blow. Justin jerked and sagged against the post.

"Stop!" Rachelle's scream ripped through the air. "Stop!" She grunted with a sob, clenched her jaw, and drove her horse into the crowd.

Villagers unprepared for a stamping, barging steed cried out and scrambled back to make way for the large Scab stallion.

"Back! Out of the way," Thomas yelled. He followed her in.

The Scab hit Justin again, unfazed by the commotion.

"Stop!" Rachelle cried.

The people separated in front of them like falling dominoes. Then they were through. Mikil and Jamous stood with several dozen of the Guard. Another thousand milled on the north side of the lake. The Horde army waited down the shore on the south side. Women and children cried softly, an eerie tone. On the post, Justin's near naked body had stilled.

They hadn't drawn blood. He'd heard of this method of torture employed by the Horde—methodically breaking the bones of a victim without draining any of his life—his blood. They wanted the drowning and the drowning alone to take the man. One look at Justin's swollen body made it clear they'd perfected their torture.

Thomas dropped to the sand and rushed forward. "What's this? Who authorized this?"

"You did," Mikil said.

Rachelle sobbed and ran for Justin. She fell on her knees, gripped his ankles, and bowed so that her hair touched his lumpy, broken feet.

"Get her off of him!" Ciphus ordered.

Rachelle spun back and pleaded. "Thomas!"

Two of the Guard leaped forward and dragged her back.

She struggled against them furiously. "It's him! It's him, can't you see? It's Elyon!"

"Don't be a fool!" Ciphus snapped. "Keep her back."

Thomas couldn't pull his eyes from Justin's brutalized body. They'd pulled his arms above his head and strapped them to the top of the post. His face was swollen. Cheekbones broken beneath the skin. His eyes were closed and his head hung limp. How long had they been beating him? It was hard to imagine that he was the boy, grown now into a man, but with a little imagination, Thomas thought he could see the resemblance.

He faced Mikil. "Release him."

She made no move.

"That's an order. This man isn't who you think. I want him released immediately!"

Mikil blinked. "I thought—"

"She can't release him," Ciphus said softly. "To do so would defy the order of the Council and Elyon himself."

"You're *killing* Elyon!" Rachelle cried.

"That's absurd. Can Elyon die?"

"Justin, please, I beg you! Please, wake up. Tell them!"

"Shut her up!" Ciphus said. "Gag her!"

Jamous pulled out a strap of leather to gag her, but he glanced up at Thomas and stopped. What had gotten into them all? Jamous would actually consider binding his commander's wife?

"Gag her!"

The lieutenant slipped the leather thong around her mouth and muffled a scream. "Thoma . . . mm! Hmmmm!"

On the post, Justin moaned.

Thomas broke from the shock that had frozen him, jerked out his sword, and leaped for his wife.

Mikil stepped forward, hand raised. "No, Thomas. You can't defy the Council."

But Thomas hardly heard her. "Let her go! Have you all gone mad?"

She moved into his path to block him. "Please—"

He swung his elbow and struck her jaw. She landed on her seat with a *thump*. Thomas thrust his sword at Jamous's neck. "Untie my wife!"

"Don't be a fool, Thomas." Mikil spoke in a hurried, hushed tone, ignoring her reddening cheek. "The verdict has been cast. The fate of our people depends on this exchange."

With those words, Thomas knew what had happened. Johan had double-crossed not only Justin, but him as well. Qurong had exchanged a promise of peace for the life of Justin, and the Council had accepted. Justin's death would satisfy the law requiring death for treason against Elyon and allow a peace to be brokered even without requiring the Horde to bathe.

"It will never work," Thomas said. "The peace won't last! You think you can trust these Scabs to keep peace? Qurong is Tanis! He's blinded by Teeleh, and he's found a way to kill Elyon!"

"*You* trusted us," Martyn said.

Thomas held the point of his sword against Jamous's neck. He knew by Martyn's tone that the people didn't know about Thomas and Martyn's agreement to betray Qurong.

"Did you hear me?" Thomas cried to the people. "Qurong is Tanis! This is Teeleh's work, this murder. Open your eyes!"

No one responded. They were deaf and dumb, all of them!

"Please, Thomas," Mikil pleaded quietly. "There's no way to undo this."

Rachelle's eyes were wide and screaming at him. *Free me! Don't let them do this! He's Elyon!*

But Thomas knew that if he killed Jamous and freed his wife, he would be forced to defend both of them against the Guard, whose allegiance to Elyon, and by association to the Council, superseded their allegiance to him. If the Council had cast their verdict, there was no way to undo the verdict without killing the lot of them.

Thomas spun around and strode for Justin's sagging body. He couldn't risk Rachelle's life, but neither could he stand by and let them work their treachery.

Is this really Elyon, Thomas? This swollen man who once served under you and dishonored you by refusing the position Mikil now holds? Elyon?

Rachelle had said so. He would die by her words.

"Stop him," Ciphus said.

This time a dozen of his Guard stepped forward. His first impulse was to fight, and he instinctively braced for them.

"If you kill one of them in the service of defending the Council's orders, then you and your wife will die with Justin," Ciphus said.

They had lost their minds over this killing! His eyes ran along the line of villagers who stood behind the Council and Guard. There was a small girl there, staring around her mother, tears running down her cheeks. He recognized her from the Valley of Tuhan. It was Lucy, the one whom Justin had singled out and danced with. The girl's mother was doing her best to keep her own sobs quiet.

"What has happened here?" he shouted.

"Finish your business," Ciphus told Qurong.

There was a light of defiance in the Horde leader's eyes. He nodded and his men leaned in to continue the beating.

Thomas tossed down his sword. "At least give me the courtesy of speaking to the general," he said. "As one warrior to another. My business is still to defend my people, and I demand a council with Martyn."

Martyn looked at Qurong, who dipped his head.

Thomas turned back to Mikil and indicated Rachelle. "One scratch on her and it will be your neck." He faced the crowd. "What's wrong with you? This is the kind of celebration you choose to end your Gathering?" Only a few seemed to hear.

Thomas gave Ciphus a parting glare, walked past Martyn, and headed toward the water's edge, away from the execution.

Martyn walked to him. Behind them another bone cracked. Thomas held his jaw firm and looked over the lake water, clear and dark in the early night. The orange flames from a hundred torches shone on the glassy surface.

"This wasn't what we agreed to." His voice was shaky, far too emotional for a warrior of his stature, but he was having difficulty even breathing past the lump in his throat, much less speaking with authority.

"It was beyond my control," Martyn said. "I didn't know that the supreme leader would offer Justin's life in exchange for peace. It wasn't our plan."

"You betray everyone except Tanis?"

Martyn didn't bother responding. *Justin had passed out,* Thomas thought. Hoped. The only sound behind them was the thudding of fists and the snapping of bones. He felt nauseated and frantic, and he spoke quickly.

"I beg you, Johan, listen to me. Your men shot a woman last night. Did you hear about it?"

"I heard something, yes."

"The woman was Rachelle. Your sister. You may not remember why you should have any allegiance to your own blood, but surely you remember simple facts. She was your *sister*."

"And?"

"And Justin found her, barely alive, with four arrows in her. He healed her. There's not a scratch on her. He told Rachelle that he has a lot riding on us. These were the same words he spoke to us fifteen years ago. Do you remember? Or has Teeleh completely consumed your mind? How could Justin have known what the boy told us? Unless he *is* the boy. You're about to kill the same boy who led us to this lake fifteen years ago, when you yourself were still a boy!"

"Even if you are right, why should I care?"

"Because he *made* you, you . . . That is your *Maker* back there!"

Martyn stared out at the lake. Thomas prayed he would come to his senses, and for a moment he began to hope that the deep sentiments of Johan's youth were rising to the surface.

Something had changed behind them. The beating had stopped.

"If that's my Maker back there," Martyn said, "then he would have made me to live with less pain."

"Your pain is your choice, not his! If you would bathe, your pain would be gone."

Martyn spit on the water. "I would rather die than bathe in this cursed lake."

He turned and walked up the shore to the execution.

Thomas could no longer contain the emotion pent up in his chest. He stared out over the lake and let tears spill down his cheeks. If he turned around, the people would see, and he wasn't sure he wanted that. But it was his Creator they were executing.

There was a pause behind him. He swallowed hard. How could it have come to this? Maybe Justin wasn't Elyon. Had Elyon persuaded Johan to enter the desert? How could Elyon's body break? Or worse, die? Elyon would never allow this!

Thomas turned around. The Scabs had strapped a rope around Justin's ankles and were preparing to hang him upside down from the platform. He averted his eyes and walked up the bank, ignoring the Scabs and Council members who watched him. He had to find Marie and Samuel! But as soon as he thought it, he saw them, kneeling beside their mother.

Rachelle lay on her face behind a row of the Guard, weeping. Thomas slipped his arms under her body and lifted her up. "Come with me," he said to his children.

They walked away from the crowd without another word.

———

It was their custom to honor the dead by facing rather than turning from their bodies at the funeral pyres. To hide one's eyes because looking at the death was painful insulted the one actually facing that death.

Thomas helped a sagging, despondent Rachelle to the closest gazebo.

Marie and Samuel had both been crying, and now Marie spoke for the first time. "Why aren't we honoring him, Papa?"

He couldn't answer her.

"Put me down," Rachelle said.

She took her children by their shoulders. "We are, Marie. We will honor him."

They hurried up the steps and gazed out over the crowd to the scene below. Thomas stepped up beside them and Rachelle gripped his arm.

They watched the proceedings in stunned silence. The pummeling of Justin's body continued. How they managed to break so many bones was beyond him.

Rachelle's fingers dug into Thomas's elbow each time they struck Justin. But she knew as well as he did that there was nothing they could do for him now.

Surely Ciphus hadn't expected this kind of brutality. The Scabs were defiling the forest with their presence. Their smell drifted over the village like a fog. Those not directly involved let their attention wander and on occasion laughed.

Many of the Forest People watched in stunned silence. Many wept quietly. Many sobbed openly.

They stopped beating him and hauled him up by his feet, so that his head hung five or six feet above the ground. Thomas watched as a Scab walked up, squeezed Justin's broken face, and then pushed him. His body swung like a deer carcass in a smoking shack. His arms hung limp, as if he were surrendering upside down.

Rachelle grunted. "Can't you make them stop? If they have to kill him . . ." She couldn't finish.

It didn't matter. He knew what she was going to say. *If they have to kill him, can't they be forced to do it quickly?* But neither of them could even say such a thing.

"It's their way," Thomas said. "They don't understand suffering like we do. They live with it every day."

"It's not *their* way," she said. "It's the way of Teeleh."

Ciphus held up his hand and walked out to the body. He walked around it, then faced the crowd.

"I know there are those among you who still think that here hangs a prophet." His voice rang over the lake. "Let me ask you, would Elyon allow his prophet to suffer like this? You see, he is flesh and blood like the rest of us. Anyone who dares say that this mess of flesh is actually Elyon has lost his sense. Our Creator could never become so uncreated! He would never let a Scab abuse him, any more than he would let Teeleh abuse him. You see?"

He faced the Horde soldiers. "Hit him."

One of the Scabs stepped forward and hammered Justin's back. No one present could mistake the loud crack.

Ciphus cleared his throat. "You see, just a man."

His words invited a fresh round of abuse from the other Horde guards. Three of them stepped forward and began slugging the body, laughing. Ciphus stepped back, surprised. In his eagerness to deflate Justin, he'd unexpectedly opened this door.

"Thomas," Rachelle pleaded.

It was all he could stand. "Wait here."

He jumped from the gazebo and ran straight for Ciphus. A murmur spread through the section of the crowd that saw him. The elder turned his head before Thomas reached the inner circle.

"Enough! To execute a man is one thing. If you insist on satisfying your blood lust, then do it quickly! But don't humiliate the man who saved the Southern Forest and the Forest Guard just a week ago. Kill him if you must, but don't mock his life."

A thousand voices rose in agreement.

Ciphus seemed relieved. He frowned at Qurong. "It makes sense. Finish this."

"The agreement was to kill him our way. Our way is to take a man's spirit be—"

"You have taken his spirit!" Thomas yelled. "Now you're taking the spirit of the people he served. Finish this!"

Qurong regarded him, then nodded at his men.

One of them grabbed a bucket of water they'd drawn from the lake earlier and splashed it in Justin's face. Justin gasped.

Thomas couldn't tell if Justin had opened his eyes, because the battered man faced the other way. But he did see something else that struck him as odd. Justin's skin was starting to gray. How long had it been since his last bathing? As with all who'd trained with the Guard, he probably bathed every morning as was required. Justin had been in the desert, restricted to canteen water, but there hadn't been a trace of the disease on him this morning.

"Drown him," Qurong said.

Two of the Scabs hastily strapped a large stone on Justin's body so that it would sink. A dozen others who had bound their legs with treated leather to protect them from the water stepped cautiously forward, staring at the lake.

"Drown him!" Martyn shouted in a sudden fit of rage.

They grabbed the tower's hastily constructed supports and began to drag the platform down the shore, to the lake.

Justin's body turned, and now Thomas saw his eyes. The left was swollen shut; the right was barely cracked. Justin's sight met his own and stopped. For a long time Justin looked at him. Even past the swollen flesh there was no fear in his face, no regret, no accusation. Only sorrow.

Was he staring into Elyon's eyes? The thought struck a chord of terror deep in Thomas's mind. This was the boy he'd met on top of the cliffs so long ago, the boy who could sing new worlds into existence. Who could turn the planet inside out, or split the globe in two for a day of play. Who could fill a lake that never ended with water so powerful that a single drop could undo any man or woman.

A tremor ran through Thomas's bones. He'd dived into Elyon's water, breathed it deep, screamed with its pleasure and with its pain. This man who hung by his feet as they hauled the device into the lake was Elyon?

Thomas's chest swelled with grief. Tears were filling his eyes, and he didn't know how to stop them. A lone child began to sob quietly behind him, and he turned. Lucy. She stood alone on the sand, crying.

Thomas impulsively stepped back, dropped to one knee, and drew her in. Neither spoke. He faced the water.

The Horde had pushed the tower ten feet off the shore, cursing bitterly as the water soaked past their leg coverings and ate at their cracked skin. The water was about four feet deep here, and Justin's hands were submerged just past his wrists. He'd closed his eyes again, but his breathing was steady. He was awake.

All except for two of the Scabs hurried out of the water. Their hands were pink where they'd touched the water, and they wiped at them madly, trying to rub them free of the poison that had discolored them. They tore the leather from their legs and beat their flesh to alleviate the pain. Above the waist, their skin was still gray.

The two who'd stayed in the lake climbed up the tower, gripped the rope with both hands, and looked at Qurong.

A small voice, barely more than a whisper, came from Justin. His mouth had opened and he was speaking!

"Remember . . ."

Thomas stopped breathing to hear. What had he said?

"Remember me," Justin said, louder this time, voice choking with emotion now. "Remember me!"

They all heard it and stood frozen.

Justin cried it out again in a terrible groan that echoed over the lake and cut straight to Thomas's heart.

"Remember me, Johan!"

Johan?

Thomas looked to his left. Martyn stood stock still, face hidden by his hood, arms folded. Qurong glanced at his general, then quickly motioned his men to commence the drowning.

Justin was sobbing now. His tears fell into the water below his head. He began to groan loudly. Then he began to scream.

What was it? Why now?

Lucy wailed in his arms, and Thomas drew her in tight, as much for his own comfort as hers. He was sure that his heart had stopped. He couldn't bear to watch this! He couldn't stand by and see any man in such a horrible state of torment.

But he couldn't dishonor the man by turning his head away.

Still Justin screamed, long terrible shrieks that cut the night like a razor. Thomas gritted his teeth and begged the sound to stop.

He noticed the change in Justin's skin just before his head touched the water. The flesh on his chest and legs was now nearly white. It was flaking.

The disease was overtaking Justin before Thomas's very eyes!

This was the source of his groans. The pain . . .

The skin on his chest suddenly began to crack like a dried lake bed.

Someone began to yell behind him. "He has the disease!" But the cry was lost in a long scream of agony from Justin.

Thomas settled to his haunches and began to weep uncontrollably.

Justin's head went under. Bubbles boiled from his mouth. His body jerked and heaved. *He's not holding his breath,* Thomas thought. He was trying to pull the water up into his lungs, but it was difficult, hanging upside down.

Just as the water seemed to take its final, terrible toll on him, the two Scabs jerked him out of the lake. Water poured from his lungs. He gasped and sputtered.

Thomas stood to his feet, horrified by their extended torture.

They lowered him again. Again, Justin's body jerked uncontrollably. Again, the water about his head boiled. Again, his diseased chest pumped deep, drawing, convulsing, spasming in rejection.

Again they pulled him from the water before he could drown.

Thomas tore for the water. "Kill him!" he screamed.

You are demanding the death of Elyon.

"Kill—"

A fist from one of the Scabs landed on his temple before he even knew the man was there. He dropped to the sand and struggled to push himself up.

"Finish it!" Ciphus said. "For the sake of Elyon, just finish this!"

"Our custom is to—"

"I don't care what your custom is! Just kill him!"

A Scab on Thomas's left suddenly rushed at the water. The general Martyn. Johan. He had a sword in his hand.

Thomas caught his breath. Something was wrong with this.

Not until Johan's feet splashed water did Thomas note the leathers on his legs. Johan's hood fell off his head, baring a face twisted in rage for all to see. He bore down on Justin, roaring with fury now.

"Die! Die!"

Before any of them knew his full intent, Johan thrust his sword into Justin's belly, jerked it to one side, and pulled it back out. Blood gushed from the gaping wound and splashed into the water.

"Drown him!" Johan screamed.

The two Scabs on top of the platform dropped the body. Justin hung suspended in the water, body jerking.

Martyn swung around, marched out of the lake, tossed his sword to one side, and pulled his hood back over his head. He walked past Qurong toward the Horde army.

Justin's body stopped jerking.

His skin was cracked and white, unrecognizable as human flesh. But it was the blood that Thomas stared at. Blood spilled for cleansing was permitted. When he'd returned from the desert nearly a Scab himself, he'd been permitted to bathe, even though he was bleeding from several of the cracks in his skin.

But this . . .

Did Ciphus realize that this might be different?

The soldiers reached down and cut the cord. Justin's body slipped into the water with a small splash and sank with the weight of the two large stones strapped to his wrists.

Bubbles rose to the surface. They watched in silence as the water slowly became glassy once again. It was finished. The lake had swallowed the brutality whole, leaving no sign except for a slick of spilled blood.

Thomas looked back at Ciphus. The elder's face was white, fixated on the water.

29

MIKE OREAR adjusted his collar mike and glanced into the camera. He'd never imagined becoming the voice of the Raison Strain, but his gall in breaking the story had somehow caught a wave of appreciation with the viewers. CNN's ratings had shot past Fox News's for the first time in years. The brass extended his airtime to six hours a day, three in the morning, three in the evening. It was the assignment of a lifetime, he knew.

A very short lifetime.

Now, with the news widely known, and after an endless parade of guests—geneticists and virologists and psychologists and the like—the threat he'd made known had come to haunt him in a very, very real way. Before, he had been as consumed with breaking the story as with what the virus meant to him personally. Now, along with the rest of America, he couldn't shake the dread knowledge that he was about to die.

That knowledge changed everything. He wanted to be home with his mother and father. He wanted to go to church. He wanted to be married and have children. He wanted to cry.

Instead, he decided to serve humanity in what way he could, which meant bringing knowledge and comfort and perhaps, just perhaps, aiding the incredible effort underway to beat this virus.

The news of the arms shipments hadn't hit the fan yet. A plea from the Pentagon and the president himself had delayed the announcement for the time being. Their argument was simple and cogent: Let the public adjust to the news of the virus for a few days, then let the president tell them the rest of the story. It had been three days. The president was scheduled to give two major addresses today: the first to the United Nations in New York and the second to the nation at six Eastern tonight. The latter address would tell America the whole story.

A clip of Nancy's interview with a social psychologist from UCLA was on its last leg. Mike scanned his notes. The source who'd given him this information on Thomas Hunter was impeccable. The story itself was beyond belief. He'd decided to hold off on the dreams, but the story hardly needed that much detail. America deserved to know about Thomas Hunter.

He looked into the camera, its red light on him. "Wise words of caution," he said in reference to Dr. Beyer's commentary on panic. "Ladies and gentlemen, I've recently come across some information that I think you'll find fascinating. I realize that under the circumstances, 'fascination' seems like a pretentious word, but we're still people and we still cling to hope, wherever we can find it, however it comes. And frankly, we may owe our hope to the man I'm about to show you. His name is Thomas Hunter."

A head shot of Hunter's stern if somewhat boyish face filled the screen for a moment—a driver's license photo from Colorado. Dark hair, strong jaw. The image slipped to the upper corner of Mike's monitor.

"'Classified' is another word that sounds a bit pretentious now, but there are details about Thomas Hunter that we can't divulge without first confirming. What we can say is that it has come to our attention that this man was single-handedly responsible for calling out the threat this nation faces while facing a sea of doubters. Indeed, if the world had listened to Mr. Hunter a week earlier than they did, we might have avoided the virus altogether. I'm sure some of you remember a story we ran two weeks ago about Hunter's kidnapping of Monique de Raison in Bangkok. It now appears that he did so in an attempt to stop the vaccine from being released."

This was where the story got a bit fuzzy. The whys and hows—and the bit about the dreams—were enough to cast suspicion on the entire story.

"We have reason to believe that many in our government consider this man critical to our ability to defeat this threat. We also have reason to believe that his life may be in danger. I promise you, we'll stay on top of this story and bring you details as soon as we have them."

He turned to Nancy, whom he'd insisted remain as his coanchor. "Nancy."

———⚬⚬⚬———

Kara Hunter left the taxi at a run and hurried up the concrete stairs to the white building in the middle of a pastoral setting outside of Baltimore, Maryland. The huge blue letters mounted overhead read "Genetrix Laboratories," but she knew that only a year ago the sign had read "Raison Pharmaceutical." The French company had sold it off when they'd centralized their operations in Bangkok.

Monique de Raison was in this building, working feverishly on a solution to her own mutated virus.

Thomas was dead.

Kara had spent the first day in complete denial. Mother had slipped into one of her terrible brooding moods. Then the news of the Raison Strain hit the airwaves and everything changed. Kara went from complete unwillingness to accept Thomas's death to the sinking realization that they were all dead anyway.

The city of New York, like all cities, had first swallowed the story in jaded silence. It took twenty-four hours for the news to sink in. The streets hadn't emptied right away, but by the end of the second day, finding a taxi would have been a chore. Wall Street was still up and running—they were saying that some semblance of life had to go on. The talking heads—the mayor, the governor, the president— all said the same thing. America had to keep functioning. Electricity, water, stocks and bonds. Food, gasoline, cars, and planes. Hospitals. If they shut down, the country would shut down. Panic would kill America as surely as any virus. Every lab in the world was frantically searching for a cure—one would be found.

But Kara knew better.

Today, Kara had developed a fresh case of denial. The news that Thomas might be some kind of hero had been picked up by every channel she surfed. They had dug up his driver's license photo, of all things. There was his young face, trying so hard to be sincere. The picture brought tears to her eyes. She missed him enough that the threat of the Raison Strain felt strangely feeble.

What if he was alive? They hadn't actually found his body, had they? Gains had been tight-lipped. He'd told her that Monique had seen him dead. But how long after his death had she seen him? Yes, the lake's power was gone over there. Yes, he'd been persuaded that this time his death would be final. Yes, it had been two days and not a word from him. Yes, yes, yes!

But this was her only brother here. She wasn't going to let him be dead, not yet.

She'd left Mother this morning, tracked down Monique through one of the deputy secretary's aides, received permission to visit her, and flown straight to Baltimore.

Kara pushed through the door. A haggard receptionist lifted her head. "Can I help you?"

"Yes, my name is Kara Hunter. Monique de Raison is expecting me."

"Yes, Ms. Hunter. This way, please."

The woman led her down a long hall and into a large laboratory. At least twenty work stations were each manned by technicians. To Kara's left, a long glass wall looked into a clean room where blue-capped, white-jacketed, masked technicians worked. Voices buzzed quietly. Intently. These were the people bent on cracking a code that couldn't be cracked in the time given. These were America's heroes, she thought. They paid her no mind as she walked through the lab into another hall and then entered a large office where Monique bent over a thick ream of photos with a scientist who vaguely resembled Einstein, bushy hair, spectacles, and all.

Monique looked up.

"Kara." Her face seemed to sag and her eyes were red. She looked at her comrade. *"Excusez-moi un moment, Charles."*

The man nodded and left.

Monique stepped to Kara and pulled her into a fierce hug. "I'm so sorry, Kara." She sniffed. "I'm so very sorry."

Kara hadn't expected such a touching reception. What had happened between Monique and Thomas? She swallowed a lump rising in her throat. "Are you okay?"

Monique pulled back and turned her face. "Not really, no. I'm not sure that I can deliver."

"They say that your encoding survived the mutation."

"It's not that simple. But yes, the genes I had isolated for modification with the introduction of my own virus did survive. We will know in a couple hours what that means."

"You don't sound hopeful."

"I don't know how to sound." She looked at Kara with sad eyes.

"I came because I'm having difficulty accepting his death," she said.

Monique's eyes watered. She bit her lower lip and eased into her chair behind the desk.

"What happened out there, Monique?"

"I dreamed," she said.

She'd dreamed. This was supposed to mean something? And then it suddenly did.

"You . . . like Thomas, you mean? You dreamed of the forest?"

"Yes. Only not as myself, but as his wife, Rachelle. And honestly, it felt to me like that was the real world and this one was only the dream."

Kara couldn't contain her surprise. "You went there? You saw him there? How?"

"We were sleeping, and I think it might have been something to do with the fact that we were in contact. Our wrists had been injured, both of ours. Maybe our blood . . . I don't know. But I do know that I shared Rachelle's life. I shared all her memories, her experiences."

"You have no doubt about this?" Kara asked, gaping.

"None. And we were both afraid that if he was killed in either reality, he would also die in the other. And also that even if he was by some miracle cured in that reality, he might not be cured in this reality."

"I won't accept that!" Kara said. Even though the same thoughts had occurred to her, she had been hoping Monique would contradict her ideas.

Monique blinked at her outburst.

"Sorry. But if you'd been through what I've been through these past weeks . . ." Kara dropped into a facing chair. "But then you have, haven't you? Then let me be straight with you. I'm not willing to accept this nonsense that he's dead."

"I saw him!"

"You saw him? Did you feel his pulse?"

"I watched Carlos feel his pulse. He was dead." Her voice was strained.

Kara considered something Thomas had told her before leaving on his rescue. He'd concluded that he was the only gateway between the two realities. If he was dead . . .

"You do realize that if your antivirus fails, then the only hope this world has is Thomas."

"Yes."

"And if he's dead, we may be in a world of hurt."

"He got me out; I have the antivirus."

"I thought you weren't so sure."

"We're working on it."

"And I'm working on Thomas."

"They've already dropped a team into the region where I was held," Monique said. She sounded as if she might snap.

"Okay, fine. Let's think this through. We both know that Carlos isn't sloppy enough to let them find him. This isn't about the tactics of special forces. This is about the mind and the heart, and I think you and I might be the ones to find Thomas's mind and heart. If he's alive."

"And if he's not?"

"As I said, I'm not willing to accept that."

Monique stared at Kara. A glimmer of hope lit her eyes. "Do you realize that if Rachelle is killed, I may die?" she asked.

"Tell me everything that happened," Kara said. "Everything."

30

THE HORDE guarded the lake that night. The custom of the Desert Dwellers required that the executed remain a night in the water to complete his humiliation. No one was allowed to enter or bathe until the body was removed.

Ciphus objected but finally capitulated, as much to control the lingering of those loyal to Justin as to yield to the Horde's demands. The beach was cleared, and those who celebrated Justin's death did so in the streets rather than by the lake. Those few who could not wait until morning to bathe did so with the small reserves held in some of the houses.

Thomas found Rachelle in their home, lying on the floor, exhausted and unmoving. Neither had slept for nearly two days. He made her wash and then did so himself. They fell into bed without talking about the execution and fell into a dead sleep.

Oddly, Thomas did not dream of the Raison Strain that night. He hadn't eaten the rhambutan fruit, so he did dream, just not of the virus and France. He should have, though. Unless, of course, he wasn't alive in the other reality any longer, in which case there would be nothing for him to dream about.

But that would mean he was powerless to stop the Raison Strain. Hopefully Monique could stop it. If not, she would die along with the rest of the world in about ten days or so. And Rachelle might very well die with her.

These were the dreamy thoughts running through Thomas's mind when he heard the screams that pulled him from deep sleep early the next morning.

He jerked upright and immediately gasped at a sharp pain that shot through his skin. A quick glance confirmed the worst. The disease was upon him. Not just a light graying, but a nearly fully advanced condition!

He bent his arm, but the pain stopped him. The gray flaking on the epidermis didn't begin to characterize the horrible agony. How had this happened? He had to get to the lake!

Again he bent his arm, this time ignoring the pain, as he knew the Desert Dwellers did. It felt as though the layer of skin just under the epidermis had turned brittle and was cracking when he moved.

Rachelle sat up. "What's that?"

The screams were coming from the west. The lake.

"What . . ." Rachelle cried out with pain and stared at her skin. "Didn't we bathe last night?"

Thomas peeled off his covers and forced himself to stand through the pain. His mind swam with confusion. Maybe they'd accidentally used rainwater instead of water from the lake. It had happened before.

Rachelle had risen and rushed to the window, wincing with each step. "It's the lake. Something's wrong with the lake!"

"Papa!" Marie ran into the room. She too! The disease covered her skin like white ash.

"Get your brother! Hurry!"

"It hurts—"

"Hurry!"

They didn't bother with slippers or boots, only tunics. Thomas and Rachelle led their two children from the house, urging them to move as quickly as possible, which resulted in tears and a pace barely faster than a walk. The screaming had spread; hundreds, thousands of villagers had awakened to the same condition. The disease had swept in over night and infected them all, Thomas thought. They streamed down the main street, desperate for the lake.

Thomas grabbed Samuel's hand and pulled him along. "Ignore it. The faster you get to the water, the sooner the pain will be gone."

"Why is this happening?" Rachelle panted.

"I don't know."

"It's everyone! Maybe it's punishment for the death of Justin."

"I hope only that."

"What do you mean?"

"I don't know, Rachelle!" he snapped.

She hurried beside him in silence. Marie and Samuel were both crying through their pain, but they too knew enough to push ahead. Elyon's lake was their salvation; they knew that like they knew they needed air to breathe. Every cell in their bodies screamed for the relief that the lake alone could give them.

The sight that greeted them on the lakeshore stopped Thomas short. Five thousand, maybe ten thousand diseased men, women, and children stood back from the water's edge, staring aghast or swaying back and forth, moaning.

The water was red!

Not just tinged with red, but red like blood.

Hundreds of brave souls had stepped into the lake and were frantically splashing the red water on their legs and thighs, but most were too terrified to even walk up to the water.

The screams weren't from the pain that would normally be associated with cleansing in such a diseased state, Thomas realized. There was terror in their voices and there were many words, but the ones that seized his mind were those that rose above the others in this sea of chaos.

"The power is gone!"

A man Thomas barely recognized as William, his own lieutenant, staggered from the water. His skin was wet but the disease clung to him like cracked, mildewed leather.

William gripped his head with both hands and looked around in desperation. He saw Thomas and lurched up the shore. "It doesn't work!" He had the look of a crazed man. "The power is gone! The Horde is coming, Thomas!"

Thomas glanced down the shore to his left. Martyn and Qurong stood with arms folded two hundred yards distant. Behind them, the thousand Scab warriors who'd accompanied them watched in silence.

"You mean these?"

William paced frantically, lost to Thomas's question.

"William! What do you mean they're coming?"

"The scouts have come in. Both armies are in the forest."

Both?

"How many? How far?"

"He was innocent! Now we will die for allowing it."

More people were running onto the shores. Even more were fleeing the lake in panic. William was hardly lucid. Thomas grabbed him by the shoulders and shook him.

"Listen to me! How many did the scouts report?"

"Too many, Thomas. It doesn't matter. My men are all diseased!"

Thomas could feel the onset of the same confusion he'd once felt when the disease had nearly taken him before in the desert. But he was still thinking clearly enough to realize what had happened.

Rachelle said it for him. "Johan knew." She gazed at the confusion before them. "He knew that Justin was pure, and he knew that innocent blood would poison the lake." She looked at him with wide eyes. "We're becoming like them. We're becoming like the Horde!"

It was true. This was Martyn's true betrayal. This was how he was waging his battle. They would take the forests without swinging a single blade. The only difference between the Forest People and the Desert Dwellers now was a lake that no longer functioned. In a matter of hours, maybe less, the Forest Guard would look, act, and think like their own enemies.

There wasn't much time. "Give me your sword!"

William stared dumbly.

Thomas reached forward and yanked the blade from William's scabbard. "Call the men! We fight now. To the death!"

His wife was staring at the red lake, eyes wide, but not with horror now. There was another look in them—a dawning of realization.

A shriek split the morning air behind them. Thomas spun and saw a woman pointing to the front gates. He twisted and looked down the main street. The front gates were five hundred yards away—he couldn't make out any detail, but enough to see that an army had arrived.

A Horde army.

"The men, William! Follow me!"

He gripped the sword in his fist and ran across the beach, toward Martyn, shoving from his mind the terrible pain he felt. Feet were padding the sand behind him, but he didn't stop to see who it was.

The plan that had emerged from the fog in his mind was a simple one, with only one end: Qurong's death. In his current condition, he wouldn't have the same advantage that he ordinarily would, but they wouldn't take him down before he killed the Horde leader, the firstborn, Tanis.

"Thomas!"

He recognized the voice. Mikil was running up the bank in a blind panic. He ignored her and raced on. The distant sound of swords clashing carried over the village. Some of his Guard were putting up a defense. But the more ominous sound of boots and hoofs—thousands upon thousands marching in cadence up the main street—made the meager defense sound like a children's sideshow.

One of the Scabs had left Qurong's army and was running to meet him. No, not a Scab warrior, but a Scab general, with a black sash.

Martyn!

"Remember, Thomas, he's my brother," Rachelle said behind him. It was his wife, not William, behind him. And she wanted him to leave Johan unharmed?

He glanced back. "He betrayed Elyon." The Council members, led by Ciphus, had finally arrived at the lake and were testing its waters. The uproar had settled in the hopes that perhaps the elder could fix this terrible problem. No one seemed to worry about the army in the streets—they wanted to bathe. Only to bathe.

Rachelle pulled up next to him. Johan was now only fifty yards from them.

"Thomas, there is another way. Do you remember what Justin told me?"

Thomas slowed and held out his sword with both hands. "The only way I know now is to take Qurong with me. If you want your brother to live, tell him to let me pass."

"You're not listening!" she whispered harshly. "'When the time comes,' that's what he said. Thomas, *this* is that time."

Martyn had withdrawn his sword and slowed to a walk. Thomas stopped and prepared to meet the general in whatever way he had in mind. His skin was crawling with fire, and his joints felt like they'd fractured, but he knew that the Horde fought through the pain all the time. He could do that and more, if not die trying.

"He said he had a better way," Rachelle said. "Justin told me to die with him."

"That's what I'm preparing to do. And with me Qurong will die."

She grabbed his arm and spoke hurriedly. "Listen to me, Thomas! I think I understand what he meant. He said it would bring me life! He knew that we would need life. He knew that he would die. He knew that the lake would no longer give us life because it would be defiled by the shedding of innocent blood. *His* blood!"

The lone figure walking toward them faded from his vision.

Die with me.

"We've died with him already," he said. "Look at us!"

"He said it would bring us *life*!"

Martyn's face was shrouded by his hood. He carried his sword loose, by his side—overconfident, taunting.

Thomas looked at the lake, at the sea of red that sent chills down his spine. Justin's message suddenly seemed quite obvious to him. He couldn't imagine actually doing it, but if Rachelle was right, Justin had asked them to die as he had died.

He'd asked them to drown in this sea of red.

Thomas had swam through a sea of red once, deep in the emerald lake that could be breathed.

A fresh cry erupted from the shore. Evidently Ciphus had failed in his task to prove that all was still fine with his lake. But there was more. Ciphus was screaming above the chaos.

"He's gone!"

Thomas cast a quick glance over his shoulder. The elder stood on the shore, dripping with water. He looked surprisingly like a Scab—with dreadlocks he would look like Qurong himself.

"There is no body!" the elder cried. "They have taken him!"

Thomas spun back to face Martyn. "He's lying," Martyn said. "The body could be anywhere under the water by now. He's setting you up."

"Thomas, you have to listen to me!" Rachelle pleaded.

The disease was making his head swim. He blinked and tried to think clearly. "You're suggesting that we run into the lake and drown ourselves?"

"You would rather live like this?"

Martyn stopped ten feet from them, head low so that shadows hid his face.

Thomas adjusted his grip on the sword. An image of Justin's swollen face filled his mind.

Follow me. Die with me.

It was an incredible demand that Justin had suggested to whoever would listen.

He spoke to Martyn. "What have you done to us?" His voice came out low and unearthly, bitter and full of pain at once.

Martyn lifted his head and Thomas saw his face.

It wasn't the scowl he expected. Tears filled the general's eyes. His face was drawn tight, stricken with fear. Fear!

Martyn was suddenly walking again, closer, sword still by his side.

"Stop there," Thomas ordered.

Martyn took two more steps and then stopped.

This wasn't what Thomas had expected. He could easily take two long steps and thrust his blade into the general's unprotected chest. A part of him insisted that he *should*. He should kill Martyn and then run for Qurong.

But he couldn't. Not now. Not with Rachelle's words ringing in his ears. Not seeing tears in Martyn's eyes. Could this be more trickery?

"I remember," the general said. The remorse in his tone was so uncharacteristic that Thomas blinked. "I remember, Rachelle. He spoke to me, and all night I've remembered."

Rachelle let out a sob and started toward her brother.

He lifted a hand, just barely. "Please, no. They can't see us."

Johan looked past Thomas toward the bank behind them. The first of the Horde army had arrived on the shores. Sporadic cries arose as villagers scattered for safety, but there were no sounds of swordplay or resistance, Thomas noted. The disease had taken most of their minds already. The mighty Forest Guard had been stripped of its will to fight by a disease none of them had defeated before.

Johan looked at Thomas, eyes begging. "I knew he was innocent. I knew his blood would defile the lake. I even knew who he was, but I couldn't remember why I should care. Now I've murdered him. I can't live with this."

"No, there is a better way!" Rachelle said.

"Please, I've decided. I will return to my army with a proposition of surrender from you, and then I will kill Qurong and publicly take the blame for poisoning the water. Ciphus will blame you. I told him that if anything went wrong with our plan, he was to blame you. He'll say that you took the body of Justin and poisoned the water. In the people's state of shock from the disease, they'll believe him. The least I can do is protect you."

"Protect us from what?" Rachelle demanded. "Not the disease."

Thomas lowered his sword. Johan glanced at it, then over his shoulder. Qurong motioned to a line of his warriors, who started to march up the beach toward them.

"Qurong suspects something. We don't have much time," Thomas said. He looked at the water. "Do you remember the boy saying that he had a lot riding on us?"

"I suggest we bow our heads in a sign of mutual agreement," Johan said. "Qurong must see that we've struck some kind of—"

"Forget your plan," Thomas interrupted. "Do you remember the boy saying he depended on us?"

"Yes."

"Justin said the same thing to Rachelle yesterday morning. Then he told her to follow him in his death. It would bring life in a better way, he said. Rachelle's convinced he meant for us to die by drowning in the sea of red, like he did."

Johan glanced at the water.

"Do you believe he was Elyon?" Thomas asked.

"I . . . I don't know. He was . . . he was innocent."

"But do you believe he was Elyon?" Thomas demanded again. "Was he the boy?"

Johan paused and stared out at the glassy red water. "Yes. Yes, I think he was."

Thomas spoke quickly now. "And is it possible to breathe Elyon's red water?"

"Perhaps." A fresh tear leaked from Johan's right eye and ran down his scabbed cheek.

"Then I think she's right," Thomas said. "And I think if we wait any longer, our minds will be confused by the disease with the rest."

Ciphus was delivering a diatribe down the shore. Thomas heard his name repeatedly, but at the moment, the elder's web of lies felt like nonsense next to the things his wife was now suggesting.

"You're suggesting we drown like he did?" Johan asked.

They were all looking at the lake now. A row of warriors had broken from the new arrivals and were approaching from their right. The ones Qurong had dispatched were drawing closer on the left. They were running out of time.

Rachelle spoke with a tremor in her voice. "I'm afraid."

"But that's what he told you?" Johan asked. "To drown like he did?"

"Yes."

Silence.

"And Samuel? Marie?" she said.

"If you're wrong, they're dead with us."

Thomas had been here fifteen years earlier, torn between fleeing Elyon's lake and diving in. Then, it had been a pool of life. This lake looked like a cold pool of death.

Johan uttered a small gasp. He was staring across the lake.

"What is it?"

But Johan didn't have to answer. Thomas and Rachelle saw them together, and instinctively Rachelle grasped his arm. Thomas's first thought was that the trees on the opposite side of the lake had sprouted a thick harvest of cherries.

But these cherries were set in black eye sockets that were attached to furry black bodies.

Shataiki!

A hundred thousand at least, clinging to the trees just beyond the nearest branches, watching them with unblinking stares.

It had been fifteen years since Thomas had seen the bats, black or white. What had changed now? Justin had been killed. The forest was now inhabited by Shataiki. Or had Justin's cry for them to remember opened their eyes as it had opened Johan's mind? Either way, it was both terrifying and revealing at once.

Johan suddenly threw back his hood. Tears slipped down his face in long ribbons now. He gave the bats one last glare and stripped off his cloak, revealing shockingly white and flaky flesh. The sight of their general standing in only a loincloth brought the Scab warriors to a complete halt less than fifty yards on either side.

In that moment Thomas knew what he must do. What he wanted most desperately to do. Whom he must follow. Why Elyon had a lot riding on him. On them.

He didn't bother discarding his tunic. He glanced to his right, caught Rachelle's wide eyes; his left, Johan's frantic stare.

"For Justin," he said.

He ran.

Despite his earlier statement, Thomas almost turned to find his children. The thought of leaving them among the Horde sickened him. But he pushed on—this wasn't the time to stop and make provision for them, no matter what the outcome. His children were now in Elyon's hands. If he survived the next few moments, he would sweep them off their feet and kiss them with joy.

They tore down the bank, Thomas first, with Johan and Rachelle hard on his heels. The Horde grunted in shock to his left and right; he could hear that much. The Shataiki screeched. He wondered if anyone else could hear them.

Then he was airborne.

He hit the water and was immediately swallowed by a cold sea.
Red.

———— ◦◦◦◦ ————

His first impulse was that their decision had been a terrible mistake. That
the disease had softened their reasoning and caused them to do something
so insane as to follow Justin in his death.

He kicked deep so that his feet wouldn't flail on the surface for the
Horde to see.

The water changed on his second stroke, less than five feet under, from
cold to warm. He opened his eyes in surprise. He'd expected a dark abyss
below him—black demons waiting to satisfy their lust for death.

What he saw was a pool of red light, dim and hazy, but definitely light!
He looked left, then right, but there was no sign of Johan or Rachelle.

Thomas stopped kicking. He floated. The water was serene. Silent.
Unearthly and eerie. He could hear the soft thump of his own pulse. Above
him, countless Scabs were watching the water for signs of his emergence,
but here in this fluid he was momentarily safe.

And then the moment passed, and the reality of his predicament filled
his mind.

His eyes began to sting, and he blinked in the warm water, but to
no relief. He was already running out of oxygen; his chest felt tight and
for a moment he considered kicking to the surface to take one more
gulp of air.

He opened his mouth, felt the warm water on his tongue. Closed it.

*It's his water, Thomas. You've been in this lake a thousand times, and you
know that the bottom has always been muddy and black. But now it's light.
You've been here before.*

But this plan suddenly struck him as irrational. What man would will-
ingly suck in a lungful of water? He'd entered intending to throw his own
life away? The disease had ruined him! He'd actually believed for one desperate moment that dying would bring him a new kind of life, but at the
moment, nothing felt quite so foolish.

What of Johan and Rachelle? Would they claw for the surface in panic?

But what choice did he have? Was returning to the living death above any less absurd? He hung limp, trying to ignore the terrible knowledge that his lungs were starting to burn. But that was just it—he didn't have the luxury of contemplating his decision much longer. He was down to a few seconds already.

A jolt of panic, a despair he'd never felt before, ran through his body, shaking him in its horrible fist.

Thomas opened his mouth, closed his eyes. He began to sob. A final scream filled his mind, forbidding him to take in this water. Justin had sucked at the water, but that was Justin.

No, that was Elyon, Thomas.

Then his air was gone. Thomas stretched his jaw wide and sucked hard like a fish gulping for oxygen.

Pain hit his lungs like a battering ram.

He tried to breathe out. In, out, like he once had in the emerald lake. But this wasn't that kind of water. His lungs felt as if they were full of stone. He was going to die. His waterlogged body began to sink slowly.

He didn't fight the drowning. If Justin was Elyon, then this was the right thing for him to do. It was that simple. Justin had told them to follow him in his death, and that is what they were doing. And if Rachelle was wrong about all of this, then he would die as Justin died to show his respect for his innocence. There was no life above the surface anyway.

The lack of oxygen ravaged his body for long seconds, and he didn't try to stop death.

Then he did try. With everything in him, he tried to reverse this terrible course.

Elyon, I beg you. Take me. You made me; now take me.

Darkness encroached on his mind. Thomas began to scream.

Then it was black.

Nothing.

He was dead; he knew that. But there was something here, beyond life. From the blackness a moan began to fill his ears, replacing his own screams. The moan gained volume and grew to a wail and then a scream.

He knew the voice! It was Justin. Elyon was screaming! And he was screaming in pain.

Thomas pressed his hands to his ears and began to scream with the other, thinking now that this was worse than death. His body crawled with fire as though every last cell revolted at the sound. And so they should, a voice whispered in his skull. Their Maker was screaming in pain!

He'd been here before! Exactly here, in the belly of the emerald lake. He'd heard this scream.

A soft, inviting voice replaced the cry. "Remember me, Thomas," it said. Justin said. Elyon said.

Light lit the edges of his mind. A red light. Thomas opened his eyes, stunned by this sudden turn. The burning in his chest was gone. The water was warm and the light below seemed brighter.

He was alive?

He sucked at the red water and pushed it out. Breathing! He was alive!

Thomas cried out in astonishment. He glanced down at his legs and arms. Yes, this was real. He was here, floating in the lake, not in some other disconnected reality.

And his skin . . . he rubbed it with his thumb. The disease was gone. He turned slowly in the water, looking for Rachelle or Johan, but neither was here.

Thomas twisted once in the water and thrust his fist above (or was it below?) his head. He dove deep then looped back and struck for the surface. He had to find Rachelle! Justin had changed the water.

The moment his hand hit the cold water above the warm, his lungs began to burn. He tried to breathe but found he couldn't. Then he was through, out of the water.

Three thoughts mushroomed in his mind while the water was still falling from his face. The first was that he was breaking through the surface at precisely the same time as Rachelle on his right and Johan on his left. Like three dolphins breaking the surface in a coordinated leap, heads arched back, water streaming off their hair, grinning as wide as the sky.

The second thought was that he could feel the bottom of the lake under his feet. He was standing.

The third was that he still couldn't breathe.

He came out of the water to his waist, doubled over, and wretched a quart of water from his lungs. The pain left with the water. He gasped once, found he could breathe easily, and turned slowly.

To his right. Water and strings of saliva fell from Rachelle's grinning mouth. She had just died as well.

To his left. For a brief moment he didn't recognize the man five feet to his left. This was Martyn the Scab, but his skin had changed. Flesh tone. Smooth. Pink like a baby's skin. His eyes shone like emeralds. This was Johan as he once had been, without a trace of the disease. He too had breathed the water.

They stood in the water, three drenched strangers facing a hundred thousand Horde, some dressed in the tunics of Forest People, some dressed in the hooded cloaks of the Desert Dwellers, all dressed in the white skin of disease.

For a while no one spoke. Qurong stood with his army a hundred yards to their right, face shrouded by his hood. Ciphus stood fifty yards to their left, lips drawn. There, directly ahead, were Mikil and Jamous and Marie and Samuel, gaping with the rest.

Thomas walked out of the lake, plowing water noisily with his thighs. In some ways he felt like he was looking at a whole new world. Not only was he a new person, drowned in magic, but the thousands he faced were different. The disease hung on them like dried dung. But when they understood what Elyon had done for them in this lake, they would flock en masse into the red waters. *He would be run over,* he thought wryly.

The Horde warriors who'd been sent to investigate stood fifty paces off. They had their answer, and Thomas doubted they understood it.

He glanced back to where he'd seen the Shataiki. Gone. No, not gone. They were still there, undoubtedly, but he could no longer see them.

He was about to speak, to tell them what had happened, when a shrill voice shattered the silence. "It was them!" Ciphus cried. "They have deceived us and poisoned Elyon's water."

Johan stepped up beside Thomas. "We will tolerate your lies no longer, old man! Are you blind? Do we look poisoned to you?"

"Look at yourselves! The water has stripped you of your flesh!"

"Stripped us?" Thomas asked, dumbfounded. He looked at the people. "It has stripped us of our disease. Can't you see that?"

"Impossible!" Ciphus said. "This is no longer Elyon's lake. This is red water, poisoned by death."

It was what one of the Horde would say, Thomas thought. Ciphus had turned completely. He searched the bank for Marie and Samuel, found them, and saw that Rachelle was already running for them. She knew as well as he, if the disease had taken them all so quickly, they might not be so receptive.

He faced the elder, who'd turned to the people. "The law states with no uncertainty that the body must remain in the water until morning, but you all saw with your own eyes. There is no body!"

Again it was Johan who took up their defense. "No one crossed my line of guards to steal the body. You hardly searched. And this is Horde law that you're quoting, not your own. Since when do you bow to Horde law?"

"It is law!" the elder shouted. "And you were complicit in their plan to steal the body. Who would have suspected the two generals were working together to enslave the entire world in one twisted plot?" He pointed at the lake. "Look at what you've done!"

Johan stepped forward and spoke directly to the people. "The lake isn't poisoned; it has only been changed. Am I dead? Does the disease still cling to my flesh? Am I a Scab? No, I'm free of the disease, and it's because I did what Justin told us to do. To follow him in his death by drowning in the lake and finding new life! This is the fulfillment of the boy's prophecy. This is the blow against evil the boy told us about, and it has come when all other hope is lost." He thrust his hand back toward the lake. "Enter the lake and find his life. Drown, all of you! Drown!"

No one ran for the lake. They stared at him as if he'd lost his senses. The great Martyn who was now Johan no longer commanded the respect he had only minutes earlier.

There was movement beside Qurong on their right. And on their left, Ciphus walked slowly toward them. "Do you hear him?"

Rachelle had shepherded Marie and Samuel to the edge of the water and was whispering in their ears. They were shivering.

"Martyn the general would complete his deception with Thomas by having us all drown!" Ciphus said. "Never!"

"Qurong is coming," Johan whispered urgently. "We don't have much time."

The Horde leader was marching up the shore with several hundred warriors.

Two men broke from the crowd of Forest People and ran down the shore—the two who had traveled with Justin through the Valley of Tuhan. Ronin and Arvyl.

Their faces were stained with tears and their eyes round with fear. "We will follow him to our deaths if we must," Ronin said quietly, looking deep into Thomas's eyes. "What must we do?"

"Swim deep and breathe the water. Let it take you. You'll find life."

They glanced at each other.

"Quickly! They're coming."

The two men stepped in, hesitated, then rushed and dove. They disappeared.

"Now his men, Justin's men!" Ciphus said. "They have all conspired to bring our ruin!"

Qurong was still marching. So then, it had come down to this. The Horde against a family. Surely his second would follow them!

Thomas ran up the shore and grabbed the hands of Mikil and Jamous. "Follow me!"

"Thomas . . ."

"Shut up and follow me, Mikil!" He kept his voice low and hushed. "Do you believe me?"

She didn't answer.

"You killed Elyon. We all did. Now give your life back to him and ride with me!"

Mikil and Jamous stared at each other.

"I think he's right," Jamous said.

"You think Justin was Elyon?" she demanded.

"He spoke to me."

She stared at him with wide white eyes.

"Dive deep and breathe the water; for Elyon's sake, move! Have I ever lied to you? Never. Run!"

It was enough for Mikil. They sprinted down the sandy bank with Thomas right behind. They dove in tandem and splashed just as Ronin and Arvyl broke the surface, flesh pink, mouths wide, retching water.

Thomas grabbed Johan's arm. "Horses, we'll need horses from the auxiliary Guard stable," he whispered. "They'll be saddled and—"

But Johan knew all of this and was already running up the bank. The diseased Forest People scrambled out of his way. He disappeared into a row of houses.

"All of you who will follow Justin in his death and find new life, drown!" Thomas cried. "Drown now!"

The Horde leader was marching faster.

Ciphus remained silent. He too saw Qurong. He too saw the Horde army that had them surrounded, many thousands, mounted on horses, sickles ready. They were under a new order, all of them.

"I beg you! Remember him! This is the day of your deliverance!" Thomas shouted. Behind him the water splashed. Mikil and Jamous had risen.

His frustration boiled to the surface. "What's wrong with you? Are you blind? It's life, you fools! Drown!"

Mikil laughed.

Two children ran down the shore. Lucy and Billy, the two from the Valley of Tuhan. They went in with Marie and Samuel. On their heels several grown men and women, maybe half a dozen, one from here, one from there. They splashed into the water and sank below the surface. One sputtered to the surface and clamored out of the lake. His skin hadn't changed. Two more broke for the lake.

"Enough!" Qurong stood with his fists on his hips, legs spread. "Enter the lake and consider yourself an enemy that we will hunt down and destroy."

"You are Tanis!" Thomas said. "You drank Teeleh's water and brought us the disease. Now you'll wage war on Elyon's children? Justin has brought us peace."

"I have brought you peace!" His voice seemed too loud for a man. It hit Thomas then—this was Teeleh speaking through his firstborn. He was playing the spoiled child who wanted to be as great as Elyon. It had always been Teeleh's way; now, having killed Justin, he would wage war on this unexpected remnant. He would kill the life that Justin had made possible in his death.

"We are one!" Qurong cried with arms spread. "I *am* peace!"

"You are at peace with Teeleh, not Elyon. Not Justin."

"Blasphemy!" Ciphus cried. "You are banished. Any man or woman or child who bathes in this lake will be banished!"

Qurong threw back his hood to expose long knotted dreadlocks over white flaking skin. "Not banished," he roared. "Killed!"

Behind Thomas, the water splashed as others came out of the lake. Oblivious to the exchange, several of the children giggled. Rachelle hurried them from the water with hushed tones.

Thomas scanned the beach. There was only one way clear of the Horde warriors, and that was past Ciphus. Even then, Qurong would give chase.

Where are you, Johan?

A lone man broke from the crowd, ran straight down the shore, and dove in defiance of Qurong's command. William? If Thomas wasn't mistaken, his lieutenant, William, had just joined them.

Where was Johan? How long did it take to open a gate for a few horses? He had to stall Qurong. "If you are with Elyon, then would you condemn women and children to death because they don't have your disease?"

"It is you who have the disease," Qurong said. "You are albinos with poisoned flesh and sickened minds." Spittle flew from his mouth. His eyes were white-hot with anger. Why so furious as this for a few naked prey? "Your disease will divide us and threaten my kingdom, and for that you will drown!"

"We just *have* drowned!" Mikil said. She burst into laughter. "You want to drown us again?"

Thomas held out his hand to quiet her. "Get them ready," he said quietly. "We ride through the forest, north."

"Horses?"

"Johan."

She understood.

"We'll see if you survive my drowning," Qurong said. "Take them!"

His guard broke around him and marched forward.

"Wait!" Thomas shouted. "I have something to exchange!" He reached into his tunic, slipped the leather book from where he'd carried it, and lifted it high.

"A Book of History."

Qurong lifted his hand, and his soldiers stopped. He took a step forward. In his own twisted mind this was a sacred book, but what would he do to own it again? It was, after all, just an artifact.

"You have said that no one is permitted to enter the lake," Thomas said. "If I throw this book in these poisoned waters, will you break your own law and enter to find it?"

"Lay it down."

Johan emerged from the village behind the people, leading a dozen horses. He took one look at the situation and kicked his mount.

Thomas spoke loudly to cover his approach.

"I will lay this book down if you will give me one minute to plead my case in front of the entire Council, as is the custom of our people in a case of this . . ."

The sound of Johan and his horses galloping down the bank was enough to turn every head. The Scabs had just made sense of his sudden appearance and were moving to intercept when their old commander thundered past Qurong.

Thomas shoved the blank Book of History into his tunic, then spun and grabbed the closest child. "Get them on the horses, hurry!"

Rachelle lifted Marie into a saddle behind William. She grabbed Samuel by the arm, jerked him from his feet, and swung him up with William's help. Then she turned for another child.

"Stop them!" Qurong shouted.

"Go, Rachelle! I'll get the others. Ride!"

But she ran for a fourth child.

They were no longer inhibited by the painful disease that slowed the Scabs. Before the first warrior reached them, they'd swung into saddles and were galloping toward the Council, which stood frozen.

All but Thomas and Rachelle, who'd helped the children.

"Mount! Hurry!" Rachelle wasn't going to make it! Thomas ran his horse at the closest warrior, who pulled up and took a meager swipe at him. He ducked the sickle easily enough. Now his wife had mounted.

"Ride! Ride!"

Out of nowhere a single arrow cut through the air and plowed into his mount's neck. The animal reared in pain and Thomas clung to the saddle.

"Thomas!" Rachelle screamed. She knew as well as he that this wound would finish the horse. And the Scabs were now rushing in. A blade struck the rear quarter of his horse.

Rachelle spun her own mount around. "Jump!" She raced up to him, released the reins, and shifted back off the saddle, holding on to the pommel with one hand.

It was a move the Guard knew well; horses often fell in battle. They learned early that at any speed, jumping from one horse to another was nearly impossible unless the rider could hold himself fast in the stirrups and catch the jumper between him and the horse's neck.

Thomas leaped, slammed into her horse's neck, and crashed into the saddle. He bent low and grabbed the reins. His wife hugged him around the waist and held tight.

But now they were going the wrong way. He reined the horse around and galloped to catch the others. It had all happened in a few seconds. Johan had just cleared the Council, but Justin's followers were far from safety.

The hundred Scabs above the beach were spurring their horses to intercept.

"Jamous, William, on your right!" Thomas cried. He veered straight for the Horde. "Hold on!" Rachelle tightened her grip around his belly.

Jamous and William broke from the others and headed for the army. Johan glanced back, took quick stock, and led the others away from the danger at a full sprint.

Thomas leaned forward and screamed as he would in pitched battle. Every Scab soldier there had undoubtedly seen this mighty warrior felling their comrades, and the sight of him and two of his lieutenants racing directly for them caused them to pull on their reins.

The delay was just enough to give Johan the time he needed to lead the others into the trees.

"Break!" Thomas, Jamous, and William veered to the left on the command and raced for the trees after Johan.

It was then, not two horse lengths from the trees, that a soft *thump* punctuated the pounding hoofs.

Rachelle groaned behind him.

Another *thump*.

An arrow smacked into a tree on his right.

Rachelle's grip on his midsection loosened.

"Rachelle?"

She grunted, and there was the unmistakable sound of pain in that grunt.

"Rachelle? Talk to me!"

In answer, a dozen arrows clipped through the branches. And then they were into the forest. His wife had been shot! He had to stop.

"Rachelle!"

The Horde was in heavy pursuit—he couldn't stop.

"Answer me!" he screamed. "Rachelle!"

Nothing. Her hands were slipping, and he grabbed them with his left hand. "William!"

His lieutenant glanced back. "Ride, Thomas! Ride!"

"Rachelle's been shot!" he cried.

William immediately pulled to the side and eased up. Thomas galloped up to him, still at full speed. They dodged several trees and broke into a meadow. William studied the limp body behind Thomas. Rachelle's limp body.

What Thomas saw in his lieutenant's green eyes drove a stake of raw dread through his heart.

Thomas veered off the path just long enough to check Rachelle's pulse. She was alive. But unconscious. Three arrows protruded from her back. He started to sob, still seated on the saddle with the sound of the Horde less than a hundred meters behind. William strapped her wrists together around Thomas's belly, and they rode hard to catch the others.

Elyon, I beg you heal her, he prayed. *I beg you save my wife.*

The others didn't know. Samuel and Marie rode ahead with Mikil and Jamous, who'd taken Marie to lighten Mikil's load. Every minute, Thomas checked Rachelle's wrist for a pulse. Alive, still alive.

William rode behind, silent. Even if they could stop, there was nothing that could be done for Rachelle. She needed rest. She needed to stop riding altogether, but with this pursuit none of that was an option.

You saved me, Justin. You will save my wife.

They had died and come back to life in the lake. Why? So that Rachelle could be killed by the Horde? It made no sense, which could only mean she wasn't going to die. He needed her! The children needed her. The tribe needed her. She was the sweetest person, the wisest, the loveliest, the most loving of them all!

She would not be dying.

William pulled up beside him after twenty minutes. "There are about two hundred in pursuit," he said. "Johan and I will lead them south and join you at the apple grove to the north."

Thomas nodded.

His lieutenant raced ahead and spoke briefly to Johan, who looked back in alarm. He veered to the right and vanished into the trees with William. They would circle back, engage the Horde, and then draw them south according to classic Guard methods.

Thomas rode hard for as long as he dared. Surely William and Johan had engaged the Horde by now. He felt his wife's pulse for the hundredth time. With the horse bouncing under them, the task was now nearly impossible. Maybe her pulse had grown too weak for him to feel without stopping.

"Mikil!"

Thomas pulled his horse up before his second could respond. She saw him stop and called to the others, who had just entered a small clearing.

Thomas untied his wife's wrists, slipped off the horse, and eased her down to the grass. She lay on her side, still. He felt her neck with a trembling hand, desperate to feel the familiar pulse he'd pressed his face against so many times.

It wasn't there.

The others had come behind him, and he heard their startled cries, but his mind didn't care about them right now. He only wanted one thing. He wanted his wife back. But she was lying on the ground and he couldn't find her pulse.

She's dead, Thomas.

No, she couldn't be dead. She was Rachelle, the one who'd been healed by Justin. The one who had led them into the lake. The one who had shown him how to love and fight and lead and live.

"Mama?"

Marie. Tears spilled from his eyes at the sound of his daughter's voice.

"Mama!"

Both of his children fell to their knees over their mother. He tried one more time to feel her pulse, and this time he knew she was dead.

He sank to his haunches and let a terrible anguish wash over him. He drew a deep breath, lifted his chin, and began to sob at the sky.

Mikil was working over the body; a woman was hugging the children, who were also crying; Thomas could do nothing but cry. He'd seen so many die in battle, but today, in the wake of breathing Elyon's water, this death felt somehow different. Raw and terrible and more painful than he ever could have imagined.

Thomas slumped down beside his wife, curled into a ball, and wept.

Mikil took charge. "Mount. Lead them to the apple grove. Wait for us there."

They left him alone. He knew he had to continue. Not all of the Horde would have followed Johan. They would be coming.

He invited them now. Come and kill me as well.

I have a lot riding on you, Thomas of Hunter.

The voice spoke crystal clear in his mind. He opened his eyes. Rachelle's back was a foot from his face. Still.

He closed his eyes, mind numb.

My daughter is with me now. I need her.

"Give her back," Thomas whispered.

"What?" Mikil's voice said.

"Give her back!" he moaned.

For a long time there was only silence. They should have left long ago, but Mikil kept watch and let him lie in grief.

Then the voice spoke again.

Ride, Thomas. Ride with me.

Something was happening in his chest. He opened his eyes and focused on a strange warmth that spread through his lungs and up his neck.

He sat up.

Meet me at the desert, Thomas. Ride.

"Thomas?" Mikil knelt beside him. "I'm sorry, it's . . . it's a terrible tragedy. We should leave."

Thomas stood. The ache in his heart throbbed, but there was this other voice, and he knew that voice. It had spoken to him in the emerald lake long ago. It had spoken in the red lake today. Justin had died. They'd all died. Now Rachelle had died again. But she was alive, because the voice said she was alive. If not here, then somewhere else.

"Help me with her, Mikil."

They put Rachelle's body on the horse in front of Thomas, facing him with her face buried in his shoulder and her arms by his side. He held his wife and he rode and he cried tears that soaked her hair.

But his mourning was for his children and for himself, not for Rachelle. Not for Elyon's daughter. She was with Justin.

When they arrived at the apple orchard, Johan and William were waiting with the others. Johan wept for his sister. He kissed her and smoothed her hair and told them all that he had betrayed her.

"Where are we going?" Mikil asked.

"To the desert," Thomas said, nudging his horse. "We ride to the desert."

31

TO SAY that the world was descending into mad chaos would not be an overstatement, not in anyone's book. Four days had passed since Mike Orear had spilled his guts on CNN, since France had declared martial law, since Monique had returned with the magic elixir firmly in mind, since Thomas Hunter had been killed by a bullet to the forehead. Whether the headlines were in English or German or Spanish or Russian or any other language, they all boiled down to one of a dozen bold statements.

RAISON STRAIN THREAT CONFIRMED

WORLD ON BRINK OF WAR

OVER 5 BILLION ESTIMATED INFECTED

GLOBAL ECONOMIC SHUTDOWN

T MINUS 10 DAYS

GOD HELP US ALL

HOPE FOR ANTIVIRUS

Seeing any such headline was a surreal experience. Neither the writer nor the readers had any clue as to what any of it really meant. Nothing like this had ever happened before. Nothing like this could possibly be happening now. The Raison Strain had been thrust upon the world, and all but a few natives hidden deep in tropical jungles had surely heard the news. But how many believed? Really believed?

Denial.

Naturally, the world was either in full-fledged denial or too stunned to react. This was why there were no riots. This was why there were no protests. This was why the typical ranting and raving on the airwaves hadn't started yet.

Instead, there was an almost disconnected analysis of the situation. The world was collectively glued to the news, praying to God for the word they all knew would soon come—the announcement that Monique de Raison's antivirus had been tested and effectively killed the virus like they all knew it would.

The president spoke to the people twice each day from the White House, calming, reassuring. Tests for the infection were assigned randomly by lottery based on Social Security number. One person in every thousand was permitted to check into the local hospital for a test. The hope that first day that certain sections of the United States had been spared the virus quickly changed to astonishment as one by one each test, each family, each neighborhood, each town and city and state came back positive. CNN used a modified electoral map to show the virus's saturation. When infection was confirmed, the town was painted red. By the beginning of the second day, half the map was red. Twelve hours later, there was nothing to see but red.

Schools canceled classes. Despite the president's pleading for life as usual, half of the country's businesses closed their doors on the second day, and more were sure to follow. Transportation had all but come to a standstill. Thankfully, the public utilities continued their service with minimal staffs under direct orders from the president of the United States.

The first sign that chaos would soon threaten daily life was a run on grocery stores at 8:00 a.m. on the second day. Naturally. Panic would soon set in. It would be impossible to get to a store, much less find one open for business.

The second sign was the tone of the United Nations meeting that the president waited to address at this very minute. Those in attendance were a motley crew if the bags under their eyes and their wrinkled shirts were any indicator. The room was stuffed, every chair filled, every aisle crawling with aides. If there was ever a time for the global community to pull together, it was now. But the responses to the impassioned speeches thus far, from Russia, England, and now France, revealed just how far apart leaders could be when the chips were down.

Organized mayhem.

The French ambassador was spitting out his plea with remarkable conviction. "We are truly the victims of these barbarous terrorists—we, the innocent people of France! Our government has acted only in the best interest of our own citizens and the world community. No matter how impossible it might seem—no matter how suicidal, even—to not yield to their demands would be our true death. Better to live to fight another day than die over a cache of arms!"

A dozen voices shouted in defiance as soon as the translation in their earpieces was complete. Some in agreement, it seemed to Robert; some in vehement opposition. The word "traitor" was in there somewhere—clear enough.

He removed his earpiece. Majority leader Dwight Olsen had been on hold for the past minute. He picked up the black phone in front of him. "Okay, patch me through."

"The president will take your call now."

"Thank you," Olsen's voice crackled. "Good morning, Mr. President."

"I'm up in five minutes. What do you have, Dwight?"

"I understand you're considering declaring martial law."

"I'll do what I think is necessary to keep Americans alive."

"I urge you to remember that people still have their rights. Martial law is pushing too far."

"Call it what you want. I'm calling out the National Guard today. Defense has drawn up a simple plan to deal with various contingencies. Curfew goes into effect tonight. I'm not going to get caught putting down a revolt at home while France is breathing down our necks."

"Sir, I strongly recommend—"

"Not today. I took this call as a courtesy, but my course is set. We'll all be dead in ten days if we can't secure the antivirus. Our best hope for finding it died three days ago with Thomas Hunter—a man you dismissed out of hand, if you remember. Let's hope his death bought us what we need. If not, I don't know what we're going to do. Our ships are halfway across the Atlantic. I've got five days to make the call, you understand. Five days! In that time we keep our citizens alive and we keep them from tearing up the country. Everything else takes a backseat."

"Still—"

"In a few minutes I'm addressing the United Nations," Blair continued. "A copy of my speech will be faxed to you then, but let me give you the gist of it. I'm going to tell them that the United States will do whatever we deem necessary to protect the lives of our citizens and the lives of all who stand with us in the respect of human life. Then I'm going to call upon France to make known to the world the exact methods and means by which it will administer an antivirus in exchange for the weapons that are now streaming to its northern shores. A guarantee. Without any such guarantee, the United States will be forced to assume that the New Allegiance intends to let us die a terrible death after we have been stripped of our weapons."

Dwight wasn't reacting. They both knew where this was heading.

"Under no circumstances will I lead my people to a needless death. If we are to be killed like sheep at the slaughter, then I will deal in kind to those who would threaten my people. With this in mind I'm authorizing the targeting of Paris and twenty-seven other undisclosed locations with nuclear weapons. In five days, short of receiving a guarantee that the United States will indeed be given an antivirus for the Raison Strain, much of France will cease to exist. The innocent citizens will have been fairly warned—make for the south. In a nutshell, you now have my speech. In light of our situation, martial is the least of your concerns."

An aide whispered softly in his ear. "Sir, I have Theresa Sumner from the CDC."

He nodded. The senate majority leader was still silent, reeling.

"If you have a problem with this, take it up with me in the morning briefing. Thank you, Dwight. I have to go."

He set the phone down and took a cell phone from the aide. The deputy secretary of state, Merton Gains, was walking toward him carrying a red folder. Judging by the man's face, the folder undoubtedly contained more bad news. The secretary of state was on his way to the Middle East for a summit with several Arab nations, but it was too soon for news from his meetings. What else could have prompted Gains's entry? Too many possibilities to consider.

The president lifted the cell phone to his ear. "Hello, Theresa."

"Good afternoon, Mr. President." Her voice sounded thin.

"Any word on the tests?"

"Yes." She paused.

Blair took a deep breath. "This isn't sounding good."

"It's not. Monique's encoding survived the vaccine's mutation, but I'm afraid it's no longer effective in neutralizing the virus."

"Meaning it doesn't work."

"Basically, yes."

"Well, does it or doesn't it? Don't give me 'basically.'"

"It doesn't work. And to make matters worse, she's gone missing."

"How could she go missing?"

"We're working on it. She didn't show up this morning. Kara Hunter is frantic. Something about Monique being able to find Thomas."

It was the worst possible news he could have received two minutes before his address. Blair lowered his head and closed his eyes.

"Um, sir?"

"I'm here."

"I just wanted to apologize. I let some details about the Strain slip to—"

"Yes, we know, Theresa. It's okay; it had to come out sooner or later anyway. It worked out. Find Monique. As soon as you do, I want to see her in Washington."

He paused. This was a bad day for news. "And if you don't mind, tell Kara that our forces found the farm Monique described to us outside of Paris. It's deserted. There's no sign of her brother. They also found the lean-to in the quarry, but no body. We had to pull our people. My condolences."

"Okay, I will. There's still hope, sir. We have over ten thousand scientists working on a—"

"Please. You've already done a good job persuading me that finding a solution in time is highly unlikely. We're going to have to find the antivirus that already exists. Assuming they have it."

"Monique thinks they do," Theresa said. "She seems quite confident it's a combination of her code and the information Thomas Hunter gave them."

Merton Gains eased into a chair next to him and shot him a glance.

"Yes, of course. Hunter. It all goes back to Hunter." He sighed. "Okay, thank you. If anything new comes up, tell them to interrupt me."

He closed the phone, mind swimming.

"It looks like it's started," Gains said. "We have reports of widespread rioting in Jakarta and Bangkok." He opened the folder. "There are a number of cities on this report, sir." He stopped and looked up at Blair. "Including Tel Aviv."

The skin at the back of Blair's neck tingled. Israel? He'd spent a full hour on the phone with Isaac Benjamin early this morning, and it was all he could do to keep the man from hanging up on him. Israel was fracturing on every fault line inherent in their delicate political system. They were the only nation with nuclear weapons not to meet France's schedule for compliance, and they'd received a new demand overnight, threatening a first strike if Israel didn't ship their weapons from where they'd been gathered in the ports of Tel Aviv and Haifa.

"Get Benjamin on the phone," he said. "If he's unavailable, I want you to speak to the deputy. We can't stop the rioting, but we'd better keep the Israelis in line."

The UN's secretary general was introducing him at the podium.

"My address is only two minutes; you tell them to sit tight until I can talk to Benjamin."

"The president of the United States."

There was no applause.

Blair approached the podium, shook the secretary general's hand, and faced the circle of countries gathered in New York for answers to this, the world's greatest crisis since man first formed nations.

"Thank you. We're gathered . . ."

It was as far as he got. One of the doors to his right slammed open. The room was deadly silent and every head instinctively turned. There in the doorway stood his chief of staff, Ron Kreet, with an expression that made Blair think he'd swallowed a bitter pill. His face was pale.

Kreet didn't offer a hint of apology. He simply tapped his lips. Meaning he needed to speak to the president. Now.

Blair glanced at the delegates. It was highly unusual, clearly, but Kreet knew this better than most—he'd spent two years as their ambassador to the United Nations.

Something had happened. Something very bad.

"Excuse me for a moment," Blair said and walked off the platform.

32

TWELVE ADULTS and five children. Seventeen. That was how many had entered the lake and escaped as outcasts.

They rode for five hours in a strange silence. Slowly the others began to talk about their experience in the lake. Slowly the others' sorrow over having lost Rachelle was replaced by the wonder of their own resurrection in the red waters. Slowly Thomas and Marie and Samuel were left to their own lingering sorrow.

In the sixth hour, Thomas began to speak to Marie and Samuel about their mother. About how she had saved their lives and the lives of the others by leading them all to the lake. About her courage in placing them on the horses first and then saving his life by coming back for him. About Rachelle's place now, with Elyon, though he really didn't understand this last thing.

They reached the forest's northern edge after seven hours, and all signs of the pursuit were gone.

There they rolled Rachelle in a blanket and buried her in a deep grave as was customary when the circumstances did not favor cremation. They set fruits and flowers by her body and then filled in the grave.

"Mount!" he cried and swung into his saddle.

A fresh determination had filled him over the hours. His destiny was now with Elyon. With every waking moment he would now honor the memory of his wife, and he would cherish the two children she'd given him, but his path was now beyond him.

He sat on his horse and stared at the blistering, red-hued dunes. They'd stopped at a creek and filled the canteens sewn into all saddles. It was spring water, clear and fresh. They wouldn't use it for bathing. Even then, they had only enough to keep them for two or three days at most.

Johan eased his horse next to Thomas. "Now where?"

He cleared his throat. "They won't expect us to leave the forest."

"No, because there's no sense in leaving the forest," Mikil said from behind. "We've never lived in the desert. Where will we find water? Food?"

"I've lived in the desert," Johan said.

"The desert," Thomas said. "All I know is that we ride into the desert."

Johan looked at him. "You say that as if you know something more."

"Only that we are meant to be there."

"The sand will show our tracks," Mikil said.

"Not in the northern canyon lands," Johan countered. "We could lose them for good there."

"We could lose ourselves for good there."

The others had mounted and now sat on their horses in a long line, staring out at the desert.

"Do you think the lakes in the other forests are . . ." Jamous stopped.

"Red?" Thomas said. "I don't know. But they won't work the way they used to. The only way to defeat the disease now is to follow Justin in his death."

"And the disease is gone forever," Lucy said.

Thomas turned to the little girl with bright green eyes. "You know this?"

"That's what I heard."

"From whom?"

"From Justin. In the lake."

He exchanged a knowing grin with the girl's mother, Alisha.

"She's right," Marie said.

"Well. Then maybe Lucy should lead us. Where do you say we should go?" he asked.

Lucy laughed. His own daughter managed a smile, which brought him hope, considering her loss. Thomas returned her smile. Her eyes watered and she turned away.

He faced the red dunes again, resisting his own sorrow.

"Will the Horde find us here, Johan?"

"Not tonight. Tomorrow they will."

"Is . . ." Samuel asked the question no one had asked yet. "Is Justin dead?"

"It depends on what you mean by Justin," Thomas said.

"I mean the Justin who drowned. Not Elyon, but Justin."

Justin. They all pondered the question.

"We saw him drown," Johan said. "And I watched the lake for several hours. He didn't come up. If his body is gone, Ciphus may have stolen it to cast blame on Thomas. But does it matter if Justin is dead or not? It's just a body he was using. Right? We all know that Elyon isn't dead."

Johan had been the one who'd shoved his sword into that body—perhaps he was easing his guilt.

They let the matter rest.

Thomas looked down the line of horses. Five experienced warriors including William and Suzan, five children, and six civilians including Jeremiah, the converted old man who'd once been a Scab. Ronin and Arvyl, of course. And the last three were from the Southern Forest as well.

An unlikely crew, but one he suddenly felt supremely proud of. From so many, these were the few who'd responded to Justin's cry. The fate of the world now rested on the shoulders of people like Marie and Lucy and Johan. Thomas glanced at his arm. The disease would never gray it again. They were truly new people. No longer Forest People, certainly not the Horde. They were outcasts.

They were the chosen. Those who had died. Those who lived.

I love you, Rachelle. I love you dearly. I will always love you.

He wanted to cry again.

"Then we make camp here tonight," he said, looking out at the red hills. "No fires."

"You're saying we waste the rest of the day?" Mikil asked. "What if I'm wrong? What if they do come after us?"

"Then we will post guards. But we wait here."

"What's that?" Samuel asked.

Thomas followed his gaze. A dot on the sand. A rider.

His heart rose into his throat. The horse was riding hard, straight toward them from the desert. A scout?

"Back!" Mikil said, pulling her horse around. "Take cover. If they see us, they'll report it."

The horses responded to the tugs on their reins and retreated behind a row of trees.

They peered from their hiding. The rider was moving as fast as Thomas had ever seen, down the slope of the last dune, leaving a trail of disturbed sand in his wake. A black horse. The rider was dressed in white. His cloak flapped behind him and he rode on the balls of his feet, bent over.

"It's him!" Lucy cried. She dropped off her mother's horse and was running before Thomas could stop her.

"Lucy!"

"It's Justin!" she said.

Thomas blinked, strained for a better view. His heart hammered. And then he knew that the man on the black horse riding pell-mell toward them *was* Justin.

His shoulder-length hair flew with his cape, and even at this distance, Thomas was sure he could see the brilliant green of his eyes. His passion was immediately infectious.

Thomas was frozen by the sudden realization that Justin was actually alive.

Had he come to give Rachelle back to him?

Justin's horse stamped to a halt twenty feet from the trees. His eyes were on Lucy, who was running out to him.

This was Elyon, and Elyon leaned over the side of his horse, grabbed Lucy under her arms, swept her up into his saddle, and spurred his horse into a full sprint. Lucy squealed. He swung the horse back less than fifty paces out and rode in a wide circle, now laughing aloud with the girl.

Thomas urged his horse forward, but he wasn't the only one; they were all rushing from the trees and dismounting.

Justin rode in, lowered Lucy to the ground, and measured them all with a bright, mischievous glint in his eyes.

"Good afternoon," he said.

None of them replied.

"How did you like the lake?"

Thomas slid off his saddle, dropped to one knee, and lowered his head. "Forgive me."

Justin dismounted and walked up to him. "I have. And you followed me, didn't you?" He touched Thomas's cheek. "Look at me."

Thomas lifted his head. There wasn't a blemish on Justin's face to show for the pounding he'd taken. Except for his eyes, he looked every bit human. Yet in those deep emerald eyes Thomas could see only Elyon.

"I knew I could depend on you. Thank you," Justin said.

Thomas wasn't sure he'd heard just right. Thank you? He lowered his head, swamped with emotion. What about Rachelle?

"Look at me, Thomas."

When he looked up, he saw that tears were running down Justin's face. Thomas began to cry. He didn't know there was anything left in him to cry, but there, kneeling, staring into Elyon's crying eyes, he began to shake with long, desperate sobs.

"You understand what you've done, and it's tearing at your mind. You want your wife back, I know. But that's not what I have in mind."

"I'm sorry!" He sounded foolish, but at the moment he only wished he could say whatever was needed to earn Justin's complete forgiveness for his doubt.

"You're a prince to me," Justin said. "I've shown you my mind and my way, but soon I will show you my heart."

"But Rachelle . . ." Thomas's heart felt as though it might explode.

"Is in good hands," Justin finished. "Laughing like she used to in the lake."

His eyes made contact with the others, pausing at each face. "The Great Romance is for you. If only one of you would have followed me, the heavens would not have been able to contain my cries of joy."

Justin's eyes grew impassioned. He hurried over to Johan, lifted his hand, and kissed it. "Johan . . ."

Johan fell to his knees and sobbed before Justin could say more.

"I forgive you." He kissed the man's head. "Now you will ride with me."

Justin stepped to the old man Jeremiah, lifted his hand, and kissed it. "You, Jeremiah, I called you out of the Horde like so many. But you came."

The old man dropped to his knees and began to weep.

Justin ran to Lucy's mother and kissed her hand. "And you, Alisha, I once told you that love would conquer death, but that it wouldn't look like love; do you remember?"

She dropped to her knees, lowered her head, and cried.

"No, no, you followed me, Alisha! You all followed me!"

He went down the line, kissing each of their hands. Their Creator had taken the form of a man and was kissing their hands. They could hardly bear it, much less understand it.

Justin stepped back from the seventeen followers, all still on their knees. He walked to his left, then to his right, like a man overcome by his first viewing of a magnificent painting he himself had painted. "Wonderful," he whispered to himself. "Incredible." His face twisted with emotion. "Wonderful, wonderful, wonderful." He paced, face stricken with emotion.

He suddenly spun from them, fell to his knees, threw his head back, and thrust both hands at the sky.

"Father!" he cried. "My father, she is beautiful!" He burst into a joyful laugh, and his brilliant eyes, full of love, traveled around the small group. "My bride is beautiful! How I have waited for this day."

Thomas immediately understood the significance of what they were watching. He could hardly see it for his own tears, and he couldn't hear too well over the crashing of his own heart, but he knew that this was about the Great Romance between Elyon and his creation. His people.

Elyon was restoring the Great Romance. Teeleh had stolen his first love, but now Justin had reclaimed her. The price had been his own life. He'd taken her disease on himself and he'd drowned with it, inviting them to embrace his invitation to the Romance by following him into the lake to drown with him. To live as his bride!

And Justin had called to his father. Until this moment, Thomas had never thought of such clear distinctions in Elyon's character. But it could hardly be clearer—somehow Elyon the father had given Elyon, his son, a bride. They were the bride. Thomas couldn't help but think that this very moment had been chosen long ago.

Justin stood, rushed to his horse, and grabbed his sword. He thrust its tip into the sand and began to run, dragging the sword. He ran around them as they watched, drawing a large circle.

This was the symbol they had once used to signify the union between a man and a woman. Half a circle on the man's forehead for a betrothal, a full circle for their marriage. He was symbolically making them his bride.

Justin finished the circle and threw his sword on the sand. "You are mine," he said. "Never break the circle that unites us. Do you understand what I'm asking you to do?"

They couldn't speak.

"Your lives have always been about the Great Romance, and in the days to come you will understand that like never before. Your love will be tested. Others will join you. Some will leave the circle. Some will die. All of you will suffer. The Horde will hate you because their hearts have been stolen and their eyes have been blinded by the Shataiki. But if you keep your eyes on me until the end"—he swallowed—"the lake will seem tame compared to what awaits us."

"None of us will ever leave you," Lucy cried.

Justin looked at her as if he himself was going to cry again. "Then guard your heart, my princess. Remember how I love you, and love me the same. Always."

He was looking at Lucy, but he was talking to all of them.

"You won't see me again for some time, but you will have my water. Go to the Southern Forest, then beyond to the farthest southern edge, where you will find a small lake. Johan knows it." He looked over their heads at the forest beyond. "I charge you to bring them to me. One by one, if you must. Show them my heart. Lead them into the red water."

A hundred questions flooded Thomas's mind. He found the courage to speak, though not to stand. "All the lakes are red?"

"All of my lakes are red. To whoever seeks, this water will represent life, just as you found life by following me. To the rest, the lakes will be a threat."

"Are the wars over?" Mikil asked.

"My peace is their war. The war will come against you. For a time, you will find safety in the Southern Forest." He ran to his horse, pulled something out of his saddlebag, and faced them.

"Do you recognize this, Thomas?"

An old leather-bound book. A Book of History!

Justin grinned. "A Book of History." He tossed it to Thomas, who caught it with both hands. "There are thousands, not just the few that Qurong carries in his trunks. This is only one, but it will guide you."

Thomas felt its worn cover and drew his thumb along the title.

The Histories Recorded by His Beloved

He cracked the book open. Cursive text ran across the page.

"Read it well," Justin said. "Learn from it. Ronin will help you discover my teachings from the Southern Forest. He'll show you the way."

Thomas closed the book. "What about the blank book?" He touched the small lump at his waist where the empty book still rested. "Does it have a purpose?"

"The blank books. There are many of those as well. They are very powerful, my friend. They create history, but only *in* the histories. Here they are powerless. One day you may understand, but in the meantime, guard the one you have—in the wrong hands it could wreak havoc."

Justin took a deep breath. "Now I must go." He put his hand on his chest. "Keep your hearts strong and true. Follow the way of the book I have left with you. Never leave the circle."

He eyed them each tenderly, and when his eyes rested on him, Thomas felt both weakened and strengthened by a stare that ran straight through him.

Justin turned toward his horse.

"Wait." Thomas stood. "If this book works only in the histories, that means the histories are real? The virus?"

"Am I a boy, Thomas?" Justin turned back, smiling. "Am I a lamb or a lion, or am I Justin?"

"You are a father and a son?"

"I am. And the water as well."

Thomas's mind swam.

"Will I dream again?"

"Did you dream last night?"

"Yes. But not about the histories."

"Did you eat the fruit?"

"No."

"Well then."

He swung into his saddle and winked. "Remember, never leave the circle." With a slight nudge of his heel, his stallion walked away, and then trotted.

Then he galloped up the same dune from which he'd first come, reared the horse once at the crest, and disappeared into the horizon.

33

THIS HAD better be important," President Blair said.

Kreet's eyes darted around furtively. This wasn't like the battle-hardened general.

"Don't tell me the Israelis have launched," Blair asked.

"They launched a missile into the Bay of Biscay. Cheyenne Mountain recorded a fifty-megaton blast fifteen minutes ago. It was a warning shot. The next one goes into the naval base at Brest. They've given France twenty-four hours to guarantee Israel's survival."

Blair didn't know what to say. They'd discussed this possibility, but hearing that it had actually happened immobilized him. Finally he cleared his throat and turned back for the door.

"Any response from Paris?"

"Too early."

"Okay, keep this quiet. As soon as I'm finished, I want our people out of here. The ambassador stays. Leave him uninformed."

"Excuse me, sir." An aide interrupted by handing Kreet a note. "A priority message."

He took the note, glanced at it. Stared at it.

"What now?" Blair asked.

"It's the French. They've answered Israel's demands."

"And?"

"They've reciprocated."

Someone had cracked the door, preparing to open it for him. One of the European delegates in the main hall was yelling about innocent citizens, but the voice sounded distant, muted by a ring that echoed through Blair's head.

"Cheyenne has picked up a missile headed over the Mediterranean. ETA, thirty minutes . . . that was four minutes ago."

Blair couldn't think straight. Nothing, not even a week of anticipation, could prepare anyone for a moment like this. France had just launched nuclear weapons at Israel.

"We don't know their target. It may be a warning shot in return," Kreet said.

President Blair stepped to the door. "Or it may not be. God help us, Ron. God help us all."

This changed everything.

The basement room used to be a root cellar—cold enough to keep vegetables from rotting. They'd plastered the walls and sealed the ducts, but it was still cold enough to serve its purpose.

Carlos stepped in, flipped on the lights, and walked to the gurney. A white sheet covered the body. He hesitated only a moment, then lifted the corner.

Thomas Hunter's blank eyes faced the ceiling. Dead. As dead as any man Carlos had ever killed. This time there would be no mistake; he'd gone out of his way to make sure of that. On both occasions that the man had seemingly come back to life, the circumstances were suspect. Carlos had never actually confirmed his death, for one thing. And the man's recovery had been almost instantaneous.

This time his body had rested in this sealed room for nearly three days, and he hadn't so much as twitched.

Dead. Very, very dead.

Satisfied, Carlos dropped the sheet over Thomas's face, left the room, and headed down the hall. It was time to finish what they'd all started.

THE JOURNEY CONTINUES
WITH **WHITE** . . .